Somewhere a Phone Is Ringing

The Collected Stories of Nancy Bourne

SOMEWHERE A PHONE IS RINGING
The Collected Stories of Nancy Bourne

Copyright © 2023 by Michael Bourne
All rights reserved

ISBN: 978-1-941066-58-4
Library of Congress Control Number: 2023903174

Book design by Jo-Anne Rosen

Front-cover photograph: Kohiko Suzu
via Unsplash

Wordrunner Press
Petaluma, California
www.wordrunner.com

This book is for Nancy's grandchildren and all the friends and family who sustained her while she wrote these astonishing stories.

Contents

Introduction

Family and friends admired Nancy Bourne's curiosity about our lives and her headlong energy, which her grandchildren called "going all Grandma Nancy." At age fourteen, she wanted to become a housewife and a writer—an unusual combination in 1953 or now. By twenty-three, she became a housewife, but she waited another fifty years to publish her first short story. Here we present all her published stories.

Why did she need half a century to become a writer? For sure, writing fiction is not easy for anyone, but Nancy's outsized energy and curiosity made it harder by attracting her to tasks that could overlap for years: marriage (59 years); three children (one or more at home, 23 years); learning to make ceramic pots, build a kiln, and run a successful pottery business (10 years); two master's degrees in English literature, at twenty-eight and at sixty-eight (4 years); law school (3 years), and then, after passing the California bar exam, practicing law (17 plus years); teaching English in high schools and a penitentiary (10 plus years), pottery in her garage (6 years), education law in universities (4 years), and writing skills to incarcerated youth (3 years).

In the 1970s, Nancy enjoyed multi-tasking, which meant raising a family, making and selling pots, and writing stories. Because magazines turned her stories down, at forty-one she sought a serious job in the great world. Practicing law tested her skills, taught new ones, and proved highly satisfying, but two decades later she retired, eager to find new challenges: teaching in prisons and colleges, organizing a hiker-birdwatcher group, campaigning for Democrats, earning the second master's degree, writing an unpublished novel. In her mid-sixties, after a twenty-five-year hiatus, she slowly returned to writing short stories. Multi-tasking and that hiatus made her more confident and furnished the broad range of experience reflected in her stories.

At age sixty-nine, Nancy set herself a lifetime goal: to publish at least one story in her lifetime. She was seventy-three when she published that first story, "Drawing Lily". (At thirty-five, she wrote the first version of that story, very different from the published version, but focused on the same old man.) During her last decade—from seventy-three until she died in 2021 at eighty-two—Nancy produced thirty-seven published stories (the last one published posthumously, in 2022), with remarkably varied settings and human predicaments. Examples: A lawyer in a small 1960s southern town pretends his political campaign is not racist ("Massive Resistance"). Touring Iran, an autistic expert on Persian art falls prey to religious police ("Stalking the Sprouted Stag"). In juvie for dealing drugs, a girl sends her friend's brother to the penitentiary and deftly punishes a teacher she distrusts ("American Girl"). A widower's demands that his daughter preserve her chastity contribute to her death, racking him with guilt ("A Case for Wrongful Death").

Characters in many of Nancy's stories find it hard to interpret or transmit messages about their own or others' inner feelings and needs. Their messages may be scrambled by differences in social class, family income, and education, or by racial prejudice, neurological disease, and sheer chance. In "Intent for Love," an unworldly, simple man who teaches laundry skills to prisoners tries hard to romance a woman who is a prison guard. Both are shy and lonely, but the friendship comes to naught because neither can transmit nor decipher their dramatically differing needs and expectations. In "Memorial Mansion," social pressure driven by racial prejudice requires that a librarian make a stark choice between keeping an innocent black woman out of jail or lying in court to protect her own son. In "Going Under," a young teenage boy, Gordy, tries to help a girl in his school, Brenda, prepare to be baptized in his church. When he sees she is worried, Brenda replies, "Gordy, you have no idea." She fails to attend the baptism, and she and her father leave town, but Gordy is too innocent to understand the girl's plight and her father's role in it.

Nancy's characters scramble, fake, or misread messages, but her prose does not. Alert readers may sniff a mystery and be saddened, amused, or even horrified but the stories offer few hints on how to prevent misreadings or alleviate the consequences. Nancy raises questions but does not pretend to know every answer.

Still, two stories do show the beneficent power of reading a message correctly. In "Drawing Lily" and "Somewhere a Phone is Ringing," clarity illuminates darkness to offer a measure of respite from the anguish of impending death. Nancy may have meant these stories to tell us that deciphering inner messages can reconcile humans, however briefly, to their inevitable crash through what Faulkner called the "wall of oblivion." Fittingly, these two stories were the first and the last she published.

Henry Bourne
Greenbrae, California
October 2022

Note:
The stories in this book are listed in reverse order of publication, from 2022 to 2012, so that her last story appears first and her first story last. Original publications are credited beneath the title of each story.

The Collected Stories of Nancy Bourne

Somewhere a Phone Is Ringing

Wordrunner eChapbooks, *Up-Ending* anthology (April 2022)
Nominated for a 2023 Pushcart Prize

My grandmother's in the mirror. Thin white hair, pulled back in a knot. Sunken, floury-white cheeks, round blue eyes staring out of puffy pouches and a skeletal face. When did it happen that I turned into her? My mother's mother, Grandmother Alice. The whiny, selfish one. I hated her.

Of course, I know how it happened and when it began. My two sons and I were on our traditional New Year's Eve hike on Mount Diablo. Ever since my husband, Fred, died of a heart attack ten years ago, we have hiked together, just the three of us, every December 31 to put an end to the old year, celebrate the new. Dick—lean, fit, always on the move, jogging, mountain climbing, backpacking, cooking, talking, talking, and Daniel—tall, blond, quiet, thoughtful. They had flown here with their wives and my two grandkids for the holidays, Dick from Oregon, Daniel from New York.

No rain on New Year's Eve, although the three of us had done this hike in the rain many times. It's part of the tradition. But this year, sunshine flooded the valleys and hills, sparkled drops of water on blue oak leaves, lit up red toyon berries. We chose the Mitchell Canyon Trail because of the waterfall, which plunges down the mountain, spewing white froth over coyote bush and the brilliant blooming manzanita, a specialty of winter.

Flat trail at the beginning, thick sludge, mud boots. Pine forests on either side. Chaparral everywhere. Two of us talking, talking. Daniel listening, smiling.

"So, what's Grace's first choice?" I asked Dick. My brilliant granddaughter, Gracie, who was waiting to hear from colleges.

"I don't dare ask," Dick said. "She's done the whole thing herself. No help from me."

I laughed. Must have been hard. Dick has always been in everybody's business, asking questions, making suggestions.

Up went the binoculars. "Quick," he called out. "Flicker. On that live oak, Mom. Left side, bottom branch. Oops, he's off. See the red shaft?"

Too late. The flicker was gone.

While Dick searched the skies, calling out red tails and Cooper's hawks, Daniel strolled along at my pace, catching me up on his son Julian's reading difficulties. Sweet Julian who at nine years old always beats me at Monopoly but struggles to read the cards. Daniel, a history professor who reads for a living, was unusually patient with his boy.

"I tell Joanie reading has nothing to do with intelligence. He's really bright."

Daniel's wife, Joanie, a lawyer, worried. She didn't understand how a child of hers couldn't read.

"I still hate reading," Dick said. He didn't read until fourth grade and now he is an orthopedic surgeon. Always was good with his hands. "Quick, Mom. That raptor way up there. I think it's a golden eagle."

I couldn't see it.

Suddenly, it wasn't flat anymore. We were climbing up the Eagle Peak trail, a narrow, rocky path, on the dizzy edge of the deep canyon. I didn't dare look down. In spring, this path is rich with golden globe lilies, shooting star, the spray of white blossoms of virgin's bower. But now in winter, it was green and fresh and soaked with spray. Alive in the sunshine.

I was straining, each step up to the top an effort. Dick had gone ahead to pick out a large rock for our picnic. Daniel was behind me, steady, silent.

My sons.

Once on the rock, we stared down at the waterfall below us, eating egg salad sandwiches, talking about the children, my grandchildren, Grace and Julian.

"Look how the sun's sparkling on the water."

"What did you say?" Dick asked.

"The sun is sparkling on the water."

"Say it again."

"Why?"

"Your 's' sound is different."

"Sounds fine to me."

But it didn't. I tried to say the word sun again and it came out fuzzy.

"I've been noticing your speech the whole hike," Dick said. "It's probably nothing, but we need to check it out."

"What do you mean, check it out?"

"Emergency room, I'm afraid. I'm sure it's nothing, Mom, but I don't want to take a chance."

"That's crazy," I said. "Daniel, have you noticed it?"

He nodded. "'Fraid so, Mom."

So, on to the New Year. Test after test, cat scans, MRIs, EKGs, echograms. Which meant cancer. Lung cancer metastasized to my brain. Luckily not the smoker's lung cancer; you don't get many months with that one. Luckily not glioblastoma; not much better than smoker's cancer. But nothing fixable, like a stroke or an abscess that can be drained. CANCER.

I am indignant. How could a healthy eighty-year-old get cancer? I'd never been in a hospital before, except to have children. I'd never been sick. I've hiked up and down Diablo, and all over Marin County. Ridden the rapids down the Grand Canyon. Climbed the dunes of Mongolia. Snorkeled in the rough water of the Pacific Islands. All in my seventies.

CANCER?

But it's real. And it's radiation, chemotherapy, pills, more pills. My heart races as liquid fills the sac around it. The pounds melt away, the cheeks sink in, the white hair thins. Six months later, still alive. But Grandmother's in the mirror.

Somewhere a phone is ringing.

All those awful years when she lived with us. In my bedroom, my large bedroom with the shelf of shells I'd collected, my high-fidelity record player, my records, my posters: Elvis, Buddy Holly, Elizabeth Taylor. I had to sleep in the double-decker above my eight-year-old brother, Brent, in his shoebox of a room.

"Why does she have to have my room?" I asked at least once a week. "It's not fair."

And Mother would explain again that our house had only three bedrooms and that Grandmother was sick and old and needed privacy and comfort. Brent's double-decker was out of the question.

She lived with us six months of the year, because she was alone and weak and needed help taking care of herself. My grandfather had died years before. So, she shuttled back and forth, twice a year, between my Aunt Mary in Kentucky and our house. As soon as she arrived, she would beg to go back to Aunt Mary, who reported that Grandmother begged for us when at her house.

But it wasn't just the sacrifice of my room, my things, my due as the oldest child. It was Grandmother. I didn't like her. No, I actively disliked her.

"It's cold in here," she'd complain.

"I don't feel like eating a thing."

"I'm weary today."

"Nobody ever writes me."

"I want to go home."

When I turned sixteen and got my driver's license, my job was to drive her to the doctor, to sit with her in the waiting room, to hear her compare our family doctor with "my man Frost" in Kentucky.

"This one doesn't know his business."

I'm being unfair, of course. Grandmother had been a beautiful woman; the photos were in the album. And she still had, even in her emaciated form, a touching fragility. She kept herself clean and sweet-smelling, wore soft cotton dresses in summer, tailored wool dresses in winter, navy blue with white linen collars. The neighbors would remark, "Mrs. Rawlings always looks so fresh."

When I complained about her, as I so often did, Mother would say, "I wish you could have known her when she was younger. She's not always been like this."

"But she is now," I would say.

I think what I held against her the most was her indifference to me. And to Brent. But to me. Grandmothers are supposed to be interested in their grandchildren, supposed to love them, give them things, knit sweaters for them, show an interest. I could have been the hired help for all the attention she paid me.

"She is selfish," Mother would admit. "But she wasn't always like that." And then the dreaded words. "If you're not careful, Judy, you may turn out just like her. You do complain a lot, and you're not very generous."

"Never!" I would reply.

And now I look in the mirror, and there we are.

A phone is ringing. Where?

I'm in the hospital. For surgery this time. Fluid is flooding the sac around my heart, squeezing my heart. It's been drained twice now, but the fluid keeps coming back. Every time I breathe, it hurts. So, back to the hospital. The surgeon, who looks like a lumberjack, stout with a belly and a sense of humor, is going to cut a "window" in my pericardial sac, where the fluid is. The idea is that it will drain permanently into the lung, which has plenty of room for extra fluid. But it's surgery, and I'm on a blood thinner, and I'm thin and sick. A glance in the bathroom mirror. Grandmother Alice in a hospital gown far too large for me with tubes and plastic cords tacked all over my body, my white hair too long, sticking out at angles. I'm a mess. Not even tidy and sweet-smelling like Grandmother.

In comes Dick. He's flown down from Portland. Smiling, laughing with the nurses, sneaking me a cup of coffee which is forbidden on the cardiology ward where they've stuck me.

"You can't concentrate on anything serious in a hospital," he says as he pulls a P.D. James novel from his backpack. "And they won't let you sleep."

I laugh. I'm so happy to see him.

"I want to hear what the doctors say," he tells me. "And I may have some questions."

When the surgeon comes in, Dick does have questions. Good ones phrased to make sure I understand what's going on.

"How big is the window?"

"What keeps it from bleeding?"

OK. He's thinking about my blood thinner.

"Where exactly does the fluid drain to?"

The surgeon explains that he's using laparoscopic surgery.

"What size is the camera?"

The surgeon explains how the camera is inserted and how it works.

"How long does it take?"

I'm amazed at Dick's quiet, respectful manner. He usually talks fast and asks too many questions. Thank God he's here.

The phone is ringing. Where am I? An empty room. No. A hallway. A small hallway. Doors leading to bedrooms. The phone is ringing. It's one of those phones attached to the wall with the receiver hanging off it.

The fog clears. A face hovers over me. It's smiling.

"You're in the ICU. You're doing great, Mom."

It's Dick.

"Daniel's up in your room waiting for you," he tells me.

"Daniel? He's here?"

"Of course, he's here."

"Are you in pain?" a voice asks.

"I don't feel a thing," I say.

The phone is ringing. I close my eyes. There is a woman I don't recognize. I see a cotton print dress clinched with a blue belt. Brown spectator pumps. Large round blue eyes, blurry, washed. White hands reach for the phone. Screams like something out of nature. Something wild.

———

Up the front steps, one at a time, holding onto Dick. The door opens, and there they are. Daniel, Joanie, Julian, Gracie on summer break from UVA. Laughing, hugging, popping champagne corks. Blinis and caviar and sour cream, scampi. More champagne. I nibble a blini, too tired to eat, too happy to go to bed. They repeat the family stories, laughing at me, at each other. The time I rolled the car down an embankment—blinded by the sun—and climbed out the window, called a cab and AAA from a neighbor's house, and took off for work. The time the middle school principal brought our model student, Daniel, home roaring drunk after he sampled some "juice" a kid gave him on the school playground. The time six-year-old Gracie made a bouquet from tulips and roses she cut from a grumpy neighbor's yard, and the irate lady called the cops claiming vandalism.

"Remember 'Duncan will flunken'?" I ask, laughing.

"What?" Julian asks.

"Some smart-ass teacher wrote it on Dick's report card when he didn't do his homework."

"But why Duncan?" Gracie asks.

I smile. "That's your dad. We named him Duncan, but he hated it. So, in high school, he changed his name to Dick."

"I never heard that," Gracie says. "Duncan's a funny name. How'd you come up with that?"

"My uncle," I tell her. "My mother's favorite brother. I did it for her. He was killed in a plane crash a long time ago."

"He was flying the plane. Right, Mom? He was the pilot?" Dick asks.

"I think so. I know he was in the Army, and it was a small plane . . . Why was he flying? I can't remember."

"What happened?" Gracie asks.

It's coming back. "He was flying to see his brother." Is that right? "His brother was dying."

"Oh my god. I didn't know that part." It's Dick.

"He never made it. He crashed into a mountain somewhere. They found the body…I was so young. Mother always said . . ."

I can't stay awake.

"Mother always said . . . Duncan was full of life . . . talking, laughing . . ."

The phone's ringing.

Mother's crying. My daddy's crying. And the woman I don't know, the one in the print dress, is crying. I'm crying. Mother takes me to her bedroom. How old am I? Three? She tells me Uncle Nelson has died from cancer. I don't know Uncle Nelson. Mother's crying. She says Uncle Duncan was flying an Army plane to visit his brother. Because he was dying. The plane was a two-seater. They found it crashed on a mountainside. I can't . . .

"Who is that woman talking on the phone?" I ask Mother.

"Don't you know?"

One phone call.

Nelson. Duncan.

Two sons.

She's there in the mirror, Grandma Alice. Looking at me. "It took you so long," she's saying. "What have you been doing that it took you so long?"

Green Spring Valley

Spotswood Virginia, Stephen F. Austin State University Press, 2021

1936

The white hair surprised him. The last time Pete was home, his father's thick, coarse hair had been brown. That was 1924, the year Pete married. But the broad shoulders stretching the seams of the blue serge suit, the thick fingers folded over the barrel chest, the shelf of brow over the closed eyes were just as he remembered. Pete knew he should cry, but he couldn't. Especially when he heard, for at least the third time, his brother's account of the old man's death.

"Luckily, I was visiting home when it happened." Preston's voice was deep, confident. "Houston came racing in the house, panting. 'Yo Pa,' he kept saying and pointed out toward the pasture. 'Fell in the creek.' I ran quick as lightning. Found him lying on his back under the willows, where Houston had pulled him out of the water. His coveralls were soaked, face gone white. When I took off my shirt to make a pillow for him, he felt stiff in my arms."

Always the same, Pete thought. Preston to the rescue.

"I asked him, 'Can you wiggle your fingers, Dad?' He just lay there, nothing moving but his lips. I put my ear next to his mouth, but all I could hear was him gulping for air. I knew right off he'd had a stroke. Next thing, he was shaking all over and making weird sounds, and his cheek next to mine was wet."

Preston paused for effect.

"He was crying."

"No!"

Pete tried to stop him. His father didn't cry.

"It happens," Preston assured him. "I've seen it in my practice, time and again. You'd be surprised. Even the most stoic patients. I talked to him like he was a child, told him he was going to be okay. When I saw there was nothing more I could do, I put Houston in charge and raced back to the house for my Ford. Drove hell for leather, bumping and bouncing over the fields to where I'd left him. His eyes were wide open, staring. I put my ear down on his chest. Like this." He leaned down to demonstrate. "Nothing. He was gone."

Pete waited for sadness to take him over or even anger at the old man lying in state in the family's dimly lit front parlor. But all he felt was resentment toward his brother. Dr. Preston, the expert. Dr. Preston, the man in charge.

Later, as he was leaving the house for the funeral, he felt a tug on his sleeve. Preston's wife, Mary Lee, pulled him aside.

"Pete, honey," she said. "I've saved up a big bag of Lee Ann's dresses. I thought your Kate might find some she likes."

"Thank you kindly, Mary Lee," he said.

He felt his sister-in-law's soft hand as she handed him a valise.

"I'm just trying to help," she whispered.

When he looked up, Pete saw his brother standing at the front door, watching him, pity in his eyes.

"Don't," he said more harshly than he intended.

Later that night, after the funeral, after the crowd of church folks and neighbors had dropped off their casseroles and pies and left the house, Pete wandered back to the tiny kitchen where his mother was sitting at the table, her blue eyes magnified by the thick lenses of old age. As soon as he came in, she jumped up and wrapped her boney arms around him. Her cheek felt dry against his neck, and she smelled like yeast bread.

"Thank you, sweet Pete," she whispered.

He smiled at the name she'd always called him.

"For what, Mama?"

"Coming all this way. I know you don't have the money."

"I manage."

"How many years has it been?"

"Since . . .?"

"Since we last saw you?"

"Let's see."

He paused, trying to figure it out. He'd just gotten married.

"Twelve years," he said. "That long?"

"I brought Margaret down, remember?"

He'd wanted to show her the farm.

His mother nodded.

He hesitated.

"It didn't work out so good."

His mother turned away.

"She was different. We didn't know how to take her."

"She was Catholic."

"I guess your father had trouble with that."

"He called her a papist."

He'd also told her a woman's place was in the home, when he knew full well she was clerking at the drug store. Pete recalled how that had rankled Margaret.

"He always spoke his mind."

Pete let that go.

"How you doing, Mama?"

"I'm okay. Feel a little broken inside. Can't cry anymore. Tears got wrung out of me."

Pete pulled her into his arms. Her body was so small. The obvious thing to say was, you're tough, you'll get through it, which was true. But those words seemed hollow, predictable. So, he said what he was feeling.

"I love you."

She smiled up into his face.

"I know."

He motioned her to follow him to the kitchen table.

"I wish I could do something," he said when they were seated, reaching across the table for her hand.

She squeezed his thick, farmer hand.

"You know what you can do," she said.

He looked away.

"I can't, Mama. You know that."

"What I know is, this place needs a farmer, now your father's gone."

He shook his head.

"I can't move. I got a job and family where I live."

"You could all live here. There's plenty of room."

He sighed and stood up.

"Can't do it, Mama."

1918-1921

He was thirteen when it struck, the illness, and in the beginning, it seemed like the usual winter cold. All of them had suffered it, had complained of a sore throat, a fever. But Pete couldn't shake it. Preston and Mabel returned to school, but Pete's temperature kept climbing. Then his knees hurt, and his shoulders, and the muscles in his legs ached so bad he couldn't walk. They all feared it was the flu, which in 1918 was in full swing and killing people. But when red bumps popped out on his chest, Dr. Bailey stopped calling it "flu." By that time, Pete was too sick to understand what was happening to him. All he remembered was hurting all over in a dark room, people whispering, his mother sitting by his bed wiping him down with a wet cloth.

He found out later he'd come close to dying. It was rheumatic fever, and there was no cure, no medicine. He just had to wait it out and hope his heart wouldn't be damaged. But his heart was damaged. Two of the valves, he found out later, were in such bad shape they weren't much use. By the time he'd finally gotten well enough to make it back to school full-time, he was fifteen years old and had missed two years. He felt left behind, lonely. Preston, his younger brother who had always looked up to him, imitated him, adored him, was now in ninth grade, while Pete, a year older than his brother, was stuck with children half his size in the eighth.

"That stuff's easy," Preston would say when Pete sought his help with complex fractions. "Wait 'til you get to ninth, and they give you algebra. Now that's hard." Or "Are you coming to the gym tonight to watch me debate? The topic is 'Should ROTC be required in high school.' I'm arguing against, which is pretty hard, don't you think? But Miss Naylor says I'm the best. So, who knows?" And home he would come with his fake-gold trophy.

At sixteen, Preston won a scholarship to the university, all expenses paid, while Pete failed geometry, bribed his younger sister Mabel to write his English reports, and increasingly found excuses to cut school. His father was not amused.

"What's the matter with you, boy? Gustafsons don't fail."

"I'm not cut out for school," Pete said.

"Well, you're not going to be cut out for anything if you don't buckle down and stop dawdling."

Pete's cheeks turned red.

"I don't dawdle," he hissed. "I'm a good worker."

Rudolph Gustafson grabbed his son's shoulders with thick hands.

"You look here, boy," he said. "I ain't talking milking cows. I'm talking studying."

"You milk cows," Pete shot back.

"Yeah. I didn't have the money for education," his father said. "But I've knocked myself out for you boys, and you are going to college. Just like your brother."

Pete pulled away, headed for the door.

"You come back here, boy," his father demanded.

But Pete slammed the front door and was gone—into the green Virginia hillsides that he loved.

Because once he had regained his strength, he loved nothing better than waking in summer at 4:00 A.M., watching the scarlet sky dissolve into blue, rushing into the valleys of velvet grass, milking the cows, washing the separator, driving the four-horse plow, picking tobacco, feeding the chickens, and gathering their eggs, soaking up the early morning sun, falling dead asleep right after supper. Often, he would feel winded or weary, but his shoulders had filled out. The muscles in his arms were long, powerful.

At seventeen, Pete stumbled on an article in *The Farm Journal* about dairy farming in Pennsylvania. It claimed that farmers were looking for men willing to work hard for good pay. He cut out the article and hid it under his pillow to read at night before blowing out the candle.

"I'm thinking of going up north to work," he told his mother.

Eva Gustafson nearly dropped the bucket of hot water she was carrying to the zinc tub in the kitchen for Pete's weekly bath.

"What on earth gave you that idea?" she asked.

Pete bent, naked to the waist, over the side of the tub.

"I'd like a change," he mumbled.

His mother dumped the hot water over his back.

"What do you mean, change?"

He stood up, water dripping into his eyes, down his neck, and looked straight into his mother's face.

"Papa doesn't want me to farm."

She looked away.

Then, "How you going to get up north?"

Pete pulled a train schedule out of his damp back pocket. He had underlined the Southern Railway times table from Richmond to Philadelphia.

"Rudy!" his mother cried out. "Get in here. This boy's talking crazy."

When Rudolph Gustafson heard his son's plan, his large square face turned red.

"You ain't going nowhere. You will stay right here, boy, and finish your education."

And he might have stayed. But he didn't. It was Christmas, and Preston was home from the university, bragging about how his chemistry professor had called him a "prodigy."

"You need to buckle down, Pete," Preston told him. "You'll never get admitted to UVA unless you take your schoolwork more seriously."

This from his little brother.

"You puffed up little weenie," Pete yelled and, without giving it a moment's thought, kicked Preston hard in the butt.

His brother whirled around, his cheeks red, and raced after Pete.

"Come on," Pete sang out. "Try to catch me."

Suddenly, he pitched forward, stumbling and bouncing down the full flight of stairs from their bedroom, a staircase he had leaped easily, gracefully countless times before. But this time, his cheek caught on an exposed nail where a framed square of his mother's embroidery had recently been hanging. Blood streamed down his face as the full weight of Preston's body came crashing down on top of him.

Then blood was everywhere, on his shirt, in his hair, pooled on the floor. He remembered the drive in the buggy, his father at the reins, his cheek smarting underneath the towel his mother had pressed against the open cut. Preston sitting next to him, apologizing, crying.

The day after the stitches came out, Pete snuck out of the house before anyone was awake, walked in the freezing January chill the eight miles to the Spotswood bus station, paid for his ticket to Richmond with money he'd saved selling eggs, and vanished.

1936

Back in Pennsylvania after the funeral, Pete stumbled in the front door, threw down his carpet bag, and nearly collapsed into Margaret as she rushed to meet him.

"Oh, sweet Jesus, I knew you shouldn't go." His wife wrapped her thick arms around him, half holding him up.

Pete leaned into her, giving himself up to her softness, her kitchen smell of tomatoes and onion, her broad hands on his back. When he had recovered his breath from the two flights of stairs, he smiled.

"I'm fine, Peg. Really. I'm okay."

"Well, you look like shit," she said as she maneuvered him over to the faded loveseat, a hand-me-down from Pete's boss. "What did they do to you down there?"

He laughed. "Killed me with kindness."

"So, you told them?"

"Why would I do that?"

"They need to know."

"I don't go begging to my family," he said.

"I'm not asking you to beg. But Preston's a doctor."

"What can he do? My valves are done for."

"He might know something our doctor doesn't."

"The arrogant son of a bitch." Pete spit it out. "I'm fine. Really. I just need some loving and a good night's sleep."

"Well, I love you," she said. "Good thing you're not too proud to ask for that."

He woke up the next morning with eight-year-old Kate balancing a cup of hot tea over him.

"Good God. What time is it?"

He threw off the quilt and looked around. Compared to his childhood bedroom in Green Spring Valley, the small, dimly lit room felt cramped. The bulky oak wardrobe he'd picked up in an auction took up most of one wall, and Kate's bed was shoved up against the wall opposite, leaving very little space on the wood floor for maneuvering. His ten-year-old son Rudy slept in the kitchen on a mattress they rolled up during the day.

"Stay where you are, Daddy," his daughter said, pulling back the curtains from the one narrow window, which looked out on a brick apartment building. "Mama says you got to stay in bed a day or two. I'm to look after you."

"Where's Rudy?"

"At school."

"What about you?"

She grinned. "Rudy reported me sick."

Pete smiled at his bone-thin daughter, his treasure, as she eased herself up on the bed beside him.

"I don't like you missing school, Honey."

"Mama wanted you shouldn't be alone," she said. "Besides, just this once won't matter. They're repeating stuff I already know."

He hugged her and laughed.

"Smarty-pants," he said and pointed to the corner. "See that valise over there? Your Aunt Mary Lee sent you some clothes."

"Uh-oh."

"Why don't you look? You might be surprised."

Kate bounced out of bed and started yanking one dress after another from the valise.

"Look a here!"

She held up a stiff pink organdy with a satin sash hanging off it. She pulled her homemade cotton dress over her head and wriggled into her cousin's hand-me-down. Her thin arms poked out of the puffed sleeves, and the skirt brushed her ankles.

"Let's have a look at you," Pete said, and he and Kate both burst out laughing.

"I'm a princess," she giggled, prancing around the room, her thin brown pigtails bouncing, one tie of the pink sash wrapped around her scrawny neck, the other trailing the floor.

"There must be some school clothes in there," Pete said.

Kate held up a soft cotton print with elaborate smocking from collar to waist.

"It's pretty, don't you think?" Pete asked.

Kate tossed it back toward the valise.

"Yeah." Her voice was almost wistful. "But I'd get laughed out of class if I came marching into school with that smocked-up thing."

"Put 'em back," Pete said. "Your mother will find some use for them."

Which meant they would be sold to a second-hand shop in Philadelphia for money the family badly needed.

1921-1936

Pete had found a good job when he first came to Pennsylvania, working a dairy farm for Ross Jennings, a gentleman farmer who sat in the state legislature. Pete loved farming, loved the vast green hills, the roomy barn with its clean stalls and freshly-cut hay, the small tenant cabin his Margaret kept spotless. His beautiful young bride. Rich, that's the word that came to him when he buried himself in all her softness, when he loosened her dark, thick hair from the untidy pile on her head and breathed its sweetness. His Margaret had none of the false modesty of the girls he'd grown up with but looked him square in the face, inviting him to pay attention, insisting with her eyes that he touch her, love her. And he did. She was part of the enchanted playground he had stumbled upon and which his two babies had rolled around in. His Papa had been wrong. Learning to farm back in Virginia was all the education he'd ever want or need.

When the family outgrew the one room cabin Mr. Jennings made available, they moved to the rented apartment in Greenwood, the town closest to the farm. Three dark rooms, parlor, kitchen, bedroom, on the top floor of a three-story building. A patch of grass out back with a sandbox. To help with the rent, Margaret went back to her old job clerking at Johnson's Drugs.

When the first attack came, it didn't stop him. He'd had a pain in his chest for months, which he'd ignored. Then a fever laid him low for a couple of weeks. The local doctor sent him to Philadelphia for tests, which confirmed myocarditis.

"Your heart's working overtime," Dr. Reynolds said. "Try to take it easy for a while."

"How'm I supposed to do that, doc?" he asked. "I got mouths to feed."

"Get yourself a desk job."

Pete laughed. As soon as he was on his feet, he was back to working fourteen-hour days, waking before light, milking, feeding, binding, plowing with the new John Deere, carrying cold biscuits in his pocket for when he got hungry, mending fences, striding the green fields.

As the years went by, there were relapses and high fevers and pain and days in bed, then weeks.

1940

Then one winter afternoon, four years after Pete's father's funeral, Mr. Jennings came to the apartment carrying a sack of Florida grapefruit.

"I hate like stink to do this, Pete," his boss said. "You're the best manager I ever met. But fact is, I need somebody full time, every day. And you need to take care of your health."

Pete protested, claimed he was getting better all the time, but he knew. Mr. Jennings was right.

"I'm not firing you, Pete. Don't get that idea. You're indispensable on this farm. But you'll be working alongside the new man."

"Sounds like an hourly wage."

"I'm afraid so."

At thirty-six, Pete still worked on the farm when he was well, and Margaret took in sewing on the weekends. And for a while, things were good again.

For one thing, Pete now had more time with his children. His own father had paid little attention to him growing up. So, his notion of being a father was to work fourteen hours a day and pay the bills. But now he had time to play catch with his son, to take long walks into the countryside with Kate, picking wildflowers and looking their names up afterward in a book he found at the county library, all the while marveling at the sharp wits of his offspring, their innate sweetness.

At fourteen, Rudy was already taller than his father. He imitated Pete's long-legged stride as he crossed the meadows rounding up Mr. Jennings' stray cows, milking them with strong sure fingers, talking soft to the horses like his dad. And Rudy was clever with his hands, turning spare boards into kitchen shelves for his mother, fashioning a boat he often sailed on the small lake near Greenwood.

But it was Kate who brought Pete to life when he was stuck in the house, too ill to work. She spent hours on the floor of his bedroom, cutting printed models out of her mother's pattern magazines. Prancing them about the bedroom, acting out scenes from her vivid imagination.

"Why's that lady up on the wardrobe?" Pete would ask.

"She's learned how to fly. And they all hate her because she won't tell them how."

"Why doesn't she?"

"They won't let her play with them."

"Why not?"

Whisper. "They think she might be a witch."

"Is she?"

"I haven't decided."

When Pete could no longer count on being well enough to farm, Margaret got a job as a receptionist in the local dentist's office. The pay was better than the drugstore job, which she still worked on Saturdays, but many bills went unpaid.

At a knock on the door, Pete struggled to sit up.

"Who is it?" he yelled.

A voice called back, but he couldn't hear the name. More knocking.

"Hold on," Pete called out. "I'm coming."

He pulled himself up, reached for his trousers which were draped over the iron frame at the foot of the bed, and fumbled his way into them. Forcing himself to walk one step at a time, he reached the door.

The brothers stared at each other. "My God," Preston burst out.

Pete stood in the doorframe, unshaven, his thin hair sticking up at angles, his undershirt stained, his pants unzipped, and he laughed. Because the man facing him, his brother, in his navy-blue suit, perfectly molded to his frame, a suitcase in one hand, a doctor's bag in the other, had the same sandy-colored hair parted in the middle, the same piercing brown eyes, the same shelf of a brow as he did.

"Well, Preston," he said. "You've got a tailor, a good barber, and a lot of money. But all the same you're an ugly Gustafson, just like me."

Suddenly Pete's knees crumpled under him. Preston dropped both bags, grabbed his brother around the waist, and half holding him, half carrying him, walked him back into the bedroom, and stretched him out on the bed.

"Is this what you came for?" Pete asked, staring up at the brother he hadn't seen for four years, not since the funeral.

"We need to get you to a hospital."

"I've been. I'm not going back."

Preston sat down on the bed next to Pete.

"You need meds," he said. "The nurses can make you comfortable, keep you hydrated. Watch over you."

Pete smiled. "I've got . . ."

"Margaret. I know. Where is she?"

"At work."

"You can't give up, Petey." Preston's voice sounded urgent. "You're only thirty-six, for god's sake."

"Petey?" Pete raised himself up on his elbows and looked hard at his brother. "Why the hell are you here?"

"I came to find out how you are."

"Now you see."

Pete collapsed back on the bed.

"Come on, tell me what's going on."

Preston shrugged his way out of his suit coat, folded it carefully over the railing at the end of the bed, then settled himself on a metal chair he had dragged from the kitchen.

"At Dad's funeral," he finally said, "you acted like, I don't know, like I'd done something wrong." He sat for a minute, staring into space, avoiding Pete's eyes. "Like you almost hated me."

So, they were going to have a real conversation. Pete felt a burst of his old energy and spit it out.

"Aside from the fact that you're rich as hell, and I'm dirt poor, that you got the stamp of approval from the old man, and I was a failure? That you haven't even visited me in all the time I've lived up here? Aside from that, why am I angry?"

Pete's outburst brought on a coughing fit so violent that for a minute he couldn't catch his breath.

Preston rushed to the kitchen for a glass of water and held it to his brother's mouth.

Pete took a sip, then whispered, "Please leave."

"I can't. You're way too ill. I may be a lousy brother, but I'm a good doctor."

"I don't want your help. I don't want your money. I don't want . . ."

Pete reached for the glass, took a swallow.

". . . your kids' cast offs."

Preston seemed to shrink into himself.

"We were close, Pete, when we were kids." His voice was soft. "What happened?"

"You know as well as I do."

"I only know you were my big brother. I looked up to you, wanted to be like you. And then you got sick, and after that you turned on me."

Pete laughed.

"That's just like you—blaming me."

He fixed his eyes on Preston.

"Don't you remember? You lorded it over me, bragging about how you skipped two grades."

"That was Dad who did the bragging."

"No, Preston, it was you."

"What I remember is trying to help you with your homework."

"How do you think that made me feel?"

"You didn't like it. But I wanted you back. You'd been sick so long."

"You're rewriting history, brother."

"Maybe. But it's how I remember it."

Pete pulled himself up to a sitting position.

"You pushed me down the stairs. Remember? And I cut my face wide open."

Preston stared. "That was a fight. We were kids. You got mad and kicked me, and I ran after you. I didn't push you. You jumped. Come on, Pete. You were always jumping down those stairs. Only that time you stumbled."

"I was covered in blood. And you were on top of me."

"I tripped and fell down the stairs behind you."

"That's your story."

Preston shook his head.

"I don't believe you're still angry because of one fight."

"It's not that."

Pete lay back on the pillow. He was so tired.

"What then?"

"You've always been the brainy one," Pete said, his voice fading. He hated bringing up all this past history.

"Even if it's true, is that a reason to hate me?"

"At least I was bigger and stronger, better at ball games."

It was as if Pete were talking to himself.

"After I got sick . . . you bragged . . . left me behind . . . I was nothing."

"You had Mama," Preston said.

Pete looked up, surprised.

"What's that supposed to mean?"

"There wasn't much love in that house. Dad pushed us to achieve. But did you notice? He never hugged us, never even touched us. You had Mama."

"And you didn't?"

"Not really. I saw it happen when you got so sick. It was after nursing you for so long, fearing you wouldn't make it, that she came to favor you over me and Mabel. We both felt it."

Preston reached over and took Pete's cold hand in his. Pete shook him off. Preston turned toward the window.

"She wants you to come home," he said. "So do I. There's room for all of you in our old house."

He looked around the crowded room.

"A lot more room than here. And I can look after you."

"She already asked. At Dad's funeral. I said no then. Nothing's changed."

"That was four years ago. What's changed is you're too sick to work."

"You come up here for the first time ever and ask me to give up . . ."

"You're sick, Pete. And you can't support your family."

"Get out!"

"No. Blame me as much as you want. Blame the old man. But it's not our fault you're too sick to work. I can get you on your feet again."

"Too late."

"It's your Green Spring Valley, Pete. You know you love it. Once you're on your feet, you can farm again. Margaret can get a job in my office at twice what's she's making here. The kids can have all that fresh air, all those green fields, horses."

He's rehearsed that speech, Pete thought, but all the same, his mind flooded with green, grass green, deep blue-green, yellow spring green, maple and dogwood spread over hills, over pastures. He could almost smell the sting of wild onion, the sweet scent of apple blossoms.

Suddenly, there was Margaret at the bedroom door, her navy straw hat plunked down to her ears, her eyebrows raised in question. Rudy and Kate just visible behind her. He smiled.

"This is home," he mumbled.

"How do you do?" Margaret walked briskly into the room and faced Preston.

"Margaret," he said, shaking her hand. "It's been too long."

"Sixteen years," she said in a matter-of-fact voice. "Rudy, Kate, come here and meet your Uncle Preston."

Rudy solemnly offered his hand to his uncle.

Kate peered up at him.

"You're Uncle Preston? I didn't expect you to look so much like my dad." She stood, patient, stiff, as Preston reached out in a clumsy attempt to hug her.

"Now then, out of here," Margaret said, pointing to the door. "Time for this man to get some rest."

And planting a kiss on her husband's mouth, she led them all to the kitchen.

It had already turned dark when Pete jolted awake, surprised to find someone's hand resting on his. Preston was sitting on the chair beside his bed watching him.

"Did you manage to sell her?" Pete asked, pulling his hand away.

"I tried."

"And?"

"She'll do what you want."

"I told you my answer."

"Just be sure you aren't turning this down because I'm the one who offered it."

"Mama did too."

"Come on Petey, aren't you just a little tempted by the valley?

He was. Not just a little.

"Look, don't just dismiss the idea. Give it . . . ."

Pete cut him off. "You staying here tonight?" he asked.

Preston smiled. "I'm a little long for that loveseat in there. I've got a room at the hotel in town. Then off tomorrow to an office full of patients."

"I'm now supposed to say thanks for coming?"

"Not if you don't mean it."

Pete struggled to sit up.

"Maybe I do. Some things need to be said."

Preston cupped his brother's shoulders in his hands and eased him back down on the bed. They watched each other in silence for several minutes.

Preston said, "They love you very much. I envy you."

Pete felt his brother touch his arm. He wanted to say something, but he was afraid of the tears he felt building up. So, he grabbed Preston's strong hand instead. But then he stopped cold, stared at his brother, then hurled the dollar bills in the air. They landed on the sheet, on the floor, on the wardrobe, in Preston's face.

"Get out!" he shouted.

In bed that night, Pete put his arm around his wife's thick shoulders, buried his head in her neck and whispered.

"Well?"

"It's your decision."

He knew her so well. "Which means you think I'm a fool not to go."

"Why'd you ask if you know what I think?"

"I can't," he whispered. "Maybe I should, but I can't."

"I figured."

"You're not going to try to persuade me?"

"No," she said.

"You know what it means."

"Yep. And I hate it."

"And it's still up to me?"

"Yes," she said and pulled him tight against her.

He lay there long afterwards, eyes open, wide awake. He could barely make out the rounded lump of his Kate, huddled under the quilt, sleeping soundly. He tried not to think about what would happen when . . . She'd be fine. The children were tough.

But he couldn't get back to sleep.

American Girl

The Briar Cliff Review (Volume 33), 2021. Nominated for a Pushcart Prize

He sits down next to me. Not the skinny old teacher with chapped lips and the caved-in chest. Not him. The young one, Jeremy. He's maybe twenty-five? Comes to juvie once a week to teach English.

He puts a book on the table in front of me. *The Girl Who Fell from the Sky.* I look around. I'm the only one. How come?

"What's this?" I say.

He smiles and says, "Read it. See what you think."

A week later, he pulls up a chair next to me. He smells like soap. He wants to know what I think about the book. I tell him it's good.

"Do you like the girl," he wants to know. "Do you like the ending?"

I shrug. I don't want to talk that bullshit.

He looks right in my face. His eyes are darker than dark.

"Okay," he says. "How 'bout you write it?"

"Write what?"

"Your opinions," he says, smiling. "I'm guessing you have a lot of opinions, JoJo."

What's he know? I keep my mouth shut in class.

But I'm thinking, Grandma sent me this notebook, says *My Life* on the cover. Clean sheets of paper, no lines. Might try writing something but nothing 'bout that book.

I been two years in this dump. Back in, back out. Mostly for dealing, I don't use. I know from my mama how that goes. Lucky she grew me during one of her dry periods. Didn't last for my two little brothers. The State took 'em, put 'em in foster care. They'll show up here sooner or later.

Jeremy's back. Sits next to me. Feels funny. Is anybody watching?

"Have you done any writing," he asks.

I pull out the notebook. Do I want to impress him?

"You've got a way with words, JoJo," he says and smiles at me.

The girls in here go on about his sexy smile.

"Keep writing," he says. "About your life, about what you do when you're outside."

> *I sell a quality product, got steady customers, money's good. I cover the high schools. Two of them. Mingle easy with the kids from the projects, the hotels, the streets. I'm an American girl top to bottom. My mom claims she's got Egyptian, Chinese, even Indian in her. Probably because so many men were hanging around back when grandma got knocked up. I got a little Hispanic and white from my dad. He's in Ironwood. Assault and battery.*

Jeremy's all over it. "Egyptian," he says. "I knew it. You've got one of those Egyptian profiles you see in the museums."

What's he on about? I'm pretty. I know that. But I don't know nothing about Egyptian profiles.

Girls in here don't miss a thing. "Lucky bitch," they say. "He hot for you, that Jeremy."

"Don't give me that," I say. "He just says I got an ear for language."

"Girl, he interested in more than your writing," they say.

And I'm noticing how he be sitting close up to me, talking so serious. Of course, he moves around the room, talks to other kids. Reads their stuff.

"What grade are you in," he asks.

"I quit," I tell him.

"How'd you manage that?"

"Signed my grandma's name on the permission form," I tell him. "I'm sixteen."

"You in here for selling drugs?" he asks.

What's he? Dumb?

I get caught. End up here. Not because the kids rat on me. It's their funeral if they do. It's the competition that does it. They want my beat, so when they get picked up selling on the street, they give the cops my name and try to steal my territory. And back here I come.

I get called into one of the little lawyer offices they got in here. A porky kind of guy is sitting in one of the two plastic chairs, his belt tight under his gut, pink cheeks. Claims he's the DA. That gets my back up right there. He points to the other chair and asks me did I know Raymond Ortez. I stay on my feet. Turns out they got Raymond on a murder charge. No surprise there.

"What's that got to do with me?" I ask.

"You know his sister, right?"

"What's it to you?"

"Just sit down and answer the question, JoJo."

I stay on my feet.

"Sister's name's Urlene. She alright. Goes to one of the high schools where I deal. She's not a customer, don't use. Smart. I figure she might go to college someday, she so smart."

The dick grins.

"You were on parole on April 5."

"So?"

"You saw a *Spiderman* movie that day."

I said, "Might be. I can't remember that far back."

He says I went to the movie with Urlene.

"Could be."

He tells me he might need me to testify.

"Not a chance. I stay away from courts. They been nothing but trouble for me."

The fat DA stares right in my face. He tells me all I gotta say is I was at the *Spiderman* movie with Urlene on April 5, and Raymond wasn't there.

I get it. I be busting his alibi.

"What's in it for me?" I ask.

He grins again.

"You testify against Ray, we cut you loose from here."

I tell him I got five more months.

"No matter," he says. "You'll walk."

"I'll think about it," I say and leave him sitting there.

I hear him calling out, "Wait!", but I'm done.

Back in my cell, I'm thinking, it's a tough one. If I snitch, I'm outta here. I could do it. Nail old Raymond. I can look a body square in the face and make up all kinds of garbage when I want to. And shit, I got no feeling for Raymond. He's a nasty piece of work.

But his sister Urlene. She's a different story.

I'm thinking, what if Raymond really didn't do it? What if he *was* with Urlene the night of the murder? What if she backs him up? Then I come along and bust him. Say I was at the movies with Urlene that day. I'm not family, like Urlene. Jury'd believe me over her. Raymond's future would snap shut, twenty-five to life, no question. That's harsh.

Of course, I'd be telling the truth to say I went to the movies with Urlene. *Could* be on the day of the murder. I don't know.

"Write about your cell," Jeremy says.

"Why?" I say.

"I want to know. It'll give you practice with descriptive prose," he says.

"Hmmm," I say.

But truth is, I want to give it a try.

> *My cell's on the second floor. You climb the stairs up out of what they call "the rec room," go along a crossway past six other rooms to get to mine. The bed's a cement block with a two-inch-thick mattress, and the light's never turned off. In the beginning, I banged my fists against the door, screamed and shouted, kicked the guards, spat on my no count lawyer. Didn't learn to sleep through the night 'til my fourth time round. It's freezing in winter. Yard's mostly dirt with weeds here and there.*

But my door is fire-engine red. Painted it myself. Shiny acrylic fire-engine red. They let me choose the color.

"Beautiful," Jeremy says. "Just beautiful." And he gives me a look.

DA's back. Puts the squeeze on me. Tells me Raymond's trial is coming up. They have to name me as a witness if I'm gonna help 'em.

I ask him what Urlene's gonna say.

He says she made up this bullshit story about how she and Raymond were watching TV at home on April 5, the afternoon the murder took place. DA says, "Nobody else was home. Nobody saw 'em go in or out of the house. Perfect alibi. Except she's lying, of course."

I think about it. She can lie, I know, because she one time saved my ass with a lie. I was at her school dealing, when a teacher asked me was I selling drugs. Urlene jumped in and said no way, I was her friend, just visiting and on my way out. Urlene would have no trouble lying to save her brother's ass.

But this is different. DA's asking me to lie to put somebody under. A kid, really. Nasty as he is, Raymond's just eighteen.

DA must be reading my mind, because next thing, he starts talking about the murder, how bloody it was. Says Raymond saw this homeless dude sleeping on the street and started stomping his head and kicking him in the stomach. Yelling like he's hella crazy. For no reason, just mean. I could see Raymond doing it. Especially when he's high.

The victim was down on his luck, the DA tells me, jerking all the strings. Had a family, a wife, and little girl.

"Think about it, JoJo. A little girl," he says. Like he cares. Then he tells me the guy died. Right there on the street in the middle of the afternoon, covered in blood.

I ask about witnesses. DA tells me Raymond disappeared before anybody could get a photo. But several witnesses saw him on the street.

"What about drawings?" I ask.

The cops always ask witnesses for drawings. DA says drawings aren't good evidence.

"You got any?" I ask, pointing to his slumped down briefcase on the floor.

I can tell he don't want to, but he pulls 'em out. I spread 'em on the metal table in front of me and pick 'em up one at a time.

I tell him I'd feel better lying on the stand if the drawings showed that little snake tattoo on Raymond's neck just below his right ear. It's not there.

They must not have seen it, DA says, because of that army jacket Raymond had on.

I get it. No witnesses. Drawings in Raymond's favor. Sister provides the alibi. These jokers really need me. Plus, it sounds fishy. Why Raymond?

DA says he got picked up running down the same street where the murder occurred. Got picked out of a line-up.

"So, you don't need me."

"Line up evidence is flimsy," he tells me. "With the sister's testimony, Raymond walks."

He reminds me of the deal. I testify. *I* walk.

"I don't want you to lie," he says, lying through his teeth. "But you saw *Spiderman* with Urlene. That's the truth."

I tell him I'll think about it.

Jeremy pulls up a chair at my table and asks me how come I go right back to selling when I get paroled.

I look straight into those dark, dark eyes and smile.

"Here's why," I say. "I like it."

He don't pull back, don't look shocked, don't lecture me. Just smiles back at me, that sexy smile the girls go on about, and says, "Write about it."

Face all smooth like he don't shave, curly hair cut close.

"Write," he says. "Write."

> *I deal because I like the respect. Like the money, like playing dumb when the cops show up at school. Like acting mainey. Even like the streets, all the crazies out there. The*

streets are cold, but they know me out there. Tell me stories you wouldn't believe. Not that I'm homeless, though I've spent a night or two under the overpass. Mostly, my grandma takes me in, fusses over me, feeds me beans and tacos, cries when I go back to juvie. Rags on me to clean up my act.

"You're so smart, JoJo," he tells me, giving me the look.

"Street smart," I say.

"That too. But I'm talking book smart. You've got potential."

"Potential?" I be mocking him.

"You could be anything you set your heart on."

"Bullshit," I say. "You seen my record?"

"You get yourself out of here," he says. "And we'll see what we can do."

"Like what?"

"Maybe write letters to get you back in school," he says. "Help you find a job so you don't have to deal."

He looking at me so serious. Then he reaches over and puts his hand on top of mine. Is anybody looking? He not supposed to do this. But I don't move my hand. His is large and warm. I feel lit up, like I'm smiling all over.

I'm hearing it now. They all teasing.

"Sexy Jerry's got the hots for you, girl. I saw you holding hands. You in love for sure."

I don't say nothing. I'm too confused.

DA's back. Writes out a witness statement for me. I sign it. I'm outta here. On my way to high school, college. On my way to . . . .

First thing I see when I come into the courtroom is Raymond's eyes looking like he'd kill me if he had a chance. The room's hot and small, only a few benches for the public. I look around. Nobody I know. Not even Urlene, who's a witness like me and can't be in here until her turn comes. The judge is up there, fussing with his papers. Face white as his hair, thin lips, no color. A ghost in black robes.

DA got on a suit, pants too short. Sweat dripping off his fat chin. Puts me on the stand, shows me my statement, asks me if all of it's true. I say yes. I don't look at Raymond. The PD, a woman, then has a go at me. Her skirt is wrinkled and too snug on the hips. I figure this kind of law's no way to get rich. She asks if I'm sure the day I saw *Spiderman* was April 5. I lie. It ain't even hard. I'm on my way out. She tries to trip me up with questions about the time of the movie, about what else I did that day. I rehearsed it all with the DA and stick to my story.

In the hall on the way out, there's Urlene.

"Traitor bitch!" she calls out.

PD pulls her off to a corner. First time I feel bad. But it don't last. I'm on my way.

DA's here with some papers. His big old face grinning.

"You did good," he says. "Scored a conviction. Judge gave him twenty-five to life."

Raymond. I don't want to think about it.

I ask when do I get out.

"Soon," he says. "Just got to do the paperwork. Soon."

First time Jeremy shows up, I tell him.

"I'm getting out."

He's smiling. Pulls me up from the table and hugs me. Just like that. I feel the muscles in his arms, smell that clean soap on him.

I feel light, happy. Don't stop. Don't stop.

"Write about it," he says. "All the things you want to do out there."

> *I'm coming out! Coming out! First thing I'm gonna do is eat nachos with lots of cheese and cookie dough ice cream and drink a supersize root beer. Then I'm gonna dump my stash outta my rubber boots where I hid it. I'm gonna cruise the streets, make all those crazies happy, handing the stuff out free.*
>
> *After that, I'm gonna call up Jeremy, ask him to get me back in school like he promised. Ask him about getting me a*

job on weekends waitressing. I'd be good at that. All those tips. Bring him to meet Grandma. She'd like that.

"Interesting," is what Jeremy says, reading it.

"How ma gonna find you?" I ask him.

"What do you mean?" he says.

"You know, when I'm out. Like your number, your email."

"I can't give you that in here," he says.

"How come?"

"Juvenile Education policy."

I'm thinking, where was that policy when you held my hand? Hugged me? But I got practical things on my mind.

"How am I gonna find you?" I ask him.

"I'll come up with something," he says.

Back home with Grandma. She all excited, filling me up with beans and rice. I try to act happy. Poor old lady. I'm all she has. Her son at Ironwood. My little brothers back in foster care. They too wild. She tried, but she's old, and they wild.

The street's too hot for me. Everybody buzzing about Raymond, how he's innocent, how I put him away. Can't sell, even if I want to. No customers. They'll be back. But I'm keeping myself scarce right now.

Tried to call Juvenile Education to get Jeremy's number. Nothing. I did find a number online for the State Juvenile Facilities and called it. Nothing but answering machines, sending me to one machine after another 'til I got a busy signal.

I try not to think about Jeremy.

I go to Central High, try to enroll. Bitch in the office takes one look at me, says school's too full. Sends me to Washington High. Same thing. Principal says District got a program for troubled youth. Maybe I could try that. Not a chance.

I try not to think about Jeremy.

I get hired for a shift at McDonalds. Quit after a week. Pay's lousy, work's disgusting.

Wake up at night, feel Jeremy's hand, warm, strong. Feel his arms.

Smell his soap clean skin. Dude from Raymond's old gang knocks on Grandma's door. All in black, hoodie pulled low. Hella scary.

"You in trouble, girl," he says. "Better make yourself scarce. They after you."

I don't waste no time. Tiptoe into Grandma's room. Kiss her cheek. Snoring, sounds like a whistle. Glad she isn't awake. Makes me sad, letting her down. Again. Kiss her. Again.

Once outside, I figure I have no choice. Juvie or else. I know the drill. I hang out till daylight, then wander down to the street. Buyers always there, day and night, some walking by casual, like they shopping, some wild-eyed crazy, all on the lookout. I wait till I see a cop cruise by. Make my move. Bingo.

Busted.

"You're back?"

It's Jeremy, acting all disappointed. I been waiting for him. Sits down beside me. Close. I'm waiting.

"So, what happened, JoJo?" Voice so sweet. "Can you tell me?"

I keep quiet.

He leans over.

"Can you write about it?"

I'm waiting. Then he does it, takes my hand, squeezes it.

"Write about it, JoJo."

I'm on my feet. I'm yelling.

"He touched me! Get him away! Son of a bitch touched me!"

Guards jumping up. Everybody watching.

Done for.

Son of a bitch. All the time telling me to write my feelings.

Here's the truth. Jeremy. You did me shady. All that bullshit about how smart I am. You were getting off on it.

Here's the truth, Jeremy. I ain't gonna change. This is who I am. I'll be back, out on the streets, ducking the red and blue lights. Selling my product. Playing my cards right. Living my life.

Trying not to think about Raymond.

A Split in the Tree

Poydras Review, November 9, 2020

A fierce crack explodes my dream. Too loud for thunder. I spring up in bed. The window is black. The clock says 4:00 A.M. Was it a bomb? I'm seventy-five years old, a widow. Live by myself. I sit, listening, afraid to move.

Screaming sirens jolt me awake. 7:00 A.M. Can't believe I got back to sleep. I throw a raincoat over my bathrobe, slip my feet into clogs and rush outside. Fire trucks block the narrow road in front of my house, red lights flashing. Slick yellow raincoats everywhere. My neighbors are packed together behind the fire trucks. What's going on? But then I see. A tree split down the middle on the bank across from my house. Half of the Monterey pine is standing, needles green, untouched. The other half is splintered into jagged logs, lying on the bank, caught in the branches of trees, blocking the road, caving the roof of a car, its window glass shattered.

"Get back in the house," a fireman yells.

For the first time, I look around me. The railing on my deck is in pieces, a log wedged between the sharp edges of wood.

"Get back in the house!"

But I don't move. I see a body's lying out there on the street. Its leg is pinned beneath a large log. The head is twisted to the side. It's a man's head, a young man's head. Thick black hair, dark skin. He's lying on something, maybe a backpack. Yellow raincoats are working to pull the log off the man's leg. I hear a moan.

The fireman approaches, scowling.

"Get in the house."

"Who is he?" I ask.

"Lady, get in the house!"

Out the window I see flashing lights. More sirens. And then, finally, quiet. They're gone. Neighbors are swarming all over the road, some are rolling logs to the side to widen the passage for cars, others are on their cell phones. Most are just gawking and gossiping. Like me.

Who was that man? Is he dead? What was he doing here at four in the morning? Was that really just lightning?

"He's a thief," my neighbor Stan yells. "He got my iPad. Check your car."

The trunk of my Prius flips open without my remote. My binoculars are missing, my Swarovski's, worth over $2000. Gone. My son Bobby gave me those binoculars for my seventieth birthday. I treasured them. And I locked the car. I always lock the car.

"The lock's broken," Stan tells me. "That man under the log stole your things."

Who is he? I want to strangle him.

Two weeks later, I open the door to a short man with thick arm muscles and squinty blue eyes. He's carrying a large satchel.

"Deputy Sheriff," he announces. He walks inside and pulls a plastic bag out of his satchel. "These yours?"

I nod. They're in there, flattened, the lenses in broken shards. I start to cry.

"We got him in custody," he says.

"He's alive?"

"Oh yeah. Broken leg, that's all. He's still in the hospital, but as soon as he's walking, he's on his way. Kaput."

"On his way?" I ask.

"To one of those Muslim countries."

"Why?" I feel a tightening in my stomach.

"You can tell just by looking at him. He's from somewhere in the Middle East."

"You think he's a Muslim?"

"Whatever he is, he don't belong here," the deputy says.

The next day, I read in the local paper that a Syrian man named Jamal Hagar is the one who stole my backpack.

> *LIGHTNING STRIKE PINS SON OF IMMIGRANT*
>
> A freak lightning flash Monday night split a Monterey Pine on West Caledonia Street in Cypress Hills. A flying log pinned Jamal Hagar, who was allegedly robbing cars at the time the tree exploded. Hagar's father, Akram Hagar, who owns a computer repair business in San Jose, is an undocumented immigrant from Syria. As a result of this incident, he is in custody with his wife for overstaying their visas. Officials are looking into Jamal's immigration status.
>
> "They are illegals," ICE officer Robert Green stated, "and will be deported." As he was led away, Akram Hagar shouted to reporters, "Jamal is a good boy. I don't know what happened. He's a good boy."

But Jamal Hagar is not a good boy. He broke into my car in the middle of the night and stole my binoculars.

Neighbor Stan stops me on the street, yanking his labradoodle's leash while the dog tries to jump on me. Stan's the kind of neighbor who gives you rides to the airport, carries your Christmas tree into the house, takes your broken washing machine to the dump. He's a retired fireman, thick body, thin hair, projects confidence. I like him despite his annoying dog.

"I want the son of a bitch deported," he tells me. "If he isn't a terrorist already, he'll become one. They all do. You've heard how they're recruiting these young Muslims on the internet. I'll bet a million our little car thief is already in their hands."

I give it some thought then ask, "Stan, what would a terrorist be doing breaking into cars in the middle of the night?"

"Who knows? Raising money for the cause?"

The cause? Could he be talking about al-Qaeda? I heard a lot about it on NBC after 9/11.

"Seems a little far-fetched," I say.

"Oh, Gracie," Stan says. "You're so naïve."

He then tells me the boy's arraignment is coming up soon, and he's going.

"Why don't you come with me?" he says. "It might open your eyes a little."

Well, why not? I've never actually been in a courtroom. Besides, I'm a victim, and I'm still pretty mad about that.

The judge, a pudgy woman with untidy red hair, flips through a stack of folders, opens one, and calls out, "Appearances for The People vs. Jamal Hagar."

A scowling young man clomps his way to the council table on crutches, his leg in a full-length cast. He looks younger than I remember.

The judge reads the charges against him in a monotone without looking up. My binoculars, Stan's iPad, several other items from my neighbors' cars.

"How do you plead?" she asks.

The man mumbles something.

Without looking at his client, the public defender asks for an early trial. And the thief is led away in handcuffs.

Two men in dark suits stand up to leave the courtroom.

"ICE agents," Stan whispers. "They're waiting for him."

"What do you mean?"

"If the jury acquits, they'll nab him. If he goes to jail, they'll arrest him when he's released."

"Is he illegal?"

"If ICE is here, it's a sure bet," he says.

As I leave the courtroom, I see two children sitting on a bench in the hallway. The boy's dark hair is curly and tangled. His jeans have holes at the knees. He looks to be about ten. A little girl in stained sweatpants stares at me with black eyes. Her skinny wrists poke out of the sleeves of her faded blue sweater. She looks to be the age of my granddaughter, Katy—eight. As I pass by, the boy jumps up.

"Lady," he says. "Did you see my brother? Jamal, my brother, is he in there?"

Before I can answer, Stan rushes me past.

"Who are those children?" I ask him.

"Who knows?" he says.

The next day the local paper has the story.

> Alleged car thief Jamal Hagar pleaded not guilty yesterday in Cypress County Superior Court to Auto Burglary. Jamal's father, Akram Hagar, owner of Hi Tech Computer Repairs, and his wife Leah have been deported as illegal immigrants to Syria, their home country, by Immigration and Customs Enforcement. Jamal will be incarcerated in the county jail until his trial. Two younger children have been placed in foster care.

A couple of months after the arraignment, Stan invites me to a meeting of a group called "Sensible Citizens" at the Cypress Hills Community Center.

"We need to make some decisions about that Muslim car thief," he explains.

"Is this one of those anti-immigrant groups?" I ask, looking him straight in the eye.

As I said, I really like Stan. He's been good to me, but I don't want to get caught up in some America First business. That's not me.

"We're not against immigrants per se," he assures me. "It's more like neighborhood protection. It's your neighbors who'll be there, Gracie. You know these folks."

Well, I can't argue with that. I think about my stolen binoculars and get angry all over again. We do need protection. So, I join a cluster of my neighbors as the president of Sensible Citizens welcomes our group. Stan whispers that the president is the CEO of a finance company.

"A big deal," he says.

What I see is a young man, maybe in his forties, about six feet, wearing Giants cap and sweatpants. A nice looking fellow. He looks around at the audience.

"Folks, I don't like to frighten you, but the man who recently victimized your neighborhood could well be a terrorist."

A gasp. A few heads nodding.

Stan takes over.

"You know from the paper that the thief's parents have now been deported and the thief has been convicted. What does that tell you?"

He pauses for effect.

"He is now parentless and ripe for the onslaught of terrorist propaganda. That is, if he isn't already a terrorist."

"The jerk's in jail, right?" A male voice. I think it's the man who bought the old Shelburn house.

"In jail for the time being," Stan says, "Unfortunately, that leftist judge agreed to reduce Jamal's crime to second degree burglary, a misdemeanor. Something about his youth, his injury, and his previously clean record. He'll be out in less than a year. Meanwhile, the jails are rife with terrorists."

Like I said, I'm an old lady. I'm not against immigrants. I'm really not, but I've known Stan for years. I trust him. And what he says has me scared.

"We need to organize," Stan continues. "Make sure this thief never returns to our community. Write to ICE, lots of letters, making sure they'll get him when he's released from jail."

"I heard he's a citizen," Matt Jefferson says. Margie Jefferson's teenaged son, a smart boy.

"Apparently there's some question about that," Stan says. "He claims he was born here, but they can't find a U.S. birth certificate. Whatever. He's a criminal. He doesn't belong in this country."

Even if he's a citizen? That doesn't sound right.

I zip my down jacket against the late autumn chill as I wait with Stan and other neighbors outside the gate of the Cypress County jail. Two men wearing sweatshirts with the words "Police ICE" across the front lean on a government car.

Stan rounded us up this morning, said it was imperative, that's his word, that the neighbors show some solidarity. So, here I am. But we're not the only ones waiting. Several women hover together, chattering in a strange language, their eyes fixed on the jail. A boy pulls one of the women toward the gate. I look closely. I'm sure he's the boy I saw at the courthouse. The girl with him stands silent, shivering. Her black hair strings down practically to her waist. She's looking at me with dark eyes, like she expects something. I look away.

Suddenly, a man emerges from the jail. Is this Jamal? I don't recognize him. He's grown a thick, dark beard and his broad shoulders stretch the fabric of his Warriors sweatshirt. I remember him in court as a slender boy; he comes out a swarthy, hairy, beefed-up man.

"You want this man back in your neighborhood?" Stan asks me.

No, I don't. He scares me.

A guard lifts a large ring of keys from his pocket and unlocks the gate. The ICE men move swiftly. But just as they grab Jamal, the two children race forward, hugging his legs, his waist.

"Jamal! Jamal!"

I watch the ICE men knock the children away, grab Jamal's arms, handcuff him, and push him toward their car.

Jamal is pleading. "I'm a citizen. I was born here. You can't do this."

"Prove it!" one of the men says, shoving him into the back of the car.

As the government car pulls away, Stan and some of the neighbors cheer.

Women are yelling at the car. The boy races after it, arms outstretched, screaming.

"Those poor children," I say.

A short, heavy-set woman glares at me.

"Those poor children are Mohammed and Rina," she says in harsh, labored English, tugging her flowered headscarf down over her forehead. "Jamal's brother and sister. Citizens," she hits every syllable, "of your country. Like Jamal. How you feel about that?"

How do I feel?

Suddenly she's in my face. I feel the heat of her breath, faint smell of garlic.

"They're children," she says. "Little children. They need their brother."

"I'm sorry," I mutter. "But he broke into my car."

"He's done his time," she hisses. "He's a poor man, needed money. And he's paid for it."

"I don't . . ."

I look around for an escape, but Stan is chatting with the rest of his group, paying no heed to this angry woman.

The boy rushes up to us, crying, fists clinched.

"Where are they taking him?" He grabs the woman's arm. "Stop them. Make them stop."

"Please, Lady."

It's the little girl, peering up at me. I feel her hand, touching mine. It's small, so soft. I take it in mine. I know this hand.

I think of endless games of Monopoly, of sewing clothes for the Barbies. Of mac and cheese. We're laughing, snuggled up together on the sofa, a book in my lap, her sweet soft hand on my arm. Katy.

"Hello," I say. "Is this your grandmother?"

"Foster mom. Temporary," the woman says. "Jamal's the brother. They need him."

"I'm sorry," I say again. What else can I say?

She's looking up at me, the little girl.

"Please, lady. I want to go home."

So, do I. I want to get away as fast as I can.

"A lawyer," the woman says, looking straight at me. "Jamal needs a lawyer."

"I can't . . ."

As I make my escape, the woman calls out, "Please. Please. A lawyer."

I want to say I don't know any lawyers. But, of course, I do. Half the elders in my church are lawyers. I've known them for years.

This is none of my business.

Several weeks later, at Stan's insistence, I attend a meeting of Sensible Citizens. He says they are going to discuss Jamal's case, and I admit I'm curious. Stan's mood is jubilant as he tells the group that we have won a significant battle in the war against terrorism.

So, that's how he sees it. I think about the kids, Jamal's brother and sister.

"Onto the next step," he crows. "I've learned that Jamal's first hearing will take place on December 3 in the San Francisco office on Sansome Street. That's three weeks from now."

Stan tells us that this hearing is called a "master calendar" hearing, and if Jamal doesn't show up, he will be automatically deported and not allowed back into the US for ten years. But since Jamal is being detained, ICE has an obligation to notify him of the hearing and tell him he has the right to an attorney at his own expense.

"And that's our ace in the hole," Stan says. "No way Jamal has money for a lawyer. And that's good."

"What would a lawyer do?" I ask.

"I guess the lawyer would try to prove Jamal is a citizen."

Stan tells us he has written to the judge describing Jamal's theft in detail and emphasizing that he is a danger to our community.

I go about my life, walking the neighborhood, volunteering at the public library, sketching live models in my college extension class. Active for seventy-five.

I hear that harsh voice screaming for a lawyer.

I find the telephone number of a lawyer I know in the Church directory.

I see the children. What were their names? The boy running after the car. Mohammed.

I pick up the phone.

I see the body trapped under that log, the dark curly hair, my shattered binoculars.

I feel a little girl's hand. Katy. No, the girl's name is Rina. *Please, lady.*

Through the window I see the tree, living and dead. Split forever.

I put the phone down. Maybe later.

A Case for Wrongful Death

Wild Violet Magazine, October 30, 2020

Connie rocked back and forth on the faded velvet sofa in her sister Lois's living room. It was summer 1940.

"Maybe you're wrong," Lois said.

"I missed twice. I never missed before."

"You might just be nervous, the wedding coming and all," Lois said.

"I threw up yesterday."

"See there. Could be nerves."

Connie reached over and clutched Lois's arm.

"Tell me what to do."

Lois was a married lady, her big sister. She'd know.

"Have you told George?"

Connie shook her head.

Lois pulled her sister close and kissed her damp cheek.

"Good. Wait 'til after the wedding. Then tell him."

"Why?"

"Just say the baby's premature. He won't know the difference."

Connie's head jerked up.

"It's his!"

Lois smiled.

"Of course, it's his. But if he doesn't know now, he'll back up your story when the baby comes early."

"It's not George I'm worried about. It's Papa."

"How's he going to know?"

"Same way everybody will. All those old ladies at the church, counting the months on their fingers. Big fat baby coming out premature? Uh-huh!"

Lois nodded.

Connie wiped her nose.

"I'm scared of Papa."

"Yeah, I know. But what's the worst he can do?"

"Disown me."

"He would never. You're his favorite."

"I wouldn't be if he knew. He'd look at me so disappointed. And he wouldn't love me anymore. That's the part I couldn't bear."

Lois thought a minute.

"You could get married early," she finally said. "Next week, say. Tell people you and George just don't want a big wedding."

"I can't. My dress is paid for. The reception's all planned. They'd start asking questions. Besides the baby would be coming way too early, no matter when I get married."

"I think you should see a doctor. Make sure you're right about this."

"I am sure."

"You never know. One time, I thought I was pregnant. I made an appointment with a doctor in Stanton."

"Really? What happened?"

"My period was late. That was all."

"Were you married?"

Lois shook her head.

Connie stared at her big sister.

"What would you have done if you were?" she asked. "I would probably have gotten a doctor to help me."

"Help you do what?"

"I don't know. It didn't happen."

"But it's happening to me."

Connie was crying.

"Maybe. We need to find out for sure. But if so, I'd advise you to have the baby."

"Papa would be so ashamed."

"Oh, sweetie," Lois moaned, holding Connie tight, rocking her on the velvet sofa.

She'd met him in the spring, May 12, 1939, to be exact, when she was still sixteen. He'd come from Ringgold, Virginia looking to set up a business. She didn't know why he picked her, he was so much older and smarter. And he had that dimple in his chin, and he was so tall. Her papa was Tabernacle Baptist and too strict to let her go out with him, so he visited her at home, on the front porch.

"You still a baby," her papa said. "You got no business with a man like that."

They lived in Goldfield, North Carolina, on the small tobacco farm her papa, Walton Reynolds, Jr., had inherited from his papa. Times being hard, all the children from five on up worked on the land, summers and after school, picking tobacco, milking the three cows, feeding the chickens. Connie was the last child of six. The seventh had died, taking her mother with her.

Three months, they sat out there, Connie pumping herself back and forth on the white wooden swing. George sitting opposite on a wicker chair, cooling himself with a fan from the funeral home, talking about his future.

Every twenty minutes or so, her papa would come out on the porch, make some comment about the weather, check his watch, and head back in. Then around nine o'clock, he'd announce, "Bedtime for this little girl." And George would disappear into the twilight of a long summer day.

Meanwhile, he talked, and he talked. About his plan to save up the money he was making at the hardware store so he could set himself up in business.

"This town is ready for a proper shoe store," he'd tell her. "Everybody orders their shoes from Sears Roebuck, you know that. And they don't fit good. Men out in the fields, they need good fitting shoes. When I get my store, they can come in and try on as many pairs as they like 'til they find one that fits perfect. Women too. I can stock pretty shoes, prettier than anything you see in the catalog. Not to mention that cheap trash they sell in the general store."

She loved to hear him talk. About securing a loan from the bank and checking out storefronts for rent and negotiating deals with boot merchandizers. She couldn't imagine how he knew so much. After a while, he started using "we" and "our" when he talked, as in, "You'll sell the ladies their spectator pumps, and I'll man the register."

By the end of the year, Connie's papa had agreed she could marry George so long as they waited until she finished high school. And that would be in June.

After the announcement in the local weekly at Christmas, her papa started letting her go out with George on Sundays after church. They'd take off in his black Ford coupe to visit friends or stop by an open field to spread a blanket and eat deviled eggs and ham biscuits. It was March when he kissed her for the first time. Sunny and warm, white apple blossoms blooming early, new grass smelling fresh.

"Come here," George said. He was lying down on his side. Connie sat down on the blanket beside him and began opening the picnic basket.

"No. Here, with me," he said and pulled her down beside him, so they were lying face to face. Connie's first thought was her papa, how he would say, "Pick yourself up right now and go home." But she found she couldn't move. She was staring into George's eyes, which seemed darker than she remembered. She tried not to notice his arm heavy on her waist, his fingers somewhere, his breath on her cheek. And he was pulling her, closer and closer, so that her breasts were touching his chest. She reached out automatically to push him away. And that's when he did it. He put his hand on the back of her head and kissed her. On the mouth. She felt herself moving closer, like something outside of her was in charge. Then she was kissing him, and her hand was feeling the soft skin under his shirt. He stopped it that time, pulled himself up, and said, "Get out the picnic, honey" in a hoarse voice she hadn't heard before.

After that, every time they took a drive, she would tell herself, I'm not gonna do it, not this time. She would not lie down beside him, she would not let him kiss her, it was a sin to even want to. And in the car, on the way, it seemed so easy, saying no. But then he would stop the car. And she would follow him and let him pull her down, down onto the blanket, down against his hard chest, and she would feel herself melting into him. Feel that place somewhere low in her body come alive. He stopped it the next time and the next. Until he couldn't.

Walton Reynolds still didn't like it. George was a good man; he'd give him that. But he was a man. Full grown. And Connie was his baby girl. Innocent as dawn. At least he prayed it was so.

In the beginning, when George first started sniffing around, there was no way Walton was permitting him to take that child out of the house, to Lord knows where, to do no telling what. His Connie was a good Christian girl. She'd be slow to temptation. But she was nuts about that man, and Walton was taking no chances. He'd prayed over the matter with Reverend Farris at the Tabernacle, and the Lord had directed him to keep that child close by. He figured George couldn't get into much mischief on the porch with the old man coming by every half hour making sure all four feet were on the ground.

It was hard being a father without a woman on hand. She'd have known what to do, how to talk to Connie about men. He didn't. As much as he loved her, he didn't know how to say things a girl needed to hear. Of course, she had sisters, but he didn't trust them to protect her. Sooner or later, they'd have given in to George. He was that persuasive.

But then, he had given in too. It was after Charlie Watson at the hardware store had told him that he didn't know how he'd manage without George. And Mr. Petty at the bank had told him George put $10 in his account every week, and it stayed right there. Meanwhile, George kept coming by, moving into the parlor when the weather turned cold, behaving himself, and Connie kept saying she wanted to marry him. So, he prayed some more, and the Lord had given His blessing.

Even then, he didn't let her go out with him at night. The Lord was pretty strong on that. Lead us not into temptation. But Sunday afternoons after church? George had started attending Tabernacle, had come forward after the service one Sunday and dedicated his life to Christian service. But even after that, the first time George offered to take Connie for a ride after church, he'd said no. Connie had begged, said they would just ride around, maybe take a picnic. In broad daylight. He's spent some time on his knees on that waiting for the Word. Because what would happen if . . . He didn't want to think about it. Because it was a deadly sin. And, as much as he loved her, more than any of the others, he might not be able to forgive her. And that would break his heart.

Finally, he gave in. No riding around after dark. Just Sunday afternoons.

But he still didn't like it.

Dr. Boyer's waiting room was full when they got there. Lois had found the office on the main street of Stanton in a big white brick house. It looked like somebody's living room with Queen Anne chairs and linen tufted loveseats. Lois settled her sister next to the front window and sat down beside her. The other women in the room glanced up, then returned to the back copies of Ladies Home Journal they held in their laps. Connie kept her head down.

Dr. Boyer was a large man, at least six feet and burly, but when he finally ushered her into his office and shook her hand, Connie was surprised at how soft it was.

"What seems to be the problem?"

Connie started to cry, so Lois answered for her.

"My sister has missed her monthly and thinks something might be wrong," she said.

Dr. Boyer nodded and began asking questions. Connie answered in monotone.

"I need to have a look at you," he said and showed her into a room just large enough for a long table, a wooden cabinet with a sink, and a stern-faced woman, bulky in her nursing uniform.

"Take off your underpants and lie down," the nurse said, pointing to the table.

Connie shivered as Dr. Boyer eased her legs apart and began to shove his fingers into her. She wanted to get up, run out of the office. He was hurting her.

"Congratulations."

She jumped up, startled.

"No wonder your periods have disappeared," he said. "You're going to have a baby."

"I want to see my sister," Connie burst out.

Back in his office, Dr. Boyer seated himself behind a highly polished walnut desk and faced the two women. He was not smiling.

"I take it you're not married," he said.

Connie shook her head, too choked up to speak.

"Not yet," Lois said. "The wedding's in September."

"Couldn't wait, huh?" the doctor said. "Well, you won't be the first," he chuckled. "Or the last."

"It's not funny," Lois said.

He looked at Connie who was digging at her eyes with a crumpled Kleenex.

"You're right. Let's see. For now, get a lot of sleep and eat a healthy diet. I'll see you in two months. You can make an appointment with my nurse."

Dr. Boyer waited. They both looked at Connie.

"I can't," Connie finally mumbled.

"What do you mean?"

"I want to . . . you know," she said.

Dr. Boyer stood up.

"I see. Did somebody tell you I do abortions? Because they're wrong."

The doctor stood by the door, twisting the knob.

"Is your intended the father?"

Connie nodded.

"Well, then my best advice is marry him. Have the baby. You'll never regret it."

"That's what I told her," Lois said.

"I can't."

"Well, then I can't help you."

"Just the name of somebody."

Connie was begging.

Dr. Boyer hesitated.

"There's a man in town named 'Wheeler.' He might be somebody to talk to."

"Where's his office?" Lois asked.

"There's an office building on South Main. You might check there."

"Thank you," Connie said.

"You're making a mistake," the doctor said and ushered them out of his office.

The overhead light in Dr. Wheeler's office was dim, the upholstery on the chairs was faded, and the carpet stained. There were no other patients.

"Who sent you?" he asked.

A rotund little man in a crumpled brown suit. Connie wanted to run.

"Excuse me, sir," Lois said, "but are you a doctor?"

"Of course," he said.

"Dr. Boyer sent us," she said.

Wheeler smiled.

"I see. What can I do for you?"

"She's expecting, and she doesn't want to be."

"You want me to terminate your pregnancy?" he asked Connie.

Connie nodded.

"Are you sure?"

"Yes, sir." Her voice was so low he had to lean forward to hear her.

"How far along are you?"

"Two months," Lois said.

"Is that right?" Dr. Wheeler stared at Connie.

She nodded.

"Okay," he said. "Let's get to work."

Connie clung to her sister's hand as she followed Wheeler into a closet-sized room with a bare wooden table and a small sink in the corner.

"You have to stay out there," the doctor said to Lois.

"No," Connie wailed.

"I'll be right outside," Lois said. "But remember, you don't have to do this."

"Look," Wheeler said to Connie. "If you don't want to, just say so."

She didn't, not here, not with this little man. But she had no choice.

"Do it," she said.

Wheeler spread a blanket over the table.

She closed her eyes and started to pray.

"God, forgive me."

Wheeler burst out, "I can't work with that kind of thing going on."

So, she prayed in her head. God forgive me—he was pulling her legs apart—I'll never, ever go against your will again – his cold hands were touching her—God, make me good, make me whole, make me good – something was going up inside of her, sticking into her, sharp, sharp– "Stop! You're hurting me"—it kept moving, up, inside, pricking her, cutting – "No! Don't!"

"It hurts. It hurts! God, make it stop!"

Pain crashed through her, wave after wave.

Then something was covering her face.

"Lois!" she yelled.

"It won't be long now," she heard him say. "Start counting backward from 100." It was the last thing she remembered.

She woke up confused. It was dark, and she ached somewhere deep. She sat up. Looked around. Then she was running out of the dark, into the next room, to her sister, hugging her, clinging to her.

"How do you feel?" Lois asked, holding her.

"I want to go home."

Wheeler suddenly appeared.

"It was successful," he said. "But she needs to rest. Make sure she has plenty of sleep tonight and aspirin for pain."

"My sweet sister, you've been so brave," Lois said as they opened the door to fresh air, yellow-green leaves, light.

Connie could barely concentrate the sun was so bright.

"We'll go home, I promise," Lois said. "But we're supposed to shop, remember? That's our excuse for coming to Stanton."

"I don't feel good."

Lois put her arm around Connie's waist and walked her to the car.

"Okay. Let's go home. I'll make up something for Papa."

On the way back to Goldfields, Connie tried to forget the dark room and the horrid little man. But she couldn't forget the pain, which kept rippling through her. She felt dizzy, like at any moment she might be sick.

They were waiting supper when she got home. Sylvia, the only sister still living at home, had cooked up pork sausage, fresh corn, and butterbeans. Spoonbread.

"You girls been spending all my money?" her papa said.

"We were just looking," Lois said. "Getting ideas for the bridesmaids' dresses."

"Well, sit down and eat," he said.

It felt good to sit, but the smell of the fried sausage disgusted her, and even sitting down, she felt dizzy, like she might faint.

"I don't feel so good," she said. "I think I just might go to bed."

Sylvia put her hand on Connie's forehead. "You feel hot," she said. "You think you might have picked up something nasty in Stanton?"

It felt good to sink into her bed. She was so tired, and her head hurt. She wanted to sleep forever.

But in the middle of the night, she woke up, shivering, her whole body aching.

"Papa!"

The light hurt her eyes, so she kept them shut. But she could hear her papa and Sylvia whispering, and then she heard Lois. What was she doing here?

"I'm so cold."

The blankets felt heavy, piled up on her. And her head hurt.

She woke herself up the next time, throwing blankets onto the floor, burning up.

Then it was daylight, and a man was bending over her. Was it Dr. Thornton?

She heard the man say, "Call an ambulance. Her fever's through the roof."

It was Dr. Thornton. She'd known him all her life. Thank God.

She didn't remember how she got to the hospital. But George was there, looking down at her, his face so serious, his hand gripping hers.

"I'm sorry," she tried to say. But it came out all wrong.

He was leaning down, his face close.

"What? I can't understand you. I love you."

"I'm sorry," she tried again.

"She's not making sense," he said to someone in the room.

"I'm so hot."

And then the pain was tearing through her. Sharp, red, jagged.

"Help me!" she screamed and fell silent.

"What happened?" Lois asked.

"I think she fainted," Sylvia said.

"No! Something happened."

Lois reached for Connie's hand; it was limp. It's that terrible little man, she thought. God, don't let it be that.

"Nurse!" she raced over to the gray-haired woman who was taking the pulse of a patient three beds away and grabbed her arm.

"Quick," she said. "Over here."

"Hold your horses," the nurse said. "Can't you see I'm busy?" She pointed to the ward full of patients.

"No," Lois said. "You have to come. Something's wrong," and she dragged her by the arm to Connie's bed, where George stood staring at the still figure.

"I'd thank you to let go of me," the nurse said.

But then she looked at Connie and her expression froze. She felt Connie's pulse, rushed from the room, and returned with two orderlies who carried Connie out on a stretcher.

"Please go to the waiting room," the nurse said. "Dr. Thornton is with her. He'll find you when he knows something."

Lois faced the nurse. "Where are they taking her?"

"I think she's in the operating room."

"What's going on?" George shouted.

"Calm down, George," Walton Reynolds said. "Dr. Thornton knows his business."

Lois's fingernails dug into Sylvia's hand as they walked to the waiting room. Why had she taken her to that awful doctor?

The waiting room was empty. The family sat huddled together in metal folding chairs next to the Coke machine and waited. George paced back and forth across the worn linoleum.

Walton was leaning forward, motionless, his hands locked together in his lap, his eyes shut. Lois figured he was praying. She bowed her head and silently begged, don't let her die, don't let her die.

Dr. Thornton at last appeared. He lowered his tall, clumsy frame into one of the metal chairs and faced the family he had been treating for decades, the family he had mourned with fifteen years before at the loss of their mother and wife. He looked exhausted.

"We need to talk," he said, putting his hand on Walton's knee. "There's a room on the second floor. It's more private."

"What's happening?" George cried.

"I'll explain everything. Would you please come with me?"

"Now!" George said. "I want to see her now!" But he followed the family down the bare corridor, into the elevator, and up to a small room with prints of Saturday Evening Post covers on the wall and an odd mismatch of armchairs and sofas.

When they were seated, Dr. Thornton said, "I have bad news."

"No!" George cried.

"I'm afraid Connie has passed away."

"I don't believe you!" George jumped up. "Let me see her."

"Please sit down, George," Dr. Thornton said. "I wish it weren't true. I'm so sorry."

Lois and Sylvia were holding each other, sobbing; their father stared at the wall of posters in front of him, stone-faced.

"I'll try to explain what happened as best I can. Then you can see her."

"What's happening to Connie?" George asked. "Right now. Where is she?"

"They're cleaning her up for you to see her. Don't worry. They'll knock on the door when it's time."

"Cleaning her up?"

"Let's start at the beginning," the doctor said, looking around. "Did you know she was carrying a child?"

"No!" Walton's cry filled the room. It was a cry so full of pain it didn't sound human. Dr. Thornton walked over and put an arm around his shoulder.

"I'm sorry, Walt," he said.

Lois couldn't stop crying.

George stared at the doctor.

"What are you saying? She was having a baby?"

"I'm afraid so."

"But she died," he said. "Why would she die?"

"I have an idea," Dr. Thornton said, "but I need to know more. Look," he said, "this is going to be hard. But you all have to hear it."

Lois moaned.

"When we picked her up, we went straight to the operating room because she was bleeding. We didn't know what was wrong then. We just knew we had to stop the bleeding. Shortly after we got her on the table . . . ."

He paused, as if he didn't want to finish the sentence.

". . . she expelled part of a fetus, maybe two months gestation, maybe two and a half."

He tightened his grip on Walton's shoulder.

"Like I said, this is hard to hear."

He paused again.

"The afterbirth was the problem. It was torn up, like something sharp had been pushed against it, cutting it. There was a lot of pus. The infection killed her."

Walton pulled a handkerchief from his pocket and covered his face. His whole body was shaking.

George suddenly turned on Lois.

"You knew, didn't you? You knew, and you didn't tell us."

They all stared at her.

"She didn't want anyone to know. She was afraid . . . ."

Lois couldn't go on.

"She didn't want me to know. Even me?"

Lois looked at the handkerchief covering her father's face.

"The shame. She didn't want the shame. She was afraid."

George's head jerked up.

"But it was my baby. Wasn't it my baby?"

"Yes."

"Then I don't understand."

"I do," Walton said under his breath.

"Did she see a doctor?" Dr. Thornton asked.

"In Stanton," Lois said.

"When?"

"Yesterday."

"We'll need his name and address."

George sprang to his feet.

"You mean? Oh my God. You mean, somebody did this to her?"

"It could be," the doctor said.

"I'll kill him," George said, clinching his fist. "Tell me the bastard's name, and I'll kill him."

"Quit that kind of talk."

Walton's voice was sharp. He wiped his eyes and put the handkerchief back in his pocket.

"If anybody's to blame, it's you."

"His name is Wheeler," Lois whispered.

Dr. Thornton nodded.

"I figured."

Walton Reynolds sat motionless beside his daughter's coffin, too angry to face her, too angry to pray.

Everything he had been taught, everything he had always believed told him he was right to be angry. His Connie, his own Connie, had destroyed all his happiness. She had sullied her body, had let that man, that man he had foolishly trusted, defile all that innocence, all that beauty. And she had done the unthinkable, sinned against God not only by degrading her body but, even worse, by killing . . . He couldn't let himself even think it.

He sat there another half hour, trying to pray, begging God to help him bear what was unbearable. At last, he forced himself to look at her, at her young face. And what he felt was a hurt so deep he could hardly breathe. For she was once again his Connie.

"You were a baby, he whispered," crying now. "You didn't know about the world. And I failed you. I'm the one. You did it because you knew I wouldn't forgive you. And you were right. God has punished me by taking you, and I don't know how I'll survive it."

As he sat beside her, talking to her, talking to God, his anger toward her began to melt. The God he worshipped had punished her for her sins. That was enough.

But anger still ravaged him, held him fast.

"God, help me!" he called out loud.

His cry shattered the hush of the funeral home.

An attendant rushed into the room, a look of practiced sympathy plastered on his homely face.

"Close it," Walton demanded, "I don't want all those busybodies staring at her. What's done is done. She's in the Lord's hands."

He returned to a house brimming with children and grandchildren, neighbors, and church members. To long faces struggling to hide the curiosity a sudden death inspires.

"Lois," he called. "Get these people out of here. We need to talk."

They sought refuge in the barn where Walton kept a small office for his accounting. He sat down behind the desk and waited until Lois was settled in a dusty kitchen chair across from him.

Then, "Tell me."

"It's my fault, Papa."

She started sobbing.

"What's your fault?"

He waited for her to contain herself.

"The doctor was my idea."

Walton's eyes were dry, and he held himself perfectly still except for his hands which fumbled with the bills and seed catalogs cluttering the desk.

"Begin at the beginning."

"She was carrying George's child."

"I heard."

"She didn't want you to know."

"Her mother should have been here," he said. "She would have seen what I missed."

"I tried, Papa," Lois said between sobs. "I told her it would be all right to have the baby. But she was afraid you would . . ."

Walton took that in. If it had come out different, if she had kept the baby, he might have . . . The possibilities sickened him.

"She was my daughter," he said and stopped because he couldn't hold it in much longer.

Just then, a barrel-chested man with deep blue eyes and a cleft chin appeared at the office door.

"Brother Reynolds," he said, "Is there anything I can do?"

The resonant voice exuded the confident assumption that Walton, or any man in trouble, would want his help.

"There's nothing anyone can do, Reverend," Walton answered.

"The Lord can lift us up, even in our most troubled times."

"He can't bring her back."

"That's true. But He can forgive her and bring you peace."

Walton didn't say anything.

"Would you join me in prayer?"

Reverend Farris lowered his bulky frame to his knees on the dusty office floor and waited.

Lois immediately dropped to her knees next to him. Walton sat at his desk, watching. He was surprised at himself, but he didn't want to pray, didn't want the intrusion of anyone, not even Reverend Farris, into his pain.

The Reverend smiled up at him.

"Won't you join us, my friend?"

Walton wanted to please him. Farris was a kind man, an old friend. He had comforted him in his agony all those years ago when his wife passed away. But his body felt heavy, stiff. He couldn't move.

"Dear Jesus," Farris began, "who brought peace to a suffering world, touch this troubled man, fold him in your arms."

"Amen," Lois breathed.

"Heavenly Father, who forgives us our sins," the preacher continued, "forgive our sister Connie. She was young and easily tempted into sins of the flesh."

Walton's mind froze as the preacher's voice droned on.

It was all true. But he didn't want to hear it. Not from other people. Not even from the Reverend.

When the preacher was finally done and back on his feet, Walton led him to the door.

"Thank you for coming," he managed to say.

He turned to Lois when the preacher was gone.

"Get hold of George. Tell him I need to see him."

Lois, still on her knees, looked up at him, her eyes bloodshot.

"What are you going to do to him?"

"Nothing to him. We'll be suing that Wheeler devil," he said. "I prayed beside the coffin over there in the funeral home, and that's what the Lord would have me do."

George didn't want to be there, didn't want to face the old man. He knew he was to blame. He had made that baby, and the dearest girl in the world had died because of it. But why hadn't she told him? That was the question that kept him awake at night. If only she had come to him instead of Lois, trusted him, he would have married her on the spot and be damned to Tabernacle Baptist and all those so-called Christians. But she hadn't. And he would never, ever see her again. And there was the baby, his baby. He couldn't let himself think about that.

He found the old man in the living room, sitting bolt upright in the worn easy chair he claimed as his own. It was red and sagging.

George took a seat in the rocking chair across from him, his gaze focused on Walton's leather slippers, flat on the carpet. He didn't want Walton to see his eyes, which were red and swollen. He did not want to be here.

"I figure we need to talk."

George raised his head and looked at the old man.

"I'm very, very sorry, if that's what you need to hear."

He hated the tears he could feel rimming his eyes, filling his nose.

Walton met his gaze.

"I know you are. So am I. She was my child, and I failed her."

"You?"

"I trusted you."

George wanted to say, yes, I'm to blame. Hate me. I deserve it. But he couldn't make the words come. Besides, couldn't the old man see how lost he was?

"We both failed her," Walton said. His voice was cold. "But that's not why I asked you here."

"What do you mean?"

"I want to sue that doctor who killed her."

"I'd rather shoot him," George said.

For the first time, the old man smiled.

"Me too. But suing is legal."

"How do you figure it?"

"I've talked to Horace Vass over at the church. He says we got a case for wrongful death."

George imagined bursting into the son of a bitch's office with a hunting rifle and shooting him in the head, the heart, the throat. Imagined the blood. He wanted to grind him into the dust and watch him suffer. But a lawsuit? He pictured himself on the witness stand in front of crowds of people, admitting he'd got his girl pregnant, being forced to talk about his beautiful Connie, crying.

"I don't like it," he said.

"Why not?"

"It's personal."

"We wouldn't have to involve you."

"Sure, you would, but that's not what I mean."

"Yeah?"

"Nobody knows about, you know, why she died. Paper gave cause of death as an infection."

"I know. I prayed on that. But the way I see it, Connie's gone. She's got no secrets to protect anymore. But that criminal of a doctor is free as air."

"You want to put him in jail?"

"Wish I could, but Vass says we'd lose. Says we'd win a civil suit."

"You want money from him?"

"I'll ask for a little money. That's the way the law works. But what I want is to put that devil out of business so that no young woman will ever suffer what happened to my little girl. Maybe then I can forgive myself."

"Are you asking my permission?"

"No. I'm telling you."

"Then I'm telling you, I don't like it."

Walton nodded and stood up. The visit was over.

The trial took place nine months later in the Madison County Superior Court in Stanton. It was March 1941 and warm enough already for the courthouse to be stuffy. Judge Aiken presided over the twelve jurors, all men, all churchgoers, but then everyone in that part of Madison County attended services.

Walton had hired Horace Vass, a prominent member of the Baptist Tabernacle, to represent the family. Which was a good thing because juries loved his country lawyer style. No matter how hard Mrs. Vass tried to keep her outsized husband looking fresh, his shirttails were forever slipping out of his trousers, and his collar was always damp. "Old Vass speaks the truth," people said.

On the day Mr. Vass made his opening statement, the courthouse was packed. Most of Stanton's doctors had come out along with members of the Baptist Tabernacle, the Reynolds family, and those too curious to stay home or go to work. Cardboard fans from Swicegood Funeral Home fluttered in front of sweaty, expectant faces. George slipped into a seat toward the back of the courtroom and kept his eyes focused on the floor.

Walton Reynolds sat with shoulders squared to Mr. Vass's right. At the other counsel table, Dr. Wheeler squirmed in his seat alongside his lawyer, Johnny Ingram, fresh out of law school and wearing a blue suit too big at the shoulders.

Judge Aiken, a lean, pointy-faced man who rarely smiled, took the bench and called the case. After dispensing with the usual logistical matters, he instructed the jury.

"The questions before you, gentlemen, are (1) whether the defendant, Dr. Wheeler, did or did not perform or attempt to perform an abortion on Connie Reynolds, and (2) if so, whether the abortion caused her death."

Horace Vass rose slowly and ambled over to face the jury. He just stood there for a minute or two without saying anything but looked each man in the eye as if to say he could count on that particular juror to see things his way. He then introduced the bereaved father.

"This man is grieving," he said in a soft voice, almost a whisper, "because the beautiful young woman he raised from a child and loved more than anyone in the whole world is not here in this courthouse. Connie Reynolds cannot be here because . . ." he paused, pointed to Dr. Wheeler, and spoke each word precisely, "...that man you see right there, cowering beside his lawyer," he paused again, "...killed her."

Wheeler shot a glance at his lawyer as if he expected him to say something, but Johnny Ingram merely patted him on the shoulder.

"That's right, gentlemen," Vass continued. "Dr. Wheeler intentionally took an illegal action that killed this young woman. Now, the evidence will show that Connie Reynolds wished to terminate her pregnancy out of a sense of shame. You are not to consider the morality of her decision."

In the back of the courtroom, George took a deep breath and stared at his shoelaces.

"The young woman," Vass continued, "is in the hands of the Lord who judges us all. But if we look into our hearts, we can understand

and sympathize with her. She was very young, very much in love, and only human."

He paused to let that sink in.

"You can, however, and you must, judge the man sitting here who calls himself Doctor..." Vass strung out the word, "...Wheeler. But this man doesn't heal the sick, he doesn't take out our appendices or hold our hands when we're dying. No, this man makes his living performing illegal abortions. That's all he does, and in this case, he performed his gruesome task so poorly that he mutilated a young woman's body and ended her life."

All eyes focused on the rotund little man who ducked his head.

Vass, with the smile of the righteous on his broad features, lumbered back to his seat, wiped his face with a rumpled handkerchief, and wrapped his arm around Walton.

Johnny Ingram then stood to face the jury.

"My client, Dr. Lonnie Wheeler, is a respected member of the medical community of this town," he began. "He is being maligned by opposing counsel for allegedly causing the death of plaintiff's daughter. Nothing could be farther from the truth. Gentlemen, this promiscuous young woman was in fact pregnant. She was an immoral woman, who . . . ."

Vass jumped to his feet. "Objection! Arguing the case."

"Sustained. You must stick to facts, not make an argument, in your opening statement, Mr. Ingram," the judge said.

"But he argued in his opening statement," Ingram answered.

"Then you should have objected," the judge said.

Horace Vass smiled.

Ingram cleared his throat and began anew.

"The plaintiff's daughter was already seriously ill when she came to Dr. Wheeler for help. She had contracted a venereal disease . . . "

Walton Reynolds jumped up, his face white.

"Objection!" snapped Vass, pulling Walton back into his seat. "Argument."

"Sustained."

"Don't let it get to you," Vass whispered to Walton. "He's

desperate, that's all."

From that point on, every time Ingram touched on the reason Connie Reynolds sought Dr. Wheeler's help, Vass jumped to his feet, and the judge sustained his objections.

The jury members shifted in their seats and looked down as if they were embarrassed for the young lawyer. But George, at the back of the courtroom, was glaring at him.

Ingram finally wound up his fractured opening statement.

"Gentlemen, when you have weighed the evidence, you will conclude that Dr. Wheeler was not performing an abortion on this young woman, but he was heroically treating her for an illness she had been suffering for some time."

Ingram smiled weakly at his client when he returned to the counsel table. Dr. Wheeler did not return the smile.

During the recess, George rushed to the counsel table.

"He's lying," he hissed. "Why didn't the judge stop him?"

"Don't worry," Vass assured him. "Nobody's going to believe it. He doesn't have a case. It's pathetic."

"You better be right," George snapped.

Vass put his hand on George's arm.

"Look, I've got it covered. I knew this line of attack was coming, and we've got the perfect witness. An expert. You'll see."

George muttered under his breath as he retreated to the back of the room.

Judge Aiken nodded to Vass.

"Call your first witness."

Vass grinned as he whispered to Walton, "Here we go."

Dr. Thornton testified that he was the Reynolds' family physician and was called to the Reynolds' house early on the morning of July 7, 1940.

"When I arrived, I found the patient, Connie Reynolds, complaining of pain and running a high fever. Her abdomen was very distended and extremely tender to the touch. I immediately called an ambulance. At the hospital, she began bleeding from her vagina, and so we rushed her to the operating room where she expelled part of a fetus, about two and a half months old, and a macerated afterbirth, which looked like someone had used an instrument to try and cut it out. It didn't come out whole and firm like an afterbirth usually does. It was all broken up, as if you would take a rake or something and rake across a piece of soft tissue and tear it to pieces."

Vass paused to let that testimony sink in with the jury.

"Oh, my God," someone hissed into the silence.

The judge banged his gavel.

"One more outburst from this courtroom, and I will empty it of all onlookers."

"Now you testified that the fetus was already dead. Did you come to any conclusion as to what caused that death?"

"The sharp object severed the placenta from the mother, causing the death of the fetus."

"Did you operate on Miss Reynolds?" Vass asked.

"I did. I opened up the abdomen with a small incision and did a complete exploration of the pelvis area."

"What did you find?"

"I found a hole punctured through the posterior wall of the uterus, large enough to insert a finger."

"And did you come to a conclusion?"

"I did. I concluded that some sort of sharp instrument had been inserted into the uterus through the vagina and had caused a rupture between them. There were between two to three pints of pus in the abdominal cavity."

"What do you believe caused the pus?"

"It resulted from the insertion of the sharp object. There is no other reasonable explanation."

"What was the cause of death?"

"Acute peritonitis caused by infection in the abdominal cavity."

On cross-examination, Ingram pressured Dr. Thornton to admit that the pus could have resulted from some other cause, but Dr. Thornton held fast.

Vass's next witness, Dr. Boyer, testified that when Connie Reynolds came to his office on July 6, 1940, she was seeking an abortion. He stressed that he advised her against this course of action then reluctantly suggested the name of Dr. Wheeler.

"And why Dr. Wheeler?"

"He is known in the medical community as someone who performs abortions."

"Objection!" yelled Ingram. "Facts not in evidence."

"Overruled," Judge Aikin said. "The witness has personal knowledge of the medical community."

Vass called Lois as his last witness. She entered the courtroom wearing a pink linen suit which fit a little too snugly around the hips, a balled up linen handkerchief in her hand. A recent perm had coiled her ordinarily straight hair into tight curls. Vass walked her through the visits to the two doctors, establishing that she had taken her sister to Dr. Wheeler expressly to get an abortion.

Despite Mr. Vass's instructions that she face the jury during her testimony, Lois never turned in their direction. Instead, she stared at the attorney, tears in her eyes, as if imploring him to let her go.

Lois testified that her sister was perfectly healthy before visiting Dr. Wheeler and described her as groggy and very tired when she came out of Wheeler's examination room.

On cross-examination, Ingram asked, "Your sister was expecting a baby, right?"

"Yes."

"Do you know whose baby it was?"

"Her fiancée's."

"Why would she want an abortion if her fiancée was the father?"

Lois looked around the courtroom as if the answer were written on the walls.

"It would be shameful to have a baby too soon after a wedding," she finally said, her voice thick with tears.

"But wouldn't it be even more shameful to have someone else's baby too soon after a wedding?" Ingram asked.

"Objection. Calls for speculation," Vass called out.

"Sustained."

"I'll withdraw the question," said Ingram with a smirk, obviously satisfied that the jury had heard the question.

"Do you live with your sister?"

"No, I live with my husband."

"So, you don't know for sure that she was perfectly healthy when you visited Dr. Boyer, do you?"

"Yes, I do."

"One more question. You didn't go into Dr. Wheeler's examining room with your sister, did you?"

"No."

"Then you don't know that he performed an abortion, do you?"

"She said he did."

"Thank you. That's all."

"Pathetic cross," Horace Vass muttered under his breath as Johnny Ingram took his seat.

To the judge, he said, "The plaintiff rests at this time but reserves the right to call witnesses in response to the defendant's case."

Even before the judge called the recess, George had rushed out of the courtroom. He was afraid if he stayed a minute longer, he would race down the aisle, take that smart-ass baby lawyer by the neck and strangle him. His face felt hot, and he was sweating all over. He had to cool off.

Lois found him sitting by himself on the courthouse steps, his head in his hands.

"What happened in there?" she asked.

"You heard it," he growled.

"They wouldn't let me in the courtroom until I testified. Some kind of rule."

"The son of a bitch is claiming Connie had a sexual disease."

The words came out hoarse like someone was choking him.

"What!"

"I knew it was a mistake. I told your old man. I begged him not to do it."

Lois put her arms around him.

He shook her off.

"He killed them! That fat butcher killed both of them."

"Go on and cry," Lois whispered. She sounded afraid. "You need to cry."

But he wasn't about to cry.

"He killed my beautiful Connie.," he hissed. "He killed my baby. You know what that's like? He killed part of me. That little baby was part of me."

"That's why we're here," Lois pleaded, "to make that doctor suffer for what he did."

"It won't be enough. Whatever happens won't satisfy me."

"I think you should go home," Lois said.

She's scared, George thought. Scared of what I'll do.

"I want to hear it," he said. "Every damned word of it."

After a recess, Ingram called Dr. Wheeler to the stand. The rotund little doctor took a minute to settle himself in the witness box then fixed his eyes on his lawyer.

After establishing that the plaintiff's daughter had visited Wheeler's office on July 6, 1940, and that he had examined her, Ingram asked, "Did you form a diagnosis?"

"Yes. She had gonorrhea," the little doctor said, sneaking a look at the jury.

George started to jump up.

Lois pulled him down and whispered, "He's lying. They won't believe him."

"And how did you make that diagnosis?"

"She told me she had a pain in her back and pain on urination. I did a vaginal examination and found the vagina full of pus, which was oozing from her everywhere. I mopped out the pus with an acriflavine solution on cotton, using an applicator, getting it out as best I could."

George bolted up from his seat.

"You should leave," Lois whispered.

"No. I have to hear it," he said, sitting down again, shoving his trembling hands between his legs.

Lois put her arm around his shoulders and held him for the rest of testimony.

"Then I put in a little drainage tube for the pus to run out," Dr. Wheeler continued. "She had a lot of inflammation, and I concluded she had an acute case of gonorrhea and treated her for that. When I was finished, she got up and seemed all right."

"Dr. Wheeler, did you at any time perform an abortion on the plaintiff's daughter?"

"I did not."

"Did you know she was pregnant?"

"No. She didn't tell me, and I didn't examine her for pregnancy."

On cross examination, Vass began, "Mr. Wheeler, you know that the only way you can determine whether a patient has gonorrhea is by examination of cells under a microscope, don't you?"

"That is one way, but I can tell it when I see it."

"How is that?"

"From the pus."

"How does the pus of gonorrhea differ from the pus of other infections?"

"Yellow and thick."

"But isn't the pus from other infections also yellow and thick?"

"Sometimes."

"Then you can't tell them apart, can you?"

"With a microscope you can."

"But you didn't do that, did you?"

"No."

"But you charged her $50 for treating her for a disease you didn't know she had?"

"I knew she had something."

"Thank you. That's all I have."

Dr. Wheeler was the only witness for the defense.

Horace Vass once again took command of the courtroom, calling a Dr. Jennings, a specialist in venereal diseases as an expert witness. His thick frame and silver hair pronounced him a man of vast self-importance with little time to waste. He testified that diagnosing gonorrhea without examining a sample of pus under the microscope was "highly unorthodox."

"Once gonorrhea has been diagnosed, how is it usually treated?"

"Doctors routinely prescribe a colloidal silver product called Protargol."

"Is that product easily available?"

"It is. Bayer manufactures it."

"Dr. Jennings, would you treat gonorrhea by inserting a drainage tube into the abdomen?"

"Never."

"Have you ever heard of that method of treating gonorrhea?"

"No, sir."

"Is the insertion of a tube, such as a catheter or a drainage kind of tube, into the womb one technique for performing an abortion?"

"That is the method commonly used by abortionists."

"Thank you, doctor."

On cross-examination, Johnny Ingram established that Dr. Jennings had not seen or examined Connie Reynolds at any time.

"Now, if a doctor discovers a large amount of pus in a patient's vagina, would it be reasonable for him to insert a tube to promote drainage of the pus?"

"Under certain sanitary conditions, that would be reasonable."

"Dr. Jennings, isn't it true that ordinarily it takes 24 to 36 hours for peritonitis, which was the cause of Miss Reynold's death, to take effect?"

"That is the usual case."

"But in this case, Miss Reynolds died of peritonitis within 16 hours of Dr. Wheeler's treatment, isn't that true?"

"I believe that is the evidence."

"Therefore, isn't there a good chance that the infection was already in her body, as described by Dr. Wheeler, when he examined her?"

"That is a possibility. But the diagnosis of gonorrhea is not."

"Thank you. That is all."

The lawyers droned on for another hour or so but added no new information.

In his closing statement, Horace Vass once again looked into the eyes of each juror.

"Connie Reynolds sought out the defendant here," Vass pointed to Dr. Wheeler, "expressly to get an abortion. This unskilled, negligent man inserted a tube into her uterus for that purpose and no other. And..." he paused for the effect, "...this poor excuse for a doctor punched..." Vass pounded his fist on the wooden railing surrounding the jury. "...a hole in the young woman's uterus. That punch..." He pounded again. "...through the wall of her uterus created an infection that caused her death. You have no choice, gentlemen. You must find for the plaintiff, the father of this unfortunate woman."

Johnny Ingram was brief.

"This is a sad story, but my client is not the villain here. Someone gave this poor woman a venereal disease which caused her to become infected and ended her life. Dr. Wheeler was in the wrong place at the wrong time, but he was only trying to heal this young woman. He did not perform an abortion. He did not end her life."

"Liar!" George yelled out.

"Remove that man," Judge Aiken ordered.

But George had already fled the courtroom.

After the jury filed out, Vass gathered the family around him: Walton, Lois, and Sylvia.

"It'll take 'em a while," he said. "It always does. You should go home, eat something, get some sleep if you can. Try not to think about it. I'll call the house if it looks like we're getting a decision."

"What's your guess?" Walton asked.

Vass flashed a grin and a thumbs up.

No one wanted to be alone. The family gathered around the kitchen table at Walton's house, staring, slightly disgusted, at the tuna fish casserole a neighbor had brought over.

"It was horrible, horrible," Lois said, "hearing all those lies."

"Nobody's going to believe it," Walton said.

"Whatever happens, I'm going to make their lives miserable," George said.

"What do you have in mind?" Walton's voice was calm, like he was asking out of a disinterested curiosity.

"I want to kill them, both of them. I want to take my hunting rifle and shoot them."

"No!" Lois cried out.

He aimed his finger at the casserole.

"Bang."

"It wouldn't help," Walton said. "You could shoot both of them. And it wouldn't help. I thought this trial would help, but even if we win, even if that bastard and his lawyer are never able to work again, it won't help."

They both stared at him.

"I'm sorry I put us through this," he said.

At 5:00 o'clock that evening, they were summoned to the courthouse.

"I didn't expect it so soon," Walton said as he and Lois joined Vass in the crowded courtroom.

The lawyer's broad forehead was creased into a frown. "It's a good sign," he said. But for the first time, his voice betrayed some doubt.

Johnny Ingram, at the defendant's table, had his arm around his client, who sat huddled next to him.

The jury took their seats looking straight ahead with solemn faces.

"Would the foreman please rise?"

The tall thin man who had identified himself as a Methodist minister when the jury was first questioned stood.

Horace Vass took a deep breath.

Walton whispered, "Didn't you say that it would be better for us if the foreman were the pediatrician?"

"Don't worry," Vass whispered back.

"Have you reached a decision?" Judge Aiken asked.

"We have."

Judge Aiken read the decision to himself with no reaction. Then he began to read aloud.

"We the jury find the plaintiff has failed to prove that the defendant performed an abortion on Connie Reynolds. Therefore, he is not liable for her death."

The room came alive. Everybody was talking, shouting.

"Quiet!" Judge Aiken slammed down his gavel.

It was over.

"Let's get out of here," Lois whispered to George.

But he just sat there, his mouth half open, his eyes staring at nothing.

"Come on," she pleaded.

But when he didn't move, Lois made herself get up and follow the excited crowd to the courtroom doors.

"What a shame," she heard someone say.

Lois felt a strong urge to go up to this woman, whoever she was, and thank her. She needed to hear someone say that the jury was wrong, their decision shameful.

But then a second voice. "Imagine! That girl was just seventeen and already in trouble."

Already in trouble?

"And that father of hers trying to blame the doctor!"

Lois wanted out. But strangers were blocking the aisles, chatting, calling to each other, in no hurry to leave the scene.

And they were using words like "immoral," "venereal," "shameful" as if they had any relation to her sister. As if anyone had any idea.

Walton sat at the counsel table, motionless. But here was Dr. Thornton. Looking down at him, his eyes full of concern.

"I'm so sorry, Walton," he said. "It's rotten."

Walton struggled to his feet, staring at his old friend.

"I'm sorry for you, Walton," Dr. Thornton said, "but I have to confess, I'm not surprised."

"You aren't?" Horace Vass asked.

"You know, somebody's got to do it. And Wheeler's the man in this town."

The next day, Walton paid a visit to George's small, spare apartment. The place looked almost empty, just a sofa and two ladder-back chairs in the main room. Walton was impressed with how clean it was. George's face was gray, and his eyes were sunk into blue-black circles.

"You been sleeping?" Walton asked.

"Off and on."

"I'm worried about you, son," Walton said.

"I'm okay."

"You don't look okay. Truth is, I'm worried you might do something rash. Somebody might get hurt."

George looked straight at the old man.

"I'm thinking about it."

"In your place, I'd be thinking about it too. But there are too many dead already. One more won't help things."

"I was thinking two."

"Well, that would get you the noose."

They sat together several minutes not looking at each other.

Finally, Walton said, "I've got a plan. It might work."

A week later, Walton paid a visit to the Tabernacle. He found the Reverend Farris seated alone in the large auditorium staring at the stained-glass window of Jesus surrounded by lambs.

He jumped up and wrapped his arms around Walton.

"Ah, Walton. I'm so glad you came."

"I've been feeling bad about sending you away that time in the barn," Walton said, disengaging himself and finding a seat in one of the pews.

"Don't mention it," Farris said, sitting down beside Walton. "You were grieving. The Lord understands."

"The fact is, it bothered me, you calling Connie a sinner when my grief was so raw."

The Reverend patted Walton's hand.

"I know it's hard to face. We just have to pray to God to forgive her."

"I've been giving it a lot of thought, Reverend, and I've concluded that there were a lot of folks, myself included, who were worse sinners than my little girl."

Farris smiled.

"Of course, we're all sinners. But surely you believe that fornication before marriage is a graver sin than most."

"I'm not sure."

"The truth is that wasn't her worst sin." The Reverend was now gripping Walton's hand. "You know that."

Walton turned to face him.

"You're referring to the abortion."

"Yes."

Walton blurted out, "But you have to understand, I drove her to it. That's what I struggle with."

"You've had a huge shock, Walton." The Reverend's voice was soothing. "That's why you're blaming yourself. But God sees all. He knows the truth. Your daughter made the decision to end her baby's life, the gravest sin of all for a mother. You're not the one at fault."

"Please." Walton was begging now. "Please try to understand, Reverend. She was afraid I would disown her. That's why she did it."

"It does not excuse her. She made the choice."

Walton stood up, shook the preacher's hand, and walked out the heavy oak door into bright sunlight.

"Wait," Farris called out. "Give yourself time. Pray. God will speak to you and comfort you."

But Walton was gone.

Two months later, Walton turned up at Horace Vass's law office.

"I've come to pay your bill, Horace," he said.

"I figured I'd hear from you sooner or later."

Vass pointed to a leather sofa across from his desk.

"I've been wanting to talk to you, tell you again how sorry I am for how the thing turned out. But I figured you needed time to make peace with it."

"I'll never make peace with it," Walton said as he lowered himself onto the stiff cushion next to the lawyer.

Vass nodded.

"How's George taking it?"

"He's leaving town. Said it was better than shooting Wheeler."

Horace smiled.

"I hear somebody else left town."

"Yeah?"

"You must have heard. Somebody put a sign up on Wheeler's office door. Said, 'UNSKILLED ABORTION DOCTOR INSIDE.' I heard Wheeler tore it up every morning when he came in, but somehow another one just like it got back up there while he was doing his business. Before long, patients stopped coming. He complained he was being harassed, but the police didn't pay him much mind. He finally closed up shop, and I hear he's moved to Greensboro."

"That a fact?" Walton said.

Both men were smiling.

After a long pause, Walton said, "Horace, I thought we were winning."

"So, did I. We had the facts, the law, the witnesses on our side. We out lawyered them. We should have won."

"What happened?"

"They believed that lying son of a bitch. Believed that venereal disease nonsense."

"But your expert?"

"Nobody believes experts. Fact is the jurors couldn't excuse her for . . . you know. They wanted to believe she had the disease. It made their decision easier."

Once again, they sat in silence, two old friends comfortable with each other.

Finally, Horace said, "You've suffered some heavy blows, Walton. Have you talked to Reverend Farris about it?"

"Not recently."

"He might could help you."

"I've put the Tabernacle behind me, Horace."

"How's that?"

"Let's just say I've graduated."

"From Baptist Tabernacle?"

Walton nodded.

"You've found another place of worship?"

"No."

"I don't get it."

Walton stood up and reached into his pocket.

"Here's the fee," he said holding out a check.

Walton turned back as he headed for the door.

"I have one more question. Those jurors, all those men, do they have daughters? That's what I'd like to know." His voice was thick. "Do those sons of bitches have daughters?"

Acknowledgment:

Much of the trial testimony comes from Richard W. Bourne's "Abortion in 1938 and Today: Plus Ca Change, Plus C'est La Meme Chose," in *Southern California Review of Law and Women's Studies,* Spring 2003, Vol. 12 Number 2.

Digging the Basement

Blue Lake Review, September 2020

"I've decided not to go to school anymore," my seven-year-old daughter, Louise, says as we drive to her mom's house.

I smile. "Why not?"

"I get stomach aches when I go."

"You know, there's a law here in Virginia says you have to go to school."

"Not if you're sick," she tells me.

"What does your mother say?"

"She says I have to go."

Louise holds up thin translucent arms as we say goodbye. I pick her up, savoring the warmth of her weightless body against me, breathing in baby shampoo. You don't know about love until you have a daughter.

Later I telephone Linda, my ex. "How come she doesn't like school?"

"She's pretty tight-lipped about it. But I think the problem is she's not reading."

"We need to talk to that teacher."

"I did. She says we should read to her."

"Jesus," I say. "I read to her all the time. She loves it."

"Yeah. Me too. Maybe she's just not as smart as you think she is."

"What are you talking about? She's plenty smart," I say.

"Just don't push her, Ronnie."

"I don't push her."

"You know what I'm talking about. The toilet training, walking her around the block when she could barely toddle, and then, of course, the bicycle."

"She loves the bicycle."

"Just don't push her."

I hang up.

Not reading? I'm on it. I do a little research—I'm a lawyer—and find out there's this new law, enacted just last year, 1975. It mandates something called "special education" for public school kids who are having problems reading. How lucky is that!

I tell the teacher, let's stop wasting time. Get her tested.

As a result of the test, she's labeled "reading disabled" and placed, for an hour a day, in a special class with other kids who can't read. The teacher tells me she'll be at grade level in no time. She better be right.

In the meantime, I take the initiative and hire a tutor. Mr. Hawkins. He's a skinny man with yellow-brown eyes, a handlebar mustache, and an office on Spring Street. The sign outside says, "Reading Clinic." Inside, there's one room with a table in the middle, a desk, and a few folding chairs. Blinds cover the only window.

"He looks like his name, doesn't he?" I say to Louise, after we meet him for the first time.

"You mean like the bird?"

"It's the eyes," I say. "They're watching you."

She giggles.

The next time I telephone my ex, she tells me Louise hates that reading guy.

"She doesn't tell *me* that," I say.

"Maybe it's because you don't always pay attention."

"What's that supposed to mean?"

"How many times have I told you? You have to listen to what people *don't* say."

I hang up.

I usually drop her off and run errands while she's being tutored. But today I ask the Hawk if I can stick around to observe. He doesn't like it, but I'm paying him. Louise spends the first half-hour, sitting at the table, sounding out words in a book from school. I can tell she's making progress. For the last half of the session, she looks at drawings of various objects. Chair. Bed. Chicken. The idea is to circle the correct name of the object from a list of words the Hawk gives her. She gets half of them right. I give her a hug. Good job, sweetie. Next week you'll get 'em all.

We're just wrapping it up when the door opens. A tall man with slicked-back dark hair, about my age, is standing there. He takes one look at the three of us and turns to leave.

"Come on in," the Hawk says.

"I was in the neighborhood, Mr. Hawkins," the man says. "Thought I'd say hi."

"We're done," I say.

As Louise and I walk past, I try not to stare. But the man looks familiar. Suddenly I've got it. Buddy Harrell. It's the sports coat he's wearing that confused me.

"Buddy?" I say.

He faces me, eyebrows raised. "That's me." His voice is deep, husky, like I remember.

"Ron Croxton. Ronnie. Remember?"

"Yeah. Been a long time," he says, brushing past us.

"It's been forever." I want to stop him, ask what happened, why he disappeared.

But the Hawk calls out, "See you next week, Louise."

We have no choice. We have to leave.

Every afternoon in the spring of my fifth-grade year, I'd hang around after school, hoping Buddy Harrell would catch my eye and jerk his thumb in the direction of the school bus. Whenever it happened, I'd grab my book bag and race after him, my eyes fixed on his wide shoulders under his tee shirt, his knotty biceps, his shiny black hair. We'd climb up on the school bus with the rest of the kids from out in the county. They'd be hollering and laughing and bouncing up and down, while Buddy sat still and silent, towering over me on the worn leather seat. I don't think I'd ever felt so important.

His house was set in the middle of a field of dandelions. It was a wood frame one story, built by his dad, he told me, with a tar and gravel roof, like all the other houses on that unpaved road. Mrs. Harrell would greet us at the front door with a thermos of lemonade, and Buddy would head directly for the toolshed, with me scurrying after him. He'd hang his clean overalls on a nail, pull on a muddy pair and cram his feet into rubber boots caked with red earth. I had to roll up the bottoms of the overalls he handed me; they were way too long. We'd choose a pick and a couple of shovels from the dozen or so hanging up on nails and head out. At the back of the house, we'd pull back a tarp, lift off the two-by-fours underneath it, then climb down a wooden ladder into a deep hole of iron-hard red mud. And start digging.

The first time I saw the hole, I asked, "What's that for?"

"A basement," he said.

"What do you mean?"

"Our house don't have a basement. I'm digging one underneath."

I didn't understand. Where I lived, on Hawthorne Lane, two blocks from Forest Knolls School, everybody had a basement. The one under our house had been turned into a family room with pine paneling, wall-to-wall carpet, a pool table and a cabinet full of board games.

"You're digging a basement all by yourself?" I asked.

"Papa helps when he's not too tired. And Chester lends a hand on the weekends, but it's mostly my job."

Chester was Buddy's older brother who worked with Mr. Harrell in the mill, which was the only industry in our town in those days.

After that, every time I came home with Buddy, we set to digging. Or rather Buddy would strike the earth with the pick, loosening it, and I would follow behind, shoveling the clumps of red earth into a wheelbarrow. When the wheelbarrow was half full, I would push it over to a pulley-like contraption with a basket, which Chester had rigged up, and shovel the mounds of earth into the basket. Buddy would climb back up the ladder, haul the basket up to ground level and dump the contents onto a large pile.

"What are you going to do with that?" I asked.

"Man down the road wants his ditch filled."

I still see him, sweat dripping off his chin, holding that pickax high above his head, then plunging it into the hard earth, over and over. I pretended he was Paul Bunyan from my book on American heroes. I couldn't believe he had chosen me, with my spindly arms and legs, as his helper. And I still don't know why. Buddy was almost as tall as my dad, and built up. All of us boys in fifth grade looked up to him. We figured he must have failed a grade or two, but we didn't care. He was our big guy, and we imitated his rolling gait and fought over him in choosing teams for ballgames.

Back then, in the 1950s, when the town was pretty small, our parents didn't worry when their children didn't show up after school. They assumed we were with friends, playing ball, shooting marbles, running the safe streets of my childhood. They didn't ask questions as long as we turned up for dinner. But after my first stint at digging Buddy's basement, Mama gave me a look.

"Where on earth did you pick up all that red mud?" she scolded.

"I went to Buddy Harrell's after school."

"Do I know him?"

"He's the tall one in our class," I said.

She looked sharp at me. "Where does he live?"

"Out in the county."

"I see."

"We were digging out his basement," I bragged. "It's hard work."

"Well, I'll be," she said. "So how did you get home?"

"His mama drove me in their truck."

That night after supper I heard her talking it over with my dad, and I worried they might stop me. But for whatever reason, they never did.

"What's that you're reading?" Buddy asked me on one of our bus rides to the county.

"*Stuart Little*," I said.

"What's it about?"

"You know. A mouse," I said.

"What about a mouse?"

Now that surprised me. Miss Robinson had handed out the books at least a month before. We were supposed to read it at home and write a report.

"Haven't you started it?" I asked.

"Not yet," he said. "Tell me about the mouse."

"He's like a human. The Little family had him instead of a child. And he has all kinds of adventures."

Buddy sat silent for a few minutes.

"Sounds dumb to me," he finally said.

"I think you'd like it," I said, "but you better get started on it. The book report's due pretty soon."

He didn't say anything for the rest of the bus ride, but when we were deep in the hole, digging and shoveling, he said, "Why don't you tell me some more about that mouse?"

So I told him about Stuart getting caught in a window blind and him sailing a model boat in a race and almost getting eaten by a cat.

Buddy never said a word, but whenever I stopped talking, he'd say, "Go on. It's dumb, but I like to hear you telling it."

And I loved it too. It felt so comfortable, the two of us down in that hole, working side by side, me talking about Stuart Little and him hacking at the earth.

"Okay, your turn." I've been reading *James and the Giant Peach* for an hour at least, with Louise curled up beside me, dressed for bed in a faded nylon nightgown of her mom's.

"I don't feel like it," she says.

"Too bad," I say. "That was our deal. I read *James and the Giant Peach* to you and you read *Green Eggs and Ham* to me."

I open the book.

"I do not like green eggs and ham. I do not like them Sam I am," she reads. Or does she?

"Good girl," I say and point to the word *green*. "What's that word?"

She looks up at me. "Eggs?"

"Try again, Louise. What does it start with?"

"G," she tells me.

I ask her to sound out 'g-r-e."

"G-r . . . g-r-e . . .green Daddy?" she whispers.

I hug her, then turn the page and point to *green* again. "What's that word, sweetie?"

She looks at the word and back at me. "*Green?*"

"Bingo!" I'm feeling on top of the world.

"Can we just read the book?" she asks.

"Of course."

She smiles and begins. "I do not like them with a mouse. I do not like them in a house."

We laugh, as we always do.

A couple of weeks after our talk about *Stuart Little*, I saw Buddy coming out of school, his cheeks a dull red and his mouth set in a line. I had asked him at recess if I could come help him with the basement and he'd nodded.

"She's a bitch," he said under his breath, as we sat side by side on the bus.

I figured from the look of him I better keep quiet. But I couldn't help myself. "Who?" I asked.

"That teacher bitch."

"What'd she do?"

"Accused me of cheating."

"Why?"

"My report."

"On *Stuart Little*?"

He nodded.

"Why'd she think you cheated?"

"Because it was written so good she said I couldn't a done it."

"You told her you wrote it, didn't you?"

"Sure."

"And she didn't take your word?"

For answer, he jerked some paper out of his book bag and tore it into strips. "I'd like to shove this right up her ass," he hissed.

We sat in silence for the rest of the bus ride.

But once in the basement, pickax in hand, he let it out.

"I never done so much schoolwork" Thunk. "in my life." Thunk. "And I ain't gonna do it again." Thunk. "It's a dumb book." Thunk. "I want to burn down the whole fucking school."

I kept quiet.

Later, when we were drinking lemonade and cooling off, Chester showed up from work. I never knew what to say to Buddy's brother; he was so big and muscular, just like Buddy, only older.

"Got your report back?" Chester asked.

Buddy didn't say anything.

"How'd we do?"

"Bitch failed me," Buddy mumbled.

"No! That was first class A+," Chester said.

"She accused me of cheating, the bitch."

"Well that's a damned lie." Chester turned to me. "I gotta say that mouse story was sort of cute. Buddy here says you told him the whole story."

I nodded.

"And I showed him how to spell the words he wanted to say in his report. That ain't cheating. That's taking the initiative."

I looked over at Buddy. He was sitting there, in his overalls and muddy rubber boots, with his back up against the toolshed wall, his face buried in his arms. He didn't get up when Mrs. Harrell came by in the truck to take me home. He didn't even say goodbye.

And that was the last I saw of him for twenty-five years.

At the reading clinic, Louise is choosing most of the words for the pictures now.

"She's making great strides," the Hawk tells me. "She's a sharp little thing."

At night, she's actually sounding out the words in *Green Eggs and Ham*.

"Let's read this one," I say, showing her another Dr. Seuss book. "We're on a roll."

"I'm too tired."

"Fair enough." I pick her up and whirl her around the room.

"What a champion!" I say.

"Put me down, Daddy," she says. She's not smiling.

On my walk from the parking lot to my law office, I pass a large truck with J. J. Harrell Construction painted in red letters on the side. It's parked next to a construction site. A young guy climbs down from the cab of the truck and starts pulling ladders out the back.

"Excuse me," I say, "I'm just wondering if you could tell me who J. J. Harrell is."

"The boss."

"I might know him," I say. "What's he look like?"

"Tall. Black hair. Nice guy."

"Is he ever called Buddy?"

"Never heard that. If you want to see him, he usually stops by around lunchtime to check up on us."

When I get to the office, I look in the yellow pages under "Construction" for J. J. Harrell. I find the ad, with a picture of J. J., all business, in suit and tie. It's him. How come I haven't seen him around? Town's gotten too big, I guess.

Around noon I see a black Buick pulling up next to the truck. And there's Buddy. Climbing out of the car, wearing an orange hardhat and lace-up boots, holding a clipboard.

I race down the stairs and out to the street.

"Buddy," I call out.

As he turns toward me, I catch a glimpse of a smile. But it instantly freezes.

"Hi Buddy. It's me. Ronnie."

"Oh, hi," he says, avoiding my gaze. "Sorry, but I'm really busy right now."

I'm not letting him by this time. "Come on. It's lunchtime. There's a Denny's on the corner. They get you out in a flash, and you have to eat."

"I brought a sandwich," he says. But he's made a mistake. He's actually looked at me. His scowl softens. "Oh, okay. But let's make it fast."

We choose a booth and order cheeseburgers and fries.

"What happened to you?" I ask. "You just disappeared."

He looks away. "I had to work."

"Work? We were in the fifth grade."

"I was thirteen." He spits it out.

That stops me for a minute. Thirteen in the fifth grade? How old was . . . ten, I was ten. I search my mind for the right words.

"All I know is you were my hero." It sounds so lame.

He laughs. "I was a stupid kid digging out a basement."

"I thought we had fun."

He takes a bite of cheeseburger, washes it down with coke. "You had fun," he says. "For me it was work."

I realize memories of the past won't keep him sitting here, and I need to find out something.

"I looked you up," I say. "That's a serious business you're running."

"You're surprised?"

"I'm surprised to see you. Twice now."

He shrugs and pops a couple of fries in his mouth.

I try again. "So how did you get in the construction business?"

"Long story." He starts to get up. "Another time."

"You haven't even finished your cheeseburger," I say. "Give me fifteen minutes. We were friends. What happened?"

He sighs, looks down at his half-eaten burger, then up at me. "Okay. Somebody saw me digging that basement way back then, offered me a job digging ditches. I was wasting my time in that fucking school and I needed the money. So I dug ditches until I got hired on in construction. One thing led to another."

"But it's a business," I say. "With machinery and employees. How'd that happen?"

He pushes his plate away and looks square at me. "You mean, how'd a dumb shit like me set up a business?" He doesn't even sound angry, just weary.

"That's not what I mean."

He laughs. "What *do* you mean?"

He's right, of course. They called it "holding them back" in those days. And we didn't question it. We just assumed . . .

I change the subject. "What school did you go to after you left Forest Knolls?"

"Nowhere. Look, I gotta go."

"Wait!" I say.

He stands up, turns to leave. Then stops.

"Look, Ronnie. I don't want to sound mean, but I need you to lay off. You understand? I can't go back there. You want to know how I got this far. And I know you mean well. Okay. The answer is hard work. And a lot of help from my brother and that reading guy. Not from that fucking teacher. And certainly not from sitting every day like a big lummox in a bunch of little kids."

"But we adored you," I protest.

"You have no idea," he says, looking straight at me.

I want to ask more questions. I want to tell him about Louise, how things are better now for kids like him.

But he's out the door.

"How was school?" It's my turn to pick up Louise.

She sits beside me, her face red.

"Hey, sunshine girl, what's up?"

No answer.

"No pouting, remember?"

No answer.

When we get to my house, she rushes to her room.

"Chocolate chip cookies," I whisper to the closed bedroom door. "If you don't eat them, I will."

She cracks open the door and stares at me with wet eyes.

"What's wrong, sweetie?"

I pick her up and carry her to the kitchen.

"I want to blow up the school!" She's suddenly so fierce it scares me.

I see Buddy in the red mud, pickax in hand. Thunk!

"Why do you want to do that?" I ask in as calm a voice as I can manage.

"I hate it."

I start talking nonsense about how everybody hates school sooner or later.

"I'm dumb," she cries. "Dumb bunny, dumb, dumb, dumb." She's sobbing.

"Of course you're not," I say, holding her, rocking her. "Who says such a thing?"

"They all do. I'm in the dumb bunny class with all the other dumb bunnies."

"It's not a class for dumb bunnies, silly," I say. "It's a class for smart people like you to get better at reading. And it's working. I'm so proud of you."

She looks up at me, tears dripping off her cheeks.

"You're smarter than all those mean kids," I say. "I'm going to talk to that teacher."

"No," Louise wails. "That'll only make it worse."

She's right. Nasty little fuckers.

"How 'bout I talk to the Hawk?"

"I hate him."

I kiss the top of her head. "But sweetheart, you're almost reading now. And you'll get better and better."

She reaches across the table for *Green Eggs and Ham* and throws it across the room.

Buddy's looking straight at me.

You have no idea.

One of Us

Bright Flash Literary Review, July 8, 2020

The singer clutches the microphone, her bright red lips wide open. Eyes closed. Voice so smooth, like molasses. Like the color of her face, dark, satiny. Amber can't take her eyes off her. She looks around the crowded Golf Club ballroom at the other wedding guests. A lot of kids from her high school. No longer chatting but staring at the singer and frowning.

Amber can see her cousin, Sterling, Jr., up front with his bride, Jodie, a brainy sort from New York. They met in Vermont working at a summer camp.

"Jodie's hired a singer for the reception," he'd told her. "She sings in Broadway musicals."

Amber had expected somebody looking like Julie Andrews or Barbra Streisand not this dark-skinned woman.

She's singing "Summertime," her voice piercing the high notes in clear, crystal sweetness. Amber loves this song. She closes her eyes and lets the music flow through her. She feels she's alone in this vast ballroom, just Amber and the beautiful singer, lost in the easy living of Summertime.

What's she feeling? Amber wonders. That black woman, singing down here in Cypress, South Carolina, in front of all these white people. She looks around. No colored faces here except on the waiters. She watches them skirt around the guests, in their starched white jackets, holding trays of shrimp high in the air.

The girls from Amber's high school in sleeveless silk dresses sip fruit punch, their bare arms and faces red from the July sun. Their mothers in pastel linen suits flutter paper fans in their faces to counter the ineffective air conditioning. Husbands and sons with jackets and ties hanging loose in their hands sweat visibly. Pink and blue balloons dangle from the ceiling. Stacks of wedding presents wrapped in silver paper overflow several tables. It has all the trappings of a summer wedding in a small southern town.

Except for that singer.

Amber hears someone say, "I think it's weird to invite a colored girl down here to sing at a wedding. I mean we've got Civil Rights and all that, but it's in bad taste. We're not ready."

Amber closes her mind to the conversations around her and fixes her eyes, large, dark brown, on the satin-skinned woman, on her wide-open mouth, on her eyes, shut tight, on her limber body swaying to the music of her song. Amber can't stop smiling.

And now the singer is bowing to the smatter of applause, nodding to Mr. Striker, the high school band instructor seated at the piano. She climbs on unsteady spike heels down the stairs from the stage, frowning slightly at the crowd of wedding guests. After a minute of searching the room, she heads off through the guests, who step aside, opening up a space for her.

The ballroom suddenly explodes with the chatter of old friends.

"The cake," someone yells over the noise. "They're cutting the cake."

There's a rush to the long table at the side of the ballroom. Amber can picture Sterling, Jr. and Jodie, her hand on top of his, as they plunge a silver knife into the bottom layer of a tiered four-layer cake, iced sugar white, the standard toy bride and groom perched on top, the wedding date, June 14, 1984, spelled out in colored icing. Cameras flash. The crowd roars.

But Amber isn't with them. She has seated herself at a small table, sipping punch, and humming to herself. She half hopes one of the high school girls will come sit with her. No one does.

And then there she is. The singer. Standing over her, watching her. Amber is stunned by the woman's beauty, the strength of her gaze. Confused, Amber looks away, her face burning.

"You," the woman says in her honey voice, "You are the most beautiful woman in the room. *You*," she stresses the word, "you are one of us." She smiles and is gone.

Amber looks around. Did anyone notice her standing there? Talking to her? A black woman making personal remarks. But everyone is still hovering near the bride and groom, crumbles of cake spilling from their fingers.

Was she making fun of her? No one has ever called Amber beautiful. Her nose is too big. Her mother says it's elegant and makes her look Egyptian. But it's too big. In fact, she is too big. Her cheeks are round, and where the collar bones of other girls stick out and their stomachs lie flat, Amber is soft, full. Her large dark eyes, her only source of pride.

But that isn't the worst. The woman called her "one of us." What did she mean by that? It scares her. What does that singer see when she looks at her? Does she see her swaying to the music, her eyes closed? Does that make her "one of us"? Or is there something else?

The singer is back on the stage, grabbing the mic, nodding to Mr. Striker. And then she is looking at Amber. She is smiling and singing right to her.

Amber looks away, her body rigid. She is terrified.

Frozen Laughter

Persimmon Tree, Summer 2020

James is emotional for the first time in his life.
Only thing, his muscles controlling both laughing and crying
are frozen. He can only make funny little noises.

I found the note in a stack of books when I was cleaning out my parents' basement, tucked inside *The World According to Garp*. My mother's loopy handwriting. She dated it September 1974, a month before my father died of ALS.

I want to talk to her. Really bad. I want to ask her how she could tell he was emotional if he couldn't laugh or cry. Ask her to describe the "funny little noises." Ask her why he didn't show emotion until the end. But I can't. She's gone too.

"He has to use a feeding tube." That's the sort of thing she told me near the end. "He can't swallow properly." "He can still write notes." "His friends are loyal. They come around."

She said nothing about frozen muscles. Nothing about laughing and crying.

Did I ask? I didn't go back to Virginia that September to see for myself.

Then he was dead.

I cried for my mother. For my father, I just felt relieved that he had escaped the prison of that cruel disease.

Mother was always laughing. That's how I remember her. The two of us laughing so hard I would collapse on the floor. And we shouted, both of us, and slammed doors. We cried in the movies, cried when we hurt each other, sobbed when my Boston bull terrier was hit by a car.

I was thirteen, and Dusty was my first and only dog. Small, mostly black with a white throat. And every time he saw me, he smiled. The houses on our street were frame, painted white, and close together, with large, grassy back yards. Perfect for children and dogs. We ran in and out of each other's front doors, usually without knocking. On that winter evening, around dusk, I dashed across the street to my friend Elaine's house to borrow a record. Just as I opened her door, I heard the screech of tires. And I knew. A man in the middle of the street was bending over what looked like a bundle of rags and a puddle of blood. I picked up my dog, held his warm, limp body close, and ran sobbing into my house.

"It's my fault," I kept screaming. "It's my fault. He followed me."

Mother put her arms around both of us, and we stood like that in the kitchen, rocking back and forth, crying, Dusty between us, his blood dripping on the linoleum, spreading into pink circles on my nylon sweater.

And my father? He stood there frowning, not with disapproval, more like puzzlement. Then he said, "It'll be all right. We can get you another dog. There are lots of dogs in the pound."

The day I left for college. I was all packed, dressed in new clothes, a print skirt and a white cotton blouse. I was scared. I'd never left home before.

"Where's Daddy?" I asked.

"At work," Mother said.

"He better get home quick," I said. "We're ready to go."

"He's not coming, honey."

I had imagined him dressed in his brown business suit, carrying my bags, shaking hands with my roommate. Being proud of me.

I raced upstairs to my room, threw myself face down on the bed. I remember clutching the knobby bedspread in my hands. By the time Mother pried me off the bed, the pillow was soaked.

"He doesn't even care that I'm leaving," I screamed at her.

"Of course, he cares. But he has to work."

I knew that wasn't true. He sometimes took off from the hardware store to play golf. Or go to baseball games.

"He doesn't love me."

But I must have loved *him*. Why else would I have cried so hard? I don't remember. What I do remember, looking back twenty years, are his stiff shoulders when I hugged him, his head tilted to the side. Not touching mine.

By Thanksgiving, his failure to take me to college that first day no longer mattered. I watched this tall, sandy-haired man, slightly stooped, carrying my suitcase into the house, frowning at pictures of Little Rock on TV, cutting into small bites the T-bone steak my mother had broiled in honor of my homecoming. And I didn't feel a thing.

Did I make a conscious decision that weekend to somehow let him go? To block out my feelings for him? I was so young, so easily hurt, so sure he had failed me.

Besides, I had fallen in love with Larry.

I didn't want to marry somebody like my father. When Larry bounced into my life freshman year in college, I fell hard. At the time, Larry was doing his best to keep from flunking out of law school while performing in campus musicals. He clowned (*South Pacific*), he danced (*Singin' in the Rain*), he sang (*The King and I*). I followed him from rehearsal to show to cast party to bars and dance halls, always on the move, laughing, yelling, hugging, fighting, kissing.

"I understand you're studying law," my father said when I brought Larry home for the first time.

"Whenever I have the time," Larry said.

My father frowned

"Joanie tells me you're in musicals," Mother said.

"It's what I live for."

"I can't wait to see you on stage," she said.

And then, after college, on an airplane trip to Atlanta to interview for a teaching job, I heard the stewardess's voice on the speaker.

"Would the passenger in seat 11B please raise your hand?"

I looked at my boarding pass.

"That's me," I said to Larry, who was sitting next to me.

"Raise your hand," he said.

The voice continued, "I have a message for the person in seat 11B."

The passenger across the aisle turned to stare at me.

"Mr. Larry Martin would like you to be his wife," the voice said. "If you accept, please kiss the man who is seated next to you."

I sat there dumbfounded, staring at Larry. People were now standing in the aisles, peering over the back of seats.

"Well," said the voice, "is it yes or no?"

"Are you serious?" I asked Larry.

"What do you think?" he laughed.

I kissed him. The passengers applauded. And I was engaged to be married.

"I'm glad he's going to be a lawyer," my father said. "You'll need a steady income."

He walked me down the aisle, his arm folded stiffly in mine, his face frozen into a smile.

After my luscious, tender baby Gail arrived, my parents flew out to Los Angeles to meet their new grandchild. We'd moved there after college for Larry's job. He represents the Screen Actors Guild, which means he gets to hobnob with actors, yell obscenities at studio executives, and occasionally talk his way into small parts in the movies. You can see why I married him.

My mother was the lively, silly grandma I expected. She sang to baby Gail, danced with her, dressed her in frilly sundresses, pushed her all over my sun-drenched neighborhood in the fancy carriage she insisted on buying.

I don't remember what my father did. Read the paper? Watched TV? I must have been hoping to shock him with my California world. My bright red sofa, slightly sagging. The faded Persian rugs. My weaver's loom plopped right in the middle of the living room. I wanted to show my father my world, wanted him to really see it. To see *me.*

One conversation sticks. I was sitting at the kitchen table in my stained yellow bathrobe nursing Gail when my father walked in, freshly shaved, a sharp crease in his blue slacks, his short-sleeved polo shirt open at the neck. He sat gingerly in the only chair that wasn't piled with clean diapers.

"Well, well. Look what we have here," he said, shifting his eyes from my uncovered breast.

"Isn't she beautiful?" I said, gazing at my child.

Neither of us spoke for several minutes.

And then, "I just want to say, Joan, that I am very satisfied with your life out here."

Satisfied?

"I know it's a challenge to have a new baby. But you are handling everything in such a sensible way."

I looked at the dirty dishes stacked all around, the tangled pile of diapers fresh from the dryer, balls of wool here and there. My messy California life, which I adored precisely because it was as different as I could make it from my father's bland orderly existence. And here he was, "satisfied" that I was being "sensible." In that moment, I thought there was nothing I could ever do to make him see me.

Now I wonder. What was he trying to say in his clumsy way? What didn't I hear?

After that, it was too late. A continent separated us.

He was in a wheelchair the last time I saw him. We were in Virginia for our yearly summer visit. His chair had a little tray on it with a pad of paper and a pen for him to write notes because he could no longer speak. Gail, who was ten, loved pushing him through the house, out into the grassy back yard. She would park him under a wooden trellis cluttered with grapevines and tell him stories she'd made up about her stuffed animals. Occasionally, he would take up his pen and scribble out a note. She would read the notes out loud and explain her answers so seriously, so tenderly. And he would nod.

Sitting on the back porch of my parents' wood frame house on those stifling July days, fanning myself with a paper plate, I watched the two of them. I remember my mother coming out to join me, her yellow-white hair hanging loose around her face, shoulders bent. Exhausted. I remember crying, the two of us, like old times.

I'm sure I talked to my father that summer. I must have.

James is emotional for the first time in his life

I hand Mother's note to Gail. She's thirty now, an entertainment lawyer like her father, and she's come to pick up her baby daughter, who has spent the afternoon with me. Gail drops her briefcase and, clutching the note, falls into the plush red sofa in my living room.

"Poor Grandpa. It must have been so awful." She's crying.

I sit down next to her, fold her in my arms, kiss her hair.

"I don't know how to read this," I say.

"It's what it says. He couldn't show emotion in the end. It's a cruel, cruel disease."

"But was he feeling it at the end? Emotion?"

She wipes her eyes and stares at me.

"What do you mean?" she says. "You saw it."

"Saw what?"

"The notes. All those notes he wrote."

"Not to me."

"To me," she says. "So many notes."

"Do you have them?"

"I wish I did. But don't you remember the one about the carrots?"

"Huh?"

"Surely you remember. He wrote something about carrots in one of the notes. I don't remember exactly what it said, but he pointed to you. You must remember."

"Carrots?"

"He was in the back yard in his wheelchair. I gave you the note." Her voice is insistent. "He told me about it once when he was first sick. He was mumbling then. It wasn't easy to make him out. But he could still talk. He said something about a garden and carrots. And he got real agitated. Don't you remember?"

I try, but it's been so many years. I do remember my father had a garden. He never spent time outdoors, except for playing golf, and he was never fond of vegetables. But that one year, when was it? I was about ten or eleven. That one year, he made a garden. I see him now, out there digging, sowing seeds from envelopes that had pictures of vegetables on them. I'm out there too. Following behind him, in shorts and a Dodgers shirt.

It's coming back. I have a garden too, a small garden patch of my own. I'm out there with him, stooping, patting seeds into the dirt, my fingernails black, feeling the cool red-brown earth as I pat it over the seeds. Warm water from the sunbaked hose soaks my sandals and shorts. I remember green, bushy plants. Carrots! That's it. I'm growing carrots. I anticipate pulling them out of the dirt, washing them, cutting them into slices. I'm excited but not because I particularly like carrots. I don't. But because I grew them.

I tell my mother, "I have a big surprise for you. You'll never guess."

I'm hopping from one foot to the other. She loves carrots.

"Is it time?" I keep asking Daddy. "Is it time?"

"Give it a few days," he says.

He's smiling at me. I see it now. We're a team.

But there's something wrong. The bushy plants are leaning to the side. I pull at one, and it pops into my hand. A broken bit of carrot hangs limp from the stem.

"Gophers," Daddy says.

I'm running from plant to plant, pulling them. Sobbing.

He holds me. Right now, I'm feeling his arms tight around me. He's kissing my hair, my cheek.

"I'm so sorry, honey," he says. "I'm so sorry."

Are there tears in his eyes?

"He showed emotion when it counted," Gail tells me. "Not just 'funny little noises.' Real passion."

What she's talking about?

"You know," she says. "The way he died."

"He died of ALS."

"That's not what I'm talking about."

"What do you mean?"

Gail looks at me, frowning.

"He was climbing out the window, fighting off the nurses."

I'm trying hard to take this in.

"He had the tube in his hand," she says. "He was gripping it. They had to pry his fingers open to get it out. By the time the doctors got there, he was dead."

"How do you know that?"

"Grandma told me," Gail says. "After we saw him at the funeral home. She was crying, and she told me about it. Didn't she tell you?"

"I remember something about a scuffle in the hospital. She was so upset when she told me, I didn't ask questions."

"Mom, he couldn't breathe without the tube. He knew that, and he took it out and tried to climb out a three-story window. He almost made it. But he stopped breathing first."

I try to picture it. My father struggling to climb out a hospital window. It's the last thing I would have expected.

But he did it. Gail says he did. He didn't want another three or four miserable years of that suffocating silence, that clumsy flesh. So, he did it. He burst free.

And I missed it.

I want to go back. I want to say I'm proud of him, proud that he pulled out that tube and ran, proud of his anger against that dark disease. Proud of his passion.

But more, I want to relive all the times he tried, in his frozen way, to reach out to me. Not just the note about the carrots. Earlier. He was trying.

And I missed it.

Author's Note:

Several years ago, a cousin sent me a letter my mother had written shortly before my father's death of ALS. The lines at the beginning of my story were in that letter. It made me cry, but it stayed with me. "Frozen Laughter" was the result. My father also tried to climb out the hospital window when he'd had enough. The rest is fiction.

Who's My Father?

The Main Street Rag, Volume 25, Number 1, Winter 2020.

"Is this Meghan Reynolds?"

I see a name I don't recognize on the screen. "Avery Burnside." Probably a cold call. But she sounds young, not like a telemarketer. I'm curious.

"If you're Meghan Reynolds, I need to talk to you."

"What about?"

"Don't hang up. It's important. Your dad. Is he Jordan Reynolds?"

I tap the red button, but not before I hear, "If he is, he might be my dad too."

It's a scam.

My cell rings again. I don't pick up, but I listen to the voicemail.

> *If you are Meghan Reynolds, please listen. My name is Avery Burnside, and I've been having my DNA checked. And it looks like Jordan Reynolds could be my dad. Please, please call me!*

"How irritating," my mother says when I play the voicemail for her. "I bet it's one of those identity theft things. We should report it. Ask your father."

I'm sitting on the wooden bench in the front hall, waiting, when my dad bursts through the door. It's summer, and he's been running in all this heat. His black curls are soaked in spite of the white bandana he's got tied around his forehead. I watch him take a towel from his backpack, wipe his sweaty face and neck. He's all wiry and athletic.

"Hi, sweetie," he says. "What's up?"

"I've had a crank call," I tell him. "Mom says you'll know what to do."

"Sure. Give me half an hour to shower and change. I'll be right on it."

That's my dad. He's not like so many fathers who work all the time. He might be the head of Spotswood Finance, but you'd never guess it when he's weeding the vegetable garden with me on Sunday afternoons in torn khaki shorts and a beat-up straw hat. He takes me to Charlottesville at least once a month during football season for the UVA games. Helps me with chemistry, edits my essays for English class.

He listens to the voicemail while we sit together on the leather sofa in the den. His hair's still wet from the shower, and I can smell Dove shampoo. For a few minutes, he just sits there, saying nothing.

Then, "It's some kind of scam, honey. I wouldn't worry."

"But maybe they're coming after you," I say.

"Not likely, but I'll put somebody on it. My office has a way of checking identity theft."

"Do I have to give you my phone?"

"I have her name and number. That's all I need."

The next evening, I ask Dad what he's found out.

"It's nothing," he says. "My people checked it out. No one's trying to steal my identity. Or yours. It's just a crank call. Forget about it."

Bur I can't because Avery Burnside has started sending texts. I don't answer them, of course. And I don't tell Dad. I'm not sure why. The texts vary:

> *I've tried to contact your father directly, but his phone lines are blocked. So, I have to keep bothering you.*
>
> *Why don't you do your own DNA research? Then I'd know for sure. I used Searchgen.*

The most disturbing text is just a photo of a teenage girl with dark curly hair and blue eyes. She looks about my age, seventeen. I delete the other texts but not this one.

They keep coming. Whenever I think she's given up, I hear the little musical phrase that announces a text, and there she is. I figure that whoever Avery Burnside is, she's not trying to steal my identity. Dad checked that out. Maybe she's pretending Dad's her father to get money?

My cell rings. It's her. Every instinct tells me not to tap the green button. But what if. . .?

"Thank God, you've finally picked up," she says really fast. "Don't hang up. Please. Just listen. I'm not trying to make trouble or scare you. But if Jordan Reynolds is my father, I deserve to know him."

I should hang up, but I don't.

"My mom told me my father disappeared before I was born."

She's talking really fast.

"She wouldn't tell me who he was. She'd only say I was better off not knowing him. Are you still there?"

I keep quiet, but I don't hang up.

"Then two years ago, Mom got sick with breast cancer. I tried really hard to get her to tell me who my father was before she died, but she wouldn't. Are you still there? The nurses finally made me stop what they called 'haranguing' her. She died last May. Don't you see? I don't have anybody. I have to meet your dad."

"He's not your dad!" I blurt it out.

"The DNA says he might be. Look. There are these little kits you can get. All sorts of companies send them. It's easy. You spit into a container, add some fluid they send you, and mail it back."

"Yuk."

"It's science. Just listen. The company emails you all kinds of information, including a list of folks who share some percentage of your DNA," she says. "Those are people, like me, who are looking for relatives. There's information about where they live and how old they are. So, you can contact the ones who live near you."

"My dad wouldn't be on any list," I say.

"Of course not. But I found a woman who lives in Virginia and shares around four percent of my DNA. Searchgen predicts she could be my second cousin. I contacted her, and she sent me a genealogy chart she'd had some company prepare. And, bingo, your dad's on it. So are you. There are no other men in her line who are the right age and live in Virginia. So, it could be he's my father."

"Stop!" I yell.

I hear her call out "Look at my photo!" before I cut the line.

Just four percent of her DNA! I don't believe it. Besides, he's not like that. He doesn't keep secrets. He would never just abandon a child, leave her out there in the world with no father. I know that because of the way he loves me.

I think about my fifteenth birthday. Dad gave me the choice of any trip in the whole world. Paris, Rome, New York. Just the two of us. I chose New Orleans because I'd watched that series on HBO, *Treme*, and I loved all the jazz and the street scenes.

Dad got us rooms on the top floor of the Monteorleans Hotel in the French Quarter. From the window, you could watch a steamboat moving up and down the Mississippi, which was muddy and brown. The hotel was really fancy. The curtains in my room were some kind of gold material, and there were crystal chandeliers in the lobby. We ate hot puffy beignets for breakfast and took long strolls on Bourbon Street where everybody was drinking just right there in broad daylight. At a music hall, my dad introduced me to Chris Thomas King, who's won Grammys. My dad knows people.

One afternoon, we wandered through Lafayette Cemetery where the tombs are as big as houses and all above ground because of flooding. We took turns reading the engravings and taking pictures. There's something about them I'm trying to remember. I take out my cell and sweep back through the photos.

John Selvedge, 1840–1892.
Long lost father of Mildred Calhoun,
Now Found, Praise be to God

Anna Rendon, born 1834
Taken by Our Lord 1870

Daughter of Louise Rendon
Father unknown

Of course. It's all those missing fathers. I even pointed it out to Dad at the time.

I remember walking the two and a half miles back to our hotel, trying to keep up with my dad, who walks really fast with his shoulders hunched forward. He threw coins in the hats of sidewalk musicians, laughing and even dancing a step or two to the beat of their banjos.

He couldn't be Avery's father. It would mean he was involved with her mother at the same rime he was getting me started. He wouldn't do that to my mom. That's not who he is.

I'm coming out of school, and I hear my name. I know that voice. She's taller than I expected but thin and wiry, and she has those thick, black curls. She's wearing jeans and a white t-shirt with Blue Ridge Mountains scrawled across it. And pink high-tops.

I walk the other way, pretending I don't recognize her. But she runs to catch up with me.

"I don't want to talk to you," I tell her, as she comes up beside me.

"I expected your hair to be darker," she says. "You don't look as much like him as I do."

"How do you know?"

"Easy. His photo's on the Spotswood Finance website."

I freeze. This girl facing me has my father's deep blue eyes, his bouncy way of walking, with the shoulders hunched forward like he's ready to take off.

"We have to talk." She sounds agitated. "Now. I've driven all the way from Charlottesville."

"Whose fault is that?"

"Look, I'm here. And maybe you're right. Maybe he isn't my father. But I have to know."

I feel sick to my stomach. I want her to disappear. But she stands in front of me, frowning, her face red.

"Can we just walk?" she pleads.

Her resemblance to my dad makes me shiver.

I start off down Jackson Street because none of the school kids live that way. Avery follows right behind me, past doctor's offices, and pharmacies, and produce stores. Neither of us says a word. There's a small park at the end of the street where tangled weeds almost hide a rusty swing set and the maple leaves are starting to turn red. On the other side of the park, there's a deserted path bordering the Red River. It's called that because it's full of red mud. She motions me to sit beside her on a bench. It's worn and dirty, and I want to run away. But I know she'll follow me. She'll find out where I live and . . . .

"Please listen," she begs.

I stand there, looking at the weeds next to the river, not willing to sit.

"I've been bugging you because I don't have a choice. I told you, my mom died. I live with my aunt outside Charlottesville. She pretends, but she doesn't really care about me. I never had siblings. That's why I have to find out."

I sit down on the bench.

"I don't know why my mother wouldn't tell me who my father was," she says. "I begged her, but she kept it secret. She did tell me one thing. He went to UVA. She met him afterwards when he would come to Charlottesville for football games. She said she wanted me to know he was educated, that I had good genes."

I have to ask. "Did he know about you?"

"She didn't say. He stopped calling her when I was born. So, he must have known."

"Why my dad? It could be anybody."

"Did your dad go to UVA?"

He did, but I don't tell her.

"Does he come to UVA games now?"

"Sure. So do millions," I say.

"I know that doesn't prove it, but there's the DNA and the genealogy charts."

She hands me a manila folder with papers inside.

"Check those out."

She grasps my hand.

"Look at me. You know I look like him."

"He says you're a scam." I stand up. "He's right. Four percent is no proof. My dad would never do what you're saying. Leave me alone."

I run back through the park toward the high school, gasping for breath.

"Check *your* DNA," she calls out. "Then we'll know."

Her voice sounds thick, like she's crying.

We're at the dinner table eating pork chops. Dad's telling a story about some kid who showed up at his office with ten dollars wanting to open an investment account, when the doorbell rings. I stiffen.

Avery follows my mom into the dining room. I can tell from her embroidered black wool mini-dress and knee-high leather boots that she wants to impress us. Impress my dad.

"I told you to leave me alone," I say.

Mom looks surprised.

"She told me she was a friend of yours."

"I'm sorry," Avery says. "But there's something I have to know. And if Meghan won't help me, I have to do it this way."

"Do what?" my dad asks. He's smiling, like having some unknown girl burst into our house in the middle of dinner is the most natural thing in the world. But surely, he sees . . . . He has to.

"I think you could be my father," Avery says. Her voice squeaks.

"Are you crazy?" Mom says.

But Dad puts his hand on Mom's arm to quiet her, then says, "That's absurd."

He's still smiling.

Avery shrugs off her backpack and digs deep inside.

"Here are your copies," she says as she pulls a sheaf of papers out of the pack and hands them to Dad. I know those papers.

He reads each page slowly, taking his time. Sitting next to him, I hold my breath. The pork chop sits uneasy in my stomach. Finally, he looks Avery full in the face and smiles.

"I'm truly sorry, young lady," he says, "but these papers prove nothing. I have one daughter, only one. And you have caused that daughter unnecessary anxiety and pain."

He puts his arm around me.

"I must ask you, from now on, to leave Meghan alone."

Avery sits down in the chair across from us. Her face is red, and she looks like she might cry.

"Look at me," she says. "No matter what you say, I look like you. I do."

He stands up.

"Please, now, leave my house."

"Give me my papers then."

"You said they were my copies. I think I'll hold on to them. If you continue to pester my daughter, I may have to use them."

He says all this in a calm, even friendly voice, like he's being patient with a defiant child. Then he hands Avery her backpack and walks her to the front door.

I hear her sobbing as the door closes.

I can't get it out of my head. The two of them. I want to believe my dad. I do believe him. He couldn't possibly have betrayed my mother. He wouldn't lie to me. But there the two of them are. Locked in my head. The same black curls, parted on the left, swirling about the ears. The eyes, deep blue, intense. The same sharp shoulders and wiry build. The way they stared at each other across the table, both hunched forward. Did Mom notice? I wonder what she's thinking.

I'm waking up in the middle of the night, arguing with myself, unable to sleep. Every time the doorbell rings, I jump. Every buzz of my phone scares me. And so, I open my computer and click on Searchgen. I'm doing this to prove Dad is telling the truth. The DNA test will put this behind me. Because I need to stop thinking about it. I order the kit. When it arrives, I hide it in my underwear drawer for a couple of weeks, afraid to take the plunge, afraid of the truth. But I've gone this far. I need to know. So, I spit into the tube, add the solution, mail it all back, and wait.

We're walking together in Charlottesville.

It's my spring vacation, and Dad is excited because I will be going to his university next September, and he wants to show me everything. Like I haven't walked all over the campus a hundred times before. The Lawn, lined with columns and a long row of one-story brick buildings, where the seniors get to room if they're lucky. The imposing Rotunda designed by Thomas Jefferson. The serpentine brick wall, the wood paneled McGregor Room in the library. The rolling hills, now yellow-green with new grass. The walnuts and maples, thick with leaves, spreading their branches over the grounds.

I watch him as he races ahead of me in jeans and an orange and blue jersey with UVA printed on the back, pointing out the room he lived in on the Lawn, the field where he-played baseball. He looks so young, my father, so full of joy.

I want to forget what I now know. That this handsome, vital man who is my father is also the father of Avery Burnside. And Avery Burnside is my half-sister. I know that because I now have my own DNA report from Searchgen. And Avery Burnside shows up on my list of relatives as sharing 24.8 percent of my DNA, which Searchgen predicts to be a half sibling. It's impossible to persuade myself that it's a coincidence.

We're staying in one of those quaint little inns so typical of Charlottesville. A small wood frame house on a back street with a wide front porch, small bedrooms, and a parlor full of eighteenth-century furniture. We're sitting after dinner in armchairs with deep velvet cushions in Dad's room which is the largest in the inn.

I blurt it out.

"Dad, I think Avery Burnside might be right."

"Goddammit!" he explodes. "I don't believe it. You're too smart to believe that pseudo-science shit."

I almost lose my courage, but I have to know.

"I want you to tell me the truth," I say. My voice breaks.

"I have. This is crazy, Meghan. I've read all about it. Those tests are full of errors. You're my only daughter."

I go into the adjoining room, my room, and bring the papers.

"Here," I say.

He flips through the pages, stopping here and there to read. I wait, my stomach churning. Don't lie, I silently beg him. I need you not to lie.

Finally, he says, "I don't know anything about this DNA business, but this has to be some kind of fluke because it isn't true."

I'm crying now.

"That's why I ordered the test. To find out the truth. There's too much similarity between us to be a coincidence."

"You don't know that," he says.

I can tell he's trying to keep his voice under control, that he's on the verge of anger. But I keep going.

"There's only one way to find out," I whisper.

"What?"

"You have them test your DNA."

"Bullshit," he spits out. "That damn girl has mesmerized you. You don't even trust your own father."

"Tell me the truth, Daddy," I beg. "I just want you not to lie."

My mother comes into my bedroom the night we return from UVA. "Your dad is very upset," she tells me. She sits down beside me on the bed and puts her hand on my arm.

"I know. Did he tell you why?"

She pulls her arm away.

"You can't believe that little bitch."

Her voice is harsh, like I've never heard it before. And I've never heard her use that word.

"It's not that I believe her," I say. "But did he tell you, I did my own DNA research?"

"How could you?" she says. "I don't believe you've fallen for it, smart as you are. But I know one thing for sure. You've hurt your dad real bad."

"I don't want to hurt him." I'm crying now. "But I want him to be honest with me."

"He is," she says. "He's the best man that ever lived."

She goes on about how he was Spotswood Citizen of the Year and Chairman of the Food Bank as if that has anything to do with it.

There's something l have to ask.

"Was Dad away a lot before I was born?"

She looks up, puzzled.

"What? "

"You know, like on business trips."

She looks in the direction of the window.

"Of course, he's always going to conferences."

I take a deep breath.

"Did you ever worry?"

"About what?"

"You know, like maybe he wasn't always on business?"

She jumps up from the bed.

"How can you even think that?"

I want to say, you're right. You're right, Mama. It's a scam. But I can't.

It's May, and I'm back at UVA for the incoming freshman tour. We've visited classes, lunched on pizza in the cafeteria, inspected freshman dorms, toured the grounds, and even attended a fraternity party. And I'm ready. Ready to shake off the dust of Spotswood, more than ready to escape the silence at home.

I'm sitting in a cafe near the university staring at the menu. And there she is. Standing beside my booth, notepad in her hand, my waitress. Avery. Her black curls are pinned back behind her ears, her shoulders hunched.

Why did I think I could avoid her? She lives here. The words on the menu run together.

"Have you decided?" she asks.

"Actually, I'm not hungry," I say. "I have to go."

"No, you don't."

She slides into the booth across from me.

"I knew one of these days you'd turn up."

Her voice sounds harsh.

My stomach is turning, and my hands feel sweaty. I want to run.

"Stay," she says. "We have a lot to talk about."

She's right.

"You're my sister, you know. Half-sister."

I can tell she's close to crying.

"I can't...."

She interrupts.

"Look at me, stuck in this lousy diner, wiping up after all these rich college kids, like you."

"What do you want from us?"

"'That's easy. A family. A father. When your name popped up on my DNA report, I thought you'd face the truth, and we could get on with it."

"I can't," I say.

"Can't what? Admit your dad . . . ."

"He won't—"

She interrupts again.

"Of course, he won't. But what's to keep us from seeing each other? Being sisters?"

Her voice breaks.

I look her in the face.

"You forced your way into our life and nearly wrecked it. I can't be anything to you. Don't you see? He's my dad. I can't lose him."

She stands up and throws her notepad on the table with such force it flies to the floor.

"You're so cold," she says, sobbing. "My father rejects me. You reject me."

People at nearby tables are staring. A man, probably the manager, comes through a swinging door and heads to our table.

I get up quickly.

"We didn't do anything to you," I say. "You're the one. You screwed up everything."

And I run from the cafe without looking back.

It's August. Hot as hell. I'm working at Dunkin Donuts, hanging out at the pool on the weekends while my friends are buying clothes for college, figuring out course schedules, packing the family car. I'm taking the year off. A "gap year," they call it. Dad tries to hide his disappointment. But I'm not sleeping. I'm gaining weight. And college seems more and more like a steep hill I don't want to climb right now. So, I bailed. I've applied for this program called City Year, where kids volunteer to work with high school kids in inner cities. It sounds kind of grim, but I have to get away. I've got a lot of things to figure out.

I haven't heard from Avery since May. I think about her a lot.

In the mornings, I watch Dad leave for work, his hair still wet from the shower, his boyish face flushed, eager, and I love him so much. At the dinner table, he spins tales of the paranoid misers and greedy millionaires he serves and secretly scorns. He makes me laugh. Now that it's clear that Avery is out of our lives, Mom has forgiven me. Everything seems normal on the surface.

But we don't go to football games. We don't garden. And we don't talk.

Dinner at the Ritz

Corvus Review, Issue 13, Winter 2019, p. 21

I sit in a restaurant facing a man I met online, in a room packed with thirty-somethings all talking at once. It's not exactly the Ritz but what passes for top-of-the-line dining in this county of overpriced houses and overpaid professionals, where I live. The man's name is Hunter, and he's slurping raw oysters at the bargain price of a dollar a piece available for patrons who show up before six in the evening. Which we did. I've been experimenting with computer-arranged "dates" ever since my husband of many years left me the house while he took off with his nurse practitioner. I'm lonely. I admit it. And this guy looks promising. Red hair going gray, neatly trimmed beard. Owns a small business, something about cameras. Loves to travel. And he's my age, forty.

I'm poking into shells with a small fork, digging out garlicky snails, when I hear someone say, "911." I put down my fork and look around. The diners are shouting at each other over the roar of conversation. Short, dark-skinned waiters in white coats rush here and there with trays of shellfish. Hunter picks his next oyster out of the mound in front of him. The noise is deafening.

A woman's back is in my line of vision. It looks like she's slumped over on the table. Her companion, also a woman, speaks into a cell phone. I put down my snail tools. A pudgy man with a pointed beard and a shaved head approaches the table. The maître d? He leans in toward the woman on the phone.

Everyone continues to shout and eat.

The maître d' turns toward the table next to the woman in distress. The man at that table looks up and nods to the maître d. Then he and his wife and two teenaged girls grab the coats and sweaters arranged on the back of their chairs and leave the room. Two waiters move their table to the side. Why does no one but me seem to notice? Meanwhile, the woman I'm watching remains motionless.

"Something weird's going on," I say to Hunter.

"Mmm?" His mouth is full of oyster.

Suddenly, waiters are everywhere, pulling empty tables away from the slumped over woman, clearing a path through the restaurant to a padded bench along the wall, where people are seated, café style, at small round tables. They pay no attention.

I catch the words "misogynist asshole" coming from nearby. Complaints about a husband? A boss?

A door to the outside opens next to our table flooding the room with freezing air. Out the window red lights are flashing. Waiters rush in and out of the room.

A young woman in a red silk blouse who is seated on the padded bench slides to the right, leaving an empty space. She never looks at the maître d nor at the three waiters who are carrying a body through the cleared space in her direction. Tables are shoved aside. I watch the waiters lay a slumped form full length on the bench. Patrons pick through their food without looking up, laughing and shouting. The motionless woman's companion remains in place still holding a phone to her ear.

In come the firefighters, in full rubber raincoats and hats, carrying a stretcher. The diners do not look up. The firefighters march across the room to the padded bench and huddle around the supine woman. Measures are taken, hidden from my view. Minutes pass. Waiters rush about. Food is consumed. The din of conversation continues at top volume. The firefighters trudge back through the room, a stretcher between them, a blanketed bulge on top. Hunter puts down his oyster shell and moves his chair as the parade passes our table. The waiters soundlessly close the door and restore the tables and chairs to their original positions.

No one looks up. The diners on the padded bench slide back into the vacated space. The four family members return, remove sweaters and coats, and reopen their menus. I hear a siren.

"My God!" I say. "What do you think happened to that woman?"

"I don't know," Hunter says. "But you better eat those snails before the next course comes. It's black cod with whipped cauliflower, sunchokes, broccoli de ciccio, and bagna cauda."

Really?

When our waiter asks if we are enjoying our shellfish, Hunter stops chewing to beam.

"Delicious."

The waiter's smile is practiced.

"The food is good," I say in a voice loud enough for my neighbors to hear me. "But the behavior in this room is appalling."

"Excuse me?" the waiter says.

Hunter smiles.

"She means that your customers were too polite to stare at the plight of that unfortunate woman. Unlike my companion here."

I drop my napkin over the whipped cauliflower and sunchokes and stand up. Now everyone is watching.

The waiter clears the oyster shells without comment.

I hear laughing and shouting and slurping as I head for the door.

Stalking the Sprouted Stag

Sweet Tree Review, Volume 4, Issue IV, Fall 2019

"Rhyton. Yes. Rhyton. Sprouted Stag. 600 BC, maybe 750."

He stands there twisting his slender, delicate fingers in the air. Murmuring.

I stare at a small clay animal in a glass case. Its squat legs support a smooth, undulating body and a head full of antlers. The top of its head is cut open to form a spout at the mouth.

"It's beautiful, isn't it?" I ask the man who is muttering to himself.

"Sprouted stag." He doesn't look at me. "Rhyton. Yes. Maybe 600."

I turn to him.

"Excuse me?"

Nothing. I recognize him. He sits by himself at the back of the van on our tour of Persia. He's small, no taller than I am, and very young looking with thick blond hair that covers his hunched shoulders. A boy, really.

I move on to a collection of urns and pitchers.

"That guy's talking to himself," I say to fellow traveler Lawton Arey, a tall man with a jutting chin and a large mole on his forehead.

"He's a weirdo," Mr. Arey says in the same nasal drawl he uses to complain about the food, the hotels, the heat, the van. Arey's a real estate developer from Memphis who travels with his wife on tours all over the world with the sole purpose, as far as I can tell, of buying up the gift shops. I've certainly not detected any curiosity about this country on the part of either of them.

After an hour of traipsing around the museum, marveling at pre-Islamic bronze lions and blown glass ewers, I return to the ceramic stag. The young man hasn't moved.

Soroya, our local guide, calls out, "Dominic, the van is here."

He stands, staring at the clay animal, still murmuring.

"Let's go," she says.

He inches closer to the glass case. I follow his gaze. For the first time, I notice a hairline crack in one of the antlers. Is that what he's looking at?

A man in uniform suddenly appears and says something in Farsi to Soroya, who shakes her head and answers quickly. The guard reaches for Dominic's arm.

"Don't touch me!" Dominic yells, and turns toward the man, his hands in front of him, palms out, thin lips quivering.

The guard backs away, yelling something. Soroya is talking fast, her dark eyes flashing under heavy make-up. She shows him her official guide's badge, points to Dominic and then us, huddled together in a group. Dominic stares into the glass case one last time, then turns sharply toward the exit leaving a wide space between him and the guard.

At dinner, Dominic sits at a table by himself and speaks to no one. After he leaves, everyone talks at once.

"What's the matter with that guy?"

"He could get us in all trouble, him yelling out like that."

Soroya tells us she's been assured by Travel Adventures, our tour company, that Dominic is just eccentric. We shouldn't worry about him.

"If it makes you feel more comfortable, I'll try to contact the head office to get more information about him. But you know," she reminds us, "we have no internet service in this country, and so far the Wi-Fi's been down in all our hotels. So, I haven't been getting calls or emails through to the company."

I marvel at her fluent English which she told me she picked up during a semester at the University of Michigan.

I wake up and can't get back to sleep. It's not late, 11:15. But it's stuffy in my little hotel room. No air conditioning. I pull a full-length kaftan over my nightgown, flip a scarf around my hair, and head down the stairs to the garden. It's quiet out here. Everyone's asleep. A shallow pool, a dim purple under the garden lights, divides the lush vegetation into two sections. I cross the narrow foot bridge into a small stand of pomegranate trees. Their red flowers are even more brilliant under the night lights than in the bright sun. I follow the winding paths through green hedges and bushes thick with pistachio nuts. The air is cool out here and smells slightly sweet. My foot scrapes something soft.

"Don't touch me!"

I jump. A dark lump in the path.

"I'm sorry," I say, "I didn't see you."

As I stumble backward toward the pool, I recognize Dominic, sitting cross-legged in the path, motionless except for his fingers which are tracing patterns in the air.

For the rest of the night, I lie sleepless, rumpled sheets tossed aside. What's he doing out there?

At breakfast, I try to pull Soroya aside to tell her what happened, but she's surrounded by my fellow travelers. When I climb into the van, I find that two couples from Dallas have co-opted the back seats where Dominic has been sitting. I watch him shuffle slowly down the aisle. Then he stops.

"Good morning, everyone," Soroya announces. "We have a long travel day ahead of us. So please, everyone, take a seat."

She's looking at Dominic, who twists around peering up and down the van, his eyes darting everywhere. Then he slides into the empty seat across the aisle from me.

"No seat in the back. No seat in the back. No seat in the back."

His delicate fingers are twitching in his lap.

He turns to face me.

"Sprouted stag," he says, then resumes his mumbling.

Sprouted stag?

I want to move my seat. I'm not the friendly type. Thirty years a lab tech. Never married, never wanted children. I don't like this. But the van is moving at a fast clip, and there are no empty seats nearby.

We're having lunch at a small restaurant somewhere in the desert. Kebobs, as usual, and some kind of dark brown stew made—we are told—from pomegranate seeds. Plus the vast platters of rice we have come to expect.

When Dominic heads off in the direction of the restroom, Mr. Arey's wife, Lorraine, who is sitting near me, pipes up.

"That young man is definitely not all right."

"What do you mean?" Soroya asks.

I notice her scarf has slipped off her silk-black hair onto her shoulders. She's obviously not worried about the country's prohibition against women showing their hair.

"My husband tried to introduce himself, you know, tried to shake his hand," Lorraine says. "And he jumped back and screamed, 'Don't touch me. Don't touch me.' And you saw the way he refused to leave the museum yesterday. Next thing you know, he'll get himself arrested for disrupting the peace or something, and the rest of us will be in trouble."

"I don't think that's likely," Soroya says.

I tell her about finding him in the garden the night before.

Mrs. Arey watches me with frightened eyes.

"See what I mean?"

Soroya sighs.

"As I've said before, the company told me he's kind of anti-social. But he's nothing to worry about. They assured me of that. Why don't you just let him be? I think he'll be fine."

As we are lining up to board the van, I see Mrs. Arey, with the Memphis crowd bunched around her, her small, heavily rouged face rigid with self-importance, whispering.

On the long drive to our next destination, I entertain myself by swiping through the photos on my iPad. I'm gazing at the clay animals we saw in the Pre-Islamic Museum when I hear the familiar mumbling.

"Sprouted stag."

I turn to look. He's just across the aisle from me again, rocking back and forth, very slightly, and nodding.

"Pre-Islamic. Rhyton. 750? 600? Before Cyrus. Ibex. Zebu."

He doesn't look at me.

Zebu?

He keeps mumbling, but I can't understand the words.

And then, "Humped."

Humped?

"Cattle. Humped cattle, zebu. Humped cattle."

I try to ignore him. But there it is, a photo of a clay animal that resembles a cow and has a huge hump. Zebu?

I steal a quick glance in his direction. Whatever his problem, this Dominic seems to know stuff.

For the rest of the ride, he talks, or rather, he mumbles. "Medes" and "Cyrus" and "Darius." I recognize those words. Before I travel to a place, I do my homework.

I steal a glance in his direction. He's staring out the window.

Later, while we wait in the Oasis Hotel lobby for our room assignments, I find myself sitting next to Mr. Arey.

"I think Dominic might know something about Persian art," I say.

"He's a nut," Arey says.

We're in Persepolis, Darius the Great's magnificent showcase palace. The ultimate goal of the trip. We enter Xerxes' Gateway, dwarfed by gigantic mythical figures with wings and long beards. We wander idly among the tall, slender columns with large capitals balanced on the top. I'm so awed by all this pomp and artistry I forget about Dominic.

On to the Apadana, a palace where Darius received officials from all parts of the Persian empire. On one side of the building, full-sized figures bearing gifts to Darius are carved into the stone wall along a stairway ascending to the palace. Some carry wine, some gold, some lambs for sacrifice. The officials' heads are covered, with crowns, with helmets, with bent conical forms, like cornucopias. I've read about this place, looked online at photographs. But the real palace takes my breath away.

As I walk slowly up the Apadana stairway, I find myself behind Dominic. He's staring at the figures, his face close to the stylized hair, the stony beards. I hear him talking, in his usual monotone. I hear the word "Darius." For the first time, it dawns on me that Dominic's not just mumbling to himself, he may be talking to *me.* I back away. Meanwhile, his thin fingers are flying in the air. He's leaning forward, close to the figures, almost touching them.

"Not so close," I say.

It just pops out, but guards are everywhere. Am I worried about him? Or is it me I'm worried about?

He ignores me, leaning into the figures, pulling a camera out of his backpack and aiming it at the struggling lambs, the elaborate urns, the chiseled faces.

"Watch out," I beg, terrified. "The guards."

Slowly, he turns his head toward me, and, without making eye contact, backs away from the stone figures.

As we reach the top of the stairs, I find Soroya waiting for us.

"Thank you," she says.

The Arey are huddled behind her, watching us.

We're in the National Crown Jewel Museum, surrounded by glass cases of the largest rubies and emeralds and diamonds maybe in the world. Jeweled crowns, tiaras, necklaces, sword handles, and sheaths. It's dark in here, lit only by the lights inside the cases. And you can hardly hear the guide's spiel for the crowd of tourists, talking, gasping, calling to one another. It's too dark, too close, too noisy. I'm ready to leave.

Then over the clamor, a loud scream.

"Don't touch me!"

The crowd parts, and there is Dominic, thrashing about, bucking and twisting, with two men in blue uniforms yanking his arms behind him. They push him toward the exit, with Soroya close behind. I snake my way through the crowd, trying to keep up. By the time I reach the dimly lit museum lobby, Dominic and the guards have disappeared, and Soroya is speaking in rapid-fire Farsi to a woman in full hijab. The tour members cluster behind me, all talking at once.

"I knew it. He's going to get us all in trouble."

"What'd he *do*?"

"He's crazy."

"He's scary."

What was Travel Adventures thinking?

Soroya turns to us, "Please, go to the van and wait," she says. "I'll be there as soon as I can."

Once inside the van, Lawton Arey takes a stand at the front of the bus.

"We're in a very serious situation," he begins. "If this man is released, which is questionable, we must insist that he be immediately flown back home. Otherwise, he will endanger all of us. I think you all know what I mean."

We nod. We do. This is the Middle East.

To distance myself from the other passengers and whatever may be happening in the Jewelry Museum, I pull out my iPad and get lost in online bridge.

When Soroya returns to the van after a two-hour wait, her shoulders are slumped, her lipstick faded, her scarf dangling. And she is alone. The chatter in the van stops cold. I watch as she picks up the microphone.

"Don't worry," she begins. "It will be all right. They are holding Dominic for questioning, but I'm sure he'll be released soon."

Her voice breaks.

"I am so sorry this is happening in my country."

"Where is he?" I ask.

Soroya shakes her head.

"I don't know."

I have an image of that fragile boy being shoved, beaten. And suddenly nothing feels safe.

"What was he doing?" Mr. Arey again.

"He was standing too close to one of the cases. The guard tapped him on the back . . . well, you know. He doesn't like to be touched. It went bad after that. I tried to convince them he was just interested in looking, but . . . ."

"I knew it! Something like that was bound to happen."

It's Lorraine Arey, her thin lips glistening red.

On the return trip to the hotel, the Arey are up front, talking at once to Soroya. Yelling past each other. Why had Travel Adventures allowed that man to go on the trip? What will happen to the rest of us? Some of the passengers want to fly home as soon as possible. One old lady is clutching her phone.

"I'm holding for my Congressman," she tells me.

I move to the back of the van to get away from the mounting hysteria. I take deep breaths, but that only makes me cough, and my face swelters from the heat of the unfamiliar scarf. A voice in my head keeps repeating. If it can happen to Dominic . . . .

A knock on my hotel room door. It's Soroya. She gives me a hug, which surprises me. I don't hug. But I've been holding myself in so tight, refusing to even imagine what was happening to Dominic, that her strong arms around me feel okay.

She tugs off her scarf and sits on the queen bed. I pull up a desk chair opposite and watch her face. Her large black eyes dart around the small, anonymous room.

"I've decided to talk to all of you separately," she says. "It's less confusing."

I nod.

"The president of our company is on his way here. He has Dominic's mother with him, also somebody from the State Department. Maybe others. James Ridley, that's the president, has spoken with several of the leaders here, and he tells me that Dominic will be released."

I want to be convinced, but I'm not.

"Dominic has done nothing wrong," she says. "There's no gain, political or otherwise, for keeping him here."

She stops and stares into space.

"But in my country, nothing is sure."

"He comes across as crazy," I say. "All that mumbling and calling out."

"I know. That's why the mother's coming. She can explain his situation."

"What *is* it, his situation?"

She pulls her iPad out of her bag.

"This is the first day I've been able to use email, and look what's been sitting here all this time."

She points.

> *To James Ridley.*
>
> *I am the mother of Dominic Whittaker, who is currently touring the Middle East with your company. In previous communications, I mentioned that Dominic is anti-social and often appears to be eccentric. At his insistence, I did not tell you that he suffers from a communication disorder on the autism spectrum. This is Dominic's first ever trip on his own, and he very much wants people not to treat him as disabled. My son is highly intelligent and very knowledgeable about pre-Islamic Persian treasures, in which he has a master's degree from Brown. He is also able to care for himself. While I respect and sympathize with my son's request, I am telling you the truth out of my concern that those around treat him with tolerance and kindness.*
>
> *I am feeling very anxious about my son and hope this message will be helpful to him and to you. Please email or call me immediately if there is a problem.*
>
> *Thank you.*
> *Adele Whittaker.*

"That's just the first one," Soroya says. "There has been an email from Dominic's mother every day since this one. But I didn't get them until today."

I feel so stupid. Autism. Of course. I've read so much about it in the news, but I've never known anybody with it.

"I keep asking myself what I could have done different," Soroya says.

I sit across from her, frightened, angry. At this country. At the travel company.

"Everyone wants out."

She takes my hand.

"You should go home. The official word is that Dominic will be released. But right now, all of you could be called in for questioning. You don't want that."

Back home, Dominic is front page news for a day or two. His hysterical mother appears on CNN begging the president to send a team to the Middle East to rescue her son.

For several weeks, I am the center of attention, at the lab, at duplicate bridge meets, in my apartment building. I'm the lady who was forced to escape the Middle East, the one on that tour where a man was captured. No one wants to know about the winged bulls of Persepolis or the sprouted stags or the blue pools of water in the desert. So, I entertain them with tales of Dominic's capture, his being swept away in front of my eyes. I tell them that I'm scared for him, that he was brave to make that trip by himself.

And then it's all forgotten. No more news coverage. My tales of adventure grown stale, I download my photos, label them, shove my guidebooks into the bookcase. It's over. Except in the middle of the night, I sometimes wake up from a nightmare of blue uniformed guards huddled together over something dark, striking it. And I can't stop it.

The papers are full of it. Dominic Whitaker released after six months in prison in the Middle East. I buy all the papers, read every word. I watch Dominic on CNN, his spare body even thinner, his hair unkempt, his fingers clutching the rail as he walks slowly down the stairs of the government plane. A stout gray-haired woman walks behind him. The mother?

The press is everywhere, pushing microphones at him, cameras flashing. A close-up reveals a face with no expression. The mouth hangs open, the eyes are half shut. There's a big reception party on the tarmac, New York's mayor and lots of officials I don't recognize. Dominic ignores them, his body stiff. No one hugs him. No one touches him. Clearly, they've been warned.

Two days later, Dominic's mother gives an angry interview on PBS. She blames Travel Adventures for allowing the capture. She chastises the White House for not bringing him home sooner.

"How is he doing?" a reporter asks.

"How do you think he's doing?" she spits out. "He's been in prison for six months." Her voice trembles.

She holds up a book on Persian art. The camera zooms in on the cover. It's the sprouted stag.

"This," she hisses, stabbing the stag with her finger, "this is the art he knows more about than most scholars. This is why he made the trip. On his own. He insisted on going alone. To see this ancient art. All by himself. I should have gone with him, but I was so proud of him."

She breaks down.

It's been months, but I still see Dominic, his nose close to the glass case, staring at the crack in the stag's antler, his fingers twisting. Hear his voice. His monotone. He picked me to talk to. Of all people. I didn't listen. I was afraid. He tried to tell me—about all those people living thirty centuries ago, all those people lost to time, building castles, shaping stags with their fingers. Tried to break through his lonely shell to *me.* I didn't listen.

The Purple Jacket

Five on the Fifth, Volume 4, Issue 9, July 5, 2019

Dede Fulton woke to fog so dense she couldn't see the trees outside her window. As she reached for the jeans that swung in a baggy lump from the doorknob, she heard Allen out front calling, "Hey, Gray Cat, where'd you hide your babies?"

Her tender boy. If there were kittens, she wanted to see them too. No, she wanted to watch Allen finding them, holding them. Her sweet ten-year-old. Slamming the screen door behind her, Dede picked her way across the cluttered front yard, side-stepping dog poop and bicycles. She found her son with his five-year-old sister, Lacy, in the field that stretched between their house and the country road, a road that led, after many twists and turns, to the Pacific Ocean.

"Look, Mama," Lacy hollered, holding up a silky blue nightgown. She twirled around, wisps of blue swinging from her skinny arms.

"Where did that come from?" Dede asked.

"From a bush. Look!" she said, pointing.

A child's pink sundress with a raspberry print lay on the damp grass. A small red bathing suit dangled from a fence post. As the fog cleared, the green field came alive with reds and blues, yellows and purples. There were dresses and panties and jackets. All new, not faded and patched. Clothes Dede could never afford. Clothes she secretly coveted for her little girl.

"Somebody left me a whole bunch of beautiful clothes," Lacy shouted, racing from one to the other.

Dede held up the sundress and watched the printed raspberries flutter in the wind.

"It's so pretty," she whispered.

"Somebody must have lost them," Allen said, picking up a stuffed kangaroo.

But they're on our property now, Dede thought.

"This fits perfect," Lacy breathed, slipping her arms into the sleeves of a purple jacket. "It's from my secret fairy godmother."

"Don't be a ditz," said her brother.

"I'll go get your dad," Dede said.

Back in the house Dede wound her arms around her husband's neck and kissed him full on the mouth.

"You'll never believe what's lying around out there in our field," she said, grinning up into his narrow face and twisting his long brown hair into a ponytail. Ron was her man, long and thin and brainy. She belonged to him and even after eleven years of living together, she still couldn't keep her hands off him. Now she watched him wriggle his feet into black scratched up boots, pull a maroon knitted hat on his head, and slam the door behind them.

As they approached the carpet of color spread all over the field, Ron whistled.

"Well, I'll be damned. Somebody's mighty generous." He winked at his daughter. "Don't just stand there, Lacy-girl. Pick 'em up."

"You think that's okay?" Allen asked.

"They're on our property," Ron said. "Go get a laundry basket."

Allen frowned and looked at his mother.

"You heard your father," she said.

Lacy began to gather her treasures, holding them up, one by one, smoothing out wrinkles, folding them into several sloppy stacks.

"What'd I say, Allen?" Ron's voice was sharp.

Later that afternoon, Dede looked up from picking blackberries out of a plastic bucket to see a man's face peering in the kitchen window.

"Ron," she called. "Better go out front. We got company."

"Where're the dogs?" he growled.

"Out back. Tied up."

"Get Growler and bring him in the house. We might need him if that man tries to come inside."

Dede returned from the back yard with a German Shepherd on a tight leash to find Ron standing on the unpainted front porch with a tall man in khaki trousers and shiny leather boots.

"You lost?" Ron asked.

"Hello," the man said, reaching out to shake the hand that Ron failed to offer. "I'm Stewart Dunning. My family is camping in that State Park up the road."

He smiled down at a small girl with red hair and large green eyes, who was tugging at his leg.

"This is Nora," he said. "I hate to bother you, but we're looking for her suitcase. It fell off the roof of our car last night, and we've been driving up and down this road all morning looking for it. We stopped here because that little girl out there in your yard is wearing a jacket just like my daughter's."

Ron scratched the back of his neck.

"A suitcase, you say?"

Dunning nodded.

"A child's plastic suitcase, with a broken zipper."

"Can't say as I have. Nope. No suitcase."

He turned to Dede.

"Me neither," she said. At least she didn't have to lie.

"That girl out there has my jacket."

Nora pointed to the yard.

The German Shepherd lowered its head in the direction of Dunning and growled.

"Have you got my dresses and my bathing suit and my kangaroo?" Nora's voice trembled. "They fell off the car roof last night."

"It was dark," her father explained. "We didn't discover that the suitcase was gone until we got to camp."

"I don't know anything about that," Ron said.

Suddenly Lacy came racing up to the house. The purple jacket now had a damp brown stain on the front.

"That's my jacket," Nora cried out. "She messed it all up."

"It's *my* jacket." Lacy's voice was defiant. "I got it fair and square."

Dunning raised his eyebrows and turned back to a woman, who was coming up the path from the car.

"That sure looks like my daughter's jacket," the woman said.

For just a moment, Dede felt a kind of relief. They could give the clothes to these folks, no questions asked. No snooping around. But the fierce frown on her husband's face stopped her.

"Maybe it *looks* like your daughter's jacket," Ron said. "But *that* jacket rightfully belongs to my daughter."

"Could I please see it?" Dunning asked.

"No. Now I'm asking you politely. Get off my land."

"Could I at least look around? Nora's clothes may be somewhere close."

"Maybe you didn't hear me," Ron hissed. "This is private land."

Dunning took one look at Growler, who was tugging at its leash and snarling, and turned to leave.

But Nora didn't budge.

"Give me back my jacket," she cried. As she reached out toward Lacy, the German Shepherd leaped at her arm. Dede yanked it back just as Dunning grabbed his screaming daughter and edged away from the dog which was straining on its leash and barking madly.

Ron motioned with his head toward the back yard, where Growler's barking had unleashed a deafening uproar.

"Like I said, you need to leave. This dog's gentle, but we got others."

"Jesus!" Dunning muttered, hurrying his family to the car.

Ron laughed as the Toyota Prius sped off in a cloud of dust.

They'd met after 9/11 at an anti-war rally in San Francisco. For Dede, a senior at Fresno High School at the time, the destruction of the twin towers in New York seemed very far away. She'd come to the city with friends to check out the latest styles in the department stores on Union Square. But while trying to cross Market Street, she got hemmed in by hundreds of people who were blocking traffic, chanting, waving signs in the air. She called out to her friends, but they were lost in the crowd. And then, a tall, thin young man with a ponytail grabbed her by the arm and handed her a poster with the slogan "Not In Our Name" splashed all over it in red. Before she knew what was happening, she was marching along beside him, calling out, "No More Wars." When they reached Hermon Plaza, her new friend snaked his way through the crowd, pulling her behind him, until he reached the speaker's platform and hopped up. Dede stared at the dozens of important looking people on the stage who were hugging him and smiling into his determined, angular face.

And then he was handed a microphone and began to speak in a deep melodious voice about all the good things his organization, Not In Our Name, stood for. Dede was too bewildered about Afghanistan and Iraq and Osama bin Laden to understand much of what he was saying. But standing there with all those people, staring up at the platform in the San Francisco sunshine, she fell in love.

Her new friend was a Berkeley dropout. And her parents hated him. Hated his ponytail and his politics and his pot. Hated him even more when their daughter, the first in the family to be accepted into a college, turned down the scholarship she had worked so hard for and moved in with him. First into a group house in the Mission, then to a dark little room of their own in Berkeley, and finally, when his animus against war had evolved into a disgust at all government, Ron moved her to a small house on two acres of land up in Mendocino which he had inherited from a reclusive old aunt who favored him. Land far away from what he now called the "corrupt, meddling society" he had grown to abhor. Land where he could hide and harvest the crop that kept them in groceries. Dede loved it all, the hillsides of golden grass, the smell of the ocean, the deer that wandered their property, her children, so full of life. And Ron, who still excited her, even when some of his ideas left her puzzled, and occasionally uneasy.

"You think they'll come back?" Dede asked Ron as she stood at the sink, sorting blackberries for jam.

"Nah," he sneered, sprawling on a ladder-back chair, his boots propped up on the oilcloth covering the kitchen table. "It's that same man from the school that came snooping 'round our place last year. You remember."

Dede nodded, even though she remembered the school district man as older and with a beard. Ron had shouted, "Get the fuck out of here," and slammed the door in his face. It was the first time Ron's behavior had actually alarmed her.

Now Ron laughed, popping berries in his mouth.

"Old Growler took care of him."

Allen sat down next to his father.

"How d'you know that man's from the school?"

"Who else comes snooping around here?" his father asked.

"Then how did those clothes get here?"

"Who knows? Maybe that school guy put them there himself as an excuse to come 'round," Ron answered. "But they're Lacy's now. That man was government for sure. Driving around this neck of the woods in that fancy car looking to put kids in that school of theirs. That little priss of a girl saw that purple jacket and made out it was hers just to give him cover to come nosing around."

"Why does he care about me and Lacy going to his school?" Allen asked.

"I've told you a million times. It's a conspiracy. They want to take away our God-given freedom and make everybody think like they do."

Ron walked over to Dede and put his arms around her.

"You and your sister got the best education in the country with your mama's home schooling."

Dede smiled and pulled him close. She loved him, loved the feel of him, loved the way he was so clever. Lately his rampages against the government had startled her, but she agreed with him on home-schooling. Actually, that had been her idea, not his, her contribution to Ron's way of life. She knew the school people would never approve of her homeschooling her children; she'd only finished high school, nothing further. But she made no apology for that. She'd always been a whiz at math, and she'd read plenty of books. Of course, there was a lot she didn't know. But she'd figure out some way to learn it.

Meanwhile, the children were such smart little things, Allen especially, and she loved it when Ron told her it was all her doing.

"Come look," Lacy called from the living room. Spread out over the rocking chair, the cracked Naugahyde sofa, the oak table, and the faded rug was a patchwork of shorts and dresses and tee-shirts and nightgowns, all different colors.

"Isn't it beautiful?" she breathed.

"Sure is," her father said. "But you best put those things in your chest of drawers before somebody else tries to claim 'em."

"What if they come back and search all over the house and find them?" Allen said.

"Stop that crazy talk," his father scolded. "Lacy found these things on our property, and that's the end of it. And if you see those people again, let the dogs loose. Okay? Can't have the government interfering with my family."

Dede bent over the blackberries, whispering, "Don't come back. Please don't come back."

The next morning, Dede saw a plump young woman in khaki slacks climb out of a jeep and walk up the gravel path toward the house. Her dark hair was pulled back in a messy bun, and she was holding a clipboard.

"Ron," Dede called. "Looks like trouble."

"Get Growler," he yelled as he yanked open the front window.

When Dede returned with the dog, Ron called out to the woman, "What's your business?"

His voice was almost drowned out by frantic barking.

The woman stopped short.

"I'm from the Park Service," she called out. "I'd like to talk to you."

"What about?"

"We got a complaint about some clothes that might have landed in your yard."

"As you can see, there're no clothes here, lady. And since this is private property, I advise you to get yourself off it."

"Don't threaten me," she said. "This is a friendly inquiry. Now come out of there like a sensible man and talk to me."

"No, ma'am. Now get, before the dogs are let out. Government's got no right to come on our land."

Dede watched the woman pull a cell phone from her pocket.

"Okay," Ron yelled. "You asked for it."

He nodded to Dede.

She frowned.

"Let him go," he demanded.

Growler came tearing out the front door, snarling and barking. The woman made a dash for her jeep, yelling into the phone.

Without thinking, Dede raced out into the yard, screaming, "Yield!" The dog pulled back, snapping and moaning.

"Now get out of here," Ron growled to the park ranger as he joined his wife. "And don't come back. Or next time we won't call him off."

The ranger backed her way to the jeep, her eyes fixed on the dog, and sped off in a roar.

"What'd you do that for?" Ron hissed at Dede when they had returned to the house.

"I'm just trying to protect us," she answered. "Suppose the dog had hurt her? We'd have the cops all over us, and we sure don't want that."

"You didn't need to go running out like that. I'd have stopped him. I just wanted to scare her."

"Well, I think you did. I just worry she'll come back with the cops breathing down our neck."

"Nah. She won't be back."

"Suppose she does though and starts searching the place. We've got more to worry about than a bunch of clothes."

She pointed to the basement door.

"I got the law on my side," Ron said. "This is private property. They got no cause for a search warrant."

"What'd that lady want?" Allen asked.

"Meddling. Just government meddling," Ron said.

"Was it about those clothes?"

"Just an excuse to mess with us."

"But those clothes aren't ours," Allen said, keeping a distance.

Ron laughed. "They are now."

Dede woke the next morning to frantic barking. She found her husband in the living room, staring out the front door, a deer rifle in his hand. Out the window she could see five patrol cars, arranged in a semi-circle in the deserted yard in front of the house.

"Oh, my God," she moaned. "Put the gun down, honey. Please. You're going to get us all killed."

"Come on, you scum," Ron whispered under his breath, ignoring her. "One step outside that car and..."

Dede rushed to the children's bedroom. She found them huddled together on Allen's mattress. He was holding Lacy, whose sobbing had left a dark damp spot on her brother's gray sweatshirt. Dede knelt in front of them, took their warm sticky hands in hers and forced a smile.

"Everything's all right," she said. "Your dad's having an argument with some people out there, but we'll work it out."

"They won't take my clothes, will they?" Lacy asked.

Allen started to cry. "Are we going to jail?"

"Of course not. You two stay here," Dede said. I'm going back out there with your dad, and we're going to settle this thing. So, don't worry, sweet things."

As she returned to the living room, Dede heard a voice bellowing over a loudspeaker. "Mr. Fulton, please come out of your house. We want to talk to you. We will not hurt you."

Dede came up close behind her husband, put her arms around his waist.

"You have to go out there, honey," she said, her voice shaky. "Just talk to them."

"They got no cause," Ron said, pushing her away.

"Listen to me," she pleaded. "Please. You're right, honey. This is our property. The government has no right to intrude."

"Damn right."

"But if you don't go out there and talk nice to them, they'll storm in here. And you know what will happen."

"Not a chance, woman. Leave me alone."

Dede's voice wavered.

"Ron, what's happened to you?"

For at least five minutes, the yard was silent. Then the voice over the loudspeaker repeated.

"Mr. Fulton, please..."

As if in answer, Ron aimed his rifle at one of the patrol cars. Allen appeared at the bedroom door.

"Here, Daddy," he pleaded, holding out the purple jacket.

"Put the gun down, Ron," Dede said in a low voice.

"Cool it," he said. "Look, I won't kill the sons of bitches. I just want to scare 'em. Otherwise, they'll come running in here, swarming all over the house, then take us in for stealing those clothes. Next thing you know, the kids will be in foster care."

Lacy ran into the room, her face white.

"Stop that talk, Ron," Dede said as she pressed her daughter close to her chest. "Don't worry, baby," she said. "Nobody's taking you anywhere."

After another interminable silence, a sheriff's deputy slowly opened the car door and squatted behind it.

"Mr. Fulton, please..."

An explosion of barking and howling drowned out the speaker. The deputy jumped back into the car as the dogs leaped against the windows, slobbering, pounding the glass with heavy paws.

"Give them the clothes," Dede yelled. "Just give them the goddammed clothes."

"Shut up," Ron snapped.

"Go back to your room," Dede whispered to the children. "I need to get your dad calmed down."

After what seemed like an hour, all five cars began to inch slowly toward the house, red lights flashing in the sunny, scruffy yard, drawing the semi-circle tighter. The dogs dropped back off the cars, avoiding the moving wheels but barking madly. The voice on the loudspeaker continued to call for Ron to come out of the house unarmed.

Another hour passed as Dede hugged the frightened children, whispering that it would be all right, that nobody would be hurt, while begging her husband to put down his gun and talk to the deputies.

"Just give them the clothes," Dede was pleading. "Think about the children."

"That's exactly the point," he spat out. "They want to take my children and turn them into government robots. Now, get out of my way."

"You don't get it," Dede said. "We can't have the sheriff's people in here."

She pointed to the basement door.

"I'm scared they'll find more than clothes."

All of a sudden, the door of one of the patrol cars opened and a deputy stepped out holding a pistol in front of him.

Out the window, Dede glimpsed a flash of purple just as the report from Ron's rifle shook the room. Then she was pushing Ron out of the way, running out the front door.

"Stop!" Ron yelled.

"Shoot me then," she hollered as she raced across the front porch into the yard and threw herself on the ground. There was so much blood, blood on the gray sweatshirt, on the sparse grass, on Dede's hands as she hugged the limp body tight against her.

Deputies poured out of the cars. One of them raced to the mother crouched on the ground, her body shaking. He gently pulled the boy's thin white arm out from the tangle of mother and son and pressed the wrist with his finger. The eyes were open, blood trickled from the delicate nose.

Then Ron was running out of the house, his face white, screaming, "You fucking sons of bitches."

The deputies quickly circled him, their guns leveled at his chest.

"Drop that," one of them said, pointing to the rifle clutched in Ron's hand.

"You killed him," Ron screamed and lifted the rifle. But the deputies were too fast for him. They knocked the rifle out of his hand and twisted his arms behind him. Surrounded by deputies, his wrists in handcuffs, Ron stared at the vacant face of his child, locked in Dede's arms.

"What's he doing here?" he moaned. "He's supposed to be in the house. He isn't supposed to be..."

Dede glared at him.

"Here," she said, pulling the purple jacket from her son's hand and holding it up. "Allen was trying to..." but she couldn't continue.

The sound of Ron's howling drowned out any thought she might have. A howling, long, loud, high-pitched—not quite human.

Runner's High

Brilliant Flash Fiction, March 2019

Chest out, head high. Arms swinging. Drawing easy breaths. Finding my stride. New sneakers, snug on my feet, bouncing smartly off the packed dirt. Wind tugging at my hair, loosening the pins, blowing the strands forward, in my face. Sweat stinging my eyes.

I breathe Douglas fir, Bishop pine. I could run for hours, up mountains, in sand. Is this what they call runner's high? Something about endorphins? I'm moving. Round the bend. Hairpin turn.

UHH!

Something hard smacks against my leg. I trip and fall on top of it. Something alive. It's warm. Blood's all over the place.

I drag myself up. Bulbous dark eyes stare at me. My chest hurts.

I look at the animal, stretched across the path, blocking my way. Nothing moving but its head.

"Get up," I say.

It doesn't move. I nudge its backside with my sneaker. It stirs.

Head full of antlers. Danger! I back off, unzip the pocket in my shorts, take out my cell. I type in Humane Society. My hands are shaking.

"You've reached the Spotswood County Humane Society. We're sorry we can't take your call at this time. If this is an emergency, call 911."

I punch 911.

"I'm afraid this isn't the kind of emergency we handle. Call the Humane Society."

It's watching me.

"Get up, you," I say.

It doesn't move.

I need help. I start to climb over it. A leg kicks out. No go. I look around. Steep hills on both sides, poison oak. I grab low bushes, rocks, roots. Up I go. It watches. I inch my way past it, slide on my bottom to the path beyond. It points its antlers at me.

Finally. Out of the woods. Panting. I ring the bell at the first house I come to. Nothing. I knock. I ring. The door opens. The man looks like he just woke up, black hair sticking up in all directions. Wonder Woman printed on his t-shirt.

"Yeah?"

"An animal." I'm panting. "Back there. With antlers."

"A deer? Woods are full of 'em."

"I knocked him down. You have to come."

He stares.

"Are you okay?"

"We need to get him up."

"Look, lady. You don't look so good. Why don't you come in for a minute and rest?"

"We've got to do something. Now!"

He disappears and comes back with a woman. She's in a long skirt that flops over her wedge heel sandals. Dangling earrings. Blonde pigtails. Snake tattoos all over her arms.

She's looking at me real hard.

"Is there somebody we can call?"

"I tried," I said. "We just need to get him on his feet."

"Who?"

"The animal. Didn't he tell you?"

"Okay," the man says. "We might as well see what's up."

Back on the path.

When we round the hairpin turn, I cry out, "Here!"

"Where?" The woman in blonde pigtails is looking at me.

I look at the ground.

"They've moved it," I say.

"What?" the man says, staring at me.

"Somebody's taken it."

They keep staring at me.

"Poor thing," I say. "All that blood. I really hurt him."

"Only blood I see is on your pants," the man says. "Look at your knees."

"Let's go, honey," the woman says. "You need to sit down and rest."

She takes hold of me. I hit out at the snakes crawling up her arms. Strong hands lift me up.

Back at their house, they sit me in a deep chair. Scarves are hanging on the walls. All kinds of colors.

"I have to go," I say.

"Hang on here, honey," she says, kneeling beside me and wiping my knee with something wet and warm. "You've had a hard day. Just relax."

"The animal," I say. "What happened to it?"

"It's okay," she says. "Don't worry." She puts a bandage on my knee.

Someone's talking on the telephone.

"Have you lost anybody up there? Old lady here claims she knocked down a deer."

"Somebody's coming," the woman says. Her voice is soft. "They'll take care of you."

"No!" I yell. "They don't get it. I have to go."

I'm out the door, my arms are swinging, my sneakers are hitting the path.

I'm a runner.

This Is My Child

Blue Lake Review, February 2019

Dorothy Winiker's daughter had fallen in love and her mother disapproved. An old story. But not for Dorothy, whose daughter had never before disappointed her. The two had clung to each other since Ray, the husband and father, left for work one morning and never returned. There were several postcards from New York City and a few from Bangkok to the effect that he was on a spiritual search. Then nothing.

To support herself and her child, Dorothy had capitalized on her hobby, painting landscapes. She landed a teaching position in the art department at an exclusive private high school, where the wealthy parents discovered her paintings. The landscapes evolved over time into outsized abstracts and arresting collages. They were now selling at a clip in galleries throughout California. Everyone who knew art, knew Dorothy Winiker.

But Dorothy's world revolved around Rachael, now eighteen. She hadn't yet started college, had practically no experience with boys, and the man, whose name was Rick, was too old for her.

Rachael had met him at the Verizon store where she was having her iPhone upgraded.

"He works there," she told her mother. "He's a wizard with computers, iPhones, you name it."

"Is he selling phones?"

"Sure."

"Well, I would think a wizard with computers would have other options."

"He'll have plenty when he finishes college."

"Oh. Where's he in college?"

"A community college in the East Bay somewhere, but he's going to get his degree. He just needs to make the money first."

"How old is he, Rachael?"

"Twenty-five."

"Oh."

When she first met him, Dorothy could see the attraction. He had the kind of chiseled upper lip and cleft chin that women find hard to resist. But he was barely taller than Rachael, his thin wisps of hay-colored hair signaled early balding, and when he talked to Dorothy, his eyes fixed somewhere above her head.

Rachael negotiated Berkeley in her usual competent way: she scored A's in her classes and ran cross-country every afternoon. But on Friday nights she drove back home to Larkspur to spend the weekend with Rick.

Dorothy struggled to contain herself. She knew an outright attack would backfire. A mother's disapproval was no weapon against the power of sex, and this was, as far as she knew, Rachael's first plunge into that heady confusion.

Second semester began and Rachael was still spending every weekend with Rick. Dorothy could hold it in no longer. They were huddled together in the former garage, transformed by skylights into a bright, spacious studio. Rachael sat, as she often did, on a paint-encrusted wooden chair close to her mother, her eyes fixed on the canvas of red-orange streaks against a background of purple swirls.

"Sunset?" she asked.

"Bingo," her mother replied. "You've got a better eye than those wannabes who write for the papers."

"I've seen it, Mom. That same sunset. You got it nailed."

Dorothy kissed the top of Rachael's head. She took a breath, and then asked, "Aren't there any boys you like at CAL?"

"Nope."

"But sweetie, you aren't giving them a chance. You keep rushing home every weekend." She didn't dare look at her daughter.

"All they do, Mom, is drink and party and whine about grades."

"At least they're in college."

Rachael pushed her thick brown hair behind her ears and glared at her mother. "Rick's dad drives a truck. His mom sells jewelry at Macy's. That's why you don't like him."

"That's not fair," her mother shot back.

"But it's true."

"I like him fine," Dorothy lied. "But you're so young."

Rachael rose slowly to her feet and looked directly into her mother's upturned face. "I love him," she said.

"You think you love him . . ."

But Rachael was out the door.

Then one night during spring break, Rachael showed up with a ring. As shocked as she was, Dorothy's first thought was, how pathetic. The tiny diamond was a mere spark on the yellow gold band.

"What does this mean?" she asked.

"I'm getting married."

"No, you're not."

"What do you mean?"

"You have three more years of college. You're much too young to settle down." Words become clichés, she thought, because they're so true.

"I'm going to marry him."

For the first time, these two women faced off against each other.

"You hate him because he's lower class."

"I don't want you to marry a loser."

"You hate him because you're jealous."

"Why would I be jealous? The point is, he's not good enough for you."

"You don't know him."

"If you marry him, I won't pay for your college."

"I don't care."

They went to bed exhausted, unresolved. But by the next afternoon, a bargain was struck. Rachael would return Rick's ring. To get that concession, Dorothy promised to pay for all four years of college.

And if Rachael still loved Rick after her sophomore year, Dorothy reluctantly agreed they could marry. She felt certain that waiting a year would bring her daughter to her senses.

The following evening Rachael burst into the studio where her mother was gluing twists of red and purple silk onto a field of black acrylic. The girl's blouse was in disarray, her hair tangled, her eyes red. She held in her palm the gold band. The diamond was gone.

"He threw it at me," she sobbed. "He was so hurt. He threw it at me and the diamond fell out. I crawled on my hands and knees, but I couldn't find it."

Dorothy pulled her daughter into her arms and held her as she had always done.

"He spent all his money for this ring," Rachael cried.

"I'm so sorry, honey," Dorothy crooned, rubbing her daughter's back, rocking her. But she was thinking, I would have expected just that.

Rachael came home rarely during the first semester of her sophomore year. She didn't mention Rick, not even during Christmas vacation. Dorothy gloated in silence.

And then late one soggy night in February the phone rang. Dorothy had gone to bed early, wrapped to her chin in her voluminous duvet, immersed in a P. D. James mystery. Rain crashed onto the tile roof, beat against the windows.

"Mom?" Rachael's voice sounded distant, frightened.

"What's the matter?"

"I'm in Reno."

"You're where?"

"We eloped. Don't be mad."

"What are you talking about?"

"Rick and I. We're in Reno. We're married."

"No." Don't panic, Dorothy told herself. "You wouldn't."

"Please . . ."

"I thought Rick was out of your life."

"He was."

"Why didn't you tell me?"

"I thought you'd try to stop us."

"You're right about that."

"Try not to be mad, Mommy."

"You're so bright; you have so much promise." Stop! Dorothy told herself, but she couldn't. "You're throwing it all away."

"Don't Mom." Rachael's voice was suddenly strong. "I'm happy. I really am. I called because I wanted you to know that."

"Well I'm glad somebody is."

They sat in silence, holding their phones.

By the end of term, Rachael could no longer hide the reason for her hasty marriage.

"When were you planning to tell me?" Dorothy asked her daughter on the first day of summer break. They were sitting on Dorothy's expansive redwood deck not facing each other.

"I thought you knew."

"That you were having a baby?"

"Are you pleased?" Rachael asked.

"It's my grandchild. I will love it." Then she added, "But how are you planning to support a baby?"

"Rick's working."

"What about you?"

"I'm taking a year off."

"I see." Her cherished daughter was leaving college to have the baby of a man who sold telephones. She choked back a rush of questions, afraid if she spoke one word, her rage would drown her.

The baby arrived in late September, a six-pound boy with chicken legs and blotchy skin. And Dorothy fell in love. She cried when Rachael told her his name, Jack, for Dorothy's father, and rushed straight to Target for a backward facing car seat.

She took a part-time position at her school so she could devote two full days a week to Jack. However, on her first visit with her grandson in Rachael's cramped one-bedroom Berkeley apartment, her daughter held her off.

"Rick's taking off from work this month, Mom, and we want to get to know Jack, just the two of us."

"But I could give you a break some afternoon. You'll both be exhausted."

"Give us a month."

"I could sleep on the sofa and give him a bottle in the middle of the night."

"No."

And so she waited. And finally one Tuesday morning in early November, in Rachael's tiny living room, she held baby Jack close to her chest, warm against her, his soft, sweet breath on her neck, and she wept.

Those Tuesdays were the happiest days Dorothy could remember, happier even than when Rachael was a baby, because back then she'd been nervous and clumsy and sleep-deprived. Happier than when she'd sold her first painting, for fifty dollars.

Every Tuesday morning Dorothy would rock the baby and sing to him until he fell asleep. Later she would drive to Lake Merritt where she pushed him in the second-hand carriage she'd found on Craig's List. She wore her binoculars around her neck and would point out the Black Crowned Night Herons nesting in the trees, while Jack's eyelids drooped over his large blue eyes.

The routine varied as he grew; Dorothy drew dogs and cats and fire trucks for Jack, read Green Eggs and Ham over and over, wiped avocado and banana off his tiny cleft chin. At the park, they whisked down the slide together, her arm circling his compact little body. He took his first step on a Tuesday and said "Grandma" for the first time in her living room.

When Rachael returned to college, Dorothy offered to take Jack two days a week.

"Thank you, Mom," Rachael said, "but I've found a daycare I like. Jack needs to be around other children."

"What about Tuesdays?"

"If you really want him, I can arrange a four-day package."

"I really want him," she said, weak with relief.

Rachael dropped out of Berkeley midway through her junior year.

"It's too much pressure," she told her mother, "writing all those papers and being a good mom."

"You have to get a degree!" Dorothy knew she sounded desperate. "You can't get a decent job with a high school diploma."

"I'll finish college," Rachael told her.

Two years later she transferred to Cal State East Bay in Hayward where she could take night courses when Rick was home with Jack. It took her three years going part-time, but she finally graduated with a degree in elementary education.

"I thought you were a history major," Dorothy said at one of their rare dinners together.

"Jobs aren't available in history, Mom, in case you haven't noticed. We need the money."

Dorothy still took care of Jack on Tuesdays, but once he was in school, her role was reduced to driving him to and from Little League practice or swimming lessons. She loved this boy, loved his wiry arms wrapped around her, loved the way he laughed at the jokes he told her that weren't funny, loved the castles he created out of Lego, loved most of all taking out the magic markers and making wild pictures together.

Just as she'd done with Rachael, beginning when her daughter was so small she had to stand on a chair in the studio to cover large sheets of butcher paper with purple and red.

"Guess what this is?" Rachael would ask.

"A Rhino?"

"Guess again."

"A Purple Spino?"

Giggles. "No, silly Mommy. A hefalump."

"I never saw a hefalump with yellow spots."

"It's the Egyptian hefalump."

"Well, you've left off the red wings."

And she and Rachael, wearing one of Dorothy's old tee-shirts, her tangled brown hair held back with barrettes, would splash watercolors onto their masterpieces spread out on the large cluttered table, giggling, admiring, inventing with rainbow fingers.

Having Jack to herself every Tuesday, for however short a time, almost made up for the loss she wouldn't yet acknowledge.

And then an email: "Rick has left me."

Dorothy sat frozen at the computer. Her hands shook when she finally picked up the telephone.

"What do you mean he left you?"

"He packed up his things and moved out."

"When?"

"On Wednesday."

She had so many questions. Was this permanent? And ten-year-old Jack? Drifting along in his pre-adolescent paradise.

"Why don't you come over tonight?"

Silence.

Then, "Not now. I need to spend time with Jack."

But I need to spend time with you, Dorothy wanted to say. I want to help. I want to be your mother. Instead she said, "How is Jack?"

"When I told him, he tore out a piece of paper from his notebook and drew a face with a downturned mouth and a tear."

"Poor baby," Dorothy said. "That's so like him."

"Yeah. Look, I don't want to talk about it now. Okay?"

Dorothy wouldn't give up so easily. She insisted on Rachael's coming to dinner the next Friday night after work.

When she saw her daughter at the front door, exhausted from working all day with third graders, her thick brown hair pulled back into a messy pony tail, her blouse stained, she reached out to take her in her arms. But Rachael rushed past.

"Do you have any wine?" she asked and Dorothy scurried off to find a bottle.

"So what happened?" Dorothy asked when she returned.

"Can I just sit down?"

Rachael followed her mother to the living room. Large canvases covered the walls on three sides, two abstract pieces with gold-green triangles on a blue background, and a favorite, from her earlier days, of cows grazing in the moonlight. Sitting beside her daughter on the worn velvet loveseat, Dorothy waited.

"Things with Rick haven't been good for a while."

"How come?"

Rachael's laugh sounded sour. "You should know."

"I don't."

"Let's put it this way. I have a college degree, I have a profession; I make more money than Rick. He couldn't handle it."

"Was he unfaithful?"

"Mom, you're so old fashioned. I don't know. Maybe. The truth is he got tired of accusing me of being tired of him."

"Were you?"

"Tired of him?" Rachael's voice quavered. "No."

"What about Jack?"

"We'll share custody. It won't be nasty, I promise."

"I love you," Dorothy said. She put her arm around her daughter's squared, muscular shoulders. She's been working out, she thought.

Silence.

"For what it's worth, honey, I know what it feels like."

Rachael looked up. "What?"

"Being left. You know, by Ray, by your dad. You feel so helpless and you don't understand."

Rachael smiled for the first time. "You? Helpless? Mom, you're a powerhouse. But you're right. You didn't understand. You left my dad no room."

Dorothy stiffened. "How do you know that?" she asked. "You were ten."

"I am your daughter."

"What does that mean?"

Rachael sighed. "Look, Mom, I'm in a bad place. I can't talk about it right now."

But Dorothy persisted. "Do you think Rick left because you're like me? A powerhouse, as you call it?"

"Good God, no!"

She's upset, Dorothy told herself, as they stared out the bank of windows at the blue-green mountain in the distance, and she held her tongue. But later, at the kitchen table as Rachael nibbled absent-mindedly at her halibut steak and downed several glasses of wine, Dorothy could no longer keep silent.

"What will you do now?"

"I don't know. Move probably."

"Move? Where?" No, she wanted to scream.

"To San Jose. Close to my school. The commute from Berkeley is killing me."

San Jose? Sixty miles from Larkspur, the traffic a nightmare.

"I'd like to help you," she said. She was begging.

"There's nothing you can do right now."

Dorothy looked directly at her daughter. "Talk to me, Rachael!"

But Rachael was standing up, dropping her napkin onto her half-eaten dinner.

"I have to go."

"I made a pecan pie."

"I'm sorry, Mom; I'm really full."

And she was gone. Dorothy sat at the kitchen table for a long time, working over and over in her mind what was happening to her daughter, to herself. There were so many possibilities.

Rachael clearly blamed her for denigrating Rick and undermining her marriage. Dorothy hated to admit it, but it was partly true. And, what was all that about being so powerful that Ray left? That seemed really unfair.

Dorothy finally dragged herself off to bed, where she lay with open eyes, her mind racing.

Rachael's move to San Jose changed everything. Not that Dorothy was completely shut off from her family. She still saw them occasionally, but Jack was always too busy, with sports or friends or band practice.

"It's not worth the drive," her daughter would email.

"But I'd like to see him," she'd email back.

"It's just not a good time."

She saw them for Christmas and the occasional birthday, always at her house, although she had visited the peach-colored adobe townhouse in San Jose. Jack always hugged her when she saw him and cheerfully answered her questions about his various teams, the books he was reading. He was a wonderful boy.

And then Rachael married again. This time to her school's assistant principal whose wife had left him with two children. Dorothy was thrilled when Rachael invited her to the wedding.

"At the courthouse, Mom, very simple. Just family."

Dorothy searched the stores for the perfect outfit. Unlike the Reno fiasco, this time she would be there, mother of the bride, celebrating. She chose a rose-colored silk dress with long sleeves and a tailored collar and black patent heels. The wedding party arrived in their school clothes.

The judge, apparently eager to return to the courtroom, hurried through the brief ceremony.

"Thanks for coming, Mom," Rachael said and gave her a quick hug.

"Can I treat everyone to lunch?" Dorothy asked.

"That's really nice," Ron said, "but I have a meeting this afternoon at school and Jack has baseball practice."

She cried as she fought the heavy afternoon traffic back to Larkspur.

Dorothy was now retired from teaching, but her experiments with fabric, found objects, and photographs kept her up late into the night, working, excited. With friends from her hiking club, she climbed the trails up the blue-green mountain, a camera in her backpack to catch unexpected bursts of color and shapes. Her wall pieces, meanwhile, were selling at exorbitant prices, in Chicago and New York. Which meant she had plenty of money for African safaris, Japanese gardens, eco-tours of Brazil and Alaska, the art museums of Europe. And she dashed off to New York at least twice a year. All first class.

Her oldest friends, whose children had grown up with Rachael, traded stories about their grandchildren, but since she rarely mentioned hers, they stopped asking. Except for Mary Lee, her long-time confidante, who wormed out the truth from Dorothy and then emailed Rachael, urging her to stay in contact with her mother, with no response.

As she grew older, Dorothy could go for months at a stretch without hearing from Rachael and Jack. She would tell herself they were busy, getting on with their lives. She knew, from a note Jack sent her, thanking her for his high school graduation present, that he was at UCLA. She had mailed him a check for a thousand dollars because she didn't know what else to give him.

Dorothy invited Rachael to her exhibition openings, and she responded with emails of congratulations. And then the emails stopped. Invitations to dinners went unanswered. Phone calls disappeared into voice mail.

When she was working or traveling, Dorothy felt good about herself. And yet, at her exhibitions she always watched the crowds, expecting that maybe, this time, Rachael would walk in, and she could say, this is my child.

Rachael never appeared. But everyone else did. That is, the critics and collectors and art aficionados who flocked to Dorothy's openings in the exclusive galleries where her work was shown.

On one rainy November afternoon, crowds clustered around a wall size image of a goat on exhibit at the JB Fine Arts Gallery near Union Square. Dorothy had first seen the photograph at a local history museum somewhere in Kentucky and had fallen in love with it. The goat seemed to be leaping out of the picture. She purchased the photograph, had it enlarged, and spent weeks staring at it propped against the wall of her studio.

"You're tired of that dead looking grass," she told the goat. "You want to escape."

So she took out her acrylics and painted the grass blue. By the time she had finished, a purple goat was leaping out of the frame on bright red legs. You couldn't not look at it.

"A stunning concept," a newspaper critic raved to the crowd. "It's so Chagall."

Dorothy smiled graciously. She knew she would read that phrase in the next morning's paper. She loved it. All of it. The attention, the excitement of an opening, the money, because her goat had sold for a tidy sum. But mostly she loved the work itself. The colors and textures and shapes and silliness; it was all play.

"I'm wild about farm animals," she explained to the crowd, "and bright colors. So I just got started doctoring up that old goat. And there you have it."

As she was talking, she caught a glimpse of a short man dashing into the gallery. Something about the way he bent his head forward under a soggy newspaper struck her as familiar.

"So this is your new stuff?" the man called from across the room.

The features in the white, fleshy face were no longer sharply chiseled and his wet head was nearly bald. But the man was unmistakably her former son-in-law.

"Rick," she said, crossing the room, taking his cold hand in hers. "How long has it been?"

"A lifetime," he said.

"What are you doing here?"

"Getting dry. I was working in the area. Got drenched and ran into the first door I saw open."

"Where are you working?"

He flashed a smile of triumph. "Autodesk. I'm in computer design. Say, what do you think about Jack?"

She smiled at him, trying not to show how little she knew, how much she longed to know.

"Look," she said. "The gallery's closing in a half hour. Could you stick around? I'd like to . . . talk. You know, catch up?"

Rick didn't seem to notice her confusion. "Sure," he said. "I need some time to dry off."

Dorothy could hardly pay attention to the chorus of admirers surrounding her. She set her mouth in a fixed smile and answered their questions mechanically. And then they were gone.

"I'll lock up," she told the manager.

"Wow!" Rick stood in the middle of the empty room, his arms spread out. "No wonder Rachael was always so intimidated by you."

"Intimidated?" The word startled her.

"You bet. You're a big deal!"

Dorothy forced a smile. "Looks like I was today. But you were talking about Jack."

"Yep. I always said that kid was a genius. Now look at him. Working for Microsoft no less."

For Microsoft? Doing what? She was tempted to beg. But she was too proud, too hurt, to do anything but nod her head.

Rick kept talking. There was something different about him, a confidence in his voice, in the way he met her eyes. "You know, I haven't been up to Seattle yet," he said. "Is Rachael's condo really as fancy as Jack says it is?"

Could he be making this up? Had her daughter really moved away without telling her? And Jack? Her legs were trembling so badly she was afraid she might crumple.

"Are you okay?" Rick was peering at her face.

"Of course," she managed to say. Her voice was stiffly polite. "Look, I'm sorry. I have to close up."

"I'm off then," Rick said. But he stood for several minutes, watching her. Then he opened the door and vanished into the rain.

After he left, Dorothy circled the room, running her fingers over the slick acrylic surfaces, willing herself to remember her joy in bringing to life all these shapes and colors. Bringing to life the goat, its beard jaunty under all that paint, its red legs leaping out of the frame. But right now, she could find no joy in it. She told herself tomorrow she would look Jack up on the internet and get in touch. He could tell her how to reach her daughter. She could write to Rachael, beg her. But not tonight.

And so she locked the door, turned out the light, and moaned into the darkness, "What did I do? What in God's name did I do?"

Faster Than a Roller Coaster

Poydras Review, January 28, 2019
Also published in *Spotswood Virginia*,
Stephen F. Austin State University Press, 2021

He's perched on that red armchair as usual. My Pierce. Surrounded by bird nests. Mud and twigs. Leaves and bark. Some are hanging from hooks in the ceiling, like purses. Orioles. And there are tidy little cups. Goldfinch, I think. He's labeled some of the nests, the ones in glass cabinets. Others are displayed on open shelves or falling apart on the scratched mahogany table his mother gave us.

"It's after midnight," I say.

He smiles up at me. I love his white hair. Premature at forty-two. I love his face, unlined, pale, boyish.

"I need an owl," he says.

"Pay attention, Pierce. She's sixteen, and it's after midnight."

But there she is, my Clare, racing up the hall toward us, her red hair half out of her ponytail, bursting into the room we call "The Museum," where Pierce keeps his collections.

"I'm sorry." She's panting. "We went for ice cream."

"That's no excuse."

"I said I was sorry."

She brushes past me and wraps her arms around Pierce's neck.

"Wayne wants to meet you, Daddy," she says. "I told him you play the clarinet. He plays piano, plays for parties and stuff."

"What kind of piano?" Pierce asks.

"Jazz," Clare says. "And dancing music, like Elvis and Buddy Holly."

"Concentrate, Pierce," I beg. "She's sixteen years old, coming in after midnight."

He pauses, looking up at me like he hears me. Then, "I *really* need a Great Horned nest."

Clare giggles. A late night, giddy sort of laugh. I give up. I love her. And she's home.

The first time it happened, I was just her age, a high school majorette from the wrong side of the tracks. And he was a short skinny boy in the band with hair so blond it was almost white and skin so pale he looked anemic. I could feel his eyes on me as I twirled my baton. He was marching along behind, tootling away on his clarinet

And then one day he just disappeared. He wasn't in class, wasn't in the band. People said he had gone to a ranch out west to build up his strength. Which made some sense because he was so pale. He was just a boy in the band then, not yet my sweetheart, but I missed him. And was glad when he came back to school, after a couple of months, with some sun on his face.

I found out all about it years later, after he stood up to his old bully of a rich daddy and married me, after he started filling up our apartment with butterflies. At first it seemed innocent enough. He knew all about nature, could whistle bird songs, could say what kind they were when nobody else could see them flitting about in the trees. He'd capture butterflies, pin them to stiff cardboard, put them in box frames with cotton. At first, it was just on Saturdays. He'd be out there tramping around in the woods with his binoculars and butterfly nets. Then it was early in the morning weekdays before work. I had my job as a secretary for Dr. Newman and didn't pay much attention until butterflies started to take over the apartment. Our place was pretty small then, living room, kitchen, bedroom. And he just filled it up with butterflies, live ones wriggling in nets, dead ones, wings all sorts of colors, plus caterpillars, dead and alive. Strange smells all over the house. He hung glass-framed butterflies on all the walls, filled the shelves with messy, broken cocoons. Pretty soon heaps of wings covered the coffee table, the top of the refrigerator, the kitchen cabinets.

And then Pierce stopped, like he had wound down. He just sat in the middle of all that mess, staring at nothing, hardly talking.

I didn't know what to do. I was afraid to tell his parents. Afraid they'd blame me. They found out anyway because he'd stopped going to the mill where his dad had gotten him a job. So, late one afternoon, old man Pierce burst in, took one look at the mess, and the next thing I knew, he carried my beautiful boy husband off in an ambulance.

That's when I found out it had happened before. It was a nervous breakdown, at least that's what his dad called it. They took him to a hospital down in North Carolina and put wires on the sides of his head and shocked him into getting better. His parents told folks he was traveling for business.

I'd done a lot of growing up before I ever married Pierce, keeping house for my hard-drinking daddy, getting myself a scholarship to secretarial school. But this was the worst. Pierce was the only person I'd ever loved except my mother who died when I was six. I loved his blunt fingers, his narrow body, the smell of starch his plaid shirts gave off, his sweet breath. I worried I'd somehow made him worse by letting him fill up the house with all that nature. That was a sign, and I'd missed it.

While he was gone, his parents bought us this house and moved me in. His mother told me she couldn't stand the idea of Pierce coming back to that tiny apartment where he'd had his breakdown. But the new place felt large and empty without him. And I was so lonely. I visited him several times before they decided to shock him, but that was worse than the loneliness. He just sat in a chair in his hospital room and stared at the TV. It didn't matter what the program was. I couldn't get him to talk or even look at me. It was awful. I thought he didn't love me anymore.

It didn't last forever. He came home and was his old self. Playing his clarinet, collecting, bird nests this time, but in an organized way in his "museum."

Then Clare was born. My girl. Named for my mother. And he's been more or less okay ever since. He's had his ups and downs, of course, and once, when Clare was little, he had to go back for a shock treatment. But he's on a new medicine now, and it's going well. To Clare, he's the perfect father. She has no idea. And I want it to stay that way.

Wayne's at the door. Polite as pie. He's a good-looking boy. Six feet at least, floppy brown hair. Dark sleepy eyes. I see why Clare likes him.

"Where you off to, baby?" Pierce asks.

"A party," she says.

"Where?"

"Hunting Club."

"No," I say.

The Hunting Club is a lump of stucco, squatting on the edge of the river. The members are mostly rednecks who shoot squirrel and rabbit and fancy themselves big game hunters.

"Wayne's playing for somebody's engagement party," she says.

"I don't like it," I say. "There'll be drinking and carrying on."

"I'll come," Pierce says.

Clare grabs him round the neck. I stare at them.

"I'll be the chaperone. Don't worry, honey."

It's only after he's climbed into the back seat of Wayne's Plymouth that I catch a glimpse of his clarinet case on the seat next to him.

Pierce plays a beautiful clarinet. He studied in New York. All the classics, "Flight of the Bumblebee," Mozart's "Clarinet Concerto." That was before we married. He'd had his heart set on being a musician, but his old man put his foot down, said you can't earn a decent living tootling on a horn. Sent him to work in one of the mill offices, where the old man was president. I never knew what Pierce did exactly, only that he didn't like it. When his dad died, he left us enough money for Pierce to stop going to the mill. He mostly stayed home and played his music and worked on his collections.

I wash the dinner dishes and pick up the *Ladies Home Journal.* But I've got that Hunting Club on my mind. I keep seeing the clarinet case on the back seat of Wayne's car. Pierce never plays in public, just has a friend or two come over occasionally to jam, as he calls it. He's a snob, really, about his music. So, I'm thinking if he's planning to play his clarinet tonight, I want to hear it. After about a half hour, I put on my coat and back the Oldsmobile out of the garage.

I've seen the Club from the outside all my life but never had reason to go in. I open the door to a barn-like room full of crêpe paper streamers with big red cardboard hearts stapled to them and lots of loud music. Men in shirt sleeves and loosened ties are bouncing around with women done up in taffeta party dresses, blues and greens mostly, with full skirts out of net and black suede high heels. I recognize some of the patients from Dr. Newman's office, where I work, but they're too busy dancing to say hello. Besides, I'm looking all around for Clare and Pierce.

Wayne's up on a stage, banging away at the piano, a Buddy Holly tune I recognize, and laughing and talking to the dancers. Then, in a flash, he turns his head toward somebody in the band and starts nodding. And that's when I see Pierce. Up on the stage with all those boys. His eyes are closed, his square-tipped fingers are flying over the keys, and his head is swaying, all in perfect time with the guitars and piano. His face so serious. And Wayne's laughing and nodding.

After a minute or two, people stop dancing and stand around the band watching Pierce, clapping to the beat, and belting out, "Going faster than a roller coaster." And there's Clare, up in front of the crowd, snapping her fingers with the others, her mouth moving. Pierce keeps playing that tune like it's the most natural thing in the world. When did *he* ever hear about Buddy Holly? The guitar player is grinning at him, and the short, skinny boy on banjo stops strumming long enough to let Pierce play solo. I push through the crowd, singing along with the rest of them, bumping into people, stepping on suede- covered toes. Trying to join my daughter. Getting the feel of it.

The clapping gets louder and louder. I see Wayne turn back to the piano. He tries a few chords but can't connect with Pierce's solo, so he stops and waits. I look at Pierce. His eyes are still closed, but now, instead of swaying to the rhythm, his whole body's jerking around. Buddy Holly is long gone. I have to reach Clare. Her eyes are fixed on her father, her cheeks are bright red, and she's stamping her feet with the beat. But the beat keeps changing and the tune seems to be lost. The noise in the room is getting louder. Pierce keeps on playing, faster and faster.

I don't know what to do.

It's Wayne who saves him. He picks up the microphone, walks over to Pierce and thanks him in a voice that drowns out the music. Pierce stops playing and looks around, like he's surprised.

Wayne says, "Well, folks, we've had a real treat here. Let's give a hand to the best woodwind player in the state of Virginia, Mr. Pierce Luther, Jr."

He puts his arm around my husband's thin shoulders. Pierce gives a sideways grin, and the two of them take a low bow.

"Thank you, Sir," Wayne says and walks him over toward me and Clare.

"What d'you think?" Pierce is beaming.

"Time to go," I say.

"No!" Clare says.

"Your mom's right." Wayne puts his arms around Clare and Pierce, one on each side, and walks them to the door with me following close behind.

"Thank you," I mutter, but he's gone, winding his way through the crowd, back to his piano.

On the way home, Clare bounces around in the front seat next to me, talking a mile a minute.

"What about Dad's solo?"

"It was great. Most of it," I say. At least that's honest.

"Maybe my improvising was a bit sophisticated for the boys, huh?" Pierce chimes in from the back seat.

"Sounded like you were improvising on Mozart," I say. "That wasn't Mozart. That was jazz."

"He was riffing on Buddy Holly," Clare says. "You're too tone deaf to hear it."

I let it go. Maybe this isn't what I think it is.

"Quick! What's the bird?"

It's early on Saturday morning, a week after the Hunting Club dance, and Pierce is peering through binoculars out the kitchen window, chirping, "Here I am—in the tree—look up—at the top."

"Red-eyed Vireo."

Clare's answer is quick, automatic. She butters her toast, half asleep.

"Bingo!" Pierce has drilled those bird songs into her from the time she learned to talk. "Get dressed. Today's the day."

She's wide-awake now, binoculars in one hand, toast in the other, heading for the door. She's spent her childhood tramping the woods around Spotswood with her daddy, listening for bird songs, inspecting the forest floor for the telltale white splashes that might mean a nest, scrambling up oaks and elms and maples, easing the empty nests out of the tree limbs and carrying them home in a wicker basket lined with velvet. Whenever there are eggs, they wait until they're sure the nest is empty before making the snatch. I know all this because I went collecting with him before she was born. And I still occasionally go along, just to watch the two of them conspiring together, standing silent in the woods, waiting. I wait with them. Holding my breath.

This Saturday, I watch him closely. Ever since the party at the Hunting Club, I've felt kind of uneasy. So, I call out, "Me too. I'm coming too."

Pierce heads the Dodge pickup south on Route 29. About thirty miles out of Spotswood, he swerves suddenly onto a dirt road. We bump along for several miles, red dust flying up in all directions, coating the windows.

"Where're you going?"

He laughs, a giddy sort of laugh.

And then he hits the brakes, jumps out of the car, and starts running.

"It's up there," he says, training his binoculars toward the top of a hill alongside the road. "Let's go."

He's running, up the base of the hill, kicking up red dust and brown pine needles.

By the time I get out of the car, he's a third of the way up the hill, hanging on to roots, a cotton mesh bag slung over his shoulder.

I look at the top of the hill through my binoculars. And there it is, on a low branch of a tree. A huge nest made of different size sticks with leaves spilling out the top. An owl's nest.

Pierce is inching up the hillside, grabbing roots, resting one foot at a time on rocks half-buried in the red dirt.

I call out in as calm a voice as I can manage, "Be careful, Pierce."

And then he's on the top of the hill, arms waving in triumph.

I look over at Clare. Her cheeks are bright. And she's grinning at her daddy. We watch Pierce stretch his hand up to the nest and carefully place it in the mesh bag. Then he starts scrambling down the hill.

In a flash, a Great Horned Owl swoops out of the air, claws outstretched. Clare and I race to the car. The mother lands on the branch of the tree where her nest was, screeching and screeching.

"Turn the motor on," Pierce yells as he half runs, half slides down to the bottom of the hill, binoculars swinging wildly around his neck, the bag held out beside him. He jumps into the front seat of the car, slamming the door just as the owl dive-bombs, crashing into the window beside him. For a split second, the bird glares in at us with large yellow eyes, then drops out of sight.

"Drive!" Pierce yells.

"Is she hurt?" Clare's voice is high-pitched.

"Of course not," he says. "That bird is flying through the pine trees right now, swooping down on mice."

He makes a perfect imitation of an owl's haunting call.

I want to scream at him, "It's not true. You know it's not true." But there's Clare.

"You think so?" she asks.

She wants to believe.

Back home, Pierce sweeps two robins' nests aside to make space on the mahogany table for his latest prize.

"Look at the inside."

Clare's voice is hushed.

I look down at downy feathers. The mother owl must have plucked them from her own breast. And there's squirrel fur in here. And then I see them. Two white perfectly formed eggs are resting on a cross hatch of downy feathers.

"What have you done?" I whisper.

Clare stares at her father. "We're not supposed to take 'em if there're eggs." She sounds close to tears.

"I'm sorry, baby," Pierce says. "I thought it was empty."

I don't believe him. I quickly put my arm around my daughter.

"Even the experts make mistakes, honey," I say. "I'm sure your dad thought the nest was old."

Pierce smiles and nods.

Now that nesting season is in full swing, Clare is up early on Saturdays, out all day with her father, armed with binoculars, telescope, Sibley's, sandwiches. They come home after dark, exhausted, her cheeks flushed. She talks all through dinner, hardly eating anything. They're watching nests and the hatching of babies, red-tailed hawks, robins, cardinals. It's June. The woods are full of song.

I watch Pierce, but he seems calm, happy. Clare wants to be with him, that's all he needs. I tell myself, relax.

The owl's nest sits there in the middle of the mahogany table, large, messy, the eggs stone cold.

"Mama!" It's Clare's voice. Coming from Pierce's collections room.

I rush down the hall. The door is open. Mud and twigs, leaves and bark, thick on the floor, stop me.

Pierce is standing near the door. He looks at me, mouth open, eyes searching mine. I realize I've been expecting this. For weeks now. I've got to get her out of here before—.

Then I see her. Her shoes are muddy, and her sweater's torn. She's smiling, and for just one minute, I hope everything's going to be all right.

But there's something in her hands, something she's holding tight against her chest.

"It's my surprise," she says. Her eyes are bright, her voice high-pitched, excited. "It's because of the raccoons. Don't you see? I had to. The raccoons."

"Clare," I speak softly. "Sweetheart?"

"It's okay, Mama," she says, kicking at the pile of broken nests on the floor. "I just need a broom. It was too crowded in here. I had to make room. I just need a broom."

I reach for her.

She backs away.

"Mama, where's the broom?"

Fear hangs heavy. Weighs me down. Stops my breath.

"Sweetheart," I manage to whisper.

"I need to sweep." Her voice is frantic. "Look at all this mess."

But I'm not looking at the mess. I'm staring at the muddy fists she's stretching out to me. A broken handle of a purse-like nest dangles from her thumb.

She spreads open her fingers.

I don't want to look. I don't want to know. I want to hold her.

"Aren't they sweet, Mama? Aren't they perfect?"

Two pink featherless creatures lie limp in her hands, their tiny legs drawn up close to their bodies.

Buried

The MacGuffin, Fall 2018, Vol. XXXIV, No. 3

I'm searching for sand dollars. Perfect circles, pristine, no chips. I have a collection. And that's when I see a shiny straight line in the sand. Black. I dig it out. A cell phone. Buried vertically. I think, some poor sucker's lost his phone. But then I think, if a cell phone just falls out of a backpack, you'd expect it to land flat. So, it's almost like the person buried it. But why would he do that?

I take a lens cleaner from my backpack and clean it off, then click the button on the side. The screen lights up with a telephone number. I try to call it. No service at the beach.

By the time I get back to the group home, the battery's dead. I try my charger cord, but the port doesn't fit. Good thing I have a photographic memory. I use my cell to call the number I memorized from the buried phone.

"Who's this?" It's a woman's voice.

"Did you lose your cell phone?" I ask.

"Who's this?"

"I found a cell phone, and it had your number on it."

"Is it a Samsung?"

"An old one," I say.

"Oh, God. It has to be Freddie. I've been calling him. He must have tried to call me. You didn't see him, did you?" Her voice is getting screechy.

"No. I was looking for sand dollars and found this cell phone buried in the sand at North Beach."

"North Beach? Where's that?

"Marin County."

"Oh, God. How did he get to Marin County? You might have seen him. He's about sixty, has gray hair, real thin."

"I didn't see him."

"He's like, disappeared. We've been calling everybody."

"I didn't see him."

I've got to call my sister. That's it. I'll call her. But where is it? I had it in my pocket. She gave me the phone so I wouldn't get lost. So, I could call her if I got lost. Or I could call Barry or Gene or Helen. She put the numbers in my phone next to their names so I could call them. I need to do that.

My phone's not in my pocket. It was there, and now it's not.

There are dogs on the beach. There are some people standing in a bunch. I try to ask them to help me call my sister, but they get on the bus. So, I do too. I try to ask them, but they just look at me.

She calls back the next morning.

"Have you gotten the phone to work?" she asks.

"I told you. It's dead. My charger doesn't fit."

"Can you take it to Verizon?"

"Why would I do that?"

"To get it working. They can get it working."

"What good would that do?"

"He might call it." She sounds so irritated. "And there are numbers in there. I could call them to see if they've heard from him."

"Why don't you call them?"

"I don't have the numbers. They're his friends. Look, take it to Verizon. Get them to charge it. I'll pay."

"If I have time."

"Look, if it's too much trouble, mail it to me. I'll take care of it."

I write down her address. It's in Los Angeles.

"Do you know my sister?"

The street is full of people.

"I don't believe I do."

The man is wearing a suit.

"What's her name?"

"Becky."

"What's her last name?"

"Benton," I say, but then I remember that was her name. She now has a different name, and I can't remember it.

The man shakes his head.

"Where does she live?"

"Los Angeles."

"I wouldn't know her then. This is San Rafael."

"Well, do you know Barry or Gene?"

"I'm afraid not."

And he walks away.

I plan to take the cell phone to Verizon. But I put it off. Becky, that's the sister, calls me every other hour. She annoys me.

"I'm going to do it," I tell her. "I'm just really busy right now."

I'm a groundskeeper at Golden Gate Park.

"Why don't you mail it?"

"I'll go to Verizon," I say. "Just hold your horses."

I go to the Verizon place. They say the phone's too old. There aren't any chargers that fit it. They even try to sell me a new phone.

That cell phone's no use. I was right. And I've had it with the sister. I could mail her the phone, but what's the use? She can't get it to work. And I'm really busy.

On the way back to the car, I drop the phone in the garbage.

I'm very tired. I'll lie down. For just a minute. Then I'll call my sister. I'll figure it out.

She keeps calling. All the time. But I don't pick up anymore. I see her number, and I don't pick up any more.

Fading

Persimmon Tree, Summer 2018

January 2010

"What's your pleasure, Mom?"

She bursts into the kitchen, all smiles. My dark-eyed daughter, on holiday break from college, her round cheeks flushed from sleep.

What's my pleasure? You, Elizabeth.

I take the croissants out of the oven, yeasty, too hot to touch. Strawberry jam. Black coffee.

"There's a new exhibit I want to see at the …"

Shit. At the …? If I wait long enough, the mouse in my brain will click on it. The letter A. I'm pretty sure it begins with A.

She's waiting.

I make a stab at it.

"You know. The fish house."

She laughs.

"Aquarium?"

I laugh with her.

"I'm losing my mind."

I didn't mean to say that.

She laughs again.

"Nonsense. We all forget names of things. For instance, last week I couldn't for the life of me remember the name of Mount St. Helens. 'You know,' I said to Tif, 'the volcano mountain.'"

"Tif?" I'm thinking, Tif? Who's Tif?

"You know, Mom. Tiffany. My housemate."

"Of course. Tiffany." I'm looking out the window. My mountain is covered in clouds. Is it going to rain? "I have to get my …"

"Umbrella? Raincoat?"

We both laugh.

July 2011

Back in Wilmington to visit my brother. In the house I grew up in. Tom and Marsha own it now.

Has Tom noticed? I can't tell. But Marsha has. I catch her watching me. Then slipping back to her iPad. Documenting?

Or am I being, what's the word? It will come.

Paranoid.

July 4th. Tom's stuffing his face, as usual. Marsha plays the martyr-wife, cooking and serving and rushing about. All these other people I don't know.

Some strange man with a double chin and eyes too close together hugs me.

"Why hello, Ellen, you look wonderful." Such a loud voice.

I pat his beefy shoulders and smile.

"Hello to you too. It's great to see you."

He's talking about Mary Louise. His wife? Sister? Cheerleading. My brother Tom.

I search his face, threading my way through the fog back to high school. Was somebody named Mary Louise a cheerleader?

Then. I know that voice. A name pops up. Where does my brain keep those names?

"Walter," I say, relieved.

Something about the senior prom. Did he take me? But Mary Louise?

September 2011

Elizabeth is here. Is it a school break?

"I'm volunteering, Mom. For Occupy." Her dark eyes are bright. "That's why I'm home."

"What?"

"Occupy. You must have heard of it."

She's loading something into her backpack. Sheets of paper. She hands me one.

"It's exciting, Mom," she says. "You should join me."

I study the paper. A young woman in a leotard is dancing on top of a bull. The text reads, "OCCUPY WALL STREET. Bring Tent."

"I don't understand."

"The 99 percent. It's in all the papers. Wall Street is strangling us."

"Wall Street?"

"It's a movement. We're occupying Market Street. Downtown San Francisco. You should come with me."

"Market Street?"

"We're blocking the sidewalk, preventing the greedy bastards from going to work."

"Why aren't you in school?"

"I have to go. Come on."

"What would I do?"

"Next time, I'll take you with me," she says. "You'll see."

And she's out the door.

She should be in school.

November 2011

It's official. I can't count backwards from 100 by sevens. But could I ever? I can't name the Supreme Court justices. Lots of perfectly intelligent people can't do that. Although I used to know them. But I don't remember words given to me an hour before. So, they put me through a brain scan. And yes, I have dementia. Early stages, Dr. Garcia says. It might be the one that starts with A. Or something else. The label doesn't matter.

"I'm too young," I tell the doctor. I'm trying not to cry.

"I know," he says and puts his hand on mine. "You're sixty-one, aren't you? I'm afraid it can strike as early as that. It's called early onset, but the symptoms are the same. I'm sorry, Ellen."

"How much time do I have?"

"It depends. You could live another eight or ten years."

He doesn't understand. He's young.

"I mean before I'm ga-ga."

He won't meet my eyes, the coward.

"Nobody knows that."

"Take a guess."

He pauses.

"You've probably had these symptoms for some time now. Maybe a year or more?"

I nod.

"I would predict within a year you could see some short-term memory loss, difficulty with directions, that kind of thing. But then again, maybe not."

"Is there anything . . . ?"

"You can do? Stay active. Read. Do you have someone you trust to help with your health care decisions?"

Elizabeth, I want to say. But not yet.

I think about my brother. Would I trust Tom to take care of me?

"No," I answer.

"You need to find somebody."

March 2012

The voice on the telephone asks, "Is Elizabeth with you?"

Is it the housemate? What's her name? It's like a dog's name.

"No. Isn't she at school?"

"She's been gone all week. I hoped she was with you."

A cold spasm grips my stomach.

"She's not here. I don't know where she is."

"I don't mean to alarm you, Ms. Foster, but maybe you should call the police."

I punch "Elizabeth" on my cell. Her voicemail sings out, "I'm out and about. Leave your number."

I try to think. She's missing. Elizabeth.

I call 911. She'll turn up, someone says. She probably just needs a break.

No!

The doorbell rings. It's dark outside. But there she is. My baby. I'm crying. It's her. I pull her into the hallway, laughing, crying. She feels cold.

"Hi Mom," she says and hugs me.

I look out the door. Is someone there? In the dark?

Elizabeth pulls away from me and calls out something to a shadow on the deck.

"I've been so scared," I say. "Where have you been?"

"It's complicated," she says.

Complicated?

"Who's out there?" I ask.

"My boyfriend," she says. "Lenny."

Lenny? Who's that? Should I invite him in? I don't want to. Instead, I pull Elizabeth into the living room. We sit down on the sofa. I touch her cheek. It's cold.

"Your friend called. Where were you?"

"I've been working day and night on Occupy," she says.

"You should be in school."

"College feels irrelevant right now, Mom."

"Why didn't you call?"

"I'm sorry. But we're lying low right now. You might have sent the police."

"What are you talking about?"

"Homeland Security. They're everywhere."

I pull her close, feel the anger, the fear.

"It's not crazy," she says, reading my mind. She starts talking about corporate corruption and Homeland Security and somebody thinking she's a Communist.

"You're going too fast, honey."

"I can't say any more. But we have a plan. We just need money."

How did we get to money?

"Can you give us some?"

"You have money in your account."

Didn't I just call the bank?

"That's long gone. We need more. It's for poor people, Mom. Please."

When did this happen? She's my sunshine girl. She goes hiking with me.

"We'll talk about it later," she says. "I can't stay. I just wanted you to know I'm okay."

"No," I beg and hold her arm. But she slips away.

I stand in the dark calling.

September 2012

I'm bending over the coffee table, fingering pieces of a jigsaw puzzle. Supposed to be good for my brain. Hah!

Tom's here. He's come about money. He's gained weight, and his beard is gray. It used to be the color of ginger. I adored him growing up. Trailing after him, picking up his golf sticks and tennis rackets, his dirty shirts.

Now he bellows, "Sis!"

He's holding me so tight I'm suffocating.

"How are you?"

"I'm demented," I say. "How are you?"

He laughs.

"I'm getting there too."

I turn to the window, toward my own green mountain, trying not to cry.

He doesn't say anything but pulls me back and kisses the top of my head.

I put my arms around his waist and feel safe for the first time since Elizabeth quit college.

"I love this house," he says. He's staring at Mother's antique cabinet in the corner. "You know it's worth a fortune, don't you?"

I nod. Here it comes.

He plops down on the sofa and points to the cushion beside him. "When's the last time you had it appraised?"

I laugh. "You want me to sell the house?"

"Hell, no. But down the line ..."

"I plan to be here for a while."

"Sure, you do. Look ..."

It's not what I expect.

"I'm worried about Elizabeth," he says.

I hug him.

"That makes two of us."

He rubs my hand with a calloused thumb while I tell him what I know. She phones me often, says she's okay. But I don't know where she's living. Not in a tent, surely not a tent, and I don't like that boyfriend.

"Look," he says, "I know you think I'm crass, but we need to be realistic."

"Back to money?"

"You're not leaving all this," his hand sweeps the room, "to her, are you?"

"She's my daughter."

"She'll burn through it in a year."

"That's my business."

"Unfortunately, she'd make it everybody's business. Those people would squander Dad's money on God knows what."

"*Dad's* money, is it? You want me to leave it to you?"

He frowns.

"That's not why I'm here."

"Why are you here?"

"I wanted to check up on you." He looks away. "Let's get real, Ellen. If you seriously have … dementia," he chokes out the word, "you need to get your affairs in order. I have a lawyer who's really good at this stuff. You could talk to him."

I pull my hand away.

"Go home," I say.

He smiles.

"Fair enough. I've said my piece. But look, Ellen, I really do care about you."

And he does. I know that.

October 2012

Elizabeth is here. Did Tom call her?

I look through her sharp, pale face, her ragged ponytail, and see my stocky fourteen-year-old Elizabeth. In jeans and a t-shirt. Running. Throwing sticks in waterfalls. Where? She's laughing at me. Why? I'm creeping, crawling up a wooden ladder. On some trail. On my mountain. Elizabeth.

I hug her now and feel her ribs close to the skin.

In the kitchen, she picks red ceramic mugs from the cupboard and pours coffee. Didn't she make those mugs in high school? I can't remember. I try not to stare at the tattooed fish swimming up her neck. Her lovely soft neck. My flesh.

"I'm glad you're home."

I reach across the kitchen table and squeeze her hand.

"I can't stay long. Lenny's got something big going."

"Lenny?" I can't …

"My boyfriend, Mom. You know."

Was that his name?

"He's the brains behind Occupy here in San Francisco," she says.

"What?"

"There are tents up and down Market Street." Something about people blocking people from going to work. "It's on TV. Haven't you seen it?"

I don't watch much TV these days. And when I do, I forget …

"Is it …?" My words get stuck.

"What?"

"Working? You know, what you're doing?"

"Occupy? You bet. Wall Street's hurting. The government's freaked out. Arresting people. Lenny got dragged off to jail in New York last week."

She sounds almost proud.

"It made the *Times*."

I struggle to find the words.

"You can't …"

"Can't what?"

How can I explain?

"You're twenty-two," is what comes out.

"I don't have a choice." Something about corporations. "I'd rather be in jail than sitting here, pretending everything is cool."

Is that what I'm doing? I have arguments. Like she's going about this the wrong way. Like this Lenny is no good. But I can't put the words around them to make her listen.

"I'm sorry, Mom," she says. "That was mean." She puts her arms around me. "I hear you're not so well."

I stiffen.

"Who told you that?"

"Never mind. Is it true?"

"In a way. Is that why you're here?"

My voice sounds far away, like it's not part of me.

"I came here to check on you."

"Can you stay?" I ask.

"Can Lenny?"

"I don't … No."

She pulls back her hand, spilling the coffee. It drips off the edge of the table. And then, "I need money. Please, Mom."

"If you come home, finish college, there'll be money."

There. That came out in one piece.

"But right now, the one percent is strangling the country. We need money to fight them."

What? I've got to keep my head clear.

Elizabeth!

May 2013

I'm climbing green hills, traipsing through mud puddles left by the winter's rain. Breathing in sunshine. Fields of small yellow flowers. Can't remember ….

Black and white wings. I know that bird. It has a clown face. Something about nuts. I know it. Begins with W. I can hear the rhythm of the syllables. It's so near the surface. It's coming; it's coming.

I am not going to cry.

September 2013

"I'm losing my mind," I tell her.

I love you, Mom."

The static on her phone is so loud.

"Come home, sweetheart. I need to know you're safe."

"I'm safe. Don't worry. Lenny takes good care of me."

"Where are you?"

"Not far. Sacramento."

"Please come home."

I'm begging.

"Soon. I promise. We're making inroads, Mom. We're going to win. You'll be so proud of me."

"I'm losing my mind."

Didn't I just say that?

"I love you, Mom."

I sit here with the dead phone at my ear.

May 2014

Tom's here. He took me to the doctor. I'm in perfect health, Dr. Garcia says. They don't count dementia when they say that. Tom hired a very nice lady to do jigsaws with me. Her name is Veronica. She's from Mexico, maybe?

Today he says, "We need to see your lawyer."

We're sitting at the kitchen table, drinking coffee. He's reading the paper.

"Why?" I'm trying to remember.

"You need help with your finances, sweetheart."

"I'm okay," I say. "And don't talk down to me."

"I'm sorry. But you really need somebody to look out for you, pay your bills, handle your money. Who's the executor of your will?"

"It's not you."

Elizabeth is suddenly here. When did she come? She's standing at the kitchen door. Her skirt comes down to her tennis shoes and has a coffee stain in front. Her hair needs cutting. She's pale. I want to take her in my arms, bring her back to life.

Tom jumps up and reaches out to her, but she backs off.

"Who is it then?" he says. "The executor?"

They stand facing each other.

"Wayne," I say.

"Wayne's been dead for ten years, honey," Tom says.

Has it been ten years?

"I mean, he was," I say.

I feel foolish.

"That's why we need to see your lawyer," Tom says.

Elizabeth slumps down on the kitchen chair next to me and takes my hand.

"I'm sorry about all this, Mom."

They're arguing. I don't understand everything they're saying because they are talking fast, and they're mad. But I understand parts of it.

"You aren't the executor. You don't get the money."

"... your mother ... protected."

"Bullshit!" Elizabeth's voice snaps. "You want to get your hands on Mom's money."

"You're running around with a bunch of lunatics who will waste your money and throw you out when it's gone."

"Stop!" I yell.

Tom's face is red.

"What's your lawyer's name?" Tom asks.

And, of course, I don't remember.

September 2014

I know I have to get some money. For Elizabeth. She's my daughter. She's here.

"Just call Arthur," she says. "He'll know what to do."

Arthur?

"You remember, Mom. Your lawyer."

"Now tell me again why you need money."

"You'll be supporting Occupy. I've explained it before."

There's more, but it's hard to follow.

How can I get money? They won't let me drive.

Tom says if I leave my money to Elizabeth, that man will get it. I can't remember his name.

Why do I need to see Arthur? Money. Elizabeth needs money.

Tom says I shouldn't.

But she's my daughter.

Elizabeth's my daughter.

Sterling Silver

Midway Journal, July 15, 2018. Nominated for a Pushcart Prize
Also published in *Spotswood Virginia,*
Stephen F. Austin State University Press, 2021

Even after all these years, Rosemary could still picture her cousin Beth, standing on the church steps, her veil swirling around her, her chin high, laughing. And Jim in white dinner jacket and tuxedo pants, clutching Beth's arm like he'd never let it go.

She'd been there. Fifty years ago. A member of the wedding. And she would go this time. All the way cross country to California. Because of the note tucked inside the invitation. *Rosie, dear, you really have to come. You're the only person besides Jim and me who was there. Beth.*

She'd been in high school. A clumsy bridesmaid, with unruly red hair, wearing light green taffeta, the bouffant skirt hitting her mid-calf, the shoulders tight on her bulky teenage frame. The dress, which she'd worn at her own courthouse wedding six years later, was now boxed up in the attic. Like her failed marriage.

But she'd been part of all that glamour. Wedding presents spread out on white linen for family and friends to admire and envy, sterling silver knives and forks, trays and pitchers, two complete sets of fine china, brocade tablecloths, toasters, and Mix-Masters. Luncheons and afternoon tea parties. Cheese straws and pink icing on the cupcakes. Rosemary had been there.

Five other bridesmaids, glossy and beautiful. Four hundred guests crowded into the Bayswater Golf Club. Nibbling shrimp and sipping punch. And she'd caught Beth's bouquet. A lone magnolia flower, pristine white petals, large shiny leaves.

Rosemary loved California, the flaxen hills, the tortured cypresses, the thundering Pacific. She loved the ruby red rhododendrons in Beth's garden, the purple salvia, blue hydrangeas, iridescent hummingbirds. And it all smelled so fresh. But best of all was Beth and Jim. They hugged her, flattered her, called her star of the show.

On the day of the party, Rosemary shivered in her sleeveless, white lace as the thick fog rolled in. Beth, her silvery hair shining, wore a long-sleeved blue silk embroidered with seed pearls and topped by a matching cashmere sweater.

"You look beautiful," Beth said.

The country club ballroom was a confusion of noise and color. Orange tiger lilies in silver buckets on the buffet, vases of red and yellow roses on the smaller tables, bevies of coiffed blond ladies shouting over each other, children racing around, bumping into knees. On one wall, wedding photos flickered, interspersed with baby pictures and photos of beach and backpacking adventures. Fifty years of a marriage.

In Beth's welcoming speech, she introduced her cousin Rosie, the guest of honor, her bridesmaid. Everyone smiled and clapped. In that moment, Rosemary no longer cared that her dress was all wrong and the hair shoved behind her ears was lank and gray.

"When I got married back there in the South," Beth continued, "lots of folks gave silver to the bride. And I collected my share."

Her laugh was silvery.

"But here in California, with a bunch of babies, I didn't have the time or inclination to polish the stuff. So . . ." She paused for effect. "I never used it. In fact, it's been packed away in the original boxes ever since. Now, fifty years later, I'm giving it away. As favors. So, please help yourselves." She pointed to a table at the back of the room. And she laughed. And everyone laughed with her.

Rosemary joined the guests as they crowded around the table covered with shiny mint julep cups and pitchers, casserole dishes and ashtrays, little bells and serving bowls. The guests studied them, held them up to the light, giggled, compared, and debated, then carried them off, remarking to each other that Beth was such an original.

"Look at this!" a woman in purple velvet exclaimed, picking up a wine goblet, its foot encrusted with elaborate silver roses, its stem entwined with sharp-edged vines.

"Who could drink out of such a thing? It's so Victorian. It hurts my hand just to hold it."

"I know," Beth laughed. "God knows where it came from."

"Could I have it?" Rosemary asked.

"Oh, but I got here first," the woman said. She held her treasure up, turning it round and round. "I have to have it. It's so ugly, it's beautiful."

Still laughing, Beth stooped to pick up a tightly folded piece of paper that had fallen out of the cup.

"Please give that to me," Rosemary pleaded, reaching for the paper.

But Beth had opened it and started reading. "Our great-grandmother . . ."

She stopped.

"Go on," the woman in purple velvet said.

"Our great-grandmother Eleanor Williams sipped sherry from the cool thin lip of this silver goblet. I want you to have it."

Beth looked at Rosemary, her cheeks flushed.

The woman in purple velvet quickly set the goblet back on the table.

"Oh, my God," Beth said. "I'm so sorry. I never saw this."

Rosemary stared at the ceiling, willing herself not to cry.

"Mother and I found it in the attic," she said, speaking in a rush, "in a hatbox, wrapped in newspaper. I thought . . ."

She reached for the goblet.

"Look," she held it up and ran her finger along the side of the cup, her voice shaking. "It's engraved. See? It says 'Eleanor.'"

And then Jim was beside her, wrapping his arm around her shoulders, folding a handkerchief into her hand.

"I want our friends to meet you," he said, and, giving her time to wipe her eyes, he led her into the crowd.

She shook hands with the guests, one at time, while Jim told stories of the wedding and how Rosemary was such a big part of it. And Rosemary smiled and smiled and clutched her great-grandmother's silver goblet until her fingers ached.

Once by the Pacific

Poydras Review, November 20, 2017

Dear Nicky,

I am your father. You probably think ill of me, if you think of me at all. But here I am. And I've been thinking about you. So, I'm writing to offer you a deal.

I've learned through the Internet that you've been accepted as a freshman at the University of Virginia. I'm guessing you could use some money.

I have the means to guarantee four fully paid years of college. But there's a condition. Before I pay the big bucks, you must fly out to California. You must meet . . .

. . . .your father.

A check for $1000, signed by Reynolds James, is folded in the letter.

"Send it back," my mother says.

"He says he'll pay for my college," I say.

"Don't trust him!" She's in my face. "He ran out on you and two-timed me."

"Mom, I want to go to college. How else am I going to get there?"

"Get a job."

"Like you, at ten dollars an hour?"

We've been over this road for months, ever since I got accepted. She doesn't want me to go to college. She's afraid I won't come back.

"You're smarter than me," she says. "You can get secretary work."

"I'm going, Mama."

She's holding onto me. I can feel how hot her face is.

"Don't go!"

I kiss the top of her head.

"It's just a visit, Mama."

"I know him," she says. "You don't."

"That's why I got to go," I say.

Because he's out there, thinking about me, waiting for me. Because he's my daddy, and I've been wanting a daddy all my life.

"What did he look like?" I ask Mama shortly before I take off for California. She'd cut all his pictures out of the album and burned them.

We're sitting together on the porch swing after dinner. She's brought a beer out from the kitchen, and every once in a while, she puts the can up against her forehead to cool herself off. Her flip-flops don't reach the floor.

"Red hair, curly. About six feet. Athletic. He was a looker. Body like a baseball player, if you know what I mean, long and thin, butt sticking out. You favor him."

"My butt does *not* stick out."

I do have one memory. He's picking me up, holding me high above his head. We're in a room, could be our same tiny living room. And he picks me up, light as a feather, he says, and holds me high until my fingers brush the ceiling. I remember looking down at Mama, so far down, so small, and she's laughing. They both are. He has a big bushy mustache, I remember that.

That's it. You don't remember much before two, when he took off and never so much as wrote a word or sent a dime's worth of support or even remembered my birthday. Every year, I'd pretend he was just about to walk in the door, holding a Barbie or a puppy or a charm bracelet. And he'd smile at me and say, "Happy Birthday, Nicky."

"How come he left?" I ask Mama.

"He two-timed me."

It's the same answer she's been giving me ever since I was old enough to ask.

"Look," I say. "I'm about to risk my life on an airplane crossing the country to see this man. I need to know more than that."

"You don't want to know."

"Yes, I do."

"Okay then. He had another woman."

That doesn't surprise me.

"What other woman?"

"In Richmond. That's where the son of a bitch lived. He just came down here for . . . ."

"Came down here for what?"

"You're no babe in the woods. You can guess what he came for. Couldn't get it in Richmond."

"How d'you find out?"

"*She* turned up one day. Fancy type. Polished leather boots halfway up her legs. Big bulky sweater and the kind of jeans that cost a fortune. I was holding you when she rang the doorbell."

"What'd she say?"

Mama starts to tear up. "She just looked at you and said, "Oh, my God. Then she told me she was his wife."

"No way! You were his wife."

"He married me, all right, but it didn't count, because he was already married to her."

I put my arm around her shoulders, which are shaking. Mama's smaller than me, a genuine petite. And she's kept herself up. She's a real artist with the cosmetics she sells at Herman's, knows how to emphasize her dark brown eyes, how to use just enough blush to seem natural. I can see how he fell for her.

"I can't believe it," I say. "Why did he marry you if he was already married?"

She blows her nose on a napkin she has in her lap.

"I was pregnant with you. I told him we had to get married. He found a preacher, and that was that. I should have suspected. He was gone a lot. But he was high up in the Herman's chain. That's how I met him. Those stores are all over the South, and I believed him when he said he had to be out of town managing them."

"What did you do?"

"I was a fool," she says.

"I mean, when she turned up."

"Oh, her. I kicked the bitch out of my house. I didn't believe her. But when he came home, he confessed. He'd been married to her for ten years. Ten years! They had two boys. I was all to pieces. I told him I was going to the police. Bigamy's a crime. But he said, what good am I to you in jail? Said he'd buy me this house, put it in my name, which he did. He put $10,000 in a savings account for me. Left me his car."

"And he was gone?"

"Yep. Just like that. I thought he'd keep up with you. He loved you. He really did. But . . . "

"You never heard from him?"

"Not a word."

"Did you try to get in touch? Get some money for me?"

"I had my pride. He broke my heart. I wasn't going to beg."

"So why do you think he wrote me now?" I ask.

"Who knows? Maybe he wants a daughter, now you're grown up so smart. But don't go. I'm warning you. He'll butter you up and let you down."

The plane slams down hard and goes racing along the ground, and I'm thinking it's going to crash into some building like a movie I saw. But it jerks to a stop, and I get my pocketbook and coat and make my way to the door.

He's out there somewhere, and I don't even know what I'm looking for. Except he's tall and has red hair. Like me.

I get out his letter, the second one. *I'll meet you at baggage claim.* No picture.

I keep one eye on the bags moving around a track and the other on the crowd. No tall redheads so far. I grab my bag.

I wait. Ten minutes. I get out my cell phone and try the number he sent me.

"You've reached the voicemail of Reynolds James."

I hear Mama's voice. "See? I told you."

A tap on my shoulder.

"Nicky?"

I whirl around to stare into the long, thin face of a man who's bald.

A chauffeur, maybe? He'd have one. But do chauffeurs wear faded navy sweatshirts and jeans?

The man reaches out. His fingers are long with prominent knuckles. Is he trying to hug me? I step away. He reaches for my bag.

"Nicky," he says again.

"Did Mr. James send you?" I ask.

He laughs.

"You could say that."

I'm frightened.

"I'm sorry," I say, "but who are you?"

"I'm your dad."

I want to grab my suitcase and run.

He smiles.

"I'm sorry," he says. "You had no idea what I look like. My fault."

He reaches into his pocket for his wallet and shows me his driver's license. Reynolds James.

But there could be other people with that name.

"I'm sorry," I say. "I was expecting. . ."

"Hair?"

I nod.

"Red, like yours. Lost it early."

"Do you mind?" I take out my iPhone and snap his photo. "My first day in California."

He laughs. "Not at all."

When he turns to go, I quickly text the photo to Mama. She'll know. I follow him to the garage. What choice do I have? He's got my bag. His car is dented, streaked with dirt. A Japanese car, I think.

"Jump in," he says, throwing my suitcase into the clutter on the back seat.

I just stand there beside him in the dimly lit garage. Afraid. I mean he found me on the Internet. He could be anybody.

"I *am* your father, Nicky. I don't know what I can do to prove it."

I'm looking around for help. But the garage is empty.

So, while we're standing there he just starts talking.

"Poor girl. You're scared. You expected a father with red hair. In a suit and tie, I bet. You expected me to drive a BMW or something. I've got one. I should have brought it."

"I don't believe you," I mutter.

"Let me tell you who I am, Nicky. I *was* the son of a bitch who ran out on your mother sixteen years ago, because I was married to somebody else. But I'm not that man anymore. I've left him behind."

"Who are you?" I ask.

We're still just standing there by the dirty car.

"A hiker, as you can see." He points to binoculars on the cluttered back seat. "Don't worry, Nicky. I don't deserve you, but I am your dad."

I don't know why, but I'm wanting to believe him. Maybe because he knows the history. Maybe because I've come so far, and I want a father.

My iPhone pings. "He sure got old," Mama texts, "but that's him."

I laugh with relief.

"Why don't you wash your car?" I ask.

He smiles.

"It just gets dirty again. Come on. Get in."

We cross the Golden Gate Bridge, driving over the blue water and all the sailboats and up winding roads into hills covered with brown grass and dusty trees.

At the top of one of the hills, we park outside a wooden gate and walk a cobblestone path through rhododendron and azalea bushes. The wood frame house spreads all over the top of the hill. Inside, the rooms all run together, living room, kitchen, dining room. All wood floors and glass. So many windows you hardly need lights.

I didn't know people lived like this.

I look up from unpacking my suitcase and see a deer out the window. I snap a photo and text it to Mama. She has to see this.

Right away, she texts back. "Does he live in the woods?"

I find my father in the kitchen.

"You must be exhausted," he says. "It's almost midnight back in Virginia."

I gobble up the tuna salad sandwich he's made for me.

"Get some rest," he says in a soft voice. "Thank you for coming."

After a restless night, I drag myself to the kitchen in search of coffee. A young woman in a black tank top and a mass of curly blond hair jumps up from the table.

"Hello. I'm Rose."

I shake her hand pretending not to notice the rose tattooed on the pale skin of her upper arm.

"Welcome," she says, handing me an outsized ceramic mug filled with coffee. "Reynolds' been counting the days."

My phone pings. A text from Mama.

"R U OK?"

"English muffin?" Rose asks, pulling one apart and dropping the two halves into the toaster. Silver rings with fake stones cover her fingers.

"Thank you."

"You're going to love it here," she says. She's really very pretty. "It's just fantastic."

I'm thinking, what's this woman doing here? Where's my father?

"I don't think I'll be here that long," I say.

"Too bad. He wants to show you around, take you hiking. He's crazy about nature."

"He is?"

"You know. Birds. Flowers."

"I don't know anything about that."

"Don't worry. He'll teach you."

"Is his wife at work?" I ask.

She looks surprised.

"What wife?"

"I thought he had a wife named Cynthia."

"Maybe he did, but he doesn't anymore."

She grins.

"I'm his girlfriend. Since Valentine's Day. He came to the studio for a full massage. And one thing led to another. He's a cool guy, your dad."

I'm thinking, do I really want to get back on an airplane and spend my summer selling shoes at Herman's? Not really. Not at all. And here I am. In California.

"I might give it a week," I say.

Hi Baby. Thanks a bunch for the photos. Looks like the scumbag is king of the mountain out there in California. What about his wife? Is she being nice to you?

When are you coming home?

We're driving along curving roads in the banged-up Nissan, past black and white cows clumped together in muddy fields, past hills that roll out to a distance of blue water.

"Why did you come out here?" I ask.

I have so many questions. It's easier to ask them riding in a car, not having to face him.

"I was running away from my life." He laughs. "That sounds like a bad soap opera."

"Why?"

"Why? I hated it. Hated driving the freeways from town to town, hiring and firing managers, checking on merchandise, supervising building projects. You have no idea."

I'm suddenly furious.

"You left my mother and me for another woman, and then you ran away from her. And now you have somebody else, and you didn't even tell me."

He looks surprised. "You mean Rose? God, I'm sorry. I thought I said she was living with me."

"Nope."

"Look, I'm a rat. I said that yesterday. But the fact is, I didn't love my wife. That's how come I got involved with your mother."

"What about your children?"

"My boys were grown when I left. But they hate me all the same."

He looks over at me.

"Look, it's no excuse, but the fact is I had to marry Cynthia. We were in high school, and she wouldn't get an abortion. It was a nightmare from the beginning. But I did love your mother. And you."

"Then why did you . . ."

"Leave you?"

I stare straight ahead and nod.

"I was a coward," he says. "I gave in to my wife, and it was the hardest thing I ever did."

"Sounds like bullshit to me."

"Yep. I guess it does."

"So, how come you invited me out here?" I ask.

"I told you. I wanted to get to know you. Besides, I have money. Why not give some of it away? The boys will have nothing to do with me. So, I looked you up."

He stops the car. We're parked beside an old barn. Branches of large evergreen trees bend toward the ground. He jumps out of the car, wiggles his shoulders into a backpack and swings binoculars around his neck.

"Grab a bottle of water. Let's go."

He strides off, squinting into the sun. I follow him along a path high above water. Far down, huge waves are crashing white.

He grins. "'The shattered water made a misty din. Great waves looked over others coming in.' Robert Frost," he says. "'Once by the Pacific.'"

I've heard of Robert Frost, but I don't know a thing about poetry.

High above us, a large bird hangs in the wind. Its wings are stretched out. Not moving.

"Red-tailed hawk," he says, handing me his binoculars. "It's called stilling. He's up there looking for food. They've got amazing vision, those birds."

The hawk is gone before I can focus the glasses, but as I swing them around, two large deer-like animals with gigantic antlers appear.

"What are they?"

"Tule elk. Handsome, aren't they?"

Flowers are everywhere, yellow, red, white. And more elk.

"Are those Redwoods?" I ask, pointing to the large trees overhead.

"Cypress. Redwoods can't survive out here. Wait! Look up. Use the binoculars. Up there in the branches."

"I don't see anything."

"There's a fork in the tree, high up. Can you see it?"

Something *is* up there. Something blurry. Then I see eyes, staring down at me.

"What is it?"

"A great horned owl. It's not every day we see the likes of him. This is your lucky day."

Is it? I breathe in sunshine and chilly air. Suddenly, I feel like I can walk and walk and never get tired.

Hi Baby. From the photos, it looks like you're out in the woods all the time. Doesn't the man work? You say he's teaching you about birds. That's weird.

And he divorced that Cynthia. What an asshole. Though I'm not sorry for her.

When are you coming home?

On the coast overlooking the Pacific. A flash of red, a white rump patch. A high-pitched "keew."

"Flicker," he says, grabbing my arm, pointing. "See him?"

He's landed on a coyote bush in plain sight. His beak is sharp and points up. He's beautiful.

"How'd you get into birds?" I ask.

"You mean, how did a business type like me discover all this?"

He sweeps his arms around.

"I guess."

"Before I was a department store guy, I was a kid. The kind of kid who climbs trees and looks for birds' nests. I got good at recognizing their songs. The department stores were my dad's idea. He owned them and made sure I followed in his footsteps."

"So, now you're into nature?"

"What I am is complicated."

That's for sure.

"So, how does Rose fit in?"

It's a question I've been puzzling over since I arrived.

"What do you mean?"

"You know what I mean. She's not interested in birds or hiking or poetry."

"I don't know. She's *un*complicated. Maybe that's it."

"Will you leave her too?"

He stops in his tracks and glares at me.

"That's mean and none of your business."

But it is my business. It's exactly my business.

It's August. Hard to believe it's only been six weeks. I've climbed Mt. Thomas, peered into tide pools at Big Sur, hiked to the top of Nevada Falls in Yosemite. With this man who whistles bird songs, who reads me poetry.

Who left my mother.

Time to go home.

"One last hurrah," he says. "Top of the mountain."

I'm game.

"How many miles?"

"Starting from the house and back, fifteen."

A month ago, I would have said no. Too long, too hard. But I'm stronger now. My legs have muscles I never had before.

A sandwich and a bottle of water in my fanny pack, my new binoculars around my neck, a baseball cap on top of my red hair. I'm ready. We start up the hill from the house, climb steps cut into the red dirt, cross bridges, zigzag through coyote brush and lupine, pennyroyal. I know some names of flowers now. We climb over rocks. At the top, we unpack sandwiches and look down on whitecaps, on Crystal Lake, on Mt. Juniper miles away. Red-tails and vultures are flying in circles. We're at the top of the world.

"I'll miss you," my father says.

Despite his ridiculous floppy canvas hat, the sun has colored his face bright red. His blue eyes search my face, willing me to say I'll miss him too.

I say instead, "Thank you for having me."

He's looking down at the ocean through his binoculars. "'The clouds are low and hairy in the skies.'"

I take it up. "'Like locks blown forward in the gleam of eyes.'"

"I taught you that poem anyway," he says.

We sit for several minutes.

"Are you glad you came, Nicky?"

"Yes."

"Will you come again?"

"Do you want me to?"

He looks at me. "Of course."

"Why?"

He laughs. "What a question. You're my daughter."

"For the past sixteen years, that didn't count for much."

"I missed you. I wanted to see you, to talk to you, to see what was becoming of you. All those years."

"Well, thanks very much."

"I don't expect you to understand, but Cynthia was so furious when she discovered your mother, I had to promise to put you out of my life."

So much weakness makes me angry.

"So, why didn't you see me after you left her?"

"I was afraid."

"That's lame."

"All the same, it's true. Afraid you'd reject me. Hate me. Like the boys."

"You could at least have sent me birthday presents."

"I told you. I'm not a good man. But I'm trying to change. And I wanted to see you. Is that so bad?"

It's too late, I think but don't say.

He looks right in my face.

"You're my daughter, Nicky. I don't want to lose you."

I turn away.

"You have a history of losing people," I say. "Or more like, discarding people."

He looks suddenly pathetic, hunched there, his red face shining in the sun.

"Nicky," he says, "try for just a minute to imagine that I have changed. That I am capable of change. That I'll be here next summer waiting for you."

I think about Mama and how she would hate it if I ever came back here. How she would make me feel guilty. I think about how much she loves me. So, I'm tempted to say, you made your bed. You got me here this summer. That's it. But here I am on top of this mountain, and . . . .

"I'm not sure," is what I say.

Thank God you're finally coming home. It's been the worst summer of my life. I got T-bone steak for your first night and French fries. I'll be at the airport. I can't wait.

We're bumping into each other, frying potatoes, broiling steaks. This kitchen is so small. It's never bothered me before. I've never even noticed the grease stains streaking the walls. And I don't want to notice now. This is home.

Mama's rushing around, setting the table, patting me, kissing me.

"I figure you might not need his money now," she says. "I got a raise."

I say, "I'm proud of you, Mama." I am.

After dinner, I get out my laptop.

"You want to see my pictures?"

"I thought I already did."

"I have a lot more. Yosemite, Big Sur, the Pacific Ocean."

"Okay," she says.

I click on slide show and watch my summer flash past. The photographs I've only seen in miniature on my iPhone jump out at me, large as life.

"Who's that?" she asks. It's the first time she's said a word. Rose smiles at the camera, one hand on the kitchen table, a cup of coffee in the other.

"That's Rose. Dad's girlfriend," I say. "I told you about her."

"Looks like he's robbing the cradle."

"You could say that."

She pulls her chair up to the computer and peers into Rose's laughing face.

"She looks cheap with all those tattoos. She'll be gone in a year, mark my words."

"I don't know."

"I do," she says.

And I'm thinking young, pretty, and...what was his word? Uncomplicated. Like Mama all those years ago.

"You may be right," I say and turn off the computer. I can watch the photos another time.

"I'm glad to be home, Mama."

It's what she wants to hear. She grabs me round the waist and holds onto me. The top of her head fits under my chin. I love her.

I'm in my bedroom, pulling out shirts, pants, sweaters from the closet, discarding one after the other. I leave for college in a week. None of my clothes seem right.

"Ta dum!"

Mama's at the door. She drags a huge suitcase into the tiny room.

"Surprise!"

Her smile looks uncertain.

"Is it all right?" she asks. "The woman in luggage said all the college kids are buying them. But I wasn't sure."

"It's perfect, Mama. Thank you."

I'm fighting tears. It must have cost so much. And not just money. I wrap myself around her. Feel her rigid shoulders, her thin arms tight around my waist.

"It's for college," she says, pulling herself away. "Not for California. It's much too big for California."

"I know."

"You're not going back there, are you?"

"You mean, ever?"

"I saw the letter," she says, "from your college. He's already paid for all four years. So, you don't need to go back."

"I don't know."

"He'll get tired of you, just like he did the rest of us. Just like he will with that Rose."

"Maybe."

She's standing there, a small figure, hanging onto the enormous suitcase she's bought with her raise, pleading with her eyes. I want to reassure her, tell her I'll never fly off to California again, never see him again. And in some ways, it makes sense. Chances are good he'll lose interest in me, like he did with all the rest.

But there are mountains out there. And oceans and birds and flowers. There's poetry out there.

And there's my daddy.

We Gather Together

Forge, Issue 11.1, November 2017
Also published in *Spotswood Virginia,*
Stephen F. Austin State University Press, 2021

Last Thanksgiving my uncle Charlie shoved a newspaperman who was taking pictures in front of our church and knocked down his camera. His picture was on television, Uncle Charlie leaning over the man, his face just furious. At the edge of the picture, you can see a policeman, all blurry, running up to stop the fight. What you don't see are all the people from Preacher Martin's church, dressed to the nines. They disappeared, just like that, before you could turn around. I know. I was there.

"It's what comes of trying to integrate," my daddy said. He was dead set against it when the Reverend Coleman announced his plan a month or so before. He stood up in the pulpit and told us he had invited the Preacher Martin's Baptist church to worship with us on Thanksgiving Day.

"I got nothing against those people," Daddy said. "But they got their own church. It's a damn fool idea to try to mix them in with us."

And Uncle Charlie said, "I don't care what those Communists on the Supreme Court say, I don't integrate. I never will."

Some of the men decided to talk to the Reverend, bring him to his senses. I know because my daddy was one of them and told me all about it.

"The Court meant for schools to be integrated, not church," they told the Reverend. "Those folks will feel uncomfortable mixing with the professional people we got here at First Baptist."

But the Reverend just smiled.

"Remember what you used to sing in Sunday School? 'Red and yellow, black and white, They are precious in His sight.'"

"Bible says nothing about mixing," the men said.

"We all worship the same God; we're all Baptists. It's time we came together in thanksgiving," the Reverend said.

I didn't know what to think. I was fourteen, and the only ones of them I'd ever known was Luther, the janitor at our church. They say Mr. Huntsman, the mayor's father, was his daddy, which is why his skin is so light. But, of course, that doesn't make Luther white. I've seen the maids on the back of the bus on the way to work, and the garbage men. But I don't *know* any of them. We don't have a maid; Mama and I clean.

When I first heard we had to go to school with the black kids, it scared me half to death. The white boys in my school are rough enough without having some boys from Calhoun Street fighting and talking dirty. And everybody says they're a lot dumber than we are. But it's been a couple of years since the Supreme Court said we had to integrate, and so far, nothing's happened to change the schools. So, I couldn't understand why the preacher wanted to make trouble at church.

On the other hand, I've always looked up to Reverend Coleman. Everybody does. I consider him as good a Christian as a man could be. Maybe because he's always so nice to me, calls me by my name, Shirley, compliments me when I play the piano at Sunday School. He always stands real straight in the pulpit and opens up his arms like the painting of Jesus, telling us that God will forgive us no matter how nasty we behave. And when it's time for hymns, he throws back his head and sings louder than anybody. So, when he asked why God would want us to turn a family away from our church just because, I didn't know what to think.

Every Sunday until the big day, Reverend Coleman read the parable of the Good Samaritan to make his point. And he wore down most of the deacons and some of the women with his arguments. Not my mama, of course. She always sided with my daddy and Uncle Charlie. And they were against it. But they got outvoted.

Uncle Charlie is the President of the Spotswood Bank and the Chairman of the School Board. He's always been my favorite uncle. He doesn't have any children himself, so he's made my brother Sonny and me his substitute children. Uncle Charlie laughs a lot, and he brings me Hershey bars, and he once gave me a little bronze statue of the Empire State Building which he had bought in New York City. He's very handsome with lots of wavy red hair, not like my daddy who's almost bald.

But mostly he's my hero. Like the time we were at a Lion's Club picnic on Luna Lake, and Daddy and Uncle Charlie took us out in a rowboat. Sonny was only two, and, of course, he couldn't swim, so Mama said he couldn't go. But Sonny kept climbing into the boat and smiling at Daddy. So, when Mama wasn't looking, Daddy pushed off.

I put my hand in the water to feel the cool on such a hot day and watched the ripples coming out from my fingers. I liked looking at Uncle Charlie's shoulders while he did the rowing. They were full of muscles and getting red from the sun. He's much stronger than my daddy whose shoulders are thin and bent forward. Maybe from bending over the cash register at the store all day.

All of a sudden, I heard a splash. I looked around, but Sonny wasn't in the boat. And he wasn't in the water. I started screaming.

Then another splash and the boat started rocking so bad I had to hold on with both hands. It was Uncle Charlie. He'd jumped in. Daddy was yelling, and I could hear Mama calling us from the shore. It seemed to go on forever. Once in a while, my uncle's head would burst out of the water, his red hair plastered to his forehead, and then back down he'd go. Finally, he pulled himself into the boat, which was rocking so bad I was afraid it would go under. He flopped down on his back, soaking wet. Sonny was spread out on top of him like a rag doll. They lay there without moving while Daddy was pulling at them, and I was screaming and screaming. Finally, Sonny opened his eyes, slowly, like in a dream, but he wasn't looking at anything.

"Row!" Uncle Charlie yelled. "Row!"

He picked Sonny up and hit him hard on the back. Nothing happened. Then he laid him down on the seat and put his mouth on

Sonny's face. I watched him breathe into my brother's mouth, then suck the breath back in. We were all quiet now, waiting, and Daddy was rowing hard. When we hit shore, Mama jumped into the water, sundress, sandals and all, crying, "Where's my baby?"

Uncle Charlie didn't look up. He just kept breathing for Sonny, hunched over him, wet and white and serious. All of a sudden, Sonny wiggled. Then he started choking and crying and spitting up water, but he was breathing for himself.

Daddy grabbed him and wrapped him in a beach towel. Mama was crying and hanging on to Daddy. I hugged Uncle Charlie, and he put his arms around me.

Daddy insisted that we leave for church right after breakfast that Thanksgiving morning to make sure we'd be seated down front.

"Don't want to sit behind the colored," he said.

I didn't want to go. But Daddy made me. He said, we'd always gone to church on Thanksgiving, and no niggers were going to keep us away. So, I put on my brown felt hat with the veil, which Mama always made me wear to church, and my white gloves.

The church slowly filled up with folks we knew until it was about five minutes before the ten o'clock service was to start. The organ was going full tilt with "Onward Christian Soldiers."

"Looks like we're safe," Mama whispered.

"Not a chance," Daddy whispered back.

They were walking in a bunch down the side aisles, the men in dark suits, the women all dressed up in bright colored dresses, red and blue with big flowers, and feathers waving off their hats. They didn't look like maids or janitors or garbage men. The girls in pigtails and stiff little skirts faced straight ahead as they followed their mamas down the aisles, hanging onto their hands. The boys were all in suits. I didn't see Luther anywhere.

"All rise."

It was Reverend Coleman. He had slipped in when I wasn't looking and was standing in the pulpit, his arms spread out, that big smile on his face. Next to him stood a tall, fat man, with rough skin the color of dark chocolate, Preacher Martin, I figured. He had on this light blue suit and a red tie, but he wasn't smiling. He didn't even look at us. He kept his eyes on his hymn book, which was open in his hands. I figured he wanted to be there about as much as I did.

Reverend Coleman spent a long time welcoming everybody to our church and saying what a glorious Thanksgiving Day God had provided. He said a prayer, and then the organist belted out "We Gather Together To Ask the Lord's Blessing," and the choir joined in. The church was full of people by this time, all the white people in the middle, Preacher Martin's people on the sides, so you would think we'd fill up that place with singing. But the sound was pretty pitiful. I didn't feel like singing, and I guess the other people felt the same. But I could hear Reverend Coleman's voice, deep and steady, way out in front of everybody. "He chastens and hastens His will to make known." I couldn't hear Preacher Martin, but his lips were moving.

After the hymn, the service proceeded as usual. The choir sang, the deacons from both churches passed collection plates, Preacher Martin read the Beatitudes from the Bible, and Reverend Coleman preached about "Blessed are the peacemakers." Except that we were what you might call integrated, it didn't seem much different from other Thanksgiving services.

Every once in a while, I'd look over at Uncle Charlie. He was sitting on the front row with the other deacons, but kind of to the side, so I had a good view of him. I noticed he wasn't singing during the hymns, which was unusual for him. He loves to sing. And whenever either Reverend Coleman or Preacher Martin started talking, he looked down at his lap.

During the last hymn, Reverend Coleman walked up the aisle through the congregation and waited at the door to greet people as they filed out. I started to join the line.

But Daddy said, "Hold on there, Shirley. Let *them* get out first."

By the time we got to the preacher, the church was nearly empty. I shook Reverend Coleman's hand and started down the stairs in front of the church. Then I stopped. The yard below was packed with people. Some I'd never seen before. And there were cameras everywhere. Big boxy cameras on stands with men crouching behind them. It was a mess. People were running away from the cameras, down Main Street, and men holding pencils and notebooks were running after them, shouting questions. I could hear them.

"How many black people were in that church today?"

"Who gave the sermon?"

"What was it like to sit next to them?"

Main Street was full of cars, but they weren't moving, and all around and between the cars, all kinds of people were yelling that bad word."

Reverend Coleman rushed past me down the stairs into the crowd.

"These are religious people," he kept saying. "Let them pass."

But the newspapermen ran past him, bumping into him, paying him no mind.

"Back into the church," Daddy ordered. "We'll go out the back way."

I stood there.

"Shirley!" his voice was harsh.

"Uncle Charlie!" I cried. Because I had just seen him, in the middle of all those people.

"You got no right to take pictures of my church," he shouted and pointed at a cameraman who was focusing on a woman in a big red hat. She was looking all around like she'd lost somebody.

The man motioned for Uncle Charlie to get out of the way. But he didn't. He walked over to the camera and with a loud crash knocked it onto the sidewalk. The cameraman started after Uncle Charlie. That's when my uncle shoved him, and he fell.

"Shirley!"

As I turned back into the church, I heard the sirens screaming.

On the news that night, they kept showing the picture of Uncle Charlie, leaning over a man, looking fierce, and the broken camera smashed beside them.

The TV announcer said, "Today, in Spotswood, Virginia, Charles Sherwood, President of the local Spotswood Bank, assaulted a *New York Times* photographer to prevent his taking pictures of the first integrated church service in the state of Virginia."

"Turn that thing off," Daddy yelled. But I kept watching.

The man on TV was talking at the top of his voice.

"Mr. Sherwood was arrested at the scene but was shortly released and is free on bail."

"Goddammit, I said turn it off."

Mama was sitting crouched over the kitchen table, her nose red and swollen. She still had on the hat she'd worn to church, the one with the black feathers. Daddy sat down beside her and put his arms around her.

"Don't you worry, sweetheart. Charlie will get off. He was just protecting our church. The judge knows him. He'll see it was self-defense."

"Why did he break the camera?" I asked.

"He didn't break the camera. The camera fell down while he was trying to keep those New York people from stirring up the crowd."

"But he knocked that man down," I said.

"Go to bed," Daddy said. "We'll talk about it in the morning."

For the rest of the Thanksgiving holiday, Daddy refused to talk about it. On Sunday, Reverend Coleman asked God to help us forgive those who revile and persecute us. I wasn't sure whether he meant the *New York Times* or all those people in the street, calling us names.

I didn't want to go to school the next Monday. I figured the kids would be asking me a lot of questions. But it turned out they were too busy arguing about whether or not Elvis's voice sounded dirty when he sang "Blue Suede Shoes."

So, when Mr. Jefferson, out of the blue, asked our Social Studies class whether we thought knocking over a newspaper camera was a violation of Freedom of the Press, I was stunned.

Henry Matthews waved his skinny arm in the air.

"He shouldn't have done it. The newspapers have the right to record the news."

That got Barry Arnold going.

"They shouldn't have let those freaks in that church in the first place."

Everybody had an opinion.

Mr. Jefferson started walking up and down the rows of desks, his head bent forward like he was listening, his hair hanging in his face, his pants dusty from chalk. Then he stopped at my desk. I sat very still.

"What do you think, Shirley?"

I looked up, scared. Did he know it was my Uncle Charlie who had knocked over the camera? I couldn't tell. But I had to defend him.

So, I said the first thing that popped into my head.

"He had to do it."

"What do you mean?" He walked back to the front of the class. "He was protecting the people at the church."

"Protecting them from what?"

"Those newspapermen were chasing the church people."

"Were you there?" Mr. Jefferson asked. He was looking at me like he was really interested.

I nodded.

"Would you tell us what you saw?"

Everybody turned to look at me.

"It was my Uncle Charlie," I said, "and he was protecting those people when they were coming out of church."

"Do you think that gave your uncle the right to knock down a news camera?"

I felt my face get really hot.

"You don't know what you're talking about," I said. "You weren't there."

I was trying not to cry.

Well, that started it. Everybody was yelling, blaming Uncle Charlie, blaming the church.

"Shirley, would you see me after school?" Mr. Jefferson said.

Then he clapped his hands. "That's enough of Current Events. Open your books to page forty-five."

I ran out of the room before the tears came. I hid in a stall in the girls' bathroom until I heard the bell ring for the end of the period. Then I ran home.

Mama could tell something was wrong the minute I got home.

"It was Mr. Jefferson," I said.

"What about him?"

"He said some mean things about Uncle Charlie."

"What things?"

"I don't want to talk about it."

I felt I was somehow to blame. I had talked back to Mr. Jefferson, which was a first for me, and I hadn't gone to see him after class. Plus, I'd cut school. I was scared of what Daddy would say, but at the same time, I was really mad at Mr. Jefferson.

So, Mama let me be, but when Daddy got home from the store, he went after me until I told the whole story.

"The son of a bitch," he said under his breath. "He'll hear about this."

And then, to my surprise, he hugged me really tight and told me I had done the right thing. And Mama hugged me. And later Uncle Charlie came over and teased me about being his lawyer. I went to bed almost happy.

The next morning when we arrived at school, Daddy surprised me by parking and jumping out of the car.

"Come on," he said. "We're going to get to the bottom of this."

I didn't like the sound of that and made a beeline for my locker.

But he reached out and grabbed me by the elbow.

"You're coming with me, honey," he said.

"I don't want to."

But it was too late.

Mr. Harrison, the principal, smiled at Daddy and shook his hand.

"Come on in, Earl," he said. "What's on your mind?"

I'd never been in the principal's office before, and I was surprised how messy it was. Textbooks were stacked on the desk, on the table, some even on the floor, and there were papers everywhere. We sat at the table on wooden chairs, Daddy and me on one side, Mr. Harrison on the other. I looked out the window.

Daddy started right in.

"Rick, you've got a teacher here who's preaching integration politics in the classroom."

"Yeah?"

He turned to me.

"You tell him what happened, Shirley."

Mr. Harrison is a short man, not much taller than the students, but he has these beady eyes that make you feel guilty no matter what you've done, and he fixed those beady eyes on me.

"I don't want to get anybody in trouble," I said.

"You won't if you tell the truth, young lady."

So, I did. I told him what Mr. Jefferson said about Freedom of the Press and Uncle Charlie. I didn't want to, but I did.

"You see?" Daddy said. "See what I'm talking about? Harassing my girl like that. You have to do something, Rick. That man has no place in the classroom."

"Thank you," Mr. Harrison said. "Why don't you go to class, Shirley?"

I was only too happy to do that. As I left the room, I heard Daddy say Uncle Charlie's name and something about the School Board.

There was a substitute in Social Studies that day. And Mr. Jefferson didn't turn up the rest of the week, which was a big relief.

At lunch period on Friday, Henry Matthews came over to where I was eating with my friend Sarah. His slide rule banged against the table as he leaned over me.

"I hope you're satisfied now that you got Mr. Jefferson fired."

"I did not."

"Well, your daddy did. He bullied Mr. Harrison into firing the best teacher we ever had in this dump of a school."

"You're lying," I said.

After Henry left, I asked Sarah, "What's he talking about?"

But I knew, and I felt sick to my stomach.

"I heard a rumor," she said, "that Mr. Jefferson was leaving, but it can't be your fault."

She hugged me.

I could have told her the truth. About my talking to Mr. Harrison. But suppose it got out. Sarah's my best friend, but still, she might let it slip. And I didn't want anybody to know about it.

So, I said, "I hate Henry Matthews."

It's January. Mr. Jefferson never came back. We've been having one substitute after another in Social Studies, and we haven't learned a thing. Even though I still blame Mr. Jefferson for what he did to me, I have to admit he made Social Studies interesting. Henry Matthews and his friends are still mad at me.

Mr. Jefferson isn't the only one leaving town. Reverend Coleman announced at the Christmas Eve service that he'd got the call to a church in Washington D.C.

"How come you're leaving?" I asked him last week. It was after choir practice, and I noticed the light was on in his study.

"Hi Shirley," he said. "Come on in."

He has a wonderful smile.

"Don't leave," I blurted out.

"I don't like leaving," he said, "but it's the right time. Besides, have you ever been to Washington?"

"No Sir."

"Well, you have a treat in store when you and your mama and daddy come to visit me."

"Is it because of Thanksgiving?" I asked.

He smiled again.

"Is that what you think?"

"I guess so."

He was quiet for what seemed like forever.

Then he said, "It's not your Uncle Charlie's fault. Don't think that for a minute. It's just time for me to go."

"I wish you wouldn't."

I started to leave, but I needed to talk to somebody about Mr. Jefferson. Maybe that's why I went to Reverend Coleman's office in the first place.

"Mr. Jefferson is leaving too," I said.

He looked up, like he was surprised I was still there.

"Mr. Jefferson, the teacher?"

"Yes, sir."

"Why is that do you suppose?"

"They say he got fired."

"That's pretty serious."

"He shouldn't have been talking about Uncle Charlie in class."

It still made me angry, just thinking about it.

The Reverend got up from his desk and put his arm around me.

"Come over here, Shirley," he said, and he sat me down beside him on this brown sofa he's got in his office.

"They say I'm to blame. That I got him fired."

I could feel tears coming, but I held them in.

"How can they say that?"

I told him about Mr. Jefferson talking about Freedom of the Press. About how I had defended Uncle Charlie. About how Mr. Jefferson had treated me.

Reverend Coleman was watching me in such a serious way.

"No wonder you're upset," he said.

I looked up into his face.

"It's because of me he got fired," I said.

My voice sounded squeaky.

"Daddy made me tell Mr. Harrison what happened. And he got fired."

Reverend Coleman sat close with his arm around me.

Finally, he said, "You didn't do anything wrong, Shirley. One of these days you'll have to decide what you think about breaking cameras and Freedom of the Press, but whatever you decide, this wasn't your fault."

He gave me a hug.

"Do you understand?"

I nodded and stood up. I wanted to believe him.

Uncle Charlie came over last night to celebrate what he called his David and Goliath victory.

"How 'bout that, kid?" he said. "Your uncle whipped the mighty *New York Times.*"

"You did?"

"You bet. They agreed not to press charges."

"Were they going to send you to jail?"

"I was never going to jail, sweetheart. Not a chance."

"Your uncle was a perfect gentleman," Mama said. "He offered to pay for the camera."

Uncle Charlie popped the cork off a bottle of champagne and poured glasses for him and Daddy. Mama, Sonny and I had orange juice.

"Let's drink a toast to Shirley." He winked at me. "She's rid this town of two trouble-makers."

I put my glass down. "Huh?"

"Your Mr. Jefferson's out on his ear. I made sure of that. And good riddance to Preacher Coleman."

"That wasn't me!" I cried out.

He picked me up and twirled me around. Laughing and laughing. I've always loved it when Uncle Charlie holds me up like that. But this time felt different.

"Put me down!" I shouted.

I struggled out of his arms and looked right at him.

"It wasn't me. It was you," I said. This time I didn't hold it in. I was sobbing. "You started it. And look what's happened. It's all a mess."

They were staring at me. Nobody was laughing.

Number 56

Five on the Fifth, Volume 2, Issue 12, October 2017

"I'll never forget," Julian begins, pushing his dessert plate away and smiling at the eight guests crowded around the dining room table. "I was in English class, senior year of high school, bored out of my gourd, as usual, when a girl in the back, someone I'd never really noticed before, raised her hand and delivered an interpretation of King Lear that was so complex, so fucking intelligent, I could barely understand it. I don't think even the teacher understood it. But he knew what the rest of us didn't, that that girl was smarter than anybody in the whole damn school."

Here it comes. Number 56. I've taken to counting them.

He's beaming in my direction.

"And there she sits. My wife Beatrice. The love of my life."

Always the same words. At academic parties, on cruise ships, at college reunions, at concert intermissions, once when he was drunk.

For the first time all evening, they've noticed me. I mean really taken notice.

I could duck my head and smile. I could say, but he was always head and shoulders above all of us. I could tell them, apologetically, when asked, that I have been his assistant for thirty years, that I edit his scholarly papers. I've said those kinds of things and ducked and smiled for years.

I watch them thinking, how generous! A nuclear physicist. And what's she done? I forget.

I watch him, talking, talking, smiling. I love him. I always have.

I feel myself rising to my feet. Slowly, the conversation stops.

I say, "When Julian and I were high school seniors, we studied calculus."

They are all looking at me, puzzled, expectant.

"It was a small class in those days. Not many high school kids were advanced enough to take calculus. Just twelve students and our teacher, Mr. Naylor."

Julian is shaking his head, trying to get my attention. I ignore him.

"Julian sat behind me. At the end of the semester, we had an hour-long test. It was fun. I chugged along, doing the calculations, figuring out the answers, lost in my own space."

Most of the guests are smiling now, but a few of the men look away, as if they are somehow embarrassed for me. I don't look at Julian.

I continue.

"Suddenly, I became aware of a scuffle behind me. I turned to find Mr. Naylor holding a piece of paper high in the air. 'You were copying Bea's paper, Julian,' he said. I looked at Julian. His face was bright red. 'I did not!' he cried. Then he jumped up, knocked over the desk, and ran out of the room."

There is not a sound in the dining room.

"Julian never came back to calculus," I continue. "But when he took it in summer school, he asked if I would tutor him. That's how we fell in love."

I sit back down and resume eating my blackberry pie and ice cream. People talk and laugh as before. But the party ends earlier than expected.

Julian says nothing on the way home. He just stares ahead, both hands gripping the steering wheel.

"Why did you do that?" he asks once we are home.

"After 56 times, I'd had enough."

"It was cruel," he says. "You could ruin my reputation, telling stuff like that."

"That would never happen," I say. "Our work is too good."

Getting Unstuck

Ursa Minor, Volume 2: Dark Matter, 2017

Just when I needed him most, he went and got himself thrown in the fucking hole. And there I was, stuck where he left me, locked up, just like him, with the Wicked Witch of Jesus standing guard. Ever since she got born-again, my life's been hell. It's not like I was boozing or doing drugs like half the kids I know. I don't do that stuff. She didn't know how lucky she was with me. I'm good. But not good enough for her.

"No dates for you, young lady," she said to me.

"No 'dates'? What kind of prehistoric word is that? You mean no fucking?"

You shoulda seen that pious face go white.

"Go to your room and stay there," she said.

"No," I said. "All I'm asking is to go to the movies with Raymond. Just the movies."

"No," she said. "You're sixteen. You got no idea what boys are like. They got one thing on their mind. Your dad ain't here to protect you, so I got to do it."

"Well, he'd let me go to the movies if he was here."

"Not if he could see Raymond," she said.

So, she marched me up the stairs to my room and locked the door. I waited until things got quiet then climbed out the window, like always, and met Raymond in the mall at Denny's, like always. He had his brother's truck, so we messed around on a back road for a few hours. But she caught me climbing back in the window.

"That's it," she said. "I know what you're doing, and I know who you're doing it with. And if it happens again, I'm going to call the cops and get you incarcerated in some juvenile facility."

"Aw, come on," I said. "I only climb out the window because you won't let me have a normal social life."

"You're not capable of a normal social life," she shot back. "And Raymond is just the type to lead you into mortal sin, if he hasn't done it already."

I laughed in her face, and she nailed shut my window with about fifty nails.

Then it got worse. On Saturday, I got so mad, I threatened to hit her, and she called the cops. The officer who showed up said I had to listen to my mom, or I'd end up like my dad. I didn't bother to tell him she was my dad's girlfriend. My mom was long gone. But I did promise to behave. She locked me in my room anyway. She'd let me out to go to school, but she'd call me on the landline at four sharp every day to make sure I was home. I thought about asking Raymond over in the afternoons, but she'd have shipped me off to juvie in a heartbeat if she'd caught me.

So, I called the prison. I had to talk to Dad to get me loose from this religious fanatic he'd stuck me with. And that's when I found out he was in the hole again. That's my dad, always in the thick of it. Nothing violent, at least on the outside. He gets put away for counterfeiting or passing checks or con games. He's a genius at that con stuff, flashing that grin of his, looking so handsome and respectable. Of course, once he gets inside, he gets knocked around, and they lock him away. He says it's the gangs that go after him, but that doesn't compute. I mean he's not black or Hispanic or anything.

Anyway, he was in no position to help me, and I could take only so much of the Jesus freak. So, I figured I'd have to bust out. Every day when I walked in the door from school, or wherever it was I went that day, the phone would be ringing its head off.

"It's Gladys," she'd say, "Where you been?"

"School. Where you think?"

"Get your homework done. You need to fry up some chicken for dinner."

Or vac the living room, clean the toilet, scrub the kitchen floor. Now that she's off the hard stuff, all *she* ever does is watch TV and

fall asleep reading the Bible. So, one day I got so fed up, I just didn't bother to come home. I hung out with Dolores and some friends at Denny's after school then went over to Raymond's house. He hadn't laid eyes on me for about three weeks, and he was some kind of horny. So, we messed around in his room until his mom got home from her job and threw me out.

"What's that little piece of goods doing in my house?" she yelled at Raymond.

"It's Cheryl," he said.

"Who's she?"

"My girl."

"Ain't she got a last name?" she yelled.

She couldn't seem to talk in a normal tone of voice. Meanwhile, I was busy getting my clothes straight and getting out of there.

"Stiggall," he said.

"Harold Stiggall's kid?"

"Might be," he said.

"Because if she is any kin to Harold Stiggall, she is bad news. That man is locked up in the penitentiary. And for good reason."

"Well, she ain't Harold."

"I don't want to see her in this house ever again."

When his mother wasn't looking, Raymond mouthed the word "Denny's," and I was out of there. I had counted on sleeping at Raymond's, but that was before I met his mom. I telephoned Dolores on my cell, and she snuck me into her house the next couple of nights after her mom went to bed, but she said her mom would call Gladys if she found me. So, I said to myself, "I can't keep this up. I got to see my dad. I don't care if he *is* in the hole. He's got connections on the outside, in that restaurant business he used to work in. Counterfeiting is just a sideline. He'll find me some place to live, safe from Gladys."

So, I took the bus to Rodeo, which is a one-horse town in the middle of nowhere about ten miles from Halifax Prison. I hadn't spent much of the money I'd lifted off of Gladys. So, I had bus fare for the trip, about a hundred dollars for food, and a metal frame bed in a rundown storefront the town called a hostel.

By then, I had started using a fake name, Doris Fernandez, that's my real mom's name. I figured Gladys had alerted every police station in California to arrest me for making off with her three hundred dollars. She'd also cut off service to my cell. I tried a couple of times to call Dolores on a pay phone, but I got the machine every time. I did get Raymond to pick up once, but he was in a rush. Didn't ask me nothing about myself. I felt more lonesome after I hung up than before I called. I had to keep telling myself I was going to see my dad. Otherwise, I might have given up.

I called the prison from a pay phone about fifteen times, but every time I got put on hold and ran out of change before anybody picked up. Finally, I found a bus that went out to Halifax. When I got to the visitor's center, the guard told me I would have to write a letter to the inmate I wished to visit and that somebody from the prison would send me a form to fill out.

So, back in town, I started to write my letter:

> *Dear Dad.*
>
> *Guess who. I need to see you bad. I've run off from Gladys who was about to ship me off to juvie.*

But then I stopped. They'll read this, I thought. They always read his mail. The minute I mail this letter, I'm toast. So, I held off.

By then, I'd met Jackie, a skinny lady with that white dried-up kind of skin and a mound of messy red hair. Jackie waited tables at the Rodeo Roundup, where I ate what meals I could afford. I must have looked lonesome because sometimes she would come over to my table when business was slow and shoot the breeze.

One day after I'd been in Rodeo a couple of weeks, she said, "We're looking for a dishwasher. You ever washed dishes?"

"All my life," I said.

"You eighteen?"

"Sure," I lied, "And I need the money."

"You're hired," she said looking hard in my face. "But I gotta ask, what's a kid like you doing in this dump of a town?"

I told her I was a relative to an inmate out at the prison, and I kept hoping to see him, but they never let him out for visiting. Which was true.

It didn't take long for Jackie to get my drift. One day after I'd been washing dishes for a couple of weeks, she sidled up to where I was standing at the grungy old dishwasher and whispered so management couldn't hear, "If you make it worth my while, I'll see to it you get to visit that relative of yours."

"How much we talking about?" I asked.

"A hundred bucks."

"Twenty," I said.

"Well, since you're just a kid, I'll make it twenty-five. What's his name?"

"Before I tell you, you need to know he's in the hole."

She thought a minute.

"In that case," she said, "it's fifty."

"Twenty-five," I said.

"Look, honey, it costs extra to get him out of there."

We settled on thirty.

"You only get the money if I see him," I said.

"Fair enough," she said. "What's his name?"

"Harold Stiggall."

"That's Stick," she said. "My old man knows Stick."

I looked up at her, surprised, though come to think of it, what else would she be doing in Rodeo?

"He an inmate?"

"Nope, he's a guard, and he can fix it."

I looked hard into her face.

"You religious or anything?" I asked.

"Sometimes at Easter."

"Good."

Maybe because she looked so tired under all that mess of hair, maybe because she'd been good to me, I decided to trust her. Besides

I didn't have another plan.

"I need to get him word," I whispered, "that his daughter is in Rodeo and wants to visit him, but it's a secret. And you have to make sure it stays secret."

She nodded.

"Everything's a secret, honey."

I told her my plan was to sign the name Doris Fernandez to the letter asking for a visit so nobody would suspect it was me, then I'd show up. For an extra twenty dollars, Jackie offered to get me a fake ID, which I needed for the forms and to get past the guards.

"You're a smart one," she said. "That Stick is a lucky man to have a daughter smart as you."

It was the first time anybody'd said anything nice to me for ages, and I almost broke out with the whole story. But I just said, "Maybe so. My dad's always bragging on how I'm going to college someday."

"Good job your dad's looking out for you, 'cause you don't want to get stuck here."

"Yeah," I said. "Just make sure you get him word."

"Don't worry, honey," she said. "You'll see your dad."

Look. I know she was making money off the deal, but somehow I got the impression it was more than the money.

While I was waiting for the prison to okay my visit, I put in a lot of hours at the restaurant, pulling in the dough, which I needed 'cause I had emptied my stash paying off Jackie for the ID. After work, she and I often shared a beer and had some good laughs at the customers. There were times I was so lonely I almost told her about Gladys and Raymond and why I was there. I wanted to spill my guts so bad. But I couldn't take the chance. I didn't think she'd rat on me, but if anyone came around looking for me, I wouldn't want her to have to lie. So, I kept my mouth shut. And Jackie didn't pry, which was a really good thing about her.

About that time, she let me know my visit permit had showed up in her post office box, which was the address we used, and I was on my way.

The folks who rode the bus out to prison that day just stared out the windows. Too deep in their own problems to take notice of much is my guess. But I did hear one old girl say to her daughter, "She looks just like a blue-jay, don't she?" referring to the blue spikes Jackie had helped me set in my hair.

I had to laugh when the daughter said back to her, "She looks cool to me."

And compared to some, I reckon I do.

I hadn't seen my dad for about five years, and I was pretty excited. I kept thinking about the times I'd visited him when I was younger. The guards used to tease me and say stuff like, "What you done wrong, little girl? You too pretty to lock up." Stupid shit like that. But the guard that day was one tough-looking bastard.

I had to say it three times, "I've come to see Harold Stiggall," before he even acknowledged I was talking.

"Well, you just got to wait," he finally snapped. "I got to check it out, and I'm busy."

Ten minutes later, he was back.

"You Doris Fernandez?"

I nodded and prayed he wouldn't pick up on how nervous I was.

"I suppose you got ID to prove it?"

I showed him the fake ID and a one-liner from the CDC saying Doris Fernandez was permitted one visit with Halifax prisoner # 383242.

He scrunched up his eyes and stared at it. The line down the middle of his forehead got real deep. I suddenly thought I bet the poor son of a bitch can't read too good, and it boosted my confidence about a hundred percent.

"Well, I guess you're Doris," he finally said, "which means you gotta be searched," and he jerked his head toward the back.

After what seemed like hours, they took me to a dingy little room with a window into another room. The walls were that slimy Army-surplus green, and there weren't any other windows.

At the door, a guard asked me, "You Harold Stiggall's visitor?"

I nodded. He ran his metal detector up and down me.

"OK. Come in and sit here."

I sat down at a wooden table facing the double glass and waited. I kept straining my eyes to see what was on the other side of that glass, but it was blurry, and the room was so still, I didn't hear a thing. All of a sudden, a shape on the other side started moving toward me.

"Daddy?" I called out.

Right then I couldn't hardly stand it, I wanted to see him so bad. But when the shape got close to the glass, I thought, what's going on here? That's not him. For starters, the hair behind the glass, what there was of it, wasn't black. And the face had lines all over it and wasn't smiling. You could always tell it was my dad a mile off from the way he smiled. I could see the mouth was moving, but no sound came out. I kept calling out "Daddy?", and the man kept moving his mouth and not making any sounds. Finally, I made out he was motioning with his hand, and that's when I saw the chains.

The guy with the metal detector said, "Use the phone, kid. That's what it's for. You ain't got forever."

I hadn't even seen the telephone sitting on the table. I was so busy peering through that blurry glass. So, I picked it up, and there for sure was my dad's voice, saying, "Hello, hello," over and over and calling out my name.

"Hi, Dad," I said. "I hardly recognized you."

"I can't believe you're here, baby. All by yourself. How'd you do it?"

"Long story," I said. It was no way to have a real conversation, over the telephone with the metal detector man staring down at me.

"This room's no good," I said. "I need to talk to you in person."

"It's all we got, baby. We gotta make the best of it. Where you been, sweetheart? I been worried sick."

I guess Gladys had written I was missing.

"Never mind," I said. "I'm here now, and I need help."

"Sure, honey."

I had to laugh.

"Oh boy, where do I start? I need a place to live. I need money, so I can go back to school. I need a daddy who's not in the goddamned prison."

"I know, sweetheart, but that's where your daddy's stuck. Anyway, I got you a place to live, and money's no problem."

I brightened up.

"Where?" I asked.

"You're not gonna like this, honey, but the only option is you gotta go back to Gladys."

I couldn't believe he said that.

"No way," I said. "You got to be kidding me. I went to all this trouble to get away from that bitch and get myself up here to see you, and you tell me I got to go back?"

"I know she pulled all that religious crap on you and locked you up and stuff, but things have changed."

"You traitor," I hissed. "Is that the best you can do?"

"Cut that out," said the metal detector, "or you're outta here."

"No problem," I said, and I walked toward the door leaving the phone sitting on the table. But I stopped. And when I turned around, there were his eyes staring through that godawful glass right at me, and his mouth was moving. I just couldn't leave. So, I went back and picked up the phone.

"Okay, Daddy, I'm not walking, but going back to that bitch is out."

"Trust me, baby. She's a different woman. She's given up on Jesus, and she wants you back."

"How come? She using again?"

"Course not."

I could tell from his voice he was lying.

"That's it. And I got to take care of her, right?"

"You gotta have a home, honey. At least till you graduate. I got plans for you, little girl. You are one smart kid. You're going to be my college girl. But you can't do it all by yourself. Gladys is all you got right now."

"No," I said. "No, no, no, no, no!"

"Please," he was begging. "I got nowhere else to send you. I can't just let you run off. I'll never see you again. You gotta do this for me. You're my little girl."

I just sat there watching while he kept on begging and begging. He looked so pathetic sitting there in his denims with his gray comb-over and the chains bunched up around him, talking into that phone. It was like I was seeing him for the first time.

I sat there for a long time thinking it over.

Then I finally said, "Okay, Dad, you win."

"You'll do it? You'll go back?"

I nodded. You should have seen his smile. Like old times, all over his face, but his eyes looked sad. I'll never forget it as long as I live.

Poor old man, he doesn't know from nothing. If I was to go back to Gladys, that would be the end of me. When she starts using, she fucks up everything and everybody in sight. I'd be scoring coke for her, picking up fake script all over the place, bouncing checks for her, cleaning up her mess.

So, that's it. Time to hit the road again. But before I go, I need to swing by Rodeo Roundup and say goodbye to Jackie.

She looks up when I walk in and nods to a booth. I slide in next to her on the slick plastic cushion. Luckily, the place is empty.

"How'd it go, kid?"

"Great."

She gives me a look.

"Great? You sure?"

"Yeah. But I have to take off. I came by to thank you."

She sits up straight.

"Like you said before, I don't want to get stuck here."

She pulls me up against her. I can smell the cooking grease on top of her perfume. And it's all I can do to keep from crying.

"That man I saw in there, he ain't my daddy. I don't know what they did with my daddy. But what was left after they finished ain't anybody I know."

She nods.

"They do that."

Then she tightens her grip on me.

"Just remember, you got this far all on your own. You'll make it."

Maybe I will. I figure I'll head north, find a job, talk my way back into some school. But right this minute, wrapped up in those skinny arms, I don't feel like going nowhere.

Trading Houses

Steel Toe Review, Issue 26, 2017

I was at Caroline Overby's house, sewing clothes for her dolls, when out of the blue I heard, "Goddammit, where the hell is Fanny?"

A man wearing a button shirt and a tangled purple tie walked in. His hair was white, and he wasn't wearing shoes.

"Oh," he said, in this really polite kind of voice. "I didn't know you had company, Caroline."

He didn't look at me.

"I'll go find her myself."

He tripped on my book bag on his way out, nearly falling.

"Goddammit!"

And he was gone.

"Who's that?" I asked.

Caroline was concentrating on cutting a piece of green satin fabric with pinking shears and didn't look up.

"That's Daddy," she said.

"Oh."

Caroline's daddy owns the mill. I know that because practically everybody in town works for him including my daddy. It's a cotton mill, and they make uniforms for our soldiers in Korea.

That's when Caroline whispered, "I'm planning to trade houses with you. It's a secret."

I stared.

"What do you mean?"

"I'll live in your house, and you'll move here."

"Why?"

"I like your house better."

Now that made no sense. Caroline's house was a mansion, solid white, with marble columns out front. I'd been looking up the hill at that big white house and pretending I lived there ever since I could remember.

My house is little. No upstairs. The living room feels crowded with just a sofa, two chairs, and the Victrola. No dining room. We eat in the kitchen. Mama and Daddy sleep in one bedroom. I share the other with my sister Becky. She's nine.

Caroline was the prettiest girl in my fifth-grade class. She had long red hair, and she wore a different dress every day.

We sometimes walked the two blocks to my house after school, but she'd never invited me to hers until that day. Linwood, her chauffeur, picked us up from school in a black Cadillac and drove us, like two princesses, up the hill to Caroline's house. The marble columns were cool and smooth on my fingers as I passed by.

When we got inside, the first thing I noticed was the quiet. Like nobody lived there. And it smelled like lemons.

"Come on," Caroline said, "my room's upstairs."

We were in the front hall, as big as my living room. No furniture except for a table where they put the mail. And so quiet.

"Can I look around down here first?" I whispered.

There were three living rooms on the first floor. Three. The biggest one on one side of the hall had four sofas—I counted them, and lots of chairs with velvet seats, like the ones in the museum in Williamsburg. It didn't look like anyone ever sat in that room. On the other side of the hall was another big living room with black shiny tables and vases with dragons painted on them.

"That's the Chinese room," Caroline told me.

The third living room was painted yellow, with lots of windows. All the furniture was white, and there were rows of flowers just outside the glass doors, which were open. It smelled like summer in there even though it was only March.

"This is the sunroom," Caroline said.

Just imagine.

Every single room, even the kitchen, had wall-to wall-carpets, which made them so quiet, I felt like tiptoeing.

Upstairs, you'd go into one bedroom, and it would lead to another one and then another one. You could get lost in all those rooms. The beds had fluffy quilts and stacks of pillows. It didn't look like anybody ever slept in any of those beds, they looked so clean and tidy.

"Which is your mama and daddy's room?" I asked Caroline.

"Mama sleeps in there." She pushed open the door, and I got a glimpse of a white filmy bedspread, maybe organdy, and somebody in the bed. Caroline closed the door fast, before I could see more.

"Daddy's up there."

She pointed to the ceiling.

"What's up there?"

"His room. Mama won't let him smoke down here."

That's how I found out there was a third floor, but we didn't go up there. I wanted to, but I felt funny asking.

Caroline's bedroom was huge. Over the bed was a baby blue, quilted canopy, and in the middle of the room was a giant table full of drawing paper and a bucket of brushes and jars of oil paints. Two walls had murals on them. On one, horses were racing, with jockeys on their backs in red caps. On the other, a girl with blond hair was smelling tall blue flowers in a garden.

"Daddy asked some famous artist he knows to paint them," she said. "It took him forever."

Caroline had a real kitchen in her room with a stove and a refrigerator that made ice. And there was a Singer sewing machine just like my mama's. I wanted that room. I wanted the whole house.

I thought she was fooling, but the very next week when we were at my house, she asked me again, "Wouldn't you like to trade houses?"

I looked at the scissors and the pot of glue and the colored paper all over my double-decker bed and said, "Who wouldn't? But why do you want to?"

"Your house is small. I like it. It's cozy."

"But you live in a mansion, and you have a kitchen in your room and a sewing machine."

She was staring out the window.

"I know. But here's what we'll do." Her voice sounded far away. "You will live there, and we can cook and sew whenever you ask me over after school."

"Your daddy won't like it."

"I bet he would if he could see your house."

I tried to imagine the owner of the mill, barefoot with a purple tie, in my little house.

"So. We're going to trade," Caroline said.

"You're making fun of me," I said.

"No. I mean it."

I didn't believe her, but I wanted to. I wanted the room with the red ceiling and the one with big ocean waves painted on the wall and her mama's room with the organdy bedspread. Wouldn't Mama love that room? It was crazy how much I wanted that house.

The next time Caroline came over, she told me her daddy was picking her up.

"Here?"

"Yeah."

"Not Linwood?"

"I asked Daddy to come after me today."

"I better tell Mama."

But I didn't have time because it was already five o'clock, and the doorbell was ringing.

Caroline ran to open it. He was wearing a gray suit this time with a vest and shiny black shoes. I almost didn't recognize him.

"Well, hello," he said with a big smile. "You must be Lorna."

"Won't you come in, Mr. Overby?"

It was my mother, and I'd never seen her so jittery. Her hair was tied back with a scarf and her apron, which she was pulling over her head, had grease stains. The whole house smelled like ham.

"Thank you, ma'am," Mr. Overby said in this really polite voice, "but I'll just collect Miss Caroline here and be off."

"I'm not ready, Daddy," Caroline said. "I have to get my stuff. You come in."

He looked like he didn't know what to do.

Then Mama said in a polite voice I didn't recognize, "Can I get you something to drink while you wait, Mr. Overby?" She'd taken off the scarf and was trying to smooth her hair into place.

"No thank you."

He just stood there for a minute staring at the blocks my sister had spread all over the living room floor like he'd never seen blocks before. Then, very carefully, he picked his way around them, trailing after Caroline. We all crowded into my room. Caroline sat on the lower bunk bed, picking her drawings out of the mess and sliding them into her book bag. Mr. Overby stood in the doorway, holding his hat. My room had never seemed so small.

Caroline smiled up at her daddy.

"Isn't this a cute house?" she said.

"Yes, indeed," he said. "Now, let's go."

And he headed out.

Just before he reached the front door, he stumbled into the three-legged footstool Becky had used as the base of a tower of blocks and fell smack down on the floor.

"Oh, Mr. Overby, I am so sorry."

Mama took his arm and tried to pull him up. I thought for a minute she might cry. He pulled himself to his feet, breathing hard, his white hair in his eyes. There was a funny smell I didn't recognize.

"Don't worry," he said to Mama. "It's my fault. I'm so clumsy."

Before that day, Caroline had been mostly a school friend. But suddenly, she was asking to come play at my house after school at least twice a week. We painted and played Monopoly like other kids, but more and more, Caroline harped on the subject of changing houses. Like all the time. Like it was really going to happen.

"I'll bring my easel to my new room," she would say, "but none of the other stuff. I can play with that when I visit you."

"Won't you miss your kitchen?"

"I won't have to. Fanny will give you stuff, and we can make brownies."

She was so serious about it. She pulled me right in. But it wasn't hard. All I had to do was imagine myself in that sunroom.

"What will you do with the mirror room?" she asked.

"I'm going to keep my clothes in there," I said. "Then when I try them on, I can see exactly how I look."

"You'll have lots of clothes to try on," she said, "because I won't be bringing many dresses to my new house. I want you to have them."

"Really?"

All those dresses, a different one every day.

"And you'll have Fanny."

"What about Fanny?"

"She'll be there," she said. "She'll cook you anything you like for dinner."

"Steak and French fries?"

"Every night if you like."

"Won't you miss having a cook?" I asked.

"She's an old grump," Caroline said. "You're welcome to her. Besides, Mama will cook for Daddy and me. And we'll eat together in the kitchen. And afterwards, we'll go to the living room and watch TV together."

"We don't have a TV," I reminded her.

"Daddy will buy us one."

Sometime that spring, Becky started complaining that blocks were missing.

"Look under the bed," Mama said.

"I did. It's the short ones that I really need. Somebody's stealing them."

"Don't be silly," Mama said. "Who'd steal blocks? I'll help you look."

But the blocks weren't anywhere. And Becky's favorite paper dolls also disappeared. And a Mary Poppins book.

Then one afternoon, I saw Caroline putting my *Anne of Green Gables* into her book bag.

"You want to borrow that?" I asked.

She smiled.

"I've read it. I'm just helping you move."

"Helping me how?"

"I thought it would be nice for you to have some of your things already in your room when you move."

That's when I knew.

"The blocks. That was you."

For a minute, she just stood there staring at *Anne of Green Gables* like she'd been caught. But then she giggled and dropped the book in her bag.

"You can't do that," I said.

"Why not? We're changing houses really soon."

"It's just pretend," I said.

"No!"

The way she said it scared me.

"Okay," I said. "You can take my things, but don't take Becky's."

Why didn't I tell Mama about all this make-believe? She'd have nipped it in the bud for sure. That's why I didn't tell her.

The next time Linwood came to pick Caroline up, he was carrying a bag with Becky's blocks. Mama thanked him, but after that, she told me I couldn't invite Caroline to our house any more.

"But she's my best friend."

"She took Becky's blocks without telling you. What kind of friend is that?"

"She brought them back."

I didn't tell her about the book.

"That's not good enough."

"Please," I begged. "She won't take anything else. I promise."

"I should call her mother," Mama said.

But she never did. I think she was afraid of Mr. Overby.

So, after that we went to Caroline's house. And that suited me just fine.

"Let's play in a different room every time I come over," I suggested.

She kissed me on the cheek.

"That's a good idea. Then you can tell your mama about every room. That will make her want to move here."

It made me feel like a cheat, letting her go on that way. But I wanted really badly to see those rooms.

So, we roamed the house.

"Sit here," she'd point to a chair. "Isn't the velvet cushion dreamy?"

She dragged me to a large picture window.

"Look out there, Lorna. Did you ever see such pretty daffodils?"

We played old maid on the dining room table in the red room and scattered Monopoly money all over the blue velvet lounge chair in the room with violets on the wallpaper.

One time, she took hold of my hand and rubbed it all over a soft, soft bedspread in one of the empty rooms.

"Try it," she said. "It's like sleeping on a cloud."

So, I climbed up on that satin-smooth bedspread and lay there, smelling the lemon smell that was everywhere.

We never went up to the third floor.

Sometimes I heard somebody walking around up there, but I didn't ask.

Mrs. Overby showed up every once in a while, dressed in a pastel dress and wearing hats with a veil.

"You girls having fun?"

That's what she always said.

"Yes ma'am," I'd say.

But Caroline would just watch her mother and not say a thing. After a few minutes, Mrs. Overby would disappear out the front door.

I was dying to spend a night in Caroline's house, to lie in her canopied bed and whisper secrets, to eat breakfast together. So, when she invited me for a Saturday night, I couldn't wait.

She met me at the front door.

"Close your eyes," she demanded.

I could feel her hand tugging me forward, through the front hall, up the stairs to a flat soft carpet. I remember hanging onto one of

Mama's shopping bags, stuffed with my pajamas and toothbrush, and trying not to stumble. Finally, I heard a door open.

"Surprise!"

I peered through the dark. All I could see were lights. Tiny lights.

"Where are we?"

"Ghost Hollow."

Her voice was all quivery.

All of a sudden, I wanted to go home.

"I can't see."

"Come in," she whispered.

I took a step and bumped my shin on something sharp.

"Come on, Caroline. Turn on the light."

"Hush! Wait a minute."

I smelled something familiar, but I couldn't figure out what.

"Turn on the light!"

This time my voice was loud.

And there we were, in Caroline's brightly lit bedroom. The curtains were pulled tight. And there were candles on the sewing machine, the stove, the refrigerator, tall red ones in silver candleholders. All burning.

"You spoiled it," she said. "It was going to be so much fun, sitting here in the dark, telling ghost stories. I've been planning it all day. But you spoiled it."

"I'm sorry. I'm scared of ghosts."

She laughed. Her old laugh.

"Then I guess it worked."

And she hugged me.

We blew out the candles and started working on the jigsaw puzzle that was half finished on her drawing table. We never mentioned the candles again.

In the meantime, Caroline kept asking to come to my house.

At first, I made excuses. "Mama's taking me shopping" or "Becky has a friend over and Mama says the house is too crowded."

But finally, I had to tell her.

"Mama doesn't want you to come to our house anymore."

We were on the playground during recess, off to ourselves.

Caroline's face went white.

"Why?"

"Because you took Becky's blocks and stuff."

"But you know why I did that."

"Sure, I do, but they were Becky's."

"I am going to move to your house."

"That's all pretend," I said.

She was staring at me in a way I didn't like.

"It's not pretend. I want your little house. We made a deal. You promised."

I didn't know what to say. I knew I hadn't made any deal, but I had led her on.

"Why don't we skip rope?" I finally said and headed off to join some girls in my class.

"Traitor!" she yelled.

I acted like I didn't hear her. But I felt just awful.

I woke up to sirens. And the smell of smoke.

I shook Becky. I was sure it was our house. The sirens were so close.

We ran to the living room and out the front door. Mama and Daddy were standing out on the sidewalk.

"Where is it?" I yelled over the screaming sirens.

Daddy pulled me close and pointed to mountains of gray smoke against the sky. You could see the smoke even though it was night because of the big red flames shooting up inside it. And my eyes were burning.

"Is it . . .?"

I couldn't say it.

Suddenly our street was full of people, some in bathrobes, some barefoot, some zipping up their jackets over pajama bottoms. I could hear them yelling at each other over the sirens.

"Is it the old man?"

I felt sick to my stomach.

"Sure, looks like it."

"You think they're in there?"

"Caroline?" I was crying.

"Let's go inside."

It was Mama's voice in my ear.

But I wouldn't budge. I kept staring at the red flames and smelling the smoke and hearing the sirens and crying.

The next morning, we all turned up to gaze at what was left of the house. The walls looked like big hunks of charcoal with sooty marble columns in front. The inside was full of water, and there was this awful smell. I stood there looking at the black, smoky mess and thought about the sunroom and the organdy bedspread and Caroline's sewing machine and all those quiet, quiet rooms.

"Don't cry," Daddy said. "I heard they got everybody out."

But I just kept crying.

That afternoon the Fire Chief drove all over town yelling through a megaphone that the Fire Department had saved everybody. The family was in the hospital recovering. Daddy took me to the hospital, but they wouldn't let me see Caroline. I sent her a card, but she didn't answer it.

There was a lot of gossip about the fire. But the rumor that Mr. Overby's leg was cut off turned out to be true. It had been so badly burned they had to amputate. Mrs. Overby was in seclusion, they said. Nobody knew where.

I didn't see Caroline again. Somebody said they were sending her to some place down in South Carolina.

Everybody in town has a theory about what started the fire.

Some blame the electric wires. Some claim grease caught on fire in the kitchen. There are also rumors.

The old man was smoking in bed.

The old man was drunk again.

Serves him right, the old bastard.

Mr. Overby told the newspaper, "I don't smoke in bed. Period."

He said it was arson, and he wanted to get to the bottom of it.

That's what scares me. Because they'll start looking around. And maybe they'll look in Caroline's room. And maybe . . .

I keep telling myself it was an accident. Of course, it was.

But then I wake up at night, and I'm back in her room with those candles. And I ask myself, suppose it wasn't an accident. Suppose . . .

But she wouldn't. Would she? She was mad because I wouldn't trade houses. She called me a traitor.

I want to tell Mama. I want to tell her everything. About Caroline's plan. About how I led her on. About the candles.

But suppose I tell her. She'll say she has to call the Fire Department. I know she will. And then something awful will happen.

And it will be my fault.

The Red Room

upstreet, no. 12, 2016

Anita was slicing smoked salmon when the knife slipped from her fingers and clattered to the floor.

Her daughter Kate looked up from *The New Yorker*.

"Hey, careful with that thing."

Anita gripped the edge of the kitchen table for a minute then resumed cutting the salmon. She could hear Emma, her five-year-old granddaughter, talking to the cat in the front yard.

"Are you okay?" Kate asked.

"I'm fine."

"You're sure?" Kate asked. "Your hands are shaking."

Anita looked down at her hands, dull white against the pink-orange of the fish, the flesh loose and flecked with brown spots.

Kate put down her magazine.

"Do you feel dizzy?"

But before Anita could respond, Ted burst into the room.

"Oh good. Lox. Let me do the sour cream and chives."

Ted, her burly, good-natured son-in-law. She smiled with relief.

"You can do the drinks while I finish up," she told him.

She wasn't sure her hands, still trembling slightly, could manage the wine.

Ted carried the tray of drinks and hors d'oeuvres to the living room. Anita loved this room, the red paint, the floor to ceiling bookcases, crammed haphazardly with books, books on top of books. It would have been claustrophobic with all that red and all those books except for the wall of windows on the far side, which opened out to the canyon of green-gray sage and live oak.

"Cheers," she said and touched Kate's wine glass with her own.

Kate raised her glass to Ted then took a deep swallow of red wine. Anita tried to catch her eye, but her daughter's cell phone buzzed, and she disappeared into the hall.

The call wasn't important, one of the nurses from work arranging a schedule change. It could wait. But Kate was thankful for the chance to escape. She didn't want to see the wine shivering in the glass as her mother held it up with both hands for a toast. Didn't want to meet her mother's eyes. Light blue like her own. And troubled.

She saw patients all the time with symptoms like this. It was routine to run through the differential diagnosis: Lou Gehrig's, Parkinson's, stroke. It was routine to ask the questions. Why not now? She didn't want to think about it.

But at the end of the evening, as they were leaving, Kate said, "Maybe you should see a doctor."

"Yeah? What do you think?"

"I don't know. It's probably nothing. But I'd check it out."

Best advice. Mistake to treat your own family. Besides she was a nurse, not a doctor.

But she suspected it wasn't good. Not good, and she didn't want to think about it. So, she concentrated on Ted's amiable chatter as they drove home and listened, with a full heart, to her daughter's sleepy monologue in the dark back seat.

After they left, Anita piled up the chocolate-smeared dessert plates and carefully carried them to the kitchen. Dirty pots and pans everywhere, although Ted, bless him, had put the dinner plates and cutlery in the dishwasher. Not Kate. Anita remembered her as a child, setting the table, begging to stir the cake batter, carefully chopping the vegetables. Eager to show her competence. Nowadays, she sat absorbed in her thoughts or chatted on her cell phone, oblivious to the bustle around her. A handsome woman, tall, regal really, with Anita's sharp nose and Roy's smooth black hair, expensively cut. Something about her made it hard to ask for help.

Roy. She missed him, now, this minute, missed his easy chatter, his joy at the taste of food, his warmth. She'd not gotten used to this dark hole in her life. God knows she'd had time to prepare. Congestive heart failure was like that. Her daughter had been there for her then, answering her questions, interpreting the doctor's evasive explanations, analyzing each medication.

Until one day, he just stopped breathing. One minute he was in the hospital bed, the great lump of him, snoring softly, his mouth open, his face gray. And the next moment, it all stopped.

And Kate was there, taking charge, asking questions—autopsy? cremation? memorial service? Paperwork, tons of it—making things happen. It was what she was good at, Anita realized, being decisive when it really mattered. So, she didn't clear the table or dress the salad. So what?

But after all the decisions were made and the rituals survived, Anita had faced down the empty house alone. Her daughter was occasionally present, efficient, whisking away her father's clothes, disposing of the hospital bed and wheelchair, informing the bank and insurance companies of his demise. But whenever Anita burst into unexpected tears, at the sudden sight of Roy's battered copy of Ulysses or his hand-carved walking stick, Kate would busy herself with some task until her mother could stifle her crushing grief, a grief that never really abated, even after she recovered her balance and moved on with her life.

The internist, who had performed her routine checkups for twenty years (but who never recognized her outside the office), ordered blood tests and a CT scan, then referred her to a Dr. Newman, a neurologist. He spent several sessions watching her move, asking questions, probing, and poking, then called her in for a consult.

"How are you, Anita?" he began, looking down at the pile of papers he was pretending to sort. Dr. Newman was almost as old as she was, with gray wispy hair, a worn white coat, and the kind of bushy eyebrows that seem ready to jump off the faces of old men.

"I don't know," she said, as she faced him across an impersonal metal desk. "How am I?"

She could feel the fear squeezing her chest.

"The good news is we can rule out heart disease, stroke, ALS."

"And?" She braced herself.

He looked at her with the weary eyes of a man who had delivered bad news too many times.

"It's very likely you are in the early stages of Parkinson's disease."

She sat very still, clutching her cold hands in her lap to stop the shaking. She knew what those words meant, and she knew where the symptoms led. With proper care and a lot of luck, she could live for years. But her death sentence now had a subject and verb.

"Do you understand?" Dr. Newman said, speaking slowly as though to a child.

"How can you tell?"

She stared at his eyebrows, not listening, as his voice droned on about her gait and her tremors.

"Are you all right?" he finally asked.

"How long?"

He smiled.

"You're in the early stages. No guarantees, but it's possible you have years ahead of you."

She didn't move.

"Look," he said. "Do you have anyone close by? Family? You need to talk to somebody."

"A daughter, I suppose," she said.

Standing on the broad redwood deck of her childhood home, Kate told herself, I can do this, I did fine when Dad died. She noticed that the brown paint on the front door was chipping. And she wondered, for the first time, who did the repairs now that her father was gone. She raised her hand, reluctantly, to knock.

Anita stood in the doorway. Kate checked her first impulse to step back. Her mother's short dark hair, recently cut and colored, and her bright purple turtleneck exaggerated the too-white face, accentuated the lines above her carefully painted mouth and the furrows in her forehead.

"Mom?"

Anita's eyes were liquid. Kate felt her body stiffen. She could tell her mother waited to be touched. The invisible audience expected it, the crowd of critics who decreed the complex rules of mothers and daughters. But she couldn't. All that raw need stopped her.

"What's wrong, Mom?" she asked.

What's wrong with me? she thought.

Following her mother into the living room, Kate fought the impulse to rush to the bank of windows and escape the stifling familiarity of this room. Instead, she eased herself onto the old blue velvet horsehair sofa next to her mother's rigid body.

"What's wrong, Mom?" she asked again.

"I'm sorry," Anita finally said, pointing to her wet cheeks.

"Don't be sorry," Kate said. "Just tell me."

She didn't mean to sound cold.

Anita wiped her eyes.

"It's Parkinson's."

"Are you sure?"

So, this is it, Kate thought. It has a name.

"Doctor Newman seemed to be."

"I'm so sorry, Mother," Kate whispered.

She knew it was inadequate from the way her mother sat there, holding herself so still, saying nothing. But she didn't know what else to say. She knew too well the touch and smell of illness and death. She could handle that. What she feared was the weakness, the emotional messiness that would transform this tough, vibrant force in her life, her mother. She was afraid, but not for her mother. She was afraid for herself.

Anita broke the silence with a little laugh.

"I need your expertise."

Her voice was suddenly steady, her expression resolute.

"Of course." This was easier. Kate was at home with the facts of Parkinson's, and she walked her mother through each symptom, each stage of the disease, each possible treatment. Anita took it in, asked questions, nodded attentively. They explored the best way to tell Emma.

Finally, Anita said, "One of these days, we'll have to do something about the house."

"Right," Kate felt relieved her mother had brought it up.

She glanced with a faint sense of distaste around the room, at the stacks of books piled on the scarred walnut coffee table, at the jumble of empty CD cases on the floor, at the red paint, faded here and there by the sun, chipping near the ceiling, and said the first thing that came to her mind.

"Mom, you don't need to do this right now, but while you're feeling healthy, you might start thinking about getting the place in shape."

Her mother's startled expression surprised her. She had meant to sound gentle, concerned.

"What do you mean, getting it in shape?"

"Forget it. I'm sorry I brought it up."

As they said goodbye at the front door, Anita leaned toward her daughter, arms slightly open. Kate's first impulse was to turn away, to escape her mother's unspoken need. Instead, she hugged her, but her embrace was swift and perfunctory, leaving her mother's arms hanging awkwardly at her sides.

From the beginning, Kate had not been an easy child to cuddle. She was too quick, too restless for sitting in laps. A little hummingbird. As soon as she learned to walk, she was off like a shot, poking into the far reaches of the playground, jumping out of her stroller to race ahead of her parents, refusing help with her clothes. And Anita loved it, encouraged her little girl's feistiness, the way she outwitted her playmates and bossed them around.

But what Anita thought about at four in the morning, as she lay staring, dry-eyed, into the darkness, was Kate at five, pulling her up from the kitchen table to wander the depths of the canyon below their house, sometimes on a path, sometimes through the dry gold grass. Kate considering the flowers with a grave seriousness, picking the ones with bright colors, delighting in the common names—blue dicks, pussy ears, purple self-heal, fiery red Indian paintbrush, crying when Anita threw them—wilted—into the trash. But what Anita remembered the best was the touching. The silky softness of Kate's hand, the warm body brushing against her, the thin arms unexpectedly circling her waist.

"I hate her already."

Anita sat next to Kate, once again on the stiff blue sofa, waiting for a real estate agent to appear. A woman named Wendy Green.

"Jesus, Mom, she's a friend. If you're going to be rude, I'll call it off."

Of course, she wanted to call it off. But instead, she said, "No. I'm sorry. I'll be good."

"Don't worry. She's just here to figure out what the house is worth and maybe make suggestions for getting it in shape for the market."

"I'm not ready for that."

Her voice was sharp.

"I know. But you've said yourself you have to sell it sometime."

"Right. Sometime."

And as it turned out, Wendy Green was not the nightmare Anita had feared. Like most real estate agents, she exuded a brisk false cheer, but she also admired things about the house Anita loved: the mimosa tree out front, the window seat in the study where you could watch the shade shifting on Mount Jude (*her* mountain), the skylights that brought the sun into an otherwise dark kitchen.

She felt suddenly embarrassed that she had been so cranky, particularly since Wendy didn't mention selling or prices. She just walked through the house, smiling and admiring everything.

But just as she was leaving, Wendy looked once more around the living room and said, "Once you're ready to sell, Mrs. Jordan, we can store the books and paint in here for the staging, and maybe something more contemporary in the way of a sofa."

"What do you mean?"

Anita could hear the defensive note of her voice as she took possession of the maligned sofa.

Wendy took her hand.

"Buyers like to imagine their own furniture in a place, and that would be a challenge in this room."

Kate smiled at Wendy and nodded.

"No," Anita said.

She and Roy had created this room together while Kate was in Paris after high school, knocked out bricks and replaced them with the wall of glass in the living room. The red paint was Roy's idea. But she had grown to love it, the slight shock of it when people first entered the room, the fiery warmth of it. And Roy had insisted on the bookcases.

"It's a living room," he had said. "And what keeps us living is books."

"Whoever buys it can change the color," Anita said. "I won't have to see it."

"It doesn't work that way, Mom," Kate said.

Anita fought back tears as she shook hands with Wendy. She didn't want to think about ever leaving this house, where she'd brought home her baby and scattered Roy's ashes in the back yard, where she'd planted the mimosa, where—she suddenly realized—she wanted to die.

When Wendy was gone, Kate muttered something under her breath.

"What?" Anita asked.

"Oh, nothing."

Kate looked embarrassed.

"What?"

More sharply.

"Okay. I was thinking about what you told me when I was homesick in Paris."

"What?"

"You said, it's time to put your feelings in your pocket."

Anita looked up, startled.

"I did?"

"Yep. Remember? I wanted you to fly me home."

"I see. You want me to put my feelings about this house, this room, in my pocket."

"Forget it, Mom."

But Anita was no longer listening. She was looking at the way the afternoon sunlight softened the red of the walls and lit up the greens and blues of the seascape in the corner.

Throughout the following year, Anita's trembling grew more pronounced, despite a regimen of exercise and Dopamine. Kate and her family visited Anita regularly. On one Saturday morning visit, as Anita was spooning out ground coffee with jerky movements, Ted turned to Kate and said, "Okay, honey."

Kate looked out the kitchen window at Emma who was bouncing a ball in the driveway. She wanted to hold that picture in the frame forever.

"Mom, we're here about the house."

Anita's body froze.

"No."

Kate had anticipated resistance, hurt feelings. But she had convinced herself that the time to fix up the house was now, before the disease took over completely and forced hurried decisions. Besides, it was a way she could help. Her mother wanted more from her. But this is what she could give.

Kate squeezed Anita's icy hand and let it drop.

"We talked about a retirement community, remember?"

"When I'm ready, not before."

Anita focused cold blue eyes on her daughter.

"Right. But when you're ready, the house has to be ready."

Anita's hand was shaking so badly she knocked over the cream pitcher. No one moved.

"Until I've sold it," she said, "the living room stays just like it is, red, with the books."

Kate looked to Ted for support, but he was dabbing at the cream with a paper napkin. Why am I doing this, she asked herself. Was it to make an extra few bucks on the house sale? Or was it that the color, the clutter of photos and shell collections, even the musty smell of the books disturbed her? For years, she'd dreamed of dismantling the bookcases, throwing stuff away, painting the walls white. Making order of the mess.

"Mom, try to be rational," she finally said.

"No. That's your department," Anita snapped.

Ted dropped the sopping napkins into the trash and left the kitchen.

"Okay." Kate had been stung. "The rational thing is to clear out that room and give it a fresh coat of paint."

For just a moment, Anita sat motionless. And then in a voice so soft Kate could barely hear her, she asked, "Why are you so cold?"

Kate looked up, startled. She had not expected her mother to put words on it. She knew that if she reached out, touched her, said she was sorry, the danger would pass. They wouldn't have to have this conversation.

"I am not cold," she said evenly, not meeting her mother's eye. "I'm practical."

"You can call it that." Anita's lip was trembling. "But you are my daughter, and you are cold to me. You are."

Kate fought a strong urge to get up and walk out. But she forced herself to stay at the kitchen table. They sat together in the silence, not looking at each other.

"I am not cold to Ted," Kate said at last, her voice a studied calm. "Ask him. I'm not cold to Emma."

Am I? she thought. The question chilled her. Her eyes sought Emma in the window frame. The child was standing perfectly still now, not bouncing the ball, but holding it tight against her chest. Kate wanted to rush out the kitchen door, to feel the child's arms around her neck.

"To me," her mother said, her voice breaking. "You are cold to me."

She was right. Kate knew it. But all the same, she felt defensive.

"Maybe you should ask yourself," she blurted out, still not daring to face her mother.

"Ask myself what? Why you're cold?"

Kate nodded.

"I have," Anita said. "I don't know." Her finger traced the outline of spilled cream. "Maybe you should tell me."

Don't cry, Kate thought. I can't handle this if you cry.

"I don't know either," she said. "It's complicated."

"Just tell me one thing," Anita insisted.

Kate paused, then without thinking, the word came,

"Paris."

"Paris?" Anita looked up, a puzzled frown on her face.

"You wouldn't let me come home."

The words, hanging between them in the silence, sounded so adolescent. Kate wished she could take them back, and yet, even after all these years, she still felt the crushing loneliness of that cold, alien city.

"But you came home," Anita said.

"You asked. You don't have to like the answer."

"I don't understand."

"It was your idea, Paris. I was just seventeen years old, just out of high school."

"But you were so self-confident. Ready for adventure. I was so proud of you."

"Dad didn't want me to go. He said I was too young. I heard him."

"He changed his mind."

"*You* changed his mind. And I went because you wanted me to."

"You wanted to study French, honey."

How could she make her understand?

"The language program you signed me up for was too hard. And my roommate would speak only Russian. And it rained, every day. My coat and shoes and hat were soggy all the time."

Anita sat silent.

"And then I got sick, and my room was freezing cold. I didn't want to call you. I wanted so badly for you to be proud of me. But, finally, I couldn't stand it any longer."

"I found you a doctor." Anita's voice was pleading.

"I didn't want a doctor. I wanted to come home." It was an admission of failure that had cost her dearly.

"But that made no sense," Anita said. "I knew you'd be well by the time you got home, and we couldn't afford to send you back."

She tried once more.

"Mom, listen to me. I hated it there. I was sick. I wanted to come home."

"But you got well in a week. I remember. I called you every day."

"I stopped going to classes. Instead, I wandered the streets, window shopping, shivering on park benches, waking up at night unable to sleep."

"What I remember is when you finally came home, you were wearing Paris fashions and speaking French. You brought me a bottle of perfume. I was so proud of you."

"I don't know what else to say."

Anita sat up straight in her chair.

"I was expecting you to tell me something I'd forgotten, something cruel. But you say you treat me this way because I made you stay in Paris and see a doctor?"

Her mother was right. It made no sense. Yet, there it was. She was their only child, and for the first time, she had felt abandoned, excluded, while her parents were home, safe, together, happily painting the goddamned living room red.

She looked away to hide the tears.

"I was miserable. You wouldn't hear me."

Her mother's feathery fingers brushed her arm.

"Oh Katie, I thought I was being practical."

She looked at her mother's square shoulders, her sharp blue eyes, heard the defensive tone of her voice. And for the first time in this tortured exchange, she smiled.

"Right," she said. "Practical. That's not how it felt."

For the next several minutes, they sat facing each other, not touching, each searching for words that would get them back to someplace safe.

Kate found them.

"I miss Dad."

Her voice broke.

Anita smiled.

"I know," she said.

They were on firm ground. Whatever connection had been made, it would do for now.

"I'm sorry," Kate said.

Anita smiled at the apology.

"Thank you," Anita said. "I'm sorry too."

Her voice was clear.

"But no painting the red room."

"Right," Kate said.

But they both knew that decision was far from final.

Act Your Age

The MacGuffin, Spring-Summer 2016, Vol. XXXII, No. 3

After the first day of rafting the Colorado River, Georgia knew she had nothing to fear. Every time a six-foot wall of water reared up and crashed down on her, she ducked her head, clutched the line alongside the raft in a death grip, and laughed out loud. The sun was so hot getting soaked was pure pleasure. And when the waves calmed down, she had the Grand Canyon, mile after mile of red and orange and blue and shiny black cliffs, towering above her. Big horn sheep leaped from ledge to ledge. Lazy blue herons swam the skies. And the boulders? They were hidden too deep in the wide waters of the Grand Canyon to crack the skull of old ladies.

For that was what she was. Seventy years old and riding the rapids. It wasn't as foolhardy as it sounds. Georgia kept herself in shape. It was her only vanity. She swam and hiked and bicycled which meant that her scrawny legs still had a few lumpy muscles, her face was a patchwork of cracks from the open air, and her white hair reflected a faint yellow from the sun.

And the training had worked. She had hiked the seven-and-a-half-mile Bright Angel trail from the canyon's rim to the river with only a skinned knee, a bruised toe, and soaking-wet hiking boots. Toward the end though, her friend Julie, who was thirty-five years younger, begged her to slow down. Her knees were beginning to tremble from the steep downhill trek, the straps of her thirty-pound pack dug into her shoulders, and more than once, she stumbled on the loose red pebbles that covered the path.

"You need a rest," Julie insisted as Georgia wobbled from rock to rock across the streams that feed the Colorado.

"No," she said and kept on wobbling.

Suddenly a lean, sunbaked man wearing faded blue nylon bathing trunks, worn Tevas, sunglasses, and a battered canvas hat appeared on the far side of a stream.

"Nicely done," he said as Julie leaped easily over the rocks toward him. Georgia noticed the deep lines in his forehead and the sad eyes. Mid-fifties at least, she thought.

Julie grinned then turned to Georgia who was beginning a slow, deliberate transverse of the rocky stream.

The man winked at Julie.

"He who hesitates is lost."

Georgia swung out her leg to jump for the nearest rock. Of course, with both of them watching, she splashed knee deep into the water. Julie quickly skipped over the rocks to reach her. But the man in the blue trunks was faster.

"Good try," he said, steadying her. "You'll need that sort of spirit if you're going to raft the Colorado."

He caught Georgia's arm and started propelling her across the stream.

"You can do it. And you're going to love it."

Georgia shook off the man's hand and proceeded alone on waterlogged boots, her wet jeans clinging to her legs. Condescending asshole, she thought.

Back on dry land, the man took off his hat, revealing thinning gray-brown hair, and smiled at Julie.

"I'm Jerry. Your river guide. Welcome to the Colorado."

"One for me. One for you," Jerry said to Lonnie when he returned to the raft.

Lonnie at sixty had been on the river rafting solo and guiding tours for forty years.

He squinted out from under the bill of his faded green baseball cap at the two women, the last of the 18-member rafting party to descend from Bright Angel.

"I take it the pretty one's mine?" he asked.

Jerry laughed.

"Hell no. You get grandma,"

"She up to it?"

"Sure. All she has to do is sit and hang on," Jerry said.

"You're captain this run. You get to keep an eye on her."

"Not so fast. I'm delegating that job to you. My eye's on the other one."

Jerry looked over at Julie unloading her backpack, stuffing her clothes into a large waterproof bag. He liked watching her long slender legs as she carried the bags to the raft.

He didn't look at Georgia. Older folks, women especially, made him uneasy. He didn't want any heart attacks or nasty falls from canyon hiking. No helicopter rescues on his watch.

Several nights later the two guides, in white shorts and fresh tee-shirts, were stretched out in Lonnie's raft, drinking beer.

"She's even better than I thought," Jerry said.

"Who?"

"You know who, asshole. Fearless Julie. You should have seen her this afternoon. Scrambling up the canyon wall to the boulder. Led the pack."

"She married?" Lonnie asked.

"What's that got to do with it?"

"You going to fuck her?"

"Jesus, man, watch yourself." But Jerry laughed. "You never know. I suggested we might try a climb, just the two of us, sometime, and she gave me a look."

"Well, like they say. Danger's a mighty aphrodisiac."

"I think that was Kissinger, and he was talking about power."

"Same thing."

They sat silent a few minutes.

"Everything OK on your hike?" Jerry asked.

"Well, we didn't lose anybody, if that's what you mean."

"You came close?"

"At one point, Georgia looked like she froze," Lonnie said.

Jerry sat up.

"You mean I shouldn't have let her go up on that ridge in the first place?"

"I didn't say anything."

"Come on. That was an easy hike."

"You're the boss."

"Go to hell."

"You might tell Georgia. . ."

But before Lonnie could finish, Jerry had pulled himself to his feet and leaped out of the rocking raft.

"Time to mingle," he said as he joined the cluster of beer-drinking passengers.

Georgia was in love with the Grand Canyon. The cliffs varied from hour to hour, depending on the angle of the sun and the cloud cover. Shiny quartz changed to granite, then to iron-red sandstone, then to black volcanic cliffs that had spilled over in red-hot sheets of lava some time in prehistory and frozen into pock-marked waves. With binoculars tucked into her waterproof shell, Georgia searched for herons, canyon wrens, dippers, red-tailed hawks, peregrine falcons.

She wasn't lonely. She had Julie, whose face had begun to shine a permanent golden-red from an excess of sun and excitement. Occasionally, Julie scaled the canyon heights and jumped from waterfalls without her. But most of the time, her friend stuck close, sitting next to her in the raft, setting up a campsite each evening, sharing bottles of wine.

And so, when Jerry encouraged her and Julie to take a swim in the river on the sixth evening out, she was game. Until that day, he had stressed that they were never—never—to swim in the Colorado, even with life jackets. Occasionally, in calm water, they were permitted to slip over the side of the raft and enjoy a cold bath in the mud-colored water while tightly gripping the line that bound the outside of the raft. And several times in really strong rapids, people were thrown into the turbulent water where they madly waved arms and legs until they were rescued. But no one could just take a swim. The current in the Colorado was too swift and unpredictable. But this was different. Jerry had been talking about it all afternoon as Julie and Georgia crouched on the floor of his raft, running the rapids, soaking up sun. Jerry sat high above them, scowling into the glare, his lean brown arms pulling first one oar, then the other.

The river god, Georgia thought.

He was talking excitedly.

"See, there's this eddy in the river just by the campsite. You catch the current at the shore, and it carries you out into the river and then circles you back home. All you have to do is lie on your belly and ride it."

"Lie on your belly?" Julie asked.

"Here's the deal. Those white foam pads you sleep on? Well, you ride 'em like surf boards."

"What about life vests?" Georgia asked.

"What do you think?" he asked without looking at her.

"It's really safe?" Julie asked.

"Come on. Would I tell you to do something dangerous?"

He grinned at Julie.

"Look, it's not about strength. It's about adventure. We wouldn't let you drown. Too much paperwork."

And he laughed as he turned his face to the river and plowed ahead.

Once they reached the campsite, Julie and Georgia quickly spread out their sleeping bags and headed for the water, white foam pads in hand. The guides lounged in their rafts close by, sipping gin and tonics. The other passengers busied themselves setting up tents.

"Tell us again how we are supposed to do this," Julie asked Jerry.

"OK. Pretend your white pad is a surfboard. Climb up on it, jump into the water, and swim upstream toward that rock."

He pointed to a black volcanic boulder looming out of the water about twenty yards upstream from camp.

"Then ride the eddy back to camp."

Julie waded into the water.

As Julie boarded her makeshift surfboard and pushed off, Lonnie kept his eyes on Jerry.

"What?" Jerry sounded defensive.

"You check the eddy?" Lonnie asked.

"I *know* the eddy."

"Then you know eddies change."

"Not this one. I been here five, six times. Always the same."

"Still."

"When did you get to be such an old lady?"

"It's the old lady I'm thinking about."

Jerry sneered.

"What do you want me to do? Tell her she's too old?"

"Do what you got to do. You're the boss."

"Look at that water. It's a bathtub out there."

Lonnie was silent. They both watched Georgia wade timidly into the river.

"She a good swimmer?" Lonnie asked.

"She doesn't need to be. She's got the jacket. Plus, it's an easy ride."

"It doesn't look like it," Lonnie said.

They watched Georgia struggle with her foam pad. Every time she tried to board it, it slipped out from under her.

Lonnie stood up, his eyes on Georgia.

Jerry was laughing.

"Oh my god, look at her. She's riding the thing like a water bug with wings."

It wasn't a bad description. Minutes before, Georgia had stood knee deep in the water watching Julie plunge into the current, her body full-length on the white pad. Using her arms to paddle, Julie had made a beeline for the black rock. It looked easy. But Georgia wasn't quite ready to abandon herself to the river. Wading carefully, she eased herself onto the pad. She was floating. But just to feel safe, she stretched her foot as deep as the white pad would allow and discovered she could no longer touch bottom. The river had made a choice. As the current picked up speed, she found she couldn't keep her foam surfboard in place. It kept slipping out from under her. Frustrated, she finally gave up and rode the pad crosswise, her arms and legs dangling in the water and the white ends of the pad flapping up on either side of her life vest. She concentrated on heading upstream in the direction of the rock, but no matter how hard she paddled, she couldn't make progress. The current was pulling her away from shore, out toward the middle of the river. Suddenly Julie swept past, several feet in front of her, riding the current downstream. She didn't look happy. But Georgia was too busy paddling and kicking and trying to get back to shore to question her. It was no use. The strong pull of the current sucked her out to the middle of the mudred Colorado. Georgia told herself not to panic. Jerry had promised that the eddy would bring her back to camp. So, she clung to the foam pad and waited for the river to save her.

But the river refused. Instead, it rushed her downstream, past the rafts where the guides were sitting. She got a glimpse of Julie, at the edge of the shore, water dripping from her hair, staring in her direction, her mouth moving without sound. The guides sat motionless, staring in her direction.

"Help!" she squeaked. "Help!"

Her voice sounded tinny. As the river swept her downstream, the scene on shore passed before her like a movie, freeze-framed and silent. Four white, stricken faces stared at the river. The bodies attached to the faces stood stiff on the narrow shore, their arms hanging limp at their sides.

"Help!" she cried again.

But she was past the camp now and moving with the current. No one could hear her. A large pile of rocks rose before her, constricting the flow of water. As the river narrowed, its surface broke into a brown and white froth. The turmoil wasn't fierce enough to be a rapid. Even in her frightened state she knew that. But the water was flowing swiftly, and even worse, she couldn't see what was beyond the rocks. Her mind shut down. She didn't think about her husband or her children. It wasn't real. She couldn't be drowning.

The white pad slipped out from under her. She grabbed it with her right hand and paddled with her left. Rushing water filled her mouth. Nothing to do but let go of the pad. It shot down the river out of sight.

Buoyed by her life jacket, she swept past the rocks and was spit out into a wider, calmer stretch of the river, a piece of flotsam isolated in the Colorado, completely alone.

This isn't happening, she thought.

She started swimming toward shore with all the strength in her body. And suddenly, the soundless film she had been watching exploded with noise and color. Lonnie was racing down the shore, a rope in his hand, his long hair flying. Julie was close on his heels.

"Swim," someone yelled.

She did her best, her arms and legs flailing like straws against the current, but the shore only receded, and she felt herself swimming backward. She struggled to catch her breath.

A rope danced in the air above her. She reached up to grab it, but it disappeared.

She heard someone yell, "Wait for the rope."

But the rope was gone, and when she looked toward shore, she saw only piles of granite. No camp. No people. She turned to face downstream. Boulders framed both sides of the narrowing river. Waves were building. The water rushed her toward the rocks. Too exhausted to swim, she focused on keeping her head out of the water.

And then she was falling, through foam, through waves, through a wall of water.

It was Jerry who pulled her out. She was floating in her orange vest in the calm water below the rapid, blood trickling from her head.

"God, don't let her be dead," he kept muttering. "Please, God."

He had jumped into the nearest raft soon after Georgia swept past, yelling to one of the younger guides to man the oars. They had to wait until she had cleared the rapids before crashing down behind her.

"Oh my god," he whispered, as the white head bobbed in and out of the heaving waves. Then down the rapid they plunged.

As he pulled her into the raft, Jerry thought, she's so light. She doesn't weigh anything. He dragged the inert body over to the plank seat of the raft and stretched it out on its back. Forgetting everything he had learned about CPR, he began to pump on the chest. He had practiced this more times than he could count but never on a real victim. Nothing happened. He felt awkward, inept. I'm going to be sick, he thought, as he leaned over the chalk-white face, but he forced himself to breathe into the slack lips. When he looked up, he saw Lonnie on the fast-approaching shore, teeth clamped tight together, eyes narrowed. He had his arms around Julie, trying to hold her back, but she pushed away from him, screaming, her skin still streaked red from the river mud.

Then Lonnie was towering above him, pulling him off the body.

"Stop. She's breathing. She's out cold, but she's alive."

Lonnie placed a sleeping bag over Georgia and began to rub her arms and legs under the cover.

Jerry straightened up. For the first time, he took in the circle of guides and passengers crowding around the raft, staring at him, silent.

Once on the raft, Lonnie turned Georgia's head, feeling for the cut, which was bleeding more profusely now that she was out of the cold water.

"Poor old girl," he said. "We'll get you out of here."

He pressed his fingers on the wound to stop the bleeding. His fingers quickly colored red.

"We've radioed for the chopper," he told Jerry. "She might wake up before it gets here, but in any case, she has to be evacuated."

The sun had begun to set. The crowd on shore was moving around now, talking in low tones. Jerry sat in the raft, chilled in his wet bathing suit, scanning the skies for the helicopter. He caught a glimpse of Julie and quickly looked away. Her face had turned an ugly shade of white. Her short dark hair stood in wet peaks from her swim.

"She's going to be okay," Lonnie said. "She's breathing."

Julie looked over at the motionless body.

"She's not okay, you motherfucker," she hissed. "She's unconscious. What do you know?"

Jerry kept his eyes on Georgia, willing her to wake up, watching for each breath, straining to hear the chopping of the helicopter. He didn't notice when someone draped a jacket around his shoulders. It didn't stop the shivering.

The first thing she saw was Lonnie's face, close to her, too close. She felt awkward and embarrassed, like she had done something stupid. She raised herself on one elbow.

"Just lie still," a voice said. "You're OK, but you need to stay put. Are you warm enough?"

She could feel her body trembling.

"I don't know," she said.

She looked around. Julie was holding her hand, squeezing it so hard it hurt.

"What's going on?" she whispered.

"You swam the rapids. That's all, but thank God you're okay. I was so scared."

Julie kept squeezing her hand and laughing. Or crying. She couldn't tell which.

Georgia heard something that sounded like a motor, humming louder and louder. Once again, she raised herself up on an elbow. Strong hands pushed her back.

"It's the helicopter," Julie said. "They're evacuating you."

"Oh, God. I feel like a fool." She struggled to get up. "I'm okay. Really."

"Good."

A young woman in a hospital-green shirt was checking Georgia's pulse and heartbeat. She then wrapped her in a cocoon of blankets. Georgia lay back and let the warmth take over. She closed her eyes. That felt better.

"Scissors, gauze, tape," she heard the young woman say.

Was she bleeding? She felt a sting in the back of her head and looked at Julie.

"You must have cut your head on a rock. It's not bleeding much. Don't worry."

The young woman asked her questions. Did her head hurt? Was she hot? Cold? Georgia kept insisting she was fine. Everything worked.

"We have to take her out," the woman said. "Do a complete physical and mental. Make sure she's okay. But from what I can see, she's none the worse for wear."

As she was being carried to the helicopter, she heard someone say, "Think of the story you have to tell your grandchildren."

Go to hell, she thought. And then she thought she had screwed up big time, and she wanted to go home.

Even after the whirring of the helicopter had faded, Jerry remained slumped in the raft, his face in his hands.

Lonnie sat down beside him and whispered, "Look, she's okay. Get a grip."

But then someone was pulling at him, lifting him to his feet.

"Hey man, you saved her. You're a fucking hero."

The passengers were swarming around, giving him high-fives.

He tried to protest, but their noisy congratulations drowned him out.

"What was she trying to do anyway? Jesus, a woman that age, swimming this river. It's crazy," one of the men said.

"What gave her the idea to ride the foam pad that way? I saw Julie. She knew what she was doing."

"Didn't I see her with a beer earlier?"

Jerry looked around for Julie. She was nowhere in sight. He started to explain, to confess his role in the near disaster but stopped himself. Why make it worse? Georgia was okay. What was the harm if they thought he had saved her? He caught Lonnie's eye and raised his eyebrows, in silent question. But Lonnie just shrugged his shoulders and looked away.

Dinner that night was almost festive. Georgia was safe. They were all safe. A disaster had been averted. They drank Jerry's health until he became slightly dizzy with too much red wine. He was feeling better. There would be the report, of course, and he would have to explain what Georgia was doing in the water. A helicopter save was a black mark. But he already had his answer. The eddy was safe. Julie had ridden it. Georgia hadn't . . . hadn't what? Followed his advice? No, that wouldn't do. He'd have to work on it.

After dinner, he wandered up a small hill overlooking the campsite, breathing in the dank river air, naming constellations, trying to block out what had happened. The night was dense black against stars so bright you could almost see by them. But he didn't see Julie sitting on the hill until he nearly stumbled over her. Good, he thought. Get it over with.

He sat down next to her and studied her profile, barely visible in the starlight. The sharp lines of her high cheekbones and pointed nose were blurred, soft even. He suddenly wanted to touch her, to lean against her in the darkness.

"Look, I'm really sorry," he began.

He could hear the need in his voice. When Julie said nothing, he continued.

"I should have gotten into the water myself and shown her how to ride that pad."

Still no response. "It seemed so simple. I mean, you had no problem. You rode that sucker like a pro."

They sat in silence for as long as Jerry could stand it.

He finally blurted out, "Say something."

"Do you know why I'm up here?" Her voice was ice. "I came to see the eddy. Before it got dark, you could see it clearly in the water from up here. And guess what?"

He ducked his head. He didn't want to hear it.

"The fucking eddy doesn't come back to the camp like you said. It goes out to the middle of the river and straight toward the rocks. You didn't check it, did you? You know, I almost didn't make it. I was a college swimmer, and I almost got washed away. That river's a killer. I made it back, just barely, but I was too late to stop Georgia. If anything is wrong with her, I'll never forgive myself."

He reached out automatically to touch her.

"It's not your fault," he said lamely.

She knocked his hand away.

"No. It's your fault," she said. "Yours."

He tried to think of something to say.

"If you'd been acting your fucking age and paying attention to your job, this wouldn't have happened."

Julie's voice cut through him. He felt the wine churning in his belly, and he was afraid he would be sick.

Scrambling to his feet, he mumbled, "I'm sorry."

But Julie wasn't finished.

"You know what I mean, don't you? I don't have to spell it out. I wouldn't have told you this if you hadn't nearly killed Georgia. I'd have let you keep on making a fool of yourself, with me and the next half decent-looking woman who came along. But I'm not worrying about your feelings now. I'm telling you straight out. Act your age."

She was sobbing now.

He found Lonnie alone in the dark on his raft.

"What she say?" Lonnie asked.

It was too painful to repeat the words.

"That bad, huh?"

"The truth."

"She told you the truth?"

"Yeah."

"About the eddy?"

"I'm old."

"Yeah? She said that?" Lonnie laughed. "You'll get used to it."

Jerry suddenly pictured Georgia's inert body, her slack lips, and scrawny, wrinkled arms. He shuddered.

"Never," he said.

Massive Resistance

The Long Story, No. 34, March 2016
Also published in *Spotswood Virginia*,
Stephen F. Austin State University Press, 2021

Massive Resistance was a policy adopted in 1956 by the Virginia State Government to block the desegregation of public schools mandated by the U.S. Supreme Court's 1954 decision in Brown v. Board of Education. Public schools were shut down in several cities throughout the state to prevent desegregation. Although the courts eventually overturned the policy, schools in Prince Edward County remained closed until the 1960s.

June 1957

Bryce Nolan breathed in the sweet scent of new grass as he headed through Harvard Yard. Buds exploded on the dogwoods. Scarlet blossoms crowned the crabapples. Like home. Almost. He glanced down at the brown bag in his dimpled fist. Another beer? Sure. He had time. He was feeling okay. Better than okay. In fact, he could almost forget the phone call last night.

"I just heard from Womack, son."

Oh shit. Just his luck his dad's campaign manager would land a job here as a Dean, snooping around, ratting on him.

"Yeah?"

"Says you're on probation."

"It's okay, Dad. I'll take care of it."

"Says you're skipping class."

Was that all?

"I spent some time in the infirmary. Missed a few classes. Nothing I can't make up."

"I'm disappointed, son."

So, Womack hadn't told him, which meant he didn't know. Bryce felt his plump shoulders relax. Those meetings *had* to be secret.

"You tell mama?"

"Not yet. You fix it, boy. You hear? We can't have your mama worrying about you."

"Yeah, I know." He wondered what she would say, his beautiful mama, if she knew the real reason he was cutting classes.

"You still swimming every day?"

"Yep."

One more lie.

"Good. Gotta go. I'm counting on you. Don't let me down."

But he would. He didn't want to, but he would. It was just too hard to keep it up. Even though the good grades and prizes were the only way he knew to assuage his father's disappointment in the soft, round bookworm that was his son. But now that he was over six hundred miles away, it no longer seemed important to knock himself out for his father's glory.

Back in his room, he tossed the empty beer bottle in the trash and studied his doughy face in the mirror.

"She's a real sweetheart," his roommate Miles had told him. Which was code for not being pretty enough to get dates on her own. "You'll love her."

"Where's she from?"

"Some place in Virginia. Culpepper?"

He knew it. Apple country. A chubby farm girl from Virginia. He glanced down at the loose white flesh rolling over the waistband of his jockey shorts as he squirmed into a navy polo shirt. Who was he to judge? And it was just as well. The pretty ones always had excuses when he telephoned for a second date.

He tugged at the zipper of his madras Bermuda shorts, dug bare feet into his loafers, and reached for his keys.

One for the road?

Better not. He got grabby when he'd had too much. On the other hand, he felt on edge. A short bourbon wouldn't hurt him.

The wind hit him full in the face, warm, humid, as he raced his Buick convertible down Route 16 toward Pine Manor Junior College. He loved that car. He'd had to work hard to persuade his dad he needed it to drive back and forth to Harvard, even though most students didn't have cars. On the radio, Elvis was growling, "I'm all shook up."

Why had he let the old man set him up as the town genius?

He was twelve when he got talked into entering the County Chess Tournament. Everybody else was older. High school slide-rule types, old guys who played in the park.

"Can't I wait 'til next year?" he'd begged his father.

"Are you kidding? Here's the thing, son. They're going to underestimate you. They'll be concentrating on each other, studying each other's plays from earlier tournaments. They won't pay attention to you, even the first time you make a smart move."

"If I get the chance."

"You will, boy. You're sharp. And by the time they've caught on to the fact that you're winning, they'll be too surprised to anticipate your moves."

"And what if I lose?"

"Don't let me hear that loser talk."

And when by some miracle he'd won, there was his father, Roger Nolan, Virginia State Senator, one arm holding him close, the other hand waiving the trophy over their heads, smiling for the photographer. The warmth and the lemony smell of his father's aftershave almost made his pre-tournament nausea worth it.

But later that night at the dinner table, as Bryce sat between his sister Liz—smiling up at him, half-shy and adoring, and his mother who had filled his plate with barbequed chicken and mashed potatoes, his favorites, Roger Nolan said, "You need to work on your Sicilian defense. The State isn't going to be as easy as this one."

He looked at his mother, waiting for her to say something like, this is Bryce's night, let's celebrate. But she just smiled.

And when he lost at the state level, because how could a thirteen-year- old win such a thing, his father was nowhere around.

What was pathetic was he'd tried. He'd tried so hard.

Liz hadn't been saddled with a superlative. "Lucky Liz," he called her. His sweet, sweet sister.

"Fuck champions," he suddenly yelled over the radio, into the wind. The noon sun streamed in the front windshield, half blinding him. Sweat dripped into his eyes. He hit the curve at sixty-five miles an hour. Too fast, he thought, slow down.

"Fuck the bookworm," he screamed. "Fuck the walking dictionary."

But his high-pitched laugh was drowned out by metal smashing, glass shattering, brakes screeching, a horn bleating.

June 1958

Betsy Nolan sat absolutely still in the spindle-backed rocking chair except to lift her hand to turn the pages of *Middlemarch* which lay open on her lap. Her dark hair, streaked with gray, was pulled back from her wide forehead into a bun. Her cheeks were thin, silky. Her large eyes, blue-gray.

If she concentrated on Dorothea and Mr. Casaubon, she could forget for hours at a time. Forget the telephone ringing that June afternoon a year ago. Ringing and ringing. The sheriff's polite voice on the line, asking for the Senator.

"He's not here. I'm his wife. Can you tell me what this is about?"

The fear rising.

"I'm sorry, ma'am, but I must talk to the Senator. Would you please tell me where I can reach him?"

She had given him the office number, the private line, the number in Richmond, every number she could think of. And still the phone kept ringing, and the sheriff kept asking for the Senator. So, when Roger finally came home, explaining that he'd unplugged his phone to write a speech, when he yelled, "No!" into the receiver, when he stared at her, still holding the phone, howling sounds beyond any meaning, she knew.

A year later and she still dreamed about him, Bryce, in the car, swerving, *not* crashing into the tree, running to her, laughing. Feeling herself light, buoyant for the split second before pulling the pillow over her face to stifle the screams.

Fortunately, there were whole days, weeks she couldn't remember. The sleeping pills, the dark rooms. Time lost.

And then the pathetic effort to resume her role as Roger's wife.

"Sweetheart, I need you," he'd said three months after the funeral. "The new governor is coming through to meet some of the school people. There's a small party."

"I don't have anything to wear."

Where did that come from?

"Call Lucile. Have her sew you something new. Treat yourself."

Practical Roger.

So, she'd numbly picked through patterns and ordered several yards of lavender lace to cover a full taffeta skirt and black silk for the top.

The stout Lucile paused to remove several pins she held pinched between her lips.

"You're a dream to sew for," she said. "Waist like a girl, and that dark hair goes so good with this black silk."

She huffed and puffed in Betsy's face, shoving pins into the delicate fabric with swollen pink fingers.

"Miz Nolan, ain't you proud of the Senator, standing up for us like he is?"

Betsy nodded. She wasn't sure what Lucile was referring to and didn't want the burden of finding out.

"Yes ma'am, he's standing firm. And you're the lady for him."

She made her first public appearance six months after the funeral at the dedication of the new high school gymnasium, a graceless brick square of a building, plopped down on a raw field of red earth. She stood next to Roger, shivering in the damp December air, arranging her face to smile up at him while he gave his speech, which she almost completely ignored.

Almost.

But then she heard him say, "Now you and I know that certain people in this town want to use this handsome facility to bring about a mixing of the races."

She was suddenly attentive.

"But I give you my solemn promise . . ."

She looked out over the starchy white faces bobbing up and down, nodding, frowning, and thought, who is this man?

Back home she confronted him.

"That sounded like segregationist talk."

He didn't meet her eyes.

"Well, I've been wanting to tell you, sweetheart, but you've been so, I don't know, distant. It's something of a feather in my cap."

"What is?"

"It's the governor's baby, you know that. 'Massive Resistance.' That's how he got elected."

"How's that a feather in *your* cap?"

But she knew.

"Well, he's asked me to play a leadership role here in Southside."

Her charismatic Roger? The idealistic Harvard student who had pulled her into his orbit and taken total possession of her years ago when she was a Vassar girl? Wooed her with his dark eyes and high cheek bones and cleft chin, his smooth spare body, his lilting southern accent.

"The way we treat the people down South is just wrong," he'd said, and something had to be done about it.

"*You're* fighting integration? You?"

"Not really."

His eyes shifted away from hers.

"Look, honey, I'm representing my part of the state, the folks who elected me."

"I thought you were supposed to lead them."

"Give me time. I can turn it around. You'll see."

He was smiling, watching her now with careful eyes.

"What happened to the man who brought me here after college to 'knock some heads together,' as you put it, and usher in the future?"

Roger flinched.

"Give me a break, Betsy. You know as well as I that you have to get elected in order to make a change."

"And you plan to make a change, as you say, by buying into racist ideas like this 'Massive Resistance'?" she said.

"I can't do anything if I can't get elected," he shot back.

She realized she was too tired to take him on. At just that moment, she no longer cared.

And so, she had quietly, permanently slipped away from the only life that was real to her husband. She avoided political dinners, stopped going to Bridge Club, which she'd always secretly hated, stayed home from the Baptist Church. Florine, the maid, told the visitors, prying do-gooders as well as the genuinely sympathetic, that she wasn't home or was ill. Roger cautioned his curious constituents to be patient, that she was taking the death hard. The retreat to the bland impersonal guest room, to George Eliot and Jane Austen and Henry James, had been gradual. At home, Florine cooked the meals, did the shopping, cleaned the house, without instruction, without asking questions. Liz had her life at the high school. So, once Betsy renounced her role as political wife, there was a vast silence. Initially, she had tried to fill it with projects, a crocheted pillow, a vegetable garden that first terrible summer. The final project, sorting through a large cardboard box of family photos, almost destroyed her.

A faded photo of Bryce, staring, unsmiling, at a birthday cake with six lit candles, his soft cheeks already too round.

"Make a wish," someone shouts. "Quick. Before they go out."

It's Roger, outside the photo, his voice ungentle. There are other faces outside the photo, small boys mostly, dressed in white shirts and brown corduroy knickers, their faces red, their hair standing up in wet clumps from racing up and down the curved staircase, throwing peanuts and popcorn at each other. At him.

"Hurry. Blow them out."

But he doesn't. He looks at her. I told you, his eyes say. His eyes already brimming with tears. Then he runs. Out of the room, up the stairs.

"Too much party," Roger says into the silence. "Who wants to blow out the candles?"

But she doesn't wait to see. She's on the stairs, in the hall, opening the door to an empty room.

"Come out, Bryce," she calls gently.

She's been here before. She reaches under the double-decker bed and runs her fingers over a soft arm.

"I'm sorry," she says. "You were right. We won't do it again."

"Daddy will make me."

And then she's sitting in the spindle-back rocking chair holding him, wiping his tears with the edge of the cowboy and Indian bedspread she has pulled off the bed and wrapped him in, humming.

"I hate them."

"They're not bad boys," she says. "They're just not your friends."

She holds him tight against her.

And she could have held Roger at bay, could have listened for words her awkward son didn't say. The details of her failure kept her staring into dark space, robbed of sleep, night after night. Signing him up for tennis lessons when she knew he hated them. Backing up his father when he begged her not to have to compete in chess tournaments. Nagging him about too many desserts.

Finally, at six o'clock one morning, the back of her eyes aching from lack of sleep, she threw the photos back into the carton, boxed up Bryce's trophies and books and shoved them all into the closet in Bryce's bedroom. She hadn't opened the bedroom door again.

She began to take naps in the upstairs guest room, then to have Florine bring her meals up there. Now she slept alone in the four-poster mahogany bed that had belonged to Roger's Alabama grandmother. Once a week, she left the house to walk the three short blocks to the public library. Then back to the dark, silent house, bearable only because she had sealed off her son's memories.

February 1959

That afternoon, like every afternoon after school, Liz lit up the house. First, the bronze chandelier in the hall. Next, the four Chinese table lamps in the living room. Then, the crystal chandelier over the dining room table. She drew back the maroon and gray flowered drapes to let in what sun remained in the late winter sky. She didn't have to light up the kitchen. Fluorescent tubes shone harshly on the straight-backed woman with cocoa-colored skin who was standing over the sink.

Florine looked up from the potatoes she was peeling.

"How you, baby?"

"I'm okay. What's for dinner?" Liz asked.

"Pork chops, scalloped potatoes, snap beans from the freezer. You hungry?"

"Maybe later. You need anything?"

"I'm short on flour and milk."

"Okay. I'll run down the street in a minute."

"Get yourself some of that butter pecan ice cream while you're there."

"You mean, get *you* some."

Florine laughed.

"How you make out on that French test, baby?"

"Lousy. Don't tell Daddy."

"What do'y'think I am?"

"Mama resting?"

It wasn't really a question, and Florine didn't bother to answer.

Liz opened the door of her mother's room cautiously as if she half expected something embarrassing to spring out of a corner. But it was the same colorless, featureless room it had always been. Beige carpet, beige curtains fully drawn, the off-white Martha Washington bedspread on Grandmother Bryce's bed, the wrought iron reading lamp, and the rocking chair where her mother now sat.

"Hi, Mama."

Betsy Nolan looked up from the book in her lap, rubbed the bridge of her nose above her glasses, and stretched her pale lips into a smile. Liz was struck, as she often was, by her mother's beauty. No make-up. No need for it. It was a beauty neither she nor her brother had inherited. Unlike her tall, willowy mother, Liz was short, her legs slightly bowed, her brown hair coarse, straight. Only her smile, her father's smile, and his dark eyes saved her from being outright homely.

"How was school?" Betsy asked.

Liz sat on the bed, as she always did, and tried to interest her mother in the latest craze of gold circle pins the girls were wearing.

"Where's your list, Mama?" she finally asked when it was clear her mother was only pretending to listen.

Betsy pulled an index card from the copy of *David Copperfield* in her lap and handed it to Liz.

"Are you going today?"

"Sure. I've got some groceries to pick up for Florine, and I can stop by the library on the way. Any returns?"

Betsy pointed to a stack of thick books with worn covers on the bedside table.

"Thank you, dear."

She settled her glasses on the narrow bridge of her thin, straight nose and returned to her book.

Some days, Liz could barely remember there had been another life, a different mother. She almost forgot the long hot summer days at Nags Head, whitecaps crashing over her, salt water in her nose and mouth, laughing, laughing with her big brother, his bathing trunks slipping below his bulging belly.

To stave off the pain, she averted her eyes from the large, framed photograph in the entrance hall of the high school where she was now a junior. "In Memory Of Bryce Templeton Nolan." The tassel from his graduation cap half-covering his pasty, solemn face, an uneasy valedictorian. At home, she rushed, unseeing, past his bedroom door, a door opened only by Florine, and only once a month, to dust and vacuum.

But sometimes, she'd see lumbering toward her, in the crowded halls of her high school, a hulking shape of a boy with a canvas book bag slung over his shoulder, and she'd feel as if she were suffocating.

She'd been in her ninth-grade history class when it happened, watching a movie about Bethlehem Steel, one of those tedious educational films where the voice was all wobbly and the picture jumped on the makeshift screen. She was taking the opportunity of the dark room and her inattentive teacher to write a note to Toby Watkins when she looked up and found herself staring into Mr. Harrison's shiny red face. The Principal. He was talking, but the roar of the projector and the narrator's gravelly voice were so loud she couldn't hear him.

And then, "I need to take you home."

"What is it?" she kept asking as he walked her out of the dark classroom into the blinding sunlight. "What's wrong?"

Begging, pleading all the way home in his Jeep station wagon.

"Don't worry. Your dad wants to see you. I'm sure it's nothing" was all he would say. She'd hated him ever since.

Then she was running into the living room. To her father, who was holding out his arms. His face all distorted, not his face at all.

She screamed "No!" and pushed against him, twisted in his grip.

March 1959

When the crushing pain began to ease, Roger Nolan experienced a lightness of being that surprised him. His slightly hunched shoulders relaxed. His smile was no longer forced. His heels, when he walked from fundraiser to ceremony to party meeting, bounced off the pavement. He had loved his son. And not just for his brilliance, although that's what Betsy believed. She was wrong. He'd loved the way the boy needed him when he was small, the way he looked to Roger for approval. The way he'd lift up his arms to be held when he was frightened. Those memories tortured Roger. But he was too honest a man not to admit that his love for Bryce had been mixed with disappointment, sometimes even fury. At his son's unhappy fat face, his unsociable nature. Most recently, at his poor performance at his own Alma Mater.

And then there was his irritating purity. This was Virginia, for Christ's sake, southern Virginia, and he, Roger Nolan, was its representative. Everyone he knew, everyone who could vote for him, wanted segregation. But history was *not* on the side of his complacent constituents. He had figured that out years ago. And he planned to pick up the pieces and lead the way when the courts and, more importantly, business interests forced the south to give up its losing battle. In the meantime, he represented southern Virginia, for better, for worse. They weren't bad people. But they hadn't gone to integrated schools, and they were damned if their children were going to.

"Folks prefer to be with their own kind," was how they put it. "Ask my girl. She'll tell you."

And it wasn't as if they didn't have schools of their own.

"Their schools aren't as good," Bryce had reminded him. Sixteen-year-old Bryce, at the breakfast table. Two years ago.

"Hold on there, boy," he'd said. "What do you know about it?"

"You got me that job last summer, mending the books at the schools. I know what I saw."

"What was that?"

But he knew. He'd seen it himself.

"The books at Luther Burbank were the books we white kids threw away. The pages were torn, the spines all broken, a mess."

He'd sat there, watching his boy stuff his fat cheeks with bacon and eggs and cereal and muffins.

"Goddammit, Bryce! Don't eat so fast."

Those were the memories that cut deep. The shamed look on the boy's face, the eyes avoiding his. He should have agreed with his son. Luther Burbank *was* dilapidated, the books out-of-date, the teachers overwhelmed. But he didn't. He couldn't. He was too caught up in the political reality of the people who put him in office.

The problem was the NAACP was organizing to integrate the schools, and the white folks in Spotswood were talking about setting up a segregated private academy for their kids. He didn't agree with them, but these were the folks who voted for him. He had to take their side. He didn't have a choice.

He wished Betsy could see it like he did. He wanted those intelligent blue-gray eyes smiling up at him as he worked the crowds. God, he loved her. It drove him crazy seeing her sitting in that room, practically in the dark, day after day.

He'd loved her right from the beginning. It was 1935, the year he graduated from high school.

She was sitting, all alone, on the expansive wooden porch of the Old Colony Inn at Nags Head. Rocking back and forth in one of the dozens of white rockers set out for guests and gazing out toward the ocean with eyes the same color as the Atlantic. Her dark hair was coiled on top of her head in thick braids, leaving her long, satin neck exposed. He even remembered what she was wearing: a high-necked white blouse and a soft dark cotton skirt. But what had stopped him, what had made him sit down in the rocking chair next to her, was the ivory white of her skin. The searing North Carolina sun hadn't touched it.

"I'm Roger Nolan," he'd said and then just stared at her, stunned by all that ivory skin into silence.

The girl's quick smile suggested she was eager to meet someone, anyone, who might provide distraction from the boredom she didn't bother to conceal.

"I'm Betsy Templeton, visiting with my aunt Evelyn. She's sweet but awfully old, and she didn't know what to do with me in Greensboro. That's where she lives. So, she packed us up and took off for the seashore. And here I am."

"Is it so bad?" he asked

"You'll think I'm horrid."

"Try me."

"Well, to tell you the truth, yes. It's my first visit to the southern states, and I don't know what I was expecting, but I find it all mystifying. And, I have to say, backward."

Roger laughed.

"You're right about backward. But don't you think the sand here is just about the finest you ever put your foot on?"

She admitted the sand was soft and white, and she liked to float in the warm waves.

But she was a New England girl, and she was bored.

"Oh yeah? What do you do up in New England to keep from getting bored?"

"I don't know. Play tennis, sail, all kinds of things."

She watched him rocking back and forth before she spoke, in a tone almost challenging.

"And I'm going to college in a month."

"Goodness me. Where?"

The girls he knew went to finishing schools. Hardly any went to a real college.

"You probably never heard of it. It's called Vassar."

He laughed out loud.

"Vassar? No kidding."

He jumped up and faced her, forcing her to stop rocking.

"Then, I bet you've heard of Harvard."

She smiled up at him with large blue-gray eyes.

"Well, pleased to meet you, Harvard," she said.

They quickly established that they were fervent New Dealers even though, or maybe because, their parents disapproved. Roger confessed his dream of one day running for the U.S. Congress. Betsy wanted, in some ill-defined way, to help the poor. But it wasn't dreams of the future that changed his life that summer. It was the taste of salt on her lips, the sting of the hot North Carolina sun, the powdery sand on the cool dunes at night. It was slogging clumsily to the top of the dunes, then racing, tumbling to the flat beach below, Betsy holding onto her wide-brimmed straw hat with one hand, the other clinging to Roger's sunburned arm. There were millions of places to hide in the dark sand, behind the dunes, in crevices on top. They couldn't stop talking. They couldn't stop touching. At the beginning, the aunt from Greensboro felt obligated to accompany her niece whenever she left the hotel for the beach, and when Roger came to call, she chose a rocking chair on the porch near, but not too near, the infatuated couple. Ultimately, however, she relaxed her vigilance, impressed by the supposed safety net of Harvard. Roger's high school friends, who had driven down from Spotswood with him, marveled at his good luck. But Roger knew it was for the rest of his life.

Once in college, they filled in the blanks, his ambition, her devotion to him, his plan to go back South and make a better world, her trust that he could do it.

In the years that followed, Roger never stopped marveling at her beauty, her cool charm, her helpless love for their clumsy boy. He loved her, and her distance after Bryce's death pained him, more, if he let himself admit it, than the boy's death.

Finally, out of desperation, he got her an appointment with Ashby Fuller, even though he thought psychiatry was baloney. And she'd gone dutifully.

"How'd it go?" he'd asked afterward.

"Fine, I guess."

"What'd he say?"

"Not much."

"Did he give you any pills or anything?"

"No."

"When are you going again?"

"I'm not."

And that was it. Roger tried to get Ashby to tell him what was wrong with his wife, but the man had refused. Patient confidentiality.

She'll come round, he thought, eventually. Meanwhile, Roger Nolan considered himself a practical man. He didn't like this Massive Resistance movement. Thought it was wrong-headed, doomed. But, like it or not, it was his only way forward. And Roger Nolan was going forward.

April 1960

Liz Nolan raced her red Schwinn down the hills and around the sharp curves of her tree-lined neighborhood. The maples were in first tender-green leaf. She couldn't get enough of the sun, the sweet air, the soft breeze in her face. The relief after the dark house, her sad mama. A stack of books was in her basket on the handlebars.

She loved the old nineteenth century house on Main Street which served as Spotswood's library, loved the smell of the books, the hush in the spacious cedar-paneled, book-lined room, the polished cherrywood tables over to the left where several women sat reading, the balcony up above with its painted white banister, and bookshelves to the ceiling. They called the old building the Memorial Mansion because Robert E. Lee was supposed to have slept there at some point during the War. Mrs. Wyatt, who had presided over the library for as long as Liz could remember, had read all those books. At least that's what Liz had concluded because she never ran out of suggestions or enthusiasm.

"I don't think your mama has read Trollope lately," Mrs. Wyatt said as Liz handed her the returns.

The diminutive, bone-thin librarian spent the next ten minutes pulling books off the shelves and whispering to Liz the delicious intricacies of each plot. Despite her fragile appearance, she moved briskly about the old building, hopping up and down ladders, stacks of books in her wiry arms.

Liz was looking forward to spending a half hour or so, sprawled on the grass in front of the library, sampling the books, then choosing one and losing herself in her mother's world of nineteenth century English manners. So, after checking out as many books as she could handle on her bicycle, she headed for the door.

But the massive oak door was blocked. Four boys stood, shoulder to shoulder, in front of it. Boys about her age, seventeen or eighteen years old, dressed in ill-fitting sports jackets and dark blue ties. They barely noticed her because they were looking all around the library, as if they'd never seen so many books, as if they didn't know what to do next.

And they were boys from Luther Burbank.

"May I help you?"

Mrs. Wyatt slipped in front of Liz pushing her back with a hand that was surprisingly strong.

"We'd like some books, ma'am."

The tallest one stared down at the librarian and thrust his hands out to his sides, palms facing backwards, as if to silence the others. Later, when her father asked her to describe this boy, Liz couldn't remember what color his coat was. All she remembered was his dark skin and big hands.

"I'm afraid I can't help you with that," Mrs. Wyatt said.

Her voice was soft.

"You must know this is a whites-only library."

"It's a public library, ma'am," the boy said. "And we're the public."

The other boys were beginning to mumble and shift from foot to foot, but their spokesman kept them in check with his long, outspread fingers.

"There's a branch of this library on Calhoun Street." Mrs. Wyatt's voice squeaked midway through the sentence. "You can get books there."

"There ain't any good books there, lady," one of the other boys said, stepping out in front of the spokesman and staring down into Mrs. Wyatt's face, which was white as powder. "It's a mess."

"I'm very sorry. But I can't let you in this library."

"We're from Burbank," the tall one said. "We need books for school."

"If you tell me what books you want, I can send them to Burbank," she said.

But it was too late. They were moving forward, shoulder to shoulder, forcing the librarian backward into the room. Liz jumped out of the way.

The handful of women who had been reading stood up and, without a word, formed a frightened huddle behind one of the library tables. Liz was sure something terrible was about to happen. But she just stood there, in a trance, and watched these boys march over to a shelf on the wall opposite the ladies. Without a word, they began to pull out books at random, glance at a few pages, then stack the books carefully on a nearby table.

Within minutes, sirens were screaming, and six policemen pounded through the door.

"Everybody stay where you are," one of them yelled.

The boys continued to pull books from the shelf, but Liz could tell from the way they looked at each other that they were frightened.

"I said stay where you are!" the policeman yelled. "And put your hands up."

One by one, skinny brown arms waved in the air.

"We have the right to be here," the tall one said. But his shrill voice lacked confidence.

"You're trespassing, you scum," the officer bellowed.

"Cuff 'em," he ordered his men.

Minutes later, the men pushed the boys out the door, their wrists handcuffed behind their backs, their heads down. One of them was crying.

A woman who had witnessed the whole thing patted the librarian on the back.

"Good for you," she said. "I was frightened half out of my wits."

The other women clustered around Mrs. Wyatt, nodding, clutching at her trembling hands. She didn't say a word, just sat down at the cherrywood table and put her head in her hands. Liz wanted to say something to comfort her but didn't know how.

Afterward, riding her bicycle back through the leafy streets of Spotswood, Liz couldn't get those boys out of her mind. They looked so scared, and they were so orderly, pulling the books from the shelves, stacking them neatly. She would have expected them to talk back or start to run once the police showed up. But they stayed polite the whole time. She knew what her father would say. Those boys had no place in the white library, and maybe they shouldn't have been there. But putting them in handcuffs? Taking them off in a police car? Suppose it had been Jess. She began to pedal faster. She needed to talk to Florine.

Florine, ready for work in her gray cotton uniform with the starched white collar and apron, stared at a tall, scrawny boy with close-cropped frizzled hair.

"You know anything bout them boys getting the white library closed?"

Jess looked up from his cornflakes.

"I heard of it."

"Well, you stay out of it, you hear me?"

"What you mad at me for? I ain't involved."

The boy got up from the metal-topped table, which was shoved up against the wall, and looked square into his mother's eyes. His mattress, a blanket tucked neatly under the sides, was on the opposite side of the room, and in between the bed and table was a wooden bench and two armchairs, upholstered in faded wool plaid. The wood floor of the small, crowded room was bare.

"You better not be. This the best job I ever had, and you ain't going to mess with it."

Jess laughed.

"The old honky!"

"That old honky's gonna pay for your college long as you behave yourself."

"I behave."

"Well, don't let me catch you making trouble for the senator."

"Mama, listen to you talk. You know them boys are right."

"I don't know nothing," she said. "I keep my opinions to myself, and I'll thank you to do the same."

After Jess left for school, Florine sat on the wooden bench for a few minutes, staring out the window at a black and white mutt running down the unpaved road in front of her house, barking.

She thought about the mothers. What they go'n do, knowing their boys are in jail and they can't do nothing about it. Mr. Nolan *could* do something about it, but he won't. He treated her decent, but he had no notion how folks lived. And with all the sadness in that house after that business with Mr. Bryce, he'd never know. Those boys were foolish going into that libary. But brave too.

"Lord, keep my boy safe," she prayed under her breath, as she pulled herself up from the bench and headed down the dirt road to the bus stop. "Just keep him safe."

"It's a damn shame," Roger announced, barging into his wife's room. "Some kids from Luther Burbank forced their way into the Memorial Mansion after school and started taking books. John Watson had to close the place down."

Betsy jumped up. "What do you mean, close it down?"

"Just what I said, honey. Mrs. Wyatt asked them to leave, they refused, and she called the police."

"Liz told me that part, but I didn't know that stuffed shirt mayor had closed the library."

She turned to face the window. She needed fresh air

"It might be good for you," Roger said, opening the window. "Get you out of this room."

You have no idea, she thought.

"What are you going to do?" she asked, her back to him, breathing in the outdoors.

"Right now, we're letting things simmer down. You remember this happened before when that schoolteacher from Luther Burbank tried to check out a book. It was a mess. All those rednecks storming the place. If we open the library now, they will be back and there'll be violence. So, we'll wait for the lawsuit and work something out."

"The law takes a long time."

"Time is on our side, honey."

"I can't," she said.

"What's that mean?"

She didn't bother to explain.

She rarely left her room after that. She still had books, in the house and on regular order from Book of the Month Club, but she didn't read the paper or listen to the radio. She didn't ask Roger about the library. She didn't want to hear it.

June 1960

Then one summer afternoon two months after the mayor closed the library, Florine announced, "Miz Nolan, there's a man at the door."

"What man?"

"I guess it's a boy. Says he wants to see you."

"You know what to tell him."

Why was the woman bothering her with this?

"Yes'm. I did already."

"Well then, would you please close my door?"

Florine just stood there.

"Miz Nolan, he says he was a friend of Mr. Bryce."

Betsy let out a sharp cry.

"Tell him to see Mr. Nolan in his office downtown," she said.

"I already done that, ma'am. He wants to see you."

She searched her maid's impassive face.

"No!"

"I told him to leave, told him you won't see him. But he won't go way."

Betsy started to close the door, but then she thought, suppose he's telling the truth. Suppose he was . . . She had to see. Her legs trembled as she started down the stairs.

"Mrs. Nolan?"

A young man was standing in the front hall, at the bottom of the stairs, peering up at her from under heavy black eyebrows, not smiling. His shoulders under his rumpled seersucker jacket were slightly hunched, his skin pale, his scrawny arms hung limp.

"Please, Mrs. Nolan."

His voice was high pitched and nasal. New York?

She called out sharply.

"Florine!"

The boy backed away, swiping at his sweaty forehead with his sleeve.

"I'm George Bradstreet, ma'am."

The words rushed out.

"Bryce's friend. I mean, *was* his friend."

She was frightened now. He could be anybody. Pretending to be her son's friend.

"What do you want?"

"I'm part of the protest, Mrs. Nolan."

Betsy walked down the stairs to the bottom and faced him.

"I don't understand."

"The protest."

His voice was insistent.

"We were down at the library, holding up signs, trying to get it back open. But the cops showed up and started arresting all the protesters. I started to protest, and the cop told me I better get my ass—sorry ma'am—out of there, or I'd go to jail too."

The cops? What was he talking about? She looked at her maid.

"I been hearing about it, ma'am," Florine said.

The boy began talking very fast.

"A bunch of us from Harvard came down here this summer to join the fight for integration."

He suddenly looked so young, so innocent.

"That has nothing to do with me," she said.

"Bryce was one of us. Only he didn't tell you because he was scared it would leak out, and somebody would use it against his dad."

No.

He pulled from his pocket a single sheet of paper folded so many times it was beginning to tear.

"This is our manifesto," he said.

Manifesto! What a child, she thought. What an absolute baby.

He handed it to her and pointed to a name at the bottom. Bryce Nolan. It was his handwriting, slanted to the left, letters close together.

She struggled to get her breath.

"Where did you get this?"

"He said you might understand -- what we're doing."

"I don't," she whispered. "I don't understand."

"He was my friend."

The boy's voice was thick.

She wanted to run back up the stairs, pick up her book, get this boy out of her house. Instead, something made her ask, "What did you say your name is?"

"George. George Bradstreet."

It sounded vaguely familiar. Maybe when Bryce was home for Christmas? He could be. She didn't know.

"Maybe some time you could visit my husband in his office," she said.

"I'll do that, Mrs. Nolan. I'm sorry to bother you."

"Take him to the kitchen," she said to Florine. "Get him some ice tea."

She heard the boy whisper, "Thank you," to Florine.

"Thank you for what?" Betsy asked Florine, her voice sharp.

"I think he meant it for you, ma'am," Florine said.

Ten minutes later, the door to the kitchen burst open. Roger Nolan filled the room, tall, imposing, fierce. His dark eyes fixed on the young man perched on the edge of a straight-backed, wooden chair. George Bradstreet sprang up and stuck out his hand. Florine disappeared into the pantry.

"I got a call just now from my wife," Roger said, ignoring the offered hand. "Says you came to my house uninvited, claiming to be a friend of my son."

"I'm sorry if I offended her, sir. But it's true I was Bryce's friend, good friend. I'm George Bradstreet. From New York."

They stood in the middle of the kitchen staring at each other.

"You in trouble with the police?"

"I hope not."

"You involved in that business downtown?"

George hesitated.

"I was part of a march."

"A lot of folks got arrested."

"I know. That's when I left."

"And ran for safety here? To my house?"

Roger's voice was sharp.

"I'm sorry, sir," George said. "I guess that wasn't too smart."

"Damned right, it wasn't smart. You put my wife, who isn't well, in a terrible position. Dangerous even."

"I'll leave right now."

George headed for the kitchen door.

"Wait."

George turned back.

"You say you knew Bryce?"

"Yes, sir."

Roger's dark eyes searched his face. "I'll check that out," he said. "Meanwhile, do not disturb my wife again. Do not come here again. Ever. Understood?"

"Yes, sir."

And he was gone.

Roger took the stairs two at a time. Betsy was standing at the window when he rushed into her room.

"I got rid of him," he said.

He tried to put his arms around her. She held herself stiff, staring out the window.

"He could be telling the truth," she murmured.

"I'll find out. But even if he did know Bryce, he had no business coming here scaring you like that."

She turned to face him.

"You're right. It scared me."

"He won't be back, honey. I promise."

He felt her body soften against him. He wanted to take hold of her, pull her into him.

She looked into his eyes.

"How do *you* feel?"

"Right now, I'm mostly angry that he came here and compromised you."

She smiled and pulled herself away from him.

"You mean, compromised *you*."

He ignored that.

"It's you I worry about," he said.

She turned back to the window.

"I want it to be true," she said.

"I love you, Betsy," he said.

She didn't answer. And Roger knew he'd been dismissed.

"You seen Jess?"

Florine was pushing through tangled knots of boys, not just brown ones, white ones too, blocking the street. Shouting, "Unlock the doors!" Shouting, "Books for freedom!" Chanting, chanting until she thought her head would burst.

Then suddenly, sirens screaming full blast. Cop cars speeding into the crowd, thick-necked bullies in uniform jumping out, waving billy sticks. A boy went down close to where Florine was standing, a kid, maybe twelve years old, his head bloody. She felt herself being shoved to the side of the road as screaming boys raced to escape the police. Jess. Where was he? They'd been doing it for two days now, the cops. Driving their cars right into the middle of the protest. Picking up the boys, children really, carting 'em off to jail. Beating up on the ones who fought back. Where was Jess?

Somebody had to stop it. Maybe the senator if he came down here with his megaphone. He'd been known to do it, get up on a stump and yell at a crowd to move back. Mr. Big Shot. But what if he spotted Jess? Or her?

Then suddenly there was Jess, standing on the outside of the crowd. Thank you, God. Staring, his mouth open.

"Get your black ass home," she shouted in his ear.

"What you doing here?"

"Getting you out of trouble."

He followed her, at a distance so it wouldn't look like he was a mama's boy, but he followed her.

Back home, safe, she could hear the sirens, the loud voice, not the senator's, on the megaphone, the screaming.

"That could be *you* screaming," she said.

Jess lay down on his mattress and stared up at the ceiling.

"I'm careful, Mama. The cops don't pay me no mind."

"You stay out there yelling and carrying on and see what mind they pay," she said.

"I gotta be involved," he said. "Dr. King, he says the time is now. And you know he's right."

She wanted to say, I know. I'm the one that sits in Reverend Martin's bible class every Sunday and hears him talk protest, protest, protest. I know 'bout the marches. I want to be out there bad as you.

But she didn't say that.

Instead, she said, "Well Dr. King's not your mama, I am, and I say you can't be out there getting beat up and going to jail."

But she knew he'd be back.

"Where you off to, honey?"

Liz stopped short. Florine was standing near the entrance hall of the unlit living room in her broad-brimmed straw hat ready to leave for home.

"I'm meeting some friends."

"At this hour?"

It was close to eight o'clock.

"What is this, the third degree?"

Florine laughed.

"Somebody got to look after you."

Poor little girl. No mama to speak of.

"Well, maybe I just won't go," Liz said, slipping out of her red cotton sweater.

"I reckon you'll just wait till I'm gone?"

Florine looked closely at the girl. Liz stood silent.

"Cause I'm betting you going to the protest downtown."

"What protest?"

"Don't you give me that 'what protest.' You know what I'm talking 'bout."

Liz sat down on the gray velveteen sofa, her sweater bunched up beside her, and looked up at Florine.

"You know you can't be out there," Florine said.

But she was thinking, I wish I hadn't seen her. Let her go on out there, show up her daddy for a change.

"Why not?" Liz asked.

Pretending all innocence.

"Well, to start with, it's dangerous."

"I want to help."

"Well, it ain't going to help nobody if you get your daddy in trouble."

"If Bryce were here, he'd go."

"If Bryce were here, he'd tell *you* to stay home."

God help me, she thought, I got to save this one too. She was dog tired. She wanted to shove the girl's sweater to the side and sit down on the sofa. But she couldn't.

"I want to do *something.*"

"Well, you can't go prancing about in public. You'll have them reporters all over you."

Course, she'd never thought of that, poor baby.

"You remember Miss Foster?"

Liz looked up, surprised.

"The old chemistry teacher, that Miss Foster?"

"That's the one."

"What about her?"

"You might look her up."

"What for?"

"I'm not saying another word."

"Look her up where, Florine?"

"I bet she's in the book."

"The phone book?"

Liz thought a minute.

"Are you saying Miss Foster's protesting?"

"I already said too much. Now go on upstairs."

Liz just sat there.

"Look here. If you go to that protest, and I saw you leaving, I'll be in hot water."

"I won't tell."

"He'll ask, and you won't lie."

Liz stood up and put her arms around Florine's neck.

"Okay. Next time I'll make sure you aren't around."

"Whatever. Now get on upstairs like a good girl."

July 1960

Two weeks after George Bradstreet visited the Nolans, he appeared at Roger's law office, once again in the rumpled seersucker jacket. But this time, he was wearing a white, buttoned shirt and striped tie.

"Come on in," Roger said, leading the way past a grand mahogany rolltop desk. Roger eased himself into a leather armchair next to a table on which stacks of paper were piled.

"Sit down," he commanded.

George backed himself onto a plush blue sofa, his eyes never leaving the older man.

"Thank you for inviting me here," he said.

"I said I'd check up on you," Roger said.

George laughed nervously.

"Yeah? Did I pass?"

"Looks like you're telling the truth. About knowing my son."

Roger's voice trembled slightly. 1960 was Bryce's class. His boy would be finished with Harvard by now.

Struggling to control his voice, Roger said, "I understand you just graduated."

"Yes sir."

George smiled for the first time and looked around the room. A red oriental carpet covered most of the dark hardwood floor. And drawings hung on the gray walls, drawings of buildings mostly. Colonial houses with columns, including one of Monticello. And one of those drawings of a tobacco barn that hangs on the wall of every white southerner's house.

"My wife tells me you boys are down here plotting to save the South from itself," Roger said.

"I don't know about that, sir, but Bryce was one of us."

"Well, the little son of a bitch," Roger muttered under his breath.

George hesitated, then spoke in a rush of words.

"Our goal is to get the library back open."

"*Our* goal?"

"A few of us from college."

Roger's eyes narrowed.

"You came to my house. I assume it wasn't just a friendly visit. What do you want from me? "

George looked directly into the black eyes.

"Nothing, sir. I was scared that day when the cops showed up at the protest. First thing I thought of was Bryce. So, I came to your house. It was a bad idea."

"It was a terrible idea."

"I know, but Bryce talked about his mother a lot. I thought she might . . ."

About *her*. Of course, Roger thought. I hate to think what he said about me.

"You can't visit her. You know that."

"I know."

"So? What *do* you have in mind?"

"I'm still marching."

"I figured. You know what they call you boys? 'Outside agitators.' Nothing gets the police more riled up than white boys coming down south and telling them their business."

George nodded.

"They've made that clear. But I'll keep protesting until the library is integrated. It's what I came down here for."

Roger frowned.

"What else are you doing?"

"Getting folks to sign petitions. Writing letters."

"What kind of letters?"

"Letters about the lousy selection of books in the black library."

Roger frowned.

"What do you know about that?"

"I've seen it myself. And I've been going to meetings at Reverend Martin's house. He's signing the letters I'm writing. And some of the Burbank teachers are signing them."

"Where're you living?"

"There are white people who put me up."

"Really?"

They sat in silence for a few minutes.

Then Roger leaned forward once again fixing George with fierce, dark eyes.

"Son, has it occurred to you that a town without a library can't attract new business?"

George grinned.

"It has now."

Roger stood up.

"You didn't hear it from me."

George jumped up and held out his hand for Roger to shake just as Roger reached out to lead him to the door. They bumped against each other and laughed awkwardly.

"Look, George," Roger said, "if it ever gets out that we've talked about this letter business, I'll deny knowing anything about it. I'll say you came here under false pretenses taking advantage of my grief. You understand?"

George nodded and picked up his jacket to leave.

"You know, he really looked up to you," he said.

Don't, Roger wanted to say. The truth is I bullied him, the poor devil.

"By the way," Roger asked, "who are these letters going to?"

"The mayor and members of the library board. The press of course."

George looked him in the eye.

"And you."

"Get out of here," Roger growled. But he smiled as he closed his office door. If these Harvard kids had to be down here messing in his town's business, at least he could make some use of them.

August 1960

Betsy Nolan, elegant in her spectator pumps, edged along the broken pavement of Wilson Street, peering at the house numbers, some of which were missing, some covered with honeysuckle. Her green paisley dress fell in soft folds from a patent leather belt. The wide collar emphasized her long, white neck not yet marred by the folds that would come soon enough.

She didn't know this street, didn't know this part of town. She stumbled on a fragment of sidewalk and quickly righted herself. Staring at peeling paint and unswept walkways, she thought absent-mindedly that this will be a mixed neighborhood before too long.

To her relief, the house she was looking for—157 Wilson—struck a happy contrast to the general state of disintegration surrounding it. Fresh-looking, off-white stucco, maroon wooden shutters, recently painted. No cobwebs, grass in front, a doorbell that worked. A stout, buxom woman appeared at the door. Her stone-white hair was piled up on her large head in a loose knot, and glasses hung from a chain around her neck.

"Well, hello, Mrs. Nolan," she said pushing open the screen door. "What a surprise."

The woman looked familiar. Did she know her?

"I'm Thelma Foster," the woman said. "I taught Bryce chemistry."

"Of course. Miss Foster. I'm so sorry. I . . ."

"Thelma. And don't worry. I've been retired so long nobody recognizes me. Come in."

"What a lovely room," Betsy said.

The sun streamed through the stained-glass oval above the door, bounced off a glass coffee table, made blue and red patterns of light on the white walls, and burnished the room in a warm honey gold.

"Thank you. Mama did it all those years ago, and I found no cause to change it after she died."

She motioned to a silk Wedgewood chair.

"What can I do for you, Mrs. Nolan?"

"I'm sorry to bother you, but I was told a George Bradstreet was staying here."

"Who told you that?"

"A friend."

Roger had let it slip that he knew where George was living. But he was adamant that no one suspect he had actually met the boy.

Miss Foster studied her for a minute.

"Was it Liz?" she finally asked.

Liz? Was she mixed up in this?

"A friend said he was here," Betsy repeated. "Would it be possible for me to see him?"

The old teacher hesitated.

"Could I ask what this is about?"

"He was Bryce's friend. I'd like to talk to him."

"I see. Wait here a minute."

When the old lady returned, she motioned for Betsy to follow her down a dimly lit hallway to a roomy closed-in back porch, paneled in cedar. George Bradstreet jumped up from a wrought-iron chair.

"Mrs. Nolan!"

"Don't look so scared," she laughed. "It's a friendly visit."

"If you don't need me . . ." Miss Foster said and disappeared.

The bright sunlight streamed in from the wall of French doors, open to afternoon breezes and the smell of newly cut grass. A round oak table dominated the room with captain chairs pushed under it. Papers were stacked all over the table. The wood floor of the original porch was painted white.

"How are you managing?" Betsy asked.

This was the first time she had seen him since he'd turned up at her house.

George's words spilled out.

"Fine, thank you. We're writing letters, using some ideas the senator gave me. But I'm being really careful, I want you to know that, so I don't get the senator in trouble."

"I know," she said, settling into one of the captain chairs, "but that's not why I'm here."

George sat back down, watching her under thick eyebrows.

"I want to know about Bryce."

"Sure."

"I know he was unhappy."

He frowned.

She leaned forward.

"The truth. Tell me the truth."

"The truth? Okay. Nobody's happy in college, especially freshman year, especially at Harvard."

"I don't mean everybody. I mean my son. What was it like for *him*?"

"He was smart, like everybody there, but he wasn't very interested in his studies. Is that what you mean?"

"Go on."

"Look, Mrs. Nolan, the world is changing. I mean the Brown decision changed everything. School is just irrelevant. I think that's how Bryce felt. I know I did. Still do."

His voice was excited.

"And the meetings you told me about, did they make you feel relevant?"

"Yes, ma'am. We wanted to make a difference."

"What about Bryce?"

"He felt the same."

"He wanted to make a difference?"

"Sure. The cause gave us something to believe in."

She smiled faintly.

"The manifesto?"

"He would have told you about it, but he didn't want to upset his dad."

Betsy thought for a moment, then blurted out, "Then, how come he was drinking?"

"Ma'am?"

"You knew him, George. Why was he drinking?"

"Everybody was drinking."

She looked away, her face drained of color.

"Not everybody ran a car into a tree."

Why had they ever agreed to let him take that car to college?

"It was an accident."

"He was drunk."

"He'd had a drink or two."

"I saw the police report," she said. "They tried to keep it from me, but I saw it."

Her blue-gray eyes were fixed on him.

George looked away.

"He didn't drink at our meetings," he said. "That was going to save him."

The words shocked her.

"Save him?"

George stood up. Betsy watched him as he circled the room, clearly agitated. He's trying to find a way to say it without hurting me, she thought. He stopped at the bank of French doors and looked out.

"He loved you both," he said.

"But he felt he was letting us down."

"I didn't say that," George said.

"But it's true."

"He loved you. Look, the meetings made him happy. We were happy, all of us."

George was looking away from her, out into the bright sunlight.

"I loved him," he said. "Not like that sounds. He was my friend."

She walked over to him, took hold of his sharp shoulders, and turned him toward her.

"Thank you," she said.

"By the way," George said as she turned to leave the room. "Was it Liz?"

"Was what Liz?"

He looked confused.

"How'd you find me? Was it Jess?"

Liz again? And Jess? Florine's son?

"What do you mean?"

"Look, Mrs. Nolan, forget I said anything."

She looked at him closely.

"Is Jess involved in this?"

"I don't know."

"Of course, you do."

"Look, don't say anything to the senator. Please."

"I know that," Betsy said. "Take care of yourself, George."

As she turned to leave, George said, "Bryce thought you would agree with him." He swept his arm over the table, piled high with papers. "About all this. He said it many times. Said you couldn't do anything because of the senator, but Bryce believed you'd understand."

"I haven't been very good at it so far," she said, her voice hoarse.

Bryce, her own Bryce, had believed she'd understand. And she hadn't. Her head hurt from holding back tears.

As she picked her way over broken concrete on the way back home, she thought, that dull, old chemistry teacher understood. Who would have guessed? And Jess. Florine's son. Florine must know. Working every day in the senator's house. And Liz? What was *she* up to? It almost made her laugh.

Liz softly opened the door to her mother's room and tiptoed in. Taking a nap? No. Instead, her mother was sitting in the rocking chair by the window, staring out. Good.

"Where've you been, honey?" Betsy asked without turning around. "Seems like I haven't seen you for days."

Liz pulled up a footstool.

"You know, Mama. Daddy got me that summer job at Johnsons, selling shoes."

"How's that coming along?"

"Lots of sweaty feet."

Betsy smiled.

"Florine says you haven't been home for dinner."

She'd noticed? That was new.

"I've been eating at that hamburger place with friends."

"What friends?"

What's she getting at?

"You know, high school friends."

"I see."

"See what?"

"Well," Betsy paused. "I thought you might be involved in what they call the 'movement'."

Liz stiffened.

"What are you talking about, Mama?"

Betsy looked at her daughter for the first time.

"I paid George Bradstreet a visit last week," she said.

"You did what?"

Was this possible?

"At Miss Foster's. She seemed to think *you* told me where he lived."

Liz didn't know what to say. She'd been so careful.

"You visited George? At Miss Foster's?"

"I wanted to know more . . . about Bryce," Betsy said. "I'm beginning to think I don't know much about either of my children."

Liz looked away from her mother, out the window. The grass stood stiff, yellow under the harsh August sun. The leaves on the maple hung dry, ready to drop with the first wind of fall.

Betsy hesitated for a minute as if she were trying to figure out what to say.

"Are you working with George?"

Might as well get it over with.

"Yes, ma'am."

"Doing what?"

"Typing. Keeping records."

"Records?"

"They're going all over town with a petition to reopen the library."

"*You're* doing that?"

"Of course not," Liz said quickly. "Daddy would kill me. But they need a record of the petitions, how many people are signing, how many are refusing to sign, what neighborhoods they're in, that kind of thing." Liz sounded excited.

"Who's *they*?"

"For the lawsuit."

"Does your daddy know?"

"That I'm involved? I sure hope not."

Betsy paused.

"How did you get started in this?"

Liz was relieved. Her mother didn't sound angry or accusing, just puzzled. Maybe even interested. But she couldn't get Florine in trouble.

"Somebody told me Miss Foster was helping open the library."

"Why didn't you tell me?"

She almost said, I didn't think you'd be interested, but stopped herself.

Betsy lightly touched her daughter's arm.

"I wish you wouldn't keep all this a secret from me."

Liz looked at her mother for the first time and smiled.

"I'm protecting you."

Betsy laughed.

"From your father?"

Liz nodded.

October 1960

It was almost ten o'clock when Roger thought he heard a knock at the kitchen door. He peered out into the dark and saw somebody tall standing there.

"Mr. Nolan, I needs to talk to you."

Florine looked directly at him, her eyes boring into his.

"Come in."

What could she want?

When he had closed the door behind her, she said, "It's my boy."

Roger took a deep breath. Thank God. It wasn't Betsy. She'd seemed so much better recently, but she wasn't out of the woods.

"They got him in the jail."

"For what?"

He remembered a small boy, shy, his thin brown arm hanging onto his mama. How old was he now?

"Some kids from the high school came by tonight. Said the police had Jess."

He must be a teenager by now. Getting into trouble already.

"What'd he do?"

"They said he was disturbing the peace."

Roger sat down heavily on a kitchen stool. Why was she coming to him? She knew he couldn't get involved.

"Have you talked to him?"

"No, sir. I went to the jail, but they say he can't have no visitors."

"I'm sure they'll let you see him later."

Florine seemed to grow taller. She looked straight at him with wet eyes.

"Mr. Nolan, I want you to get him out of there."

That's all he needed. He could see the headlines. Nolan backs protest movement. Gets agitator out of jail.

"You know I can't do that."

"They beating up boys in there," she said.

"That's just talk, Florine. The out-of-town press makes up that stuff to sell newspapers. Don't believe it."

"I seen the bruises myself. I seen the blood."

"When?"

"Last week. Not Jess. Other boys."

She was right, of course. He'd tried to talk to the chief, told him it was hurting the town's reputation which, as a state senator, was his concern. But that good old boy just denied it.

"Hell," he'd said, "we ain't laying a hand on 'em. We're only asking questions. Sons of bitches are lying."

"Look, Florine," he said. "I'd like to help, but my hands are tied."

The easy cliché embarrassed him.

She turned away.

"I know all bout that, sir."

He leaned forward to hear her; her voice was so soft.

"It was crazy to come here asking you. I could get myself fired. But, he's my boy. He might be out there protesting, but he's not breaking the law. That's the God's truth, Mr. Nolan."

He sat there, gazing at her skinny back, silently cursing her for locking him into this straitjacket. The newspapers were all over this goddamn business. If they found out Senator Nolan's maid was somehow part of it, he'd have to do something. Fire the maid, for sure. And that's the last thing he wanted to do. He'd have hell to pay from Betsy and Liz. And if he pulled strings to get her boy out of jail, and somebody found out, it would be even worse. He didn't want to think about that.

"I'm sorry, Florine," he said.

"You mighty smart, Mr. Nolan. That's why I come here."

He smiled.

"Not that smart."

But it got him to thinking about Police Chief Williams and how he'd pulled his butt out of the fire several years ago when the chief got a little overzealous in his search and seizure practices. Roger had quietly, effectively, put an end to an investigation, and the Chief owed him one and knew it. But was this the time to play that card?

"Go on home, Florine. The jails are overflowing right now. They'll have to let your boy out in a day or two."

"But they'll charge him, and the judge will send him back."

They were both standing now, facing each other.

"Look, Florine, there's a possibility he could get out without any charges against him. If that happens, we never had this conversation. Do you understand?"

"Yes, sir. Thank you."

"I haven't done anything."

"Yes, sir."

After she'd gone, Roger headed up to bed and found Betsy standing at the top of the stairs.

"What are you doing out here, sweetheart?"

"I heard you talking to somebody."

"It was Florine. She was just leaving. Go on back to bed."

"What's Florine doing here at this hour? It's about Jess, isn't it?"

"What do you know about Jess?"

"Nothing. I'm guessing."

Roger put his arm around Betsy's shoulders and started walking her back to her bedroom.

"He's in trouble, isn't he?" she said.

Roger stopped abruptly.

Betsy turned to face him.

"I'm only guessing, but Jess is just the right age to be out there protesting. And the police are rounding up kids like him right and left and hauling them off to jail."

"That's what the papers say."

"Come on, Roger. You know it's true. And Florine is asking you to help Jess, isn't she?"

"How do you know . . ."

"I'm right, aren't I?"

She's so smart, he thought, she's always been smarter than anybody.

He nodded.

"You have to help her."

"I can't."

"Yes, you can."

"Go to bed."

"Only if you'll promise to help her."

"Go to bed," he said again, and turned to leave.

But she was smiling. She knows, he thought. She knows me better than anybody in the whole world.

The next evening when Florine opened her front door, she found Jess sprawled out on his mattress. Asleep.

"Thank you, sweet Jesus," she whispered and sat down on the floor next to him.

Rocking back and forth, she ran her fingers lightly over his bare arms, over his scrawny neck, through his tightly curled hair, feeling for cuts, looking for bruises.

Then he was throwing his arms around her, this large almost-man who was her boy. Squeezing her so tight she had to pull herself away to catch her breath.

"I was so scared. Mama, I was so scared."

Over and over.

Finally, "How'd you get out?"

"I was in this cell with a bunch of other guys, and this cop opened the door and yelled out, 'Which one of you assholes is Jess?' Scared me to death 'cause they been calling boys out and beating on 'em. Somebody pointed at me. So, I stood up. 'Come on,' the cop said. Next thing I knew, I was out the jailhouse door and heading home."

"Nobody told you why they were letting you go?"

"No, ma'am."

"They say anything about charges?"

"No'm. Said I was free."

They struggled to their feet, still tangled up together.

"You hungry?"

"What do you think?"

They sat together at the metal-topped table, eating warmed over spoonbread, drinking milk.

"You gotta stop," Florine finally said.

"Stop what?"

"Don't play dumb with me. Next time you be staying in that jail."

"You talked to him, didn't you, Mama?"

"Who?"

"You know who."

"No."

"You not going to get fired, are you?"

She smiled.

"Not if you keep clear of those protests."

"I mean to," he said.

But she knew how young he was, how innocent, even now, and she could only pray he'd listen to her this time.

The following evening after work, when Roger opened the front door, he found Florine inside waiting for him.

"My boy's home," she said.

"Well, that's good news."

"Thank you."

"What for?"

"I just wanted to say it."

"Well, thank *you* for all the help you give this family," he said.

"You're welcome," she said.

February 1961

Betsy stood perfectly still, staring at a stack of letters on the table. Her hair was almost entirely gray now, and there were lines on her broad forehead and along the sides of her eyes. Since her first visit to Thelma Foster's house, she had come several times with Liz. She told herself she was keeping an eye on her daughter, making sure she was safe, but in fact, Betsy was becoming more immersed in George's work, editing letters, tallying petitions, making suggestions for his meetings in the black churches. George was now working for the N.A.A.C.P. all over Virginia. But his focus for the moment was on the Spotswood library.

Thelma Foster reached over with spindly fingers and picked up a letter and handed it to Betsy.

Betsy ran her eyes over the letter.

"Do you think this will do it?" the teacher asked, watching Betsy with hooded green eyes.

"You got a better idea?" George asked her.

"No."

"Look," he said. "None of those Neanderthals actually wants to live in a city without a public library. It's embarrassing. That's why we're pushing the risk-of-losing-business angle. It's the argument Mr. Nolan's using with the mayor to get a settlement."

"Preaching won't do it," the old lady said.

"We're not preaching. We're pointing out the facts."

"And the facts are?"

"No commercial enterprise will look at a town without a library."

Betsy was still staring at the letter.

"The facts," she suddenly said. "Here's one. It's not about the books."

"Huh?"

"No one actually minds them reading books. At least that's what the mayor says."

"Just not in our library," Miss Foster said.

Betsy turned to face the window. Outside dark limbs of a maple were silhouetted against the gray sky.

"What they don't want is the mixing," she murmured. "That's the important fact. We keep forgetting it."

They both stared at her.

"It's chairs," she said.

They waited, puzzled.

"If you can't sit down in the library . . . ."

George finished her sentence.

". . . . you can't stick around to mix."

He started laughing, a high whinny of a laugh. Betsy realized she'd never heard him laugh before.

"Brilliant," he said. "You get your books, and you go home."

Betsy smiled.

"It's just an idea."

June 1961

Roger waved the newspaper in the air.

Betsy sat on the rose velvet sofa, watching him, her shoulders, as always, straight. Her slender, veined hands rested in her lap.

He pointed to the headline, "Library Opens With No Chairs, No Fanfare," and began to read aloud:

The library in the Memorial Mansion opened its doors today for the first time since April 1960 when Mayor John Watson was forced to close it to prevent racial conflict. The reopening of the library resulted from the settlement of a lawsuit brought against the city by the N.A.A.C.P. According to the terms of the settlement, all chairs have been removed from the library premises. The library opened quietly without disturbance.

Contacted in his office, Senator Roger Nolan stated, "I am pleased we have resolved this unfortunate lawsuit in a peaceful manner. My family and I intend to patronize the library on a regular basis."

"Chairs," Roger said. "Just brilliant. Wish I'd thought of it."

September 1961

Roger knocked softly on his wife's bedroom door.

"Can I talk to you?"

She opened the door wide and smiled.

"Come in."

"The governor just called."

Betsy's smile vanished. She nodded in the direction of the green damask daybed and eased herself into the rocker.

"He wants me to run in the '62 election."

"For?"

"The Senate."

"You're in the Senate."

"The U.S. Senate."

Her smile was back.

"Congratulations. I can see the library settlement paid off."

But Roger wasn't smiling. He was watching her carefully.

"You know why I'm here."

"Yes."

Of course. The inevitable. And she dreaded it with her whole being.

"The Senate is big, you know that. I have to be seen and heard. Every day. For the next year. And if my wife doesn't show up now and then, people will ask questions."

"What exactly do you want?"

"I need you next to me when I make speeches. Not every time, of course. And I need you at fundraisers."

"Is the governor writing the speeches?"

"Of course not."

"You know what I mean."

"You mean, do I have to support the governor's stand on school segregation?" he asked.

She nodded.

"Jesus, Betsy. Be realistic."

"I am realistic. I'd like to help you. But I can't. And you know it."

Roger stood up, reached for her hand, and pulled her to her feet. They stood facing each other, not touching.

"It means I can't run."

"I don't think so."

"They'll say we're estranged. Or that you're depressed or worse."

"I'm not depressed. I *was* worse. But not now."

"Then why can't you do this for me?"

"It would destroy me."

He paused a minute, then, "You're too strong for that. But if you don't, it might destroy me."

"No, it won't. You're too clever. You'll figure out some story. I'm no longer hibernating. I'm back in the world. I'm working on Bryce's scholarship fund. Use that. Use my grief. That's always available."

She gave a small laugh.

"You'll at least come to fundraisers?"

"Only if they're local and only if they don't involve segregation politics."

He laughed.

"I'll see if I can organize one."

He took her hands and pulled her to him. She felt his chest, hard after all these years, his stomach, flat. He'd been exercising. How nice it would be to stay there, breathe in the mix of fresh laundry and aftershave.

"You know," he murmured in her ear, "that I agree with you."

She pushed him away.

"When you say things like that, I get crazy. I know you used to agree. That's why I can't watch you make those awful speeches about 'mixing the races.'"

"You know I have to support the governor's position to get elected in this state."

"Yes, and I know you can't resist running for office. I just don't have to be a part of it."

"But you are."

"Not anymore. Every time you make one of those feel-good southern speeches, all I can think about is Bryce."

"Don't!" Roger moaned.

"We need to talk about it, and we never do. You know, as well as I, that he was fighting against your governor . . ."

"Stop, goddammit. You're using him against me."

"I hate what you stand for."

Roger glared at her, his eyes dark, fierce.

"What do you mean by that?" he hissed. "You know what I stand for, what you and I have always stood for."

"And what's that?" she asked.

"A world that's fair and equal for everyone."

"You should hear yourself, Roger." Her voice was soft, tired. "That's just cant. You know you haven't believed that for a long time."

"I still do believe it," he said. "But I can't do anything about it if I'm not elected. We're stuck with a losing cause here in the South, but somebody smart's going to find a way out. And that's what I'm good at."

"I wish I could believe you."

"You don't have to believe me. Just don't hate me."

She looked into his eyes.

"I don't hate you."

He put his arms around her slender shoulders and pressed her against him.

"I used to be good at loving," he said. "I was good at loving you."

"I know," she said, pulling away.

"I still do."

She looked up at him, her college sweetheart, handsome still, earnest, his dark eyes begging her. She knew every contour of his back, could feel, this minute, the strength of his arms, knew he loved her.

"But love doesn't save us anymore," she said. "It died with…."

"Don't," he cried.

"Running for Congress saves you. The scholarship fund saves me. I think, all things considered, we're lucky."

"So, do we have a deal?"

"I'm here, I'm your wife through the election. But be careful not to let the press near me."

"What do you mean, through the election?"

His voice was sharp.

"We'll see."

"No. It's not worth it."

He pulled her close, held her hard against him.

"Nothing's worth losing you. I'll tell the governor, no. That's final."

When she didn't respond, he kissed her forehead then turned and left the room.

But she knew it wasn't final. He would run. He couldn't help himself. After that? Who knew? Right now, it didn't matter. She felt alive. That's what mattered.

October 1962

Liz stood at the back of the crowd, peering around the heads in front of her, straining to see the speaker.

"Let me tell you, I am *proud* to be a Virginian. Just like every one of *you*. Proud of this state. *Our* state. And you know? We have the right to be proud. George Washington was a Virginian. Thomas Jefferson was a Virginian. James Madison was a Virginian. Virginians fought the American Revolution for our right to independence. And today, we're still fighting for our independence."

The crowd cheered.

Liz tried to tell herself it wasn't him.

She'd come up to Farmville, Virginia, this October morning, with a busload of students from Duke. She'd been riding the Freedom Bus every weekend since she'd joined the Students for Racial Equality, visiting towns all over North Carolina and southern Virginia, picketing segregated movie houses and restaurants and swimming pools, walking alongside colored boys, carrying signs. It felt scary, and she was always worried she'd run into somebody from home. Although, how could she? At the same time, it felt right to be on those picket lines. Bryce would have been there. She imagined him, her big brother, walking just ahead of her, a bag full of petitions slung over his shoulder. Like when he was a paperboy.

They'd wanted her to go with them to Spotswood. That town's as redneck as they come, they'd said. Schools still lily white. And you know it inside-out. But, brave as she felt on all those picket lines, she wasn't ready to face her hometown. Even more, she didn't want to make trouble for her daddy.

Farmville wasn't home. The students planned to picket the all-white private high school the county had been supporting since 1959 when it closed the public schools to avoid desegregation.

As they drove into town, they saw a large crowd gathered in front of what looked like a courthouse. Everybody was white, and there was a lot of yelling.

"Okay," Dickie Sutherlin, the group leader, shouted. "Let's check it out."

Liz waded into the crowd behind Dickie, edging herself past the swollen bellies of middle-aged men in plaid flannel shirts open at the collar. The men were clapping and hollering.

The amplified voice broke through the din.

"Our state has the right under the United States Constitution to make its own decisions about public education. You in this town, in this great Prince Edward County, are fighting for that constitutional right."

It *was* him. No mistaking. Liz turned and started inching her way back through the crowd. But Dickie was raising his fist in the air and yelling, "Integrate!" in a shrill voice that cut through all the cheering, and the other students started yelling with him.

Liz felt a hand on her shoulder jerking her so hard she fell back into a mass of arms and legs. She was breathing hard, trying not to cry, when the area around her suddenly cleared, and a policeman, his round face dirty with sweat, yanked her wrists in front of her with one large fleshy hand and pulled her to her feet. He held a billy club in his other hand.

"Let me go!" she screamed as she twisted back and forth, but he just glowered at her.

But then he suddenly twisted his head in the direction of the speaker's stand. She followed his gaze. Her father had stopped speaking and was walking down the stairs, wading into the crowd toward the policemen, who stood frozen, watching.

Liz started to call to him, to acknowledge him, to let him rescue her. To cry out the word, "Daddy." But there were her friends, their wrists in handcuffs, watching her with puzzled frowns, waiting to see what she would do.

Liz looked straight at her father and began to sing in a low voice.

"We shall overcome. We shall overcome."

Then her friends joined in, louder and louder.

"We shall overcome some day, ay, ay, ay."

"Let 'em go," her father said to the policeman who was holding her wrists. "They're just kids. I don't want trouble from some college."

The tension broke. The fat cop let go of Liz. Her fellow students rubbed their wrists as the handcuffs came off. Roger Nolan squared his shoulders, marched back to the speaker's stand, and picked up the microphone.

"We're supposed to be at that private school," Liz said. "Let's get out of here."

And to her relief, they followed her.

What in the hell was Liz doing here? It wasn't easy to make these damn speeches, encouraging these rednecks to defy the Supreme Court, and keep their schools closed. He hated it. Hated every minute of it. Surely, she knew that. Knew he had no choice. If he wanted to be elected, these speeches were mandatory. And he wanted to be a United States Senator. That was real power. But she was too naïve, this daughter of his, too full of misplaced idealism. She couldn't, or wouldn't, see that once he was a senator, he could work behind the scenes, work with Virginia, get all the goddamn schools back open. Like he did with the library.

He'd been warming up his audience, watching the faces smile, watching the eyes follow him, watching the heads nodding at him. Then out of the corner of his eye, he'd seen some movement in the crowd, heard someone yelling. A disturbance. Police. It broke the rhythm of his speech. Made him stop, assess the damage. It was okay. He'd been here before. He knew the drill. Give 'em a gracious smile. A calm voice. Nod at the policemen to step aside.

Then, "Come on up to the platform, young man. Let me finish my speech, and then you can give yours."

It had always worked before. Rabble-rousers liked the comfortable anonymity of a crowd. They backed away from standing up front. And then he'd seen her. Some cop pulling at her. No time to think. He'd had to rescue her.

But she'd rescued *him*. She'd looked right at him and started in on that singing. If she had called out to him, called his name, or let the police drag her off, he would have been lost. It would have been on the front page of every morning newspaper. "Nolan Sides with Protesters against Farmville Police. Protects His Integrationist Daughter." His campaign would have been over. But she'd started singing, and in that split second, he knew she didn't *want* to be rescued. She wanted to make a statement, poor misguided creature. So, he'd called off the stupid cops then turned back to the podium and picked up his microphone.

"Looks like we have some folks who don't agree with us," he said with a smile. "Well, they have a right to their point of view. And we have a right to ours."

The crowd cheered. They were with him.

"They don't have a right to disturb the peace though."

More cheers.

That did the trick. Liz and her crowd turned tail. Disappeared. Thank God. He'd have time afterward to square it with the police, who'd have questions. The governor would take care of the press.

Meanwhile, Liz. What in God's name was she doing running around the country with a bunch of troublemakers? He'd make sure it didn't happen again.

SENATOR RUNNING FOR OFFICE
DENIES SON'S ACTIVISM

State Senator Roger Nolan put to rest on Thursday rumors that his son Bryce had been involved in the integrationist movement before his tragic death in 1957. A reporter for the Washington Post raised the question during a speech Mr. Nolan was giving in Alexandria, Virginia as part of his campaign for the U. S. Senate.

"Wasn't your son a member of the Integrate the Schools movement while he was at Harvard?" the reporter asked.

"My family is off- limits," Mr. Nolan politely replied.

"Not if your family opposes your views on integration," the reporter persisted.

"My son Bryce died three years ago in a tragic automobile accident," the Senator said, "and I refuse to answer any questions about him or any of my family."

"Senator Nolan, I have right here a document signed by a Bryce Nolan of Harvard University stating his opposition to segregated schools."

"I don't know what you have, and I don't care," the Senator replied, his voice rising in anger. "My son Bryce signed no such document. He was just eighteen years old when he was killed. A young boy, immature. He didn't know his own mind. He was behind in school and too busy catching up to be involved in politics."

The reporter, however, would not be silenced.

"So, you deny your son's involvement in the integrationist movement?"

"Yes, I do," the senator stated.

The day before in Farmville, Virginia, out-of-state student agitators raised their fists and booed Senator Nolan in an attempt to disrupt a campaign speech. As the local police closed in to disperse the students, the senator waded bravely into the crowd and calmed the students who departed peacefully.

After the disruption, Mr. Nolan returned to the podium to give a rousing speech in support of Massive Resistance.

"You seen the paper?"

Jess handed Florine the morning edition of the *Spotswood Dispatch*.

"I seen it."

"I told you."

"Told me what?"

"He's a racist."

Florine sat down heavily on the wooden bench, the newspaper in her lap.

"He's lost," she said. "He's got some good inside him. I got evidence for that. But he's lost."

Going Under

The Carolina Quarterly, Volume 65.2, Winter 2016
Also published in *Spotswood Virginia,*
Stephen F. Austin State University Press, 2021

You see, I really loved her. Not like the others. All the guys who *told* her they loved her. When all they really cared about was taking advantage.

Her name was Brenda. Brenda Hill. She came to our town last summer. Right before we started eighth grade. The summer of 1954. The summer I decided to take Jesus as my personal savior and be baptized at First Baptist.

That day I was picking up my stack of papers for my afternoon route in front of the Langston Apartments, the way I always did, and there she was, out front on the concrete steps, just sitting there.

"Hi there, paperboy," she said.

It was sticky hot, and she had on white shorts and a pink-checked halter top. And she was barefoot. Her brown hair was short and brushed back in what they call a "duck tail." And her eyes were deep black brown.

"Hi." I said. "I'm Gordon. Are you new here or just visiting?"

"Moved in yesterday," she said. "And I'm about to *melt.*"

Her face and shoulders were sunburned, not tanned brown like the rest of us. So, I figured she was new to the southern weather.

"Where you from?" I asked.

"All over." she said. "We move a lot."

I liked her from the first. She was friendly and pretty, and we had some nice talks. She was usually sitting on the steps when I came by to pick up my papers, and I would sit down beside her to roll them. Then she'd help me load up my bike basket with the rolled-up newspapers. That's how I've been saving for college. They pay me to ride my bicycle through town and throw newspapers onto the front porches without having to stop. It's good money.

Brenda told me she had lived in Washington D.C. and Florida and even California. Her dad was retired military. And her mama was a secretary.

She started bringing me a glass of lemonade every afternoon, and I'd tell her about the teachers at school and who the nice kids were and the ones she should avoid. I told her about Reverend Keeling at our church, how he was somebody you could talk to, and he'd listen. I was too shy to ask her for a date. I was too shy to ask anyone for a date. I just liked her, liked talking to her. And looking at her. She was so pretty.

I didn't see much of her after school started that fall. She showed up now and then on the steps to chat, but I had to wait until after football practice to deliver my papers, and it was too cold by that time for sitting around.

Then one afternoon after practice, Joey Kinser, a ninth grader and the J.V. quarterback, started talking about how that new girl Brenda was a hot ticket. He said he'd taken to going to her apartment after practice, and her mama worked. So, she wasn't home. They'd drink lemonade or something first and pretend to do homework. Then they'd start French kissing.

"No shit!" Bobby Crumpton said.

"Scout's honor." Joey said. "She starts it. She drops her pencil or something and slides over close to me to pick it up. Then she takes off my glasses and says, 'You got such blue eyes, Joey.' Which makes me turn and look at her. Then she laughs and looks closer, right into my eyes. I get the message she wants something, so I lean forward and put my hand on her tit. You know."

We didn't, but we wanted to.

Joey held back a minute, pulling us in.

"Aw, I shouldn't tell you this stuff. She wouldn't like it."

So, we begged.

"You get a hard-on?" Bobby asked.

Joey laughed.

"How else do you think I get it in, dickhead?"

"I don't believe you," I said.

I thought of Brenda and how pretty she was and how much I liked her.

'You're such a kid, Gordy," he said. "She loves it."

"Where's her dad?" I asked.

"I never saw any dad," Joey said. "I don't think she has one."

"She does," I said, but nobody listened.

After that, I'd see them together in the halls at school or after the games. I'd see her rushing onto the field with everybody else. Joey would be all sweaty, and his uniform would be muddy, and he'd put his arm around her shoulder and walk off the field waving at his friends like some hero. And she'd be looking up at him and laughing. I wanted to kill him.

No. I wanted to tell her what kind of things he was saying about her. All the lies and bragging. But I didn't get a chance because Joey's mama put an end to it. Somehow, she got wind of what Joey was up to and started making him come right home after practice. I still didn't believe him, but then other guys, Bobby Crumpton and Billy Sizer and other guys, whose mothers didn't go to First Baptist like the rest of us, started talking.

"You going up to Brenda's today?" one of them would say.

"Nah. It's your turn."

And they'd laugh.

Bobby would look at me and say, "How 'bout it. Gordy? All you have to do is tell her you love her. And then watch out for your braces."

I hated him.

But it started me thinking. I'd never kissed a girl, never even had a girlfriend. Maybe Brenda was the place to start. She was the only girl I'd ever felt comfortable just talking with. I thought I might tell her what the guys were saying and promise to set the story straight. But if she was the kind of girl they said, maybe she would kiss me too.

So, I worked up my courage, and the next time I picked up my papers at the Langston, I rang the doorbell of her apartment. After a long time, she opened the door. She was wearing a blue terrycloth bathrobe.

She took one look at the stack of papers in my arms and said, "Oh. It's you."

"Who'd you think it was?"

"Nobody. Never mind. Want to come in?"

I'd never been inside her apartment before, and I was surprised at how empty it was. There was a sort of saggy brown sofa and a couple of chairs. A TV, of course. But there were no pictures on the walls and no lamps or rugs or figurines. Just a bare wood floor and a ceiling light.

She walked over to the sofa, sat down, and patted the cushion next to her. I pretended not to notice that the belt on her robe had come untied, and I could see her leg all the way up to her underpants.

I sat down next to her, my bundle of papers in my lap.

"Were you expecting Bobby Crumpton?" I asked.

She laughed.

"Maybe. It's OK. I'm glad to see you. It's been a while."

She nodded toward my papers.

"Look, you want help with those?"

"Sure," I said and handed her a stack.

We sat rolling papers while I worked up my courage.

"Look," I finally said. "I don't want to upset you, but I thought you should know Bobby's been spreading lies about you."

She sat up real straight and pulled her robe around her.

"What'd he say?"

I took a deep breath and blurted out.

"He says if he comes here and tells you he loves you, you'll...."

I couldn't say the words.

"...let him do things."

The silence was awful. She just kept staring at the rolled-up papers.

Finally, she said, real low, "Do you believe him?"

"I said it was lies."

She turned toward me. She looked so good, sitting there like that in her blue bathrobe, her brown eyes so dark and wet-looking.

"You're really pretty," I said.

I didn't know it was coming. It just popped out.

"You think I'm going to let you do things now?" she asked, laughing a kind of nasty laugh.

I felt my cheeks getting hot.

"No. I'm sorry. I didn't mean it like that."

"How *did* you mean it?"

She looked suspicious.

"I don't know," I mumbled. "I just mean you're pretty."

"Wait a minute," she said and got up and left the room.

I sat there for about ten minutes, wanting to leave, not wanting to leave.

When she came back, she was wearing a blue and black plaid skirt and a red sweater, white socks and brown loafers. Her school clothes. She sat down on the sofa facing me and put her hands on either side of my face. I could feel her soft fingers on my cheeks. She smelled good, like Ivory soap. I wanted to kiss her, to touch her. I'd never felt this way before.

It looked like she'd been crying, at least her eyes were red. I didn't know what to say, so I just sat there hoping she wouldn't move her hands.

She looked right into my eyes and said, "Will you do something for me?"

"Sure."

I didn't care what it was, I'd do it.

"Promise?"

"Of course."

"Okay," he said. "I want you to take me to that church of yours."

Just then, the door burst open, and this short, stocky man walked in. He had on a blue business suit like my dad wears, but I thought he could use a haircut. He smiled at Brenda. She looked down at her lap, and she wasn't smiling.

"Well, who is this?" he asked nodding his head in my direction.

"It's Gordy," she said. "A friend."

"Nice to meet you, Gordy," he said and reached out to shake my hand.

His hand was softer than I expected, and I noticed his fingernails needed clipping. But he seemed pretty nice.

"I like this one," he said.

I looked over at her, but she just sat there, which I couldn't figure out, because her dad was watching her like he was waiting for her to say something.

"I better go," I said.

"Yeah," the man said. "You better go. It's getting late."

As I was heading out, Brenda suddenly looked up and said, "Remember what you promised."

Her voice was cool like it didn't really matter what she said, but her eyes looked different. She was begging me.

So, that's how she started coming to First Baptist. In the beginning, Mother was against it.

"How come she wants to go with us?" she asked. "Where's her family?"

"I guess they don't go to church."

"Well, I don't think much of that," she said.

"Look," I said. "Jesus welcomes everybody. Reverend Keeling is always saying that."

"Yeah, but I've heard rumors about that girl."

"Maybe she wants to change."

"Maybe she's after you."

I could only hope.

The next Sunday morning, we found her waiting on the steps in front of the Langston Apartments. She had on a blue wool coat I hadn't seen before and a little rose-colored hat with a veil and white gloves. She thanked Mother for picking her up and sat in the back seat real still all the way to church.

First Baptist is the biggest church in our town. Of course, like any town, there are Methodist and Presbyterian churches, but they're pretty small. Most people go to First Baptist, and that's because of Reverend Keeling. He's a big man, real tall, and he says complicated things in a simple way you can understand. You can tell him anything, and he says no matter how bad it is, Jesus will forgive you if you are truly repentant. We all sit there every Sunday in this big sanctuary with flowers on the altar, the sun shining through the stained-glass window of Jesus with the lambs, and we just feel good. I know church is boring for most people, but First Baptist is different.

The first time Brenda came, everyone was staring, trying to figure out what she was doing there, especially with me. But she paid no attention and just smiled and sang the hymns and bowed her head when we prayed. So, after a while folks stopped staring.

Meanwhile back at school, Bobby Crumpton and his buddies were complaining.

"Brenda's got religion. She's no fun," they'd say.

Bobby claimed he still went to her place after school and messed around, but I knew he was lying because I was there. After I delivered my papers every afternoon, I'd ring her doorbell. She always met me dressed in her school clothes. I never saw that blue bathrobe again. We'd do our homework or play Monopoly or just talk. I told her about my mama, how she had to work as a nurse since my dad died. She liked hearing about her, but when I asked her questions about her mother, she just said she was a secretary and then changed the subject.

The first time she let me kiss her, I got all dizzy and didn't know where to put my hands. All I could think was how soft her mouth was. How much I loved her. But that was it. If I tried anything funny, like putting my hand on her chest, she'd push me away.

"Come on. You let Joey."

"Look. I've been bad. I admit it. But Reverend Keeling is going to cleanse me of all that."

So, I held back. I tried to tell her how I felt about her several times, but she told me to hush, she didn't want to hear it. So, I held it inside.

I always tried to leave before her mama and dad came home, but every once in a while, her dad would show up.

"Hi, kid," he'd say and mess up my hair or give me a mock punch in the chest. "How's Brenda getting on at First Church?"

"She's doing great, sir." I'd say, feeling confused. There was something about him that seemed to be making fun. But he was friendly enough, and he was awfully fond of Brenda.

"How's my girl?" he'd say.

I always packed up my books when he showed up and left. I never saw her mama. Not once.

As I said, I had made the decision to take Jesus as my personal savior and join the church the summer I met Brenda. The time for my baptism had now come. It wasn't actually such a big decision. Everybody in our town joined the church when they were about my age, fourteen. But Reverend Keeling didn't just let you join up. He made sure you understood the step you were taking. There were bible study classes you had to attend on Friday afternoons, and you had to have a private conference with Reverend Keeling. Finally, there was the baptism. Total immersion.

On the first Friday of bible study, I rang Brenda's doorbell after I'd delivered my papers to tell her I couldn't see her that day. But when she opened the door, she had her coat on.

"I'm going too," she said. "I'm joining the church."

"Are you sure?" I asked. "You've only been going about a month. Most people take longer than that."

"I want to be really saved," she said. "I want Reverend Keeling to wash away all my sins forever."

So, every Friday afternoon for the next two months, we met in a Sunday school classroom with about ten other kids to prepare to take Jesus as our savior. We learned about twenty psalms by heart and played this game where you would open the bible at any place and read the scripture out loud and try to figure out what it meant. Brenda was a whiz. She memorized the bible passages faster than anybody else in the class, and she never goofed off.

On the last afternoon of bible study, Reverend Jones asked us to come back to the church that night so that he could meet with each one of us separately. He said he was going to ask us about our lives and why we were making this decision. He talked about the seriousness of the step we were taking and how proud he was of all of us for choosing the Christian path and how he expected us to hold fast to our faith. He said the baptism would take place on Sunday night. Then he gave everybody a bible with a red leather cover.

I walked Brenda home as usual that Friday afternoon. It was March, the beginning of spring, and you could smell apple blossoms, and the air was warm and sweet.

"How come you're so quiet?" I asked her.

She looked down and muttered something under her breath.

"What's that?"

She still didn't look at me, but I heard her this time.

"I'm afraid," was what she whispered.

Now that surprised me. She'd never struck me as scared of anything. Certainly not a pool of waist-high water.

I'd seen dozens of baptisms and had studied the way it was done. We don't go to a river to be baptized in our church like the primitive Baptists out in the country. We have a baptismal font right at the front of the sanctuary about the size of a bathtub, only deeper. Most of the time, it's empty, but when they do baptisms, they fill it with water. They do the baptisms on Sunday nights after the sermon. Reverend Keeling and all the people being baptized wear choir robes over their underwear. But Reverend Keeling also wears hip-high rubber boots under his choir robe. He showed them to me once.

"Look. Brenda," I said. "There's nothing to be afraid of. When it's your turn. Reverend Keeling will take your hand and lead you down the stairs into the water. Which is warm, like in a bathtub. He'll take both your hands in his and say, 'I baptize thee, Brenda Hill, in the name of the Father, the Son, and the Holy Ghost,' then he'll put his hand over your face. You're supposed to hold your nose with your fingers, which are under his, and he'll tip you back into the water until it covers you. He'll bring you right back up and say to the congregation, 'Lord, it has been done as Thou hast commanded and yet there is room.' That's it."

"I'm talking about tonight."

'Tonight?" It made no sense. 'We're just talking to Reverend Keeling tonight. You're surely not afraid of him?"

"Suppose you're too full of sin even for him." she said.

"That's why you get baptized," I said. "To wash your sins away."

"Suppose they won't wash."

"But they *will.* That's the whole point. You'll feel better after you talk to the Reverend tonight."

She smiled then.

"Promise?"

"Promise."

I kissed her then, just on the lips, and she kissed me back.

That night, I went by her apartment. I waited a long time, and finally Brenda's dad opened the door. He was in his undershirt, and I realized it was the first time I'd ever seen him without the blue suit.

"What do you want?" he asked.

"I came for Brenda."

He smiled this strange kind of smile.

"She's not going."

"But the conferences with Reverend Keeling start in about fifteen minutes."

"I heard," he said.

And then I saw her. She was standing behind him in the dark living room.

"I'm sorry," she said.

Her voice sounded strange.

"I can't."

"Why?" I asked, peering around Mr. Hill to get a better look.

"She's not going," he repeated, and he shut the door in my face.

She didn't show up on Sunday night for the Baptism either. I was so sick at heart I could hardly pay attention. I do remember the water being colder than I expected. I kept trying to concentrate on Jesus, but I couldn't stop shivering, and all I could think about was Brenda.

The next day at school, she acted like she was avoiding me. So, I waited by her locker after school.

"What happened?" I asked when she finally showed up.

"I told you before."

"You said you were afraid. But there wasn't anything to be afraid of."

"You don't get it."

"You would have been fine. Reverend Keeling would have held you up the whole time."

"Nobody's strong enough for that." she said. "Not even Reverend Keeling."

"What do you mean?"

She looked away.

"Gordy," she said, "you have no idea."

That afternoon, when I rang her doorbell, nobody answered. I even thought I heard voices inside, so I banged on the door and called out to her. But nobody came.

A week later, when I went to pick up my papers, there was a moving van out front. I went into the building. Brenda's front door was wide open, and the living room was full of boxes. No furniture. I was about to leave when I saw something red sticking out of a pile of trash. I dug out Brenda's bible and stuffed it in my jacket pocket.

I managed not to cry then, but that night at home in bed, I cried. And that wasn't the only time.

I loved her so much.

Not a Word

Forge, Issue 9.2, November 2015
Nominated for a Pushcart prize

"When did you stop talking?" she asks sitting there all wrapped up in a red shawl with a long, ugly skirt watching me with dark gypsy eyes. A spy. Mother hired her, like all the others, and drives me to see her to make me talk. And I go because I don't wish to tell her I won't. Of course, I could let her drag me out of the house like somebody's cat. But I don't. I don't know how that might end. This way, I know what I'm doing. This one's a little weirder looking than the others, but it will all come out the same.

At least she plays it straight. No trick questions. I could say I didn't stop. Not technically. I still answer questions in school, for instance. Obvious answers to factual questions, like how many got killed at Appomattox or what's an isosceles triangle. And I can say the right words when the girls in my school go on about new shoes and cool boys and those fantasy books they all read. That's not really talking. I could tell her this, but I don't.

She reads my mind.

"Oh, I know you still talk to your teachers," she says. "But when did you stop talking to your mother?"

Two years ago, when I was ten, I think but don't say. Why should I? She already knows. My mother has bent her ear for hours.

She fills up a big leather chair. It's brown, and her red shawl spills out the sides of it. I sit on an ugly green sofa across from her. There's a wood table, like the art tables at school, near the window with some plastic chairs shoved up to it. The curtains are closed, so it's dark in here, but the rug is pretty. It's Persian, I think. She smiles at me. I stare back. I like watching her trying to figure out what to do next.

In the next session, she tries something different.

"I want you to remember a time you were happy," she says.

She's wearing boots under her skirt with the big red shawl wrapped around her. And it's warm. I'm wearing shorts and my lavender Gap shirt with the V-neck and my baseball cap.

"Aren't those shorts too small for you?" Mother asked when we were leaving.

She hoped I'd get mad enough to talk back. Fat chance.

Maybe *she's* fat, the spy. Like me. Maybe that's why she wears all those clothes when it's warm. Maybe there aren't any skinny jogger-type psychiatrists. At least I haven't seen any. Maybe they get fat sitting all day listening to people talk. Or not talk.

"Why don't we start with a house," she says when I don't answer. "Think about the house you lived in when you were happy."

In the first place, it wasn't a house. It was a trailer, the kind they call a "double wide." We lived there for two years, until I was nine. It had a kind of porch extended out the side where I kept Mother's dollhouse, the one she had when she was little. Daddy fixed it up, and we painted it together. Not that I played with dolls. I played with trolls with weird-colored hair, bright pink and chartreuse, that stood on end. I spent hours out on that porch making furniture out of milk cartons for that troll house, pasting on popsicle sticks for the chair legs, which were especially tricky. Daddy bought me acrylics, so I could paint them. All kinds of wild colors. We sit for a long time. I can see she's trying to figure me out, but I don't make her nervous like the others.

After a while, she gets up and comes back with a shopping bag full of empty milk cartons and some scissors and scotch tape and dumps them on the table.

"Do you think you could make a model of the house, the one you lived in when you were happy?"

That's smart on her part. I give her that. I figure I can probably wait her out just making and furnishing a milk carton double wide.

Mother usually gives up on one of these spies after ten sessions, or maybe the insurance cuts off.

There were stacks of CDs all over the living room in that trailer. Daddy likes music, bluegrass, rock and roll, country, you name it. And the speakers had wires running out of them that I was always tripping on. There were posters of Creedence Clearwater and the Beatles on the walls and a black cast-iron woodstove, which kept the room really warm in winter. At night, Daddy and I would sit on the sofa, which was brown and soft, and listen to music and play games like Monopoly and be warm.

But it was even better outside the trailer. We lived on an apple farm. There were a few cows and chickens and a horse. And this mean peacock. It was a real farm. We lived there because Daddy's job was to manage the farm. The owner lived someplace else. I was the only kid and had the farm to myself. Mother left for the hospital every day. She's a nurse. When I wasn't in school, I climbed trees and played with my trolls and helped Daddy feed the chickens and pick apples and brush the horse and lots of other things.

At night, the three of us would eat dinner, outside if it was warm, or in the kitchen. And Mother would tell us stories about the hospital, about the babies she took care of. She was like a different person then. She'd tickle me and tease my daddy and laugh.

I take the scissors and cut wheels out of one of the milk cartons and tape them onto the bottom of the other one. The spy pretends to be impressed.

"That's a trailer, isn't it?" she says.

As if she didn't know all about it from Mother.

"You're good with your hands. Would you like to tell me about it?"

I smash the milk carton with my fist.

"I guess not," she says. "It's okay. I'm sorry you smashed it though. Was it that important?"

Fat cow.

Back home, Mother tries to talk to me about my dad.

Lies, lies. I cover my ears.

"You have to talk to me, Lucy."

I shut my bedroom door and tune in the Beatles on my iPod. I know she's screaming. I turn up the volume. John and Paul are singing. "Lucy in the Sky with Diamonds."

His favorite song.

She hands me a bag of colored pens while she watches me with those dark gypsy eyes.

"Could you draw your family?" she asks. I know what she's after. I draw three stick figures. The one in the middle is shorter than the other two and has a big smile on her face. The other two, one with a ponytail, the other with some messy hair hanging out the back of a baseball cap, are also smiling.

"Is that your family?" she asks.

She knows it's not. Not now anyway.

Then she surprises me. She takes a piece of paper and starts to draw. At first, I pretend not to notice, but after a while I have to look. She's drawing a girl who is wearing a yellow tee-shirt with blue flowers and a pair of blue pants. The girl has the same dark hair as me. The spy's a pretty good drawer. She looks at me for a minute then draws an upside-down smile for a mouth. I laugh.

"Okay," she says, and smiles. "We're agreed. That's you. And you're not very happy. Now let me do your mom."

And she starts drawing a woman next to the girl. She's got on a tennis dress, and her hair is pulled back. She's looking at the girl, and there are lots of lines across her forehead.

"Hmm," she says. "She looks worried about you."

Good, I think.

"There's someone else in your family," she says, "but I don't know what he looks like."

She's lying. I bet Mother's shown her that picture she used to keep on her chest of drawers. The man in the white shirt with a collar, his dark hair slicked down, cut short. A man made to dress up to have his picture taken. I hated that picture and was glad when she took it down. My daddy's hair is messy and long on his neck. And he's always laughing at something. Or singing Elvis songs, like "Blue Moon of Kentucky."

She puts her drawing in front of me.

"You draw him."

I stare at the curtains.

"You're a tough cookie," she says and smiles.

He disappeared after we left the trailer, after we moved to Bon Air. I was nine when we moved, and I didn't want to leave the farm, but Mother told me I'd like it better in town where there'd be other girls to play with. She said my new school had "state of the art" playground equipment. That's how she put it. Like playground equipment would substitute for the apple trees and the horse.

Even at the time, I knew the move had nothing to do with me. It had to do with Daddy and the fights she was having with him. The way she was picking on him. Wanting him to be different. For one thing, she didn't like his smell.

"Into the shower," she'd say when he'd come into the trailer at the end of the day. "You're disgusting."

"That's not what you used to say."

He'd laugh that big laugh of his.

"You planning to fumigate me with some of that Bon Air?"

I liked the way he smelled, sweet and sour, like cows and apples and sweat all at the same time.

"Draw your daddy," she says again.

I pick up the red-colored pencil and scribble all over her drawing.

He lost that smell after we moved. After she made him cut off all his nice messy hair that grew down to his shoulders. Made him go out looking for a job in an office.

"A management position with a future," she called it.

He laughed. He always laughed. Or whistled some Beatles song. He didn't argue.

"You're a dreamer," she said. "A boy."

I shut my door and played with my trolls, but I could hear them. Not him. Her. Her voice, cutting through the air, sliding under my door.

He lost the smell, and then he was gone. Like that, he was gone.

Mother got really skinny. She left for a run every day before I woke up, then she'd burst in the door while I was eating my fruit loops at the kitchen counter, her face red, her hair in a scraggly ponytail, dark circles of sweat under her arms. She looked awful. She'd pull up a stool beside me and eat a piece of cantaloupe or a banana with yogurt and start asking me about school and had I made any friends.

I hadn't.

She was all over that. She said I needed some interests to make friends. I was ten and not quite sure what she meant by "interests." She pointed out that she was making friends, playing tennis with one group, doing yoga with another, jogging with the neighbors.

In those days, I wanted her to be happy, so I made up the Troll House Club and described the club members who were my new friends, the twins Vanessa and Teresa. That worked for a while. Mother stopped asking questions, and I could entertain myself, for hours at a time, cutting up milk cartons for troll house furniture and eating mint chocolate chip ice cream.

The truth was Vanessa and Teresa were real. They were in my fourth grade class, and they were not my friends. In fact, they paid no attention to me at all. No one did. Until I brought my two favorite trolls to school.

"Why don't you show us your dolls?" Miss Veronica said, and just from the way she said it, all false and sweet, I knew I was in for trouble.

But I went up to the front of the room anyway, like she asked me to, Pinky in one hand, Rola Moncola in the other. It was show and tell, and I figured I better get it over with.

"My name's Pinky," I said in a real high voice, "and this is my friend, Rola Moncola. Our talent is singing, and we're going to sing 'Yellow Submarine.' And we'd like all of you to sing with us."

Nobody said a word, but Miss Veronica was nodding and smiling at me, so I couldn't back down. I stuck the trolls out in front of me and bobbed them up and down and started singing. If any of the kids joined in, I didn't hear them because Miss Veronica drowned them out. She had a really terrible voice. I thought it would never end.

Miss Veronica clapped when it was over, and most of the girls did too. But afterward, on the playground, I could hear them laughing. And one time when I was walking home from school, one of the boys called out, "Hi. Rola Pola Moncola."

Miss Veronica must have said something to Mother, because after that, she started paying more attention. She started watching me when I was eating. I could feel her eyes on me whenever I was finishing up a carton of ice cream or making chocolate chip cookies for myself. By that time, I was ten and weighed almost ninety pounds.

That's when the lessons began.

"I hate tennis," I told Mother after the first session.

"Of course, you don't," she said.

She kept telling me I was getting better when I wasn't.

"You have to run after the ball," Mother would say when she came to watch my lessons.

"I hate running," I'd say.

"You're just being difficult."

"No, I just hate tennis."

One time after the tennis lessons, she found me in my room making sinks and bathtubs out of play dough for the troll house.

"Let's go for a run," she said.

She was wearing her running shorts and the orange tank top and her purple headband.

"No, thank you."

"You can't just sit all day and eat ice cream and play with dolls," she said.

"I want to go home," I said.

She looked sad.

"You are home."

"No, I'm not."

I saw her watching me.

"You won't find him back at the farm," she said.

"Get out!" I yelled.

"Draw a picture of you and your mother the day you stopped talking to her."

I pick up a pencil and draw two figures. One is a stick figure. The other is made of big fat circles.

She studies the drawing.

"You think that's how she sees you?" she says.

Like I said, she's smart.

I was ten. Mother opened the door to my bedroom, ignoring the "No Trespassing" sign, and said, "We need to talk."

I was on the floor cutting up magazines to wallpaper the troll house. I didn't look at her.

"What happened to the doughnuts?"

Of course, she'd noticed. She snoops around the kitchen whenever she comes home from work. Why does she keep buying doughnuts anyway?

"You ate them, didn't you?"

I carefully placed the magazines and scissors and paste on the shelf with the trolls and lay down on my bed. She came over and sat next to me.

"You did, didn't you?"

Her voice felt like a drill.

"Look, honey, you can't keep on eating like this."

I lay there staring at the cracks on the ceiling.

"I worry about you," she said. "You've put on fifteen pounds since school started. Your pants are tight. Look at your stomach."

I turned over on my stomach, my face in the pillow.

"Don't you even care?"

Her voice was edging up, squeaking.

I pulled the ends of the pillow up around my ears, but I heard her anyway.

"I care about you. You know I do. You're my little girl. But if you keep sneaking food and gaining all that weight, you won't have any friends."

I could feel her wanting me to cry. And there was a part of me that *was* crying, but I concentrated on holding my face very still, and the tears stayed back.

"Say something," she said.

I had to hold really still and clinch my fists against the pillow, but I didn't say a thing.

"Talk to me," she said.

Her voice was getting louder.

"Do you think that will bring him back?"

She was so mad at me.

"Eating everything in sight and cutting me off?"

I lay there hoping she'd leave.

"It won't, you know."

She was still there. I put the pillow over my head.

"Say something!" Her voice was muffled by the pillow, but I could tell she was yelling at me.

After a while, she got up off the bed. I figured she was gone, but I didn't move. I was afraid if I moved, I'd start screaming and wouldn't be able to stop. So, I stayed like that, holding myself in for a long time. I don't know how long.

I knew she'd be back, and I was right.

"I'm sorry, Lucy."

She was begging.

"Please, honey, talk to me."

But I didn't.

The spy opens an envelope and pulls out a photograph. She's up to something. It's the ninth session, and she's running out of time.

I turn away.

"The person who mailed this letter says this is a photo of your father," she says.

I refuse to look.

"What are you afraid of?" she asks. "You're very strong, Lucy. Anybody who can keep herself from talking for such a long time has to be strong. You can't be afraid of a photograph."

I look her in the eyes. She's daring me.

I glance at the man in the photograph. It's not him. This one's laughing at somebody who isn't in the picture. He's wearing a suit, one with stripes. Like a businessman. His hair is cut real short. Definitely not him.

"You don't think it's him?" she says.

She looks at the picture again and puts it back in the envelope.

"Okay."

She puts the envelope on the table. I see the words "Daniel Fralin," his name.

"Your mother gave this to me," she says. "She wanted to tell you about it, to show you, but you wouldn't listen."

Show me what? I want to yell, "Bitch! That's not my daddy!"

"There's a letter," she says. "To you. Would you like to read it?"

No, I don't want to read it. Some stupid made-up letter from some old guy in a suit. Not my daddy, not my daddy, not my daddy. I feel the words in my throat, I want to scream them at her. My face feels hot. I have to do something. I pick up a pen and throw it at her.

"Cut that out!" she says real sharp.

It scares me a little. But I smile and leave the room, slamming the door.

I'm pretty sure it's our last session. And it's a good thing because the first thing I see when she opens her office door is that man's photograph propped against the lamp on her desk.

"This is the letter from your father," she says, shutting the door, holding out a piece of paper. "It's to you, and you're strong enough to hear what he says."

Why does she keep saying that? I head for the door and turn the knob. She hasn't locked me in. Good.

I stand there, my back to her, ready to run.

The spy keeps on talking.

"You need to hear what he says. Since you won't read the letter, I'll read it to you."

I don't want to hear it. I want to leave. But I don't. I put my hands over my ears, but I can still hear her voice. Why don't I leave?

Dear Lucy in the sky with diamonds. I miss my big girl.

Lies, lies, lies.

What do you think about your old dad, all dressed up fit to kill? Just like your mom wanted, huh? I'm in the auto business down here in L.A., making a go of it. I want you to come visit me real soon. I'll take you to Disneyland. How 'bout that?

It's a lie. It's all a lie. I feel those words bursting in my throat. But I force them back. I choke on them.

I feel real bad about how I treated you and your mom. I just hope I can make it up to you someday, and I hope you'll forgive.
Your loving Dad

I rush at her and rip the letter from her hand, tearing it, and throw it on the floor. I hit at her, at her face, her chest. The spy grabs my arms and pins them to my side. She wraps her own arms around me. I'm surprised how strong she is underneath all those shawls. She smells like lemonade. I try to fight her, but she's too strong.

"You're okay," she says.

Mother's in the room. How come she's here? She's watching us, looking scared.

"He misses you," she says. "That's in the letter. He loves you."

The spy holds onto me.

"Please leave," she says to Mother.

She sounds angry.

"You shouldn't be in here."

I break away and face them. They're watching me, waiting.

I walk over and pick up the photograph. I start singing. It just comes out. I'm singing, loud, louder, singing to the man in the picture.

"Blue moon of Kentucky, won't ya keep on shining."

Louder and louder. They're talking, but I can't hear them. They watch me. They don't know what to do.

The Columbia

The South Carolina Review, Volume 48, Number 1, Fall 2015
Also published in *Spotswood Virginia*,
Stephen F. Austin State University Press, 2021

Reva Hamm's big toe stuck straight up. No one in Spotswood suspected. They just thought that the bulky brown shoes she always wore were the style up North, where she'd gone after high school on a piano scholarship. Reva played like an angel, all the classical pieces and hymns. No show tunes though. But she didn't stay in New York after she graduated from Julliard. She just turned up back in Spotswood and practiced her piano pretty much all day. You could hear her out on the street. The hymns mostly. Sounded like she went through the whole Broadman hymnal, end-to-end, at least once a week. People who saw her in town, carrying groceries in a faded cloth bag, picking up her father's starched white shirts at the cleaners, waiting for prescriptions at Johnson's Drugstore, said she was surely a treasure to her mother, who rarely left her bed.

But Birdi knew about the toe because she'd seen it. She was visiting her friend Mrs. Hamm in that second-floor bedroom with all the windows shut and the blinds drawn. It was hot enough to melt, but the old lady had pulled the cotton blanket with the cornflower pattern up to her waist and was propped up, as always, against three or four pillows in the four-poster mahogany bed. Her gray hair was pinned into a knot on the top of her head, and her face was white as flour and quilted-looking. Birdi sat on the stool close to the bed, her eyes fixed on the old lady. And they were both laughing out loud at the antics of the Banks family as Mrs. Hamm read from *Mary Poppins*.

"Time for your medicine, Mama."

It was Reva, standing at the bedroom door, clutching a pill bottle in her hand, her voice shrill. She was wearing lime green shorts and a white pique halter. Her limp brown hair was pulled back in a ponytail. And she was barefoot. Which is why Birdi stared. She'd only seen Reva in the brown shoes. The big toe on her right foot was stuck up straight as a ruler. The other toes were ordinary, just lying there on the hardwood floor flat as you please.

"Just put it here."

Mrs. Hamm pointed to a small table beside her bed cluttered with crumpled up tissues and a couple of empty drinking glasses.

But Reva was giving Birdi a hard look. "Mama, you know you're not feeling well enough for visitors," she said.

"I said to put the bottle here." Mrs. Hamm's sharp tone startled Birdi.

"Now, Mama, the doctor said for me to administer your medicine." Reva shook out two small white pills from the bottle and handed them to her mother.

"What does he know? Put the bottle over here. I can count out pills myself."

Reva frowned, then placed the bottle on the table. She turned to Birdi. "Now don't stay long," she warned. "Mama needs her rest."

"Oh, I'm never too tired for my Birdi," the old lady said.

Reva stood beside the bed for a minute, her fingers twitching at her sides like she was playing the piano.

Then, "Do you need anything else, Mama?"

But there was no answer.

After Reva left the room, Birdi interrupted *Mary Poppins* to ask, "What's the matter with her toe?"

"She's a musician, dear."

Birdi gave that some thought. Had she injured it on the piano pedals? But she didn't have time to pursue the subject because Mrs. Hamm downed several pills with a glass of water and said, "Birdi, dear, I bet you'd like a bicycle."

And that's what Birdi wanted more than anything in the world. She was almost seven, long past time for a girl to have her own bicycle, but her daddy had told her the bicycle factories were too busy making tanks for the soldiers to fight the Germans. Cheap junk. That's all there was out there, cheap junk, and her daddy wasn't one for that. She'd just have to wait until the war was over, he said.

"I sure would, Ma'am, but there's nothing but junk in the stores," Birdi said.

"Maybe there's one that's not for sale," Mrs. Hamm said.

"I wouldn't know about that, Ma'am."

"Maybe there's a bicycle right now in the garage that's not junk," Mrs. Hamm said.

"Whose bicycle?"

"Maybe it's yours."

Her voice sort-of sang it.

Birdi was confused.

"I don't think so," she said.

"Go on out there," Mrs. Hamm said. "If you find a bicycle in that garage, it belongs to you."

And there it stood near the door of the spotless garage, all by itself, clean and fresh, ready to go. It was painted black with cream-colored stripes, not red and shiny like the Schwinn she dreamed about. It was second-hand, she could tell, but the tires and steel handlebars looked new. It was a girl's bike. It was a Columbia. It was the most beautiful thing Birdi had ever seen.

When she went back upstairs to make sure this bicycle was really hers, the old lady was lying on her back, her mouth open, snoring. Birdi took hold of one of her velvety-soft old-lady hands and cradled it against her cheek.

"Thank you," she whispered. "I love it so much."

Mr. Hamm was Harris Reynolds' boss, the Hamm of Hamm Hardware, the Hamm of "If you're handy, go to Hamm." And Harris Reynolds was Birdi's daddy. He had worked for Hamm since high school and knew the business top to bottom. No other hardware store had ever succeeded in Spotswood, a sleepy town of about forty-thousand in southern Virginia, because Harris took care of Hamm's customers.

The old man was an enigma to most of Spotswood. Silent and stiff-faced, his balding head bent slightly forward, his light blue eyes fixed on the papers before him. He shut himself up in the inner office most of the day, rarely looking up from the large book he scribbled in.

Harris, on the other hand, bounced around the cluttered store, shaking hands, giving advice, demonstrating power tools, laughing, talking. He was a robust young man, a little heavy around the middle, with thick red-brown curls, large brown eyes, and the beginning of a double chin. The kind of young man people trusted.

Once a year, at Christmas, Hamm invited Harris and his family to a dinner of roast chicken, mashed potatoes, carrots, and chocolate cake, all of which had been purchased in cardboard cartons from the Spotswood Hotel dining room. On these occasions, Mrs. Hamm left her bed and appeared downstairs in a navy-blue silk dress and black and white spectator pumps.

Before they sat down to eat, Reva always played the Steinway piano which dominated the living room. She sat with a straight back on the piano bench, her light blue eyes, her father's eyes, fixed on the music stand, while her audience perched uncomfortably on faded Queen Ann chairs and a brown velveteen horsehair sofa. First, there would be Christmas carols, then selections from Handel's *Messiah*, and always at the end, a rousing rendition of the "Alleluia Chorus."

The first time Birdi was invited, she responded by contributing her thin four-year-old voice to the concert. But no one joined her, and no one smiled or looked in her direction except Mrs. Hamm, and so, midway through "Away in a Manger," she stopped singing and never raised her voice again. Instead, she focused on Reva's heavy shoes pumping the pedals. Reva dressed for these occasions, like her mother, in a blue silk dress, but the fabric seemed softer, and the skirt swept low over her legs, almost hiding the shoes, but not quite. Her hands, thin and bony with prominent blue veins and long fingers, spread out along the keys, lifting, arching, crashing down.

After the concert, they filed into the dimly lit dining room which was barely large enough for the walnut table. Geneva, the maid, had to hold her breath as she squeezed herself between the guests and the dark green walls, serving the dinner with a weary smile. The centerpiece of plastic plums and bananas in a silver-plated bowl was an annual fixture. Time had yellowed the lace cloth.

At the table, Mrs. Hamm sat herself next to Birdi and made sure she got plenty of mashed potatoes and chocolate cake.

It was after one of these dinners that Birdi began her visits to Mrs. Hamm's sick room. She was five at the time, and Mrs. Hamm told her she had lots of wonderful books she would like to read to her. And so, the weekly visits began, with Mrs. Hamm sitting up in bed, a stack of books beside her, and Birdi on a stool close by.

"What's wrong with you?" she once asked.

"Nerves, dear," Mrs. Hamm said.

"Where do they hurt?"

"My head mostly.

"Do those pills make it feel better?"

"Most of the time."

"Will you read to me even after you get well?"

"I'll read to you forever if you like."

Birdi smiled at the old lady and scooted her stool even closer to the bed.

"Where'd that come from?" her daddy asked the day Birdi first rode the bicycle home.

"Mrs. Hamm gave it to me."

"For goodness sakes," her mother said.

"You sure she gave it to you? She didn't ask you to pay for it?" her daddy said.

"She didn't say anything about paying her. It's old. I think it was Reva's."

Mrs. Reynolds picked up the telephone right then and asked Mrs. Hamm about it.

"She's welcome to it, dear. No one's ridden it for years."

"Are you sure, Maddie? We'd be happy to pay you for it," Birdi's mother said.

"Don't be silly. You know I'd do anything for that child," was her reply.

The next day at the store, Harris told Hamm he thought he should pay for the bike.

"You'll have to ask the wife about that," Hamm said. "All I know is she asked me to clean it up. And I did."

Birdi was small for her age, with a sharply-pointed nose and large black eyes. That's why they called her "Birdi." Her real name was Roberta.

Now that she had the Columbia, she took flight, racing around town, running errands for her mother, ringing the bell her daddy put on the handlebars, her thin brown hair streaming in wisps behind her, her skinny legs pumping.

She was riding down South Main under green-leafed maples one spring afternoon on the way home from school when she nearly collided with a yellow rubber raincoat. Reva Hamm was inside the raincoat, crossing the street against a red light, and Birdi had almost hit her.

"Watch where you're going!"

Reva's voice was harsh. But then she stopped and stared.

"Oh, it's you, Birdi," she said in the sort of polite tone adults use when talking to a child, and, smiling, she reached out and grabbed hold of the Columbia's handlebars.

Birdi was relieved. The harsh tone had startled her.

"Where'd you get your bicycle?" Reva asked.

"Your mama gave it to me."

Reva's smile was gone.

"When was that?"

"Last month."

"Well, how 'bout that?" Reva said. She paused a minute, then said, "Are you sure?"

"Yes ma'am."

Birdi was feeling uneasy.

Reva suddenly smiled and released her grip on the handlebars.

"Well, you run along now, and try to be more careful."

Birdi almost said, "Who wasn't being careful?"

But instead, she hopped on her bike and raced home.

The next morning, when Birdi's father opened the front door for his morning paper, he found Jerry Batson, a local policeman, standing on the front stoop.

"Morning, Harris," the policeman said. "I'm wondering if you got a Columbia bicycle anywhere around here?"

"Sure. It's Birdi's bike."

"Well, I'd like to take a look at it. We got a report of a stolen Columbia."

"Help yourself. But ours isn't stolen."

"Yeah? Hamm's daughter called it in."

"That's mighty peculiar, Jerry. Mrs. Hamm *gave* Birdi the bike."

The policeman raised his eyebrows.

"Peculiar's the word for that girl all right. The mother too. But I got orders to take possession. You can settle things with Hamm. Sorry 'bout that, Harris."

Harris stood silent for a minute.

"Look, Jerry," he finally said, "I myself offered to pay Hamm for that bike. How 'bout you hold off until I talk to him?"

Birdi appeared from behind her daddy, peering up at the policeman with tears in her eyes.

"I guess that's okay," he said, looking down. "But I better not hear about it again."

As soon as the policeman was gone, Birdi raced to the garage and jumped on the bicycle seat, one foot on the cement floor, the other tucked around the black and cream frame.

"It's mine," she pleaded when her father approached. "Mrs. Hamm gave it to me."

"Maybe she meant to just lend it to you for a while," he said.

Her lower lip began to tremble. "She *gave* it to me."

"Okay. But I think we need to talk to her."

Birdi's mother came out from the house and put her hand on Birdi's head.

"Let me do it," she said. "I know her better."

"You're right," Harris said.

Birdi saw him look at her mother in a way she didn't understand.

"You're not taking my bike," Birdi said, winding her arms around the handlebars and pressing her cheek against the bell.

"All right," her mother said. "We'll both take it."

"No!" Birdi screamed.

Her mother pulled her off the bicycle with fingers stronger than they looked and wiped her face with a washcloth.

"I'm sure there's a mistake, and we'll bring your bike back home. But the policeman says we have to make sure the bike's yours. I'm sorry, but that's how it is."

They headed together over to the Hamm's house. When they got to the front door, Birdi rested the Columbia on the kickstand, carefully locked it, and dropped the key deep in the pocket of her shorts.

Geneva let them in.

"No company, Geneva."

It was Mrs. Hamm's feeble voice coming from upstairs.

"It's just me and Birdi," Ms. Reynolds called back. "We need to see you."

"Geneva, tell her to come back later."

Something about Mrs. Hamm's voice struck Birdi as different, and she wanted to leave right then. But Birdi's mother yelled out, "It won't take a minute, Maddie," and pulled the reluctant Birdi up the stairs behind her.

They found Mrs. Hamm in her bed as usual, her hands nervously twisting the blanket with the cornflower pattern. Her gray hair hung loose around her colorless face, her watery blue eyes seemed puzzled. The room smelled funny to Birdi, slightly sweet and not pleasant.

Birdi's mother cleared her throat and announced in a loud voice, "Maddie, look at me."

Mrs. Hamm stared in the direction of the visitors.

"Maddie," Birdi's mother repeated. "Reva claims Birdi stole her bicycle."

Birdi stood very still beside her mother and looked at the floor. She knew something terrible was going to happen.

The old lady's eyelids fluttered.

"Why Birdi," she whispered, "I can't believe you'd do such a thing."

Birdi looked up, startled. "Do what?" Her face suddenly felt hot, and she was crying. "I didn't steal anything. It's mine. You gave it to me."

"Really?"

Mrs. Hamm frowned like she was trying to remember something that had happened a long time ago.

Birdi's mother looked closely at the old lady.

"But I thanked you for it, Maddie," she said. "On the telephone. And you said you'd do anything for my girl."

But Mrs. Hamm was no longer watching them. Her eyes had fixed on the door.

"Did you bring it back?"

It was Reva, standing in the doorway, her limp brown hair pulled back from her face with bobby pins, her light blue eyes shining out of dark hollows.

Mrs. Hamm reached out and gripped Birdi's arm with icy fingers, but her eyes were still fixed on her daughter.

"Did I give Birdi your bike, dear?" she asked.

"Of course not," Reva spat out.

"We'll return the bicycle," Birdi's mother said. "Now."

She was standing very stiff, and Birdi could tell by her voice she was angry.

"No," Birdi wailed. "It's my bike." She pulled her arm away from the old lady. "You gave it to me. It's mine."

But Mrs. Hamm wasn't listening.

"Did you bring my medicine?" she said, her voice low, pleading.

"Yes, Mama." Reva grinned as she turned to Birdi.

"Now then," she said. "Please go away. You're making her sick."

Without another word, Birdi's mother took hold of her daughter's hand and pulled her out of the room. Birdi fought her all the way down the stairs, but her mother's anger was stronger than her own.

Reva followed them out the front door.

"Where should we leave the bicycle?" Birdi's mother asked in a cold voice.

"No," Birdi screamed. "I won't."

"Just leave it here, by the front door." Reva looked at the bicycle. "It's locked. Where's the key?"

"You can't have it!" Birdi cried.

"You got no choice, honey," her mother said. "Hand it over."

Birdi threw the key at Reva and wrapped her arms around the Columbia's handlebars and kissed each one. Then carefully, lovingly, she leaned her bicycle back up against the kickstand and walked away. She held her mother's hand all the way home because she was crying too hard to see.

Early the next morning, Harris Reynolds found the bicycle on his front stoop, its spokes bent and broken, the fender smashed, the tires flat.

"Keep Birdi inside," he whispered to his wife who was standing behind him, her hand over her mouth. But it was too late. Birdi pushed past both of them and threw herself onto the battered bicycle, pressing her hands against the busted wheels and crying out in jerky gasps. When her daddy tried to pick her up, the bicycle came with her. So, he swooped them both up, laid them carefully in the back of his Dodge truck, and headed for the Hamms.

Hamm opened the door before Harris had even rung the bell. He was dressed, as usual, in his blue suit and starched white shirt, but his shoulders sagged, and his usually sharp blue eyes were bloodshot.

"It's busted," Harris announced, thrusting the Columbia out in front of him. "How come?"

Hamm stared at the bicycle. He opened his mouth as if he were about to say something, but nothing came out.

They heard someone calling weakly from upstairs.

"Who is it?"

"Never mind, dear," Hamm called back to her.

"It's Birdi, isn't it? Tell her to come up."

The voice was soft, pleading. Birdi stared up at Mr. Hamm. She was crying, and her nose was running unchecked.

"Birdi?" The voice from upstairs.

The child shook her head from side to side.

"Please, please, Birdi, come up."

Birdi turned back toward her wounded bicycle.

"I've got some new books," the voice promised.

But Birdi was crouched over her Columbia, caressing the fenders, kissing the pedals, her wet cheek resting on the seat.

"Birdi, come back. I miss you . . ."

But the rest of whatever Mrs. Hamm was going to say was drowned out by a sudden crash of chords on the piano. Someone was playing a hymn, except it was too harsh, too loud, like one hand was banging fiercely on the piano while the other was picking out a tune.

Birdi peered around Hamm into the living room. Reva sat at the piano, smiling. Her eyes were focused on the sheet of music before her. Her hands pounded the keys. Her feet on the pedals were barefoot. And the big toe on her right foot was standing straight up.

Dirty Dora

Thin Air Magazine, Volume 21, Spring 2015
Also published in *Spotswood Virginia,*
Stephen F. Austin State University Press, 2021

I seen the papers. I know what they say about me, what they call me. "Dirty Dora." Just because I danced one dance with one of them. Just one dance. This whole town's been in a tizzy ever since some fancy court said we got to go to school with them. So, they make *me* out to be some kind of criminal and shut me up here in the courthouse. It ain't exactly a jail, at least there ain't no bars. But the door's locked, except when they bring me food or let my mama in to see me, which I wish they wouldn't, she's so shamed.

I been here a month, mostly in this room, sitting on this bed, looking out the window at the statue of Mayor Woods, white as chalk, up in front of the courthouse. Dead now. I ain't seen Trish or Faye since they picked us up, but I reckon they got them stashed away in rooms like this too. They supposed to get me a lawyer, but I ain't seen one yet.

Dirty Dora. It's not even my name, which is Doreen. But they don't care 'bout that. They just want to make a joke out of me, that's all. All those little pipsqueak boys in my class. The girls ain't a lot better. Much shorter than me with thin little arms and no chest at all. Some of them are nice though and ask me to draw things, horses mostly or girls all dressed up in pretty clothes.

One thing about being shut up in here, I don't have to go to school. I been going for eight years, seems like forever, and I never got no further than sixth grade. Had to repeat first. Then nasty old Miz Brown failed me in fourth. I'm fourteen now and stuck in sixth grade, second time around, and I can't read the science book or the history book or any of the books. I can do the arithmetic good as the boys so long as they ain't written out problems. Numbers has always been easy for me. That's how I know I'm not dumb. But, since I'm no good at reading, they'll probably flunk me again. All I can say is two more years I'm outta there. No more school.

Long about fifth grade, I started changing. Got tall, got myself a bra. The other girls in my class stayed little, even the ones in sixth who had been in my class before Old Lady Brown flunked me. I could see them trying not to look when we changed clothes for gym. Funny thing was those same little girls were all friendly to me in gym class. We'd line up to choose sides for kickball, and whoever was captain would yell out, "I want Doreen."

"No fair. You had her last week," the other captain would say.

So, they'd draw straws, and the long straw would get me. And good for them because we won every time. So, I liked gym class. But I liked art best. You give me a subject and a pencil and some paper, and I can make it look so real. Dogs, cats, pretty girls with curved lips and long hair, like in the comics.

"Bet you can't draw a monster," Joey Kinser said just last month in that smart-alecky voice of his.

"What kind of monster you want?"

"I don't know. With fangs and stuff."

"Piece a cake," I said.

Fact is, I could do it with my eyes shut. I'm that good. But I still hate that Spotswood Grammar School. Every time I had to read out loud, I'd say all the big words wrong, and people laughed. I heard 'em call me "Dumb Dora." Teachers too.

Back when I was in fourth, my mama took off from her job at the mill to see why I was doing so bad. She made me sit there while she asked Miz Brown straight out, "How come Doreen ain't moving up with her class?"

"I hate to tell you, Miz Harris," the old witch said, "but your daughter is behind in her reading."

"Well, whose fault is that?" my mama asked.

"I've done my best with her, but she just doesn't seem to progress."

"You think another year in fourth will help?"

"If she applies herself, I don't see why not."

But I been applying myself, and it don't do no good.

"Why can't I quit Spotswood and go to beauty school?"

"Law says you gotta stay till you're sixteen," Mama says.

So, I kept on going, kept on getting bigger. At recess, when all the girls were playing hopscotch or jumping rope, I'd sit on the steps and draw pictures. That's how I met Trish.

She's this big, red-headed girl who turned up one day during lunch period and sat down next to me on the stairs.

"You a good drawer," she told me after she been watching awhile.

"Thank you," I said. "You ain't in this school, are you?"

"Nope. I'm in seventh over there."

She jerked her thumb toward the junior high across the street.

"How come you over here?"

"I got permission to go home for lunch, but I usually mess around instead."

"Messing around at a grammar school don't sound like fun to me."

"Yeah. Well, I seen you over here all the time and couldn't figure out what somebody so grown-up was doing at this baby school."

"I don't read so good," I said.

"Me neither," she said. "Draw me."

I looked sharp at her long carrot-colored hair, her icy white skin, her purple dress bulging at the top with the biggest bosom you ever saw, and I said, "I need colored pencils for you."

Well, Trish rescued me. Mama says she ruined me, and I have to admit she got me into this mess. But I don't blame her. I didn't have no friends 'til she showed up. Early on, I'd had a couple of girlfriends at Spotswood Grammar, but they'd moved on to the junior high and didn't have nothing more to do with me. Anyway, Mama said they was trash, and maybe she was right. All I know is 'til Trish showed up, I was lonesome all the time. Mama was working the afternoon shift at the mill and didn't get home till after I went to bed. I don't have no daddy. He joined the army when I was a baby and never come back. There was another baby before I was born, but he died.

The drawing was what did it. Trish loved the picture I did of her with the colored pencils I borrowed from the art teacher. I say "borrowed" because I meant to give 'em back. Anyway, Trish had me draw a picture of her friend Faye in Green Street Park after school. Faye's a short little thing with a dirty blond ponytail and skinny legs. So, now I had two friends.

"You like dancing?" Trish asked me one day when we was smoking cigarettes in the park.

"Sure do," I said, although I had never danced a step in my life.

"You got a radio?"

"Yeah?"

"They play all kinda good music on WKRM. Elvis, Buddy Holly, Bill Haley."

"Sure do," I said, bluffing.

What did I know? Mama told me she'd wear me out if she ever caught me listening to that dirty music.

"Let's go over to your house and do some dancing," Trish said.

"My mama wouldn't like that," I said.

"Is she home?"

"No."

"What she don't know won't hurt her."

"What 'bout your house?" I asked.

"My mama's home. You don't want to mess with her," Trish said.

Faye nodded like she knew.

"Come on, Doreen, let's go to your house."

I wanted to say no, but I didn't want to lose the only friends I had.

"Mama'll know if we leave a mess," I said.

"We won't leave no mess."

And we didn't. Most afternoons after school, we'd have our smoke in the park. It was April and getting warm, and it felt good to sit on the benches with my friends like other people and smoke our Camels. Sometimes the grownups gave us dirty looks, but we just laughed. Then we'd walk over to my house, which is one of those houses the mill rents out to its workers. They're all alike, wood frame, most of them needing a paint job, a little patch of grass out front. My bedroom is small, just enough room for a single bed and a chest of drawers. But the living room is big enough for dancing. We'd shove the sofa up against the wall and carry the two chairs and the rug into the kitchen. The rug was easy, just a small, rag rug Mama made. Trish found the radio in the kitchen and turned on WKRM.

I'll never forget that first time. This voice was singing, "Get out from that kitchen and rattle those pots and pans," and Trish just started bouncing all over the room, waving her arms and singing. She grabbed Faye's hand, and they bounced together, twisting and turning and laughing and singing. I hadn't heard that song before, which is hard to believe, but remember, I was in sixth grade with all those little kids.

"Come on, Doreen," Trish called out and grabbed my hand.

I started hopping from foot to foot.

"Ain't you even been dancing?" she asked.

It was pretty obvious I hadn't.

"Come on, Faye," she said. "We gotta teach her."

They started me out just bouncing to the beat, not even moving my feet, just bending my knees up and down and waving my arms. Once I got the beat, they showed me how to move my feet. We practiced a while, and pretty soon, I got it. I got better and better at it. I didn't want to stop. Mama never guessed because we fixed up the living room good as new every time.

That summer, Trish and Faye came over to my house every afternoon as soon as Mama left for work. We didn't always dance. Sometimes we played rummy or double sol. Sometimes we read love comics.

One day, Trish said, "I'm sick of dancing with girls. Let's find some boys to dance with."

"How do you mean?"

"I hear there's some dancing in the pavilion in Boyle Park," Faye said.

Trish perked up.

"Yeah? When?"

"Friday nights."

"I can't," I said. "Mama won't let me."

Truth is Mama played bingo at the church on Friday nights. She wouldn't know. But I was scared to be out in that park at night.

"Whose gon' tell your mama?"

"Somebody might see me."

"Somebody's gon' see you, alright, but they ain't the type to tell your mama."

I see now I was dumb to listen to her. But I loved that dancing. And, to tell the honest truth, I didn't know no boys, and I was itching to dance with one. If I hadn't listened to her, I wouldn't have met Tommy.

It was August, and steaming hot that first time, even at eight o'clock at night. Trish, Faye, and I walked through the park to the Pavilion, talking and laughing real loud to cover up how nervous we were. I was wearing my white pedal pushers and those cheap ballet shoes that look like Capezios, and I was sweating under my arms. Once we got there, we hung around on the sidelines for a few minutes watching couples close dancing to "Love Me Tender," which was playing on somebody's radio. I looked around to see if I knew anybody. I didn't, and it made me feel easier.

Trish and Faye started dancing with each other, showing off, hoping to attract some boy's attention, which they did pretty fast.

Then this soldier come up and asked me, real polite, "May I have this dance?"

He was taller than me and had this blond curly hair and blue eyes. I mean I couldn't believe somebody so handsome was asking me to dance. "All Shook Up" was playing on the radio, and he took my hand and swung me out and pulled me back to him, his feet hopping to the beat and me right along with him.

"I haven't seen you here before, sugar," he said during the commercial break.

"This my first time."

"You in high school?"

I nodded. You couldn't tell a man old enough to be soldier that you're in sixth grade.

"You in the Army?"

"Fort Dix."

"Where's that at?"

"North Carolina, about an hour from here. Name's Tommy," he said, "and if you have no objection, I'm gonna monopolize your company tonight."

I kept staring at him and breathing in a lemony smell like from shaving lotion and smiling like a big fool.

"Not much of a talker, are you, sugar?" he said.

"What do you want me to say?"

He laughed.

"Anything you want to say."

"I can draw," I said.

He looked at me so solemnly.

"Well, you have to draw me some time," he said.

I was having trouble breathing he was so close. I wanted right then to draw him. I wanted to take my blue pencil and color in those deep violet eyes. I wanted to use the side of my pencil to shade in his cheekbones. I wanted to touch his ears that were so small and perfect. I wanted to feel the skin of his white neck against my mouth.

"I'm Doreen," I said.

I saw him every Friday night after that. We jitterbugged and slow danced. He would pull me right onto the front of his starched khaki uniform and rock me back and forth, whispering right in my ear, and every part of my body would be singing. We took breaks from the dancing, of course. Out in the dark where there were lots of trees. I let him do whatever he wanted. It felt so good. We didn't go all the way. I held him off there. But I wanted to. I still think about it. I loved that man.

Now here comes the bad part. School started, and after a couple of weeks, it got cold out there in the park. People stopped coming on Friday nights. But we wanted to keep dancing.

I thought about Tommy in my house, sneaking up to my bedroom, shutting the door. I almost said yes.

But then, "Too many people," I said. "Besides the neighbors would tell my mama."

"I know a place," this GI said. His name was Dwayne, and I never seen him before.

"What place?"

I could tell Trish was all for it.

"Called Dix Dance Club. Other side of town."

"What other side of town?"

He named a street I hadn't heard of. The cops don't believe me, but I had no idea.

"What's it like," I asked.

"It's a guy's living room. He got hundreds of records, and he charges a dollar a person to let people dance there."

"How come I never heard of it?" I asked.

"Come on, sugar," Tommy said. "It'll be just fine. You know you want to."

He was right. I wanted to real bad.

So, the last Friday night in September, Trish, Faye, and I met Tommy and a bunch of soldiers in the park, like always. Only this time, the soldier named Dwayne had a Ford car. We all squeezed in, the girls sitting on the boys' laps. We was so busy giggling and carrying on, I didn't pay no attention to where we was going.

"Here we are," Dwayne said as he slammed on the brakes.

There weren't no streetlights, no lights in the houses, no car headlights even. It was dark.

"It's okay," Tommy whispered, kissing my ear. "You're with me."

He pushed me off him and out the car.

Suddenly, I heard *Peggy Sue* coming from somewhere, and I seen Dwayne standing in the open door of one of the houses, motioning us to follow him.

"Hurry up," he called out in a voice we could barely hear.

Now, what choice did I have? We couldn't just stand out there in the dark.

Inside, the room was bare. No furniture. Shades over the windows. The floor was scuffed up, and some of the boards was cracked. The only light come from a bulb hanging from the ceiling. And it smelled. Not real bad. Just like yesterday's dinner.

And then we saw them. Standing in a line against the wall, an old man, maybe fifty, two young ones about my age, and a small woman with a rag around her head.

They was dark as ink. All of them.

"We're leaving," Trish said.

We rushed back out the door, but Dwayne had gone off. Left us high and dry.

Tommy came outside.

"Come on in, sugar. You can't stay out here. I promise we won't be here long."

"How we gon' get home?"

It was all I could think about.

"Dwayne'll be back. I promise."

I wanted to believe him.

What happened next I can't explain. One of the colored boys put a record on the record player, which was in the kitchen, and the soldiers started dancing, first by themselves, turning and twisting and singing. Then they was pulling Trish and Faye out into middle of the bare room. Tommy and I just watched. A few minutes later, some more girls turned up, girls we'd seen dancing in the park. White girls. But they didn't act surprised like we was. It was like they'd been there before.

The old guy was handing out paper cups of lemonade, and we all started drinking it. We was thirsty. Now I know that it had something in it, but at the time, I didn't even suspect. Tasted like lemonade. After a while, the beat of the music just got to me, and I found myself hanging onto Tommy and swinging round the room.

Then I somehow lost hold of Tommy, and he was dancing with Faye, and it didn't even bother me. I just kept on dancing by myself. And then those dark skin boys was in the middle of us, shaking their shoulders and their hands in time with the music, moving their feet in a kind of shuffle. And the music wasn't Elvis or Buddy Holly anymore. It was this dirty song called "Work with me, Annie" that WKRM wouldn't play on the air. But I'd heard about it. And I didn't know what to do with that dirty music and those boys shaking their hips and laughing. Then one of 'em grabbed my hand and swung me round so hard I got dizzy.

I was standing in the middle of the room with that boy hanging onto me, crying out for Tommy, when the door burst open.

Mama says they gon' send me away to reform school. Says they gon' reform me, so I never dance dirty again.

"What happened to that lawyer?" I say.

"He's the one got you reform school instead of jail," she says.

She keeps on crying every time she shows up.

"What'd I do wrong for you to turn out so delinquent?" she says.

I reckon she got that big word from the newspaper.

"Weren't your fault," I tell her.

"It was them girls. They the ones made you so wicked. You stay away from them in that reform school. You hear me?"

"Yes, ma'am," I say, but I'm glad to hear Trish and Faye will be with me. Makes me less scared.

Mama says the cops only arrested the folks who were in the house that night, including all the girls. They didn't bother with the soldiers. I wrote to Tommy, but I didn't hear nothing from him. I figured the guards was throwing his letters in the trash. I missed him so much I started drawing him. They gave me paper and a pencil, and I drew him over and over.

I said to those pictures, "Hurry up, Tommy. They gon' send me away."

But he didn't come.

Then I figured it out. Tommy's done with me. He don't really love me. He'd visit if he did. Or at least write. I try not to be mad at him, but he's the one put me in that man's house. If anybody's dirty, it's him.

I know I ain't. I may not be good at reading, but I ain't the Dirty Dora they talk about in the papers. And I can draw. Nobody can draw like me.

The Intent for Love

Shadowgraph Insiders, Spring 2015

She didn't like it, the way they laughed at him. The way they whistled "Simple Simon met a pie man" when they saw him coming. They were bruisers, most of them, heavy on their feet. Like the inmates they bullied. Of course, they were also her pals, her coworkers. And they were harmless, really. Just beefy guys kidding around. But she didn't find it funny.

She knew what they meant, of course. His name was Simon, and he did look a little like the illustration in the Mother Goose book. It was the hair. It angled out from a center part in a straight line on both sides of his head, rather like a haystack. But could he help it that his hair was so straight and fine and really lifeless that it wouldn't conform to his skull? He *could* do something about the bangs, which hung in wisps over his forehead. He could, but he didn't. And why should he? It's *his* hair. Live and let live.

Maybe the chemicals had something to do with it. They smelled pretty strong coming out of the dry-cleaning shop. That's where he taught. She figured chemicals that smelled as foul as that could take all the life out of your hair, although she'd never noticed this phenomenon in dry cleaning establishments on the outside.

But it wasn't just his hair. It was his rimless glasses and the way he walked through the yard, chin in the air, arms swinging from the shoulders, smiling. He seemed oblivious of the inmates in their orange jumpsuits, some hand-cuffed, some squatting over outdoor toilets. She hated that, always avoided looking in that direction. He didn't seem to see any of it, but breezed along the ground on invisible skates, his mouth curved in a perpetual smile. The officers imitated him behind his back, sliding their feet along the ground, swinging their arms, grinning like jackasses.

She felt sorry for him. And yet, why? He didn't seem unhappy. Just the opposite. And the men learning the dry-cleaning trade, his inmate students, didn't complain.

He stopped now.

"Well, hello," he said.

His voice was pitched higher than most men's and went up at the end like he was asking a question.

"Hello, Simon," she said, and then, "Well, have a good day."

And she smiled.

She seems interested, he told himself. Definitely interested. She always smiles and says hello. I need to strike while the iron is hot. But he had no idea how. What did the books say? *The Intent For Love. Tracking the Right Partner. Men Are From Mars, Women Are From Venus. 101 Ways to Find Love.* He'd have to do more research.

Her name was L. Winters. He knew that from her nametag. "L." Louise? Laura? Linda? Lee? He liked all those names. And he liked her blond hair which hung in a ponytail out the back of her officer's cap. She was a big woman. Her arms packed the sleeves of her uniform. Her thighs filled out the tops of her trousers. He didn't mind. She had a lovely smile. And she was interested. He was pretty sure of it.

Sailing across the ball field and ducking behind the machine shop, he pulled from his pocket a heavy chain of keys. The laundry, where he taught, was a beat-up white frame building in bad need of a coat of paint. He signed in at the desk without acknowledging the scowling officer presiding there. The dry-cleaning room was empty. He liked it here, in this room. Liked the order, the identical olive-green wool coats lined up in plastic bags, hanging from the metal rack, the large gray machines, silent for now, the steam pressers.

He was a good teacher. He was sure of it. And it was more interesting than running a dry-cleaning business on the outside. He'd done that for ten years or more and made a decent living.

But he'd always dreamed of being a teacher, so when he'd seen the prison job advertised, he thought, well, why not? He liked the idea of giving the inmates a way to earn a living when they paroled. So, in most ways, his life was ideal. He just hadn't met the right woman. But he knew she was out there. He just had to be patient and concentrate on his intent. The books all talked about that. A man finds love only when he intends to find it. He'd lacked that intention while he was so busy running his business. But now he was ready. Thirty years old and ready for love.

She had this ticket. It was a birthday present from her brother, a ticket to a Giants game. Just one ticket. So typical. It's what he would want for his birthday, her brother, Dale. It never occurred to him to ask her what she wanted, or even if she liked baseball, which she didn't. Why didn't he know that? But. he had remembered her birthday. Give him credit for that. Anyway, she wasn't going to ruin a Saturday afternoon sitting in the sun by herself watching a ballgame.

On her way to the cafeteria, ticket in her pocket, she saw Simon walking toward her, chin in the air, whistling, swinging his arms. Not far behind him, Barney Knute, the knucklehead, was mimicking him, exaggerating the sway of his head, the bounce in his step. Simon walked on, oblivious.

Without knowing what she was about to do, Laura came to an abrupt stop right in front of Simon.

"Would you like a ticket to the Giants' game on Saturday?" she blurted out.

He never would have imagined it, never for a minute, but there she was, L. Winters, offering him a ticket to a baseball game.

"Do you have an extra one?" he had asked, not quite sure what she was offering, not at all interested in sporting events.

"I have one," she said. "Just one. Do you want it?"

And then he understood. Only one, and she was giving it to him.

"Yes, yes," he stuttered. "Thank you."

"There's one condition."

"Of course."

He smiled broadly.

"You have to tell me about it. You know, who won, whether there were any homeruns. That kind of thing."

He blushed. Not only a gift from the lovely L. Winters, but she wanted more. She wanted future contact.

"Oh, absolutely," he said. "I'll give you a full report."

And to cover his confused delight, he took an envelope from his pocket and carefully stowed the ticket inside.

"Saturday," he said. "I'll be there. You're very kind."

He wanted to say more, to ask her why she wasn't using the ticket herself, perhaps to ask her to have lunch with him. But she rushed off. Overcome by her own boldness, he thought.

He turned abruptly around, intending to follow her, and bumped headlong into Officer Knute.

"What she give you?" the officer asked.

"A ticket to the Giants game."

He tried not to sound too pleased with himself.

"Well, I'll be goddamned."

It hadn't been her intention to give Simon the ticket, it had just happened. But she felt good about it. She figured he didn't get out much. He certainly looked as if he didn't have a social life with that god-awful haircut and the white cotton shirts buttoned to the collar. Do him good to sit in the sun with a bunch of regular folks and see some baseball.

It never occurred to her to wonder if he liked ball games. Men just did, at least the ones she knew. Her ex sure did! That's all he ever talked about. Buster Posey, Pablo Sandoval, homeruns, and RBIs, then the silence at dinner, followed by an hour or so of shouting at the TV. She figured all men were like that. So, she put up with it. Until that night she caught him with that waitress from Denny's. That was it. She was finished. Not forever, of course. She wanted a family, wanted children. But not yet. She was only twenty-seven. She had her dog. She had time.

The next Monday, she dropped by his shop during his break to find out how it went. She wanted enough information to thank Dale properly. He jumped up from his desk when she walked in, his eyes practically closed from the sheer energy of his smile.

He does look like Simple Simon, she thought. Poor sucker.

"Thank you!" he beamed. "The game was...very lively."

It had been deadly, of course, just as he'd expected. Sitting in the stands with all those noisy men, women too, yelling obscenities, jumping up and down, knocking into him, sloshing their beer onto his clean trousers. He kept jumping up and cheering at the wrong time when the other team—which one was it? —hit the ball. He left before it was over.

But he had done it, braved the ordeal, because he knew this was his big chance. L. Winters had made the first move. It was his job to follow up, to grab the initiative. And he was primed.

Capture her interest with stimulating conversation. That's what the books said. *Begin with* a *subject you know something about, preferably something in which you excel.*

Gardening. That was the thing. Women love flowers, and he was an expert. But how to tum a ballgame into roses. He'd think of something.

But she was asking, "Who won?"

"The Giants, of course."

He knew that much from all the shouting.

"Were there any homeruns?"

"I don't think so."

He was already regretting his early departure.

"Don't you know?"

"I didn't see any."

"What was the score?"

"Let's see. I wrote it down, but I must have left it at home."

"Are you sure you went to the game?"

This wasn't going well. He had to change tactic quick or he'd lose the initiative.

Suddenly, he had it.

"I kept notes," he said. "In my book. My gardening book."

"Gardening book?" she asked. "You're a gardener?"

It had worked.

"Yes. A passionate gardener."

He blushed at the word passionate.

"I'm partial to roses."

His cheeks felt bright red.

"Really?"

"Would you like to see them?"

He'd done it. He'd taken the leap.

"See what?"

"My roses."

"Maybe, sometime," she said, opening the shop door, inhaling the fresh air.

"How about this Sunday?"

You'd need to smell roses after this place, she thought, glancing back into the room at the large machines. The sharp smell of cleaning fluid was giving her a headache. She needed air.

She didn't want to go to this man's house any more than she wanted to go to a baseball game. Especially to see roses which always smelled to her like too much perfume. So, she was on the verge of saying no. Politely, of course. She wouldn't hurt his feelings. But before she could speak, she saw two of her comrades, bouncing along, swinging their arms, grinning like maniacs.

She'd always hated it when people made fun. She'd start feeling the hurt herself. And so, she turned back to Simon and said, "Okay. Thanks. But just for a minute, you know. To look at the roses."

"Make it 3:00 o'clock?"

She nodded, and without another word, she walked out into the blinding sunlight.

"I was right!" he told himself as he bounded about the shop, turning on machines, turning them off, picking up papers, putting them down. "She's interested. I knew it! All I had to do was take charge of the conversation. She was ready."

He could hardly wait to get home that night and start preparing. This was big.

"The first time she comes to your home, you must be prepared," he read in *The Intent For Love*. "Your home should feel welcoming, gracious. And, of course, it must be clean. Nothing discourages love quite so completely as cobwebs and dust."

No problem there. Cleaning was his business. His house was spotless. He looked around the living room, his confidence growing. Welcoming? Gracious? If that's what it took, he was on the road to love. It was a small house, three bedrooms, two baths. Paid for with profits from his laundry business. But the living room was a happy place, full of color, reds and oranges and yellows on the curtains, the sofa, the pillows. There were books and houseplants and a framed Cezanne print.

He tried to picture L. Winters in the red and yellow plaid armchair. He saw her blond ponytail. Sticking out the back of her officer's cap? No. She'd probably wear it down on weekends. And what would she be wearing? He tried to imagine her in anything other than the khaki uniform. A dress maybe, or more likely a nice blouse and sharply pressed pants. He could see her sitting there, her full-fleshed arms resting on his chair. In his living room.

He continued his research.

"Too many would-be lovers pack their lives so full they leave no space for love," he read. "If you have the true intent for love, you must make room for the other person."

Simon looked around his gracious, welcoming, dust-free living room and panicked. Too many things. Luckily, he had time.

On Saturday, up early, he tackled the living room first. Standing on a stepladder, he pulled books by the handful from the shelves. A French dictionary, three books on how to eat healthy food, five fat gardening books, a well-thumbed copy of "How To Win Friends and Influence People," "Lady Chatterley's Lover"—what would L. Winters think of that trash? —five Asian cookbooks. When he had finished, each shelf of his bookcase was at least a quarter empty. He carefully bagged his discards and drove them to the local library.

"On to the bedroom."

Simon was a fastidious dresser, the result of a lifetime of handling and admiring the expensively tailored garments of stylish customers. But he never bothered to throw anything away. God forbid she should catch a glimpse of that closet on the way to the bathroom, he thought. He plunged into the clutter, tossing shirts, trousers, shoes, hats, jackets into piles on the floor and spent the rest of the afternoon carrying trunk loads of his cast-offs to Goodwill.

"If you have the true intent for love, you must make room for the other person," he chanted as he flipped open his bedroom drawers and gazed into the half empty closet.

If not L. Winters, he said to himself, then surely someone. I've opened my space to love. I have the intent.

Why on earth did I agree? she asked herself as she washed her face and pulled her hair into an untidy ponytail that Sunday afternoon. She had spent the morning with Tombo at the dog park. Still a puppy, he absolutely shook with excitement every time they got near the park. He chased the other dogs and yelped and ran after the ball she threw him. She'd always had dogs. But this black lab, Tombo, was the most satisfactory dog she'd ever owned.

When she returned from the park, she needed a shower. But it was already 2:30 in the afternoon, and the drive to Simon's place would take a half hour. Jeans and the gray sweatshirt would have to do.

Maybe he wasn't serious, she thought, though he had drawn a map. Maybe he was just being polite. And then I'll show up, and he'll be embarrassed, and he'll have to show me his garden. It sounded grim.

Maybe I should phone, she told herself. But she didn't want to, felt it would be awkward. He did invite me, she reminded herself. It's what comes from feeling sorry for somebody.

The house surprised her. What had she expected? A little white cottage with a picket fence, straight out of Mother Goose. It wasn't like that at all. Lavender bushes and a ground cover of periwinkle surrounded a small redwood house. And wasn't that a lemon tree in the front yard? It all smelled delicious.

Oh my God, Simon thought as he opened the door to a woman in a sweatshirt and slicked-back ponytail. He pasted a smile on his face.

"I should have changed," she blurted out.

"Welcome," he said. His voice went up a pitch at the end as usual.

"It's the dog," she said. "I'm sorry."

"Excuse me?"

"I have this dog, and I took him to the park, and it was late, and I didn't have chance to ...."

She stopped.

"I'm sorry."

"Won't you come in?" he said, looking past her, trying to pretend that this plump woman in gray drab was the L. Winters for whom he had so carefully prepared. He squared his shoulders and led her through the front door into a sunny inner courtyard. Roses everywhere, each bush different. The colors flowed in a circular pattern from dead white to pink to a creamy peach color to orange-red, and finally, to a red so dark it was almost black, then abruptly back to white. He breathed in the smell he loved so much. Not cloying or too sweet, more like fruit, like very fresh peaches.

"My god," she said. "I didn't . . . I never saw .... You did all this yourself?"

There it was, just as he had hoped. L. Winters rendered speechless by the color and aroma he had created. He did his best to savor the moment. After all, why should clothes matter? But for all his trying, the moment felt flat.

So, this must be what he means by passion, Laura thought. When he had used the word at the prison, it had embarrassed her, but here in the middle of all these roses, it struck her as just right. And because it was just the right word, she found herself really looking at him, at Simon, as he stood there in in his crisp white trousers and bright blue cotton shirt. Why hadn't she taken the time to change? He still had that dopey, expectant look in his eyes, and his hair still angled out from his scalp, straight and thin. But something was different. She didn't feel sorry for him.

"Could I offer you a glass of cold lemonade?" he asked.

"If it's no trouble," she said and followed him into the house.

Inside, the house was as colorful as the garden. She'd never paid much attention to fixing up a house, even during her brief, dull marriage. When later she'd taken the prison job, she'd found an apartment nearby, in one of those wood-frame complexes that clutter American suburbia. One place was as good as another in her mind. She'd made a couple of trips to Ikea to supplement her few furnishings, cheap and not too ugly. But there was no color. The wood was blond. The sofa and bedspread were brown. There were no curtains, just shades. This living room sort of glowed. It made you want to stay. And there were pictures on the wall. She had a few family photos on the kitchen shelves at her place, but the walls were bare.

"You've done a bang-up job here, Simon," she said, settling into the deep red and yellow chair, clutching the arms with her large hands, the folds of her sweatshirt drooping over the sides.

"Why, thank you," he replied as he placed a plate of brownies on the glass top coffee table in front of her. "Please have one."

They were good, the brownies, moist and buttery in the center and not too sweet with lots of pecans and powdered sugar on top.

"These may be the best brownies I ever ate," she said.

But he wasn't thinking about brownies. He was staring at the dog hairs, drifting from Laura's sweatshirt onto the arms of the chair, down to the carpet.

"Yum," she said, scattering crumbs as she took a second brownie from the plate. "What's the brand?"

"Brand?"

"You know, on the box?"

"Oh, I see. No, they're from scratch."

"Oh." She looked around. "You're not married, are you?"

He blushed. Now we're getting to it, he thought.

"No," he said. "The right woman hasn't come along."

He blushed even deeper.

"Your mom, then?"

He frowned.

"What about her?"

"She made the brownies?"

She helped herself to a third one.

Without thinking, Simon thrust the plate under her brownie to catch the crumbs.

"I made them."

"No kidding," she said. "A real gourmet. A man who can cook. Now that's a new one on me."

They sat in silence while she chewed.

"You must be quite a reader," Laura finally said. She'd never been in a house with so many books, had never known anyone who spent much time reading. She bought magazines from time to time, but there were really no books in her apartment.

"What's your favorite?"

She leaned forward, full of curiosity, watching his face. She wanted to know what kinds of books a man who taught dry cleaning in a prison liked to read. He was full of surprises.

He hesitated.

"I like biography. You know, I like to read about famous people, heroes, people who've accomplished something with their lives."

"Like Lincoln?"

"Sure. Him. And others. People like Martin Luther King and heroes back in history, like Queen Elizabeth. The first one."

As he talked, the pitch of his voice went higher. He sounded excited, and she didn't know what to say.

"Martin Luther King?" she finally said. "That's awesome."

"Do you like to read?" he asked.

"I like a good murder mystery," she said.

Simon smiled politely.

"Maybe you'd like to borrow something?"

He pointed to the shelves.

"I don't know where I'd start," she laughed.

She looked over at him expecting some response, but he was staring at the shelves, and his smile had faded.

"How'd you end up in dry cleaning?" she asked.

He told her about the business he had inherited from his father.

"It was okay," he said. "It gave me a chance to meet the public, you know. I'd look at all those silk shirts and suits and dresses they brought in, and I'd imagine them, out in the world, creating a good impression at business meetings, livening up cocktail parties."

"You don't say," she said smiling up at him.

"A family from Vietnam now runs it, a man and his daughters. Hard workers. But I still own it. So, I take the profits and get to do what I love. Teach."

For the first time that afternoon, his face began to glow. He told her he loved to demonstrate to his students how to remove stubborn spots, how to operate the pant presser without scorching the fabric.

"People think I'm courageous and good-hearted. 'Aren't you the kind one?' they say, 'Giving those men a second chance in life!'"

He blushed.

"I feel like it gives me a certain stature," he said, looking into her face for the first time all afternoon. "Do you know what I mean?"

Laura nodded even though she had no idea what he was talking about.

"People ask me if I'm afraid," he said. "I tell them there's nothing to be afraid of. The inmates are just men, like you and me."

"Maybe in the dry-cleaning shop," she said. "But remember, there's the killers in that prison. You just don't see them. But I do. My mom and dad thought I was nuts applying to be a prison guard, said it was a man's job and dangerous. Which it is. Course when they learned about the benefits and the pay, I never heard another peep out of either of 'em."

Simon smiled politely and stared at his hands which were folded in a pale lump in his lap.

"Well, I came to see the roses, Simon," Laura said, finally. "So maybe another look before I leave?"

He jumped up and led the way out to the garden. She followed behind, reading aloud from handsome, handmade signs the names of each variety.

"'Crimson Glory,' 'Sunset Jubilee,' 'Irish Gold.' They fit, don't they?" she said. "The names and the roses. I bet they're a world of trouble to grow."

Simon was too busy pulling off dead blossoms and inspecting for insects to respond.

"I wouldn't have the patience," she said. "I guess you have to have the passion, like you said."

"It makes a difference," Simon said, nodding.

That night Laura couldn't sleep, which wasn't like her. Her mind wouldn't relax. It kept running off in different directions. Something had happened, and she didn't understand it.

"One thing's sure," she said aloud in the darkness. "Simple Simon isn't simple."

She had accepted his invitation to be kind because she was a kind person. But the house and the roses with the beautiful names and all those books had thrown her. He read books, and he knew about all kinds of things, like art and fixing up a house and flowers, of course, and history. It should have made her feel small, stupid even. But she didn't. She felt wired. That was the best word she had for it. Too wired to sleep.

She told herself she'd drop by the dry-cleaning shop tomorrow. She'd thank him for the afternoon. Maybe he'd suggest they go for coffee sometime. Or even dinner. The guys would laugh, of course. Well, let 'em. What did they know?

After she left, Simon sat motionless on the rust-colored sofa frowning at the bookcase. All those empty spaces. What had he expected? That just any woman he happened to pick, someone like L. Winters, for instance, would be the right one, a woman who would fill his shelves with books, would fill his house, this treasured house, with new life, with love?

He roused himself grimly and began to attack the living room carpet and armchair with his vacuum cleaner. With a damp cloth, he scrubbed the arms of the chair for fingerprint smudges that didn't exist, trying to erase from his memory the gray sweatshirt, the dog named Tombo, the crushing defeat of his afternoon.

Exhausted, he reheated some leftover curried chicken in the microwave and ate it at the kitchen table, a new biography of Roosevelt propped up next to his plate. But he couldn't concentrate, and long after he had finished the chicken, he sat at the table, motionless, staring through rimless glasses into the courtyard, his shoulders drooping, his hands, small, manicured, defenseless, folded together in his lap.

Memorial Mansion

Persimmon Tree, Spring 2014
Also published in *Spotswood Virginia*,
Stephen F. Austin State University Press, 2021

So, there was my Jimmy sitting in the den with his bare feet on the coffee table watching the news on the TV. It made me happy just to see him, unexpected like that.

"You're home early," I said.

"You know what they're saying?"

He jerked his head toward the TV. It was Governor Byrd talking.

I sat down beside him on the old blue linen sofa which has gotten awful faded, and ran my fingers alongside his arm.

He pulled away.

"All those integrationists up north? Governor says they'll be heading this way, making trouble down here."

"I don't think they'll come here."

His upper lip twitched.

"We got restaurants, don't we?"

That made me smile.

"You calling that hamburger place out on River Road a restaurant?"

"Don't laugh. They mean to put their brown butts at restaurant counters."

"Don't tell Grandpa," I said.

He squinted at me.

"Grandpa! What about you? They'll come to the library."

"I doubt it."

"Sure, they will."

"They won't, honey. It's not a restaurant. Besides, they'll be marching in the cities. Atlanta, Birmingham, places like that."

"But if they come to the library, what will you do?"

I put my arm around my son's wide shoulders and stretched up to kiss his cheek. It's still soft, that cheek.

"I'll cross that bridge when I come to it."

"I worry about you, Mama. I do. They're troublemakers, those outside agitators. You're so naïve."

"It's a library, honey, for children. At least my part is. They won't come."

"It's the Memorial Mansion, for God's sake."

"All the more reason," I said.

They called the public library the Memorial Mansion because of General Lee. He was supposed to have spent a night upstairs in the blue room in a four-poster bed when it really was a mansion, back during the War. The general had taken up old Harrison Langhorne's offer of a rare good night's sleep in that room when the Rebel troops were advancing or retreating, I can never remember which. When old Mr. Langhorne finally died at the age of ninety-three, he left the place to Spotswood. The town fathers christened it the "Memorial Mansion" and turned it into a library. What else could you do with it?

"Shouldn't you be at work?" I asked.

He stood up abruptly and turned off the TV.

"Well?"

"I can't do it anymore, Mama. Crawling around on my hands and knees, shoving all those stinking feet into bargain basement shoes. I gotta find something more suitable."

I felt the old familiar tide of worry rising in my chest.

"Did you get fired, son?"

"They got this new girl, Liz something. Said they didn't need me. Anyway, I hated it."

I gave him a look.

"I'll get something better, something where you don't crawl around on your hands and knees."

I figured it would do no good to remind him how hard it was to find a proper job without a college education. No need to remind him of how many times his grandpa had pestered friends to take him on, to give him a chance. He knew all that. Nagging wouldn't change anything. He was twenty years old, and I loved him more than anybody in the world.

I work all over the library, but I prefer the children's section, maybe because I'm not much taller than the children. They put us in the basement, which would be gloomy except for the movie posters I've tacked all over the walls. *Treasure Island* and *The Secret Garden.* Makes things colorful. I love the smell of old paper and library paste almost more than I love the books and definitely more than I love the white marble statue of General Lee that lords over the grounds out front of the Memorial Mansion. The mayor's nephew, who's an artist in New York City, got paid to create the statue, which is the general to the life, or so they say. For me, he looks pompous.

Now that Saturday morning, I was demonstrating the dinosaur exhibit I'd set up on the front table for several of the children, when something made me look up. A colored lady was just standing there, in the middle of the library, watching me. I was too shocked to speak. She looked to be about thirty, a clean-looking woman for all her dark skin, and she was wearing a blue-flowered cotton dress with large black buttons in the front. She didn't look like anybody's maid. No colored people are allowed in the library, except of course the cleaning lady and Harvey, the janitor. It's not that there's a "Whites Only" sign, like there is at the Spotswood swimming pool. Everybody just knows. And what I knew was I had to get this lady out of the library before somebody saw her.

"I'm sorry," I said when I finally found my voice. "But I'm afraid you can't use this library. There is a library over on Calhoun Street, and I'm sure it's open today."

I spoke softly, hoping the children wouldn't hear me.

The woman didn't move.

"I would like to use this one," she said. She spoke her words carefully, like an educated person.

"I'm afraid that's not possible."

I walked to the door and held it open. Several of the children looked up, watching to see what she would do.

"Why?"

The woman still didn't move.

"This is a whites-only library," I said.

I'd never had to say anything like that before. In Spotswood, the colored knew their place.

The woman looked at me out of scared, dark eyes.

"I am a high school teacher," she said. "Here in Spotswood. And I need some books for my classes that are not in the Calhoun Street library. You have them here."

I could hear the children beginning to react.

"Who's she?"

"She don't belong here."

I had to act quick.

"Look, Ma'am," I said. "Please leave. You're going to get into all kinds of trouble if you don't leave right now."

"I'll leave when I've checked out my books," the woman said.

She was standing up real straight, like she belonged there, but her voice sounded squeaky.

"If you don't leave, I'll have to call the police," I said.

"Why don't you just give me the books? Then I'll leave."

I could see it was up to me. She wasn't going to budge. I knew I was much too small to force her out, and the adult part of the library wouldn't open for another hour. I considered phoning the cops, but I knew the local guy would call in all the squad cars and probably the fire department too, and there'd be no end of trouble.

"Look," she said, "all I want is *Great Expectations* and *Call of the Wild*."

That made me stare.

"Surely they've got those in the Calhoun library."

"Maybe they did at one time but not now."

I knew right then it was the wrong thing to do, but I had to get her out of there, and nothing else came to mind.

"Okay," I said. "But stand by the door while I get the books."

She smiled for the first time, and I could see she was almost pretty in a sad sort of way. Her mouth was thinner than what I'm used to, and her hair had been straightened and was neat.

Meanwhile, I could hear the children talking among themselves, getting louder. The woman turned toward the children, and they broke off mid-sentence. I quickly grabbed the two books off the shelf, checked them out to myself, and handed them over.

"Now, go. Please," I begged. "Leave the books in the return box outside when you finish. Don't come back in here. Please."

The woman backed out the door, clutching the books.

"Thank you," she whispered.

"Hurry," I said.

I don't know who was more scared, that teacher or me. I mean I would have lost my job if I was caught giving books to that woman, and we need the money. Not to mention I'd be bringing shame on my family.

"What's that woman doing in our library?"

It was Dexter, of course. He's got no breeding, comes from the mill side of town. Some of the other children were staring at me, waiting for me to say something.

"She was wrong to come," I said, as calmly as I could manage, because you can bet I wasn't calm. "But now she's gone. And don't you use that word, Dexter."

"What word?"

He shouted that word again and again and again.

I knew how to handle him. I took him by the arm and pushed him ahead of me out the door.

"Come back when you've learned how to behave in a library," I said.

Daddy had barely seated himself at the head of the table that night when he shouted out, "Irma Mae, how come you let that bitch in the library?"

He gets more ornery by the day. My husband, James, looked up from serving the meatloaf and sighed. Jimmy stared down at his plate.

"How'd you hear about that, Daddy?" I asked, keeping my cool.

"Don't matter how I heard about it. Why'd you do it?"

"I didn't let her in. She walked in by herself. The door's not locked. I got her out."

"That's not what I hear."

"She's a teacher."

"I don't give a good goddamn what she is. She's got no right at all to set one toe in the Memorial Mansion."

White flecks of spit clung to the corners of the old man's lips.

"Calm down, Daddy," I said.

How many times in my life had I said that. Calm down, Daddy. I looked over at James, trying to signal him for some help. But he just smiled his tired old smile at me.

"Have some meatloaf?" he said.

"I told you it would happen," Jimmy said. "I warned you. You're in deep shit now."

"Watch your language, Jimmy," I said.

"You're acting like a goddamn fool, and you're telling your boy to watch his language?"

Daddy stood up, knocking over his chair, and limped out of the room on his stiff knee.

We sat in silence, not looking at each other, taking small bites of meatloaf.

"He's right, Ma," Jimmy finally said.

"He's a bitter old man," I said.

"Everybody's talking about it. That kid from the mill is spreading it around town. I worry about you."

"Well, don't. I took care of it."

James reached across the table and patted my hand.

"It'll be all right," he said.

Jimmy looked at his father with disgust.

"It won't be all right," he said. "She'll be back, this schoolteacher lady, and Mama will let her in, and this town will go wild."

"Calm down, honey," I said.

But I have to say, he made me nervous. It wasn't that I mind the folks who live in the Calhoun Street area using the library, especially the better class like that teacher. What's wrong with that? But it's against the law, and I'm not one to break the law.

A week passed. Mr. Talbot, the head librarian, demanded an explanation about what had transpired between me and the schoolteacher, and he warned me never to let her or anybody like her into the Mansion. I chose not to tell him I'd given the teacher books. I just prayed we'd get them back without anybody knowing who'd been reading them.

The following Saturday morning, I looked in the return box for the books, but no luck. That made me antsy, but I figured she'd bring them back sooner or later. I was re-shelving books when I heard a commotion outside. Thinking the children were lining up, I unlocked the door and opened it.

There stood that schoolteacher, clutching the books tight to her chest, her dark eyes wide, begging. About twenty yards behind her, at least a dozen men were milling about on the grassy lawn. I figured Dexter's daddy had been watching for her. I tried to close the door, but she stuck her foot in and stopped me.

"Let me in, *please*," she whispered.

"I can't," I said. "I told you."

"Please," the woman begged.

The men moved closer. I knew some of them, Buck Poindexter who manages the Buick lot and Eddie Williams who pumps gas at the Esso station.

"Hey, Buck," I called out. "What's going on?"

"We're here to protect the Mansion from scum."

But it wasn't Buck who answered. It was a man I didn't recognize.

I could see them moving slowly in my direction and some of them were yelling, "Keep the bitch out!"

"Whites only."

It was a sorry sight.

The teacher grabbed my arm with her free hand. Her eyes looked wild.

"Let me in," she begged. "They gonna kill me."

I'd never been this close to a black person before. I could see the dark circles under her arms. I could smell the sweat on her. It was mixed with some gardenia kind of perfume. I felt like I was about to faint. Meanwhile, the men over on the lawn kept bellowing and coming closer. And I could see that a couple of them were carrying sticks.

I just couldn't leave her out there with all those riled-up men. That's the truth. So, I let her in and shut the door.

"Quick," I said, pointing to the stairs that led up to the main library. "You can get out that way."

But she just backed herself against the wall like a cornered animal and hissed at me.

"Lock it. Quick. Lock the door."

The words came in short, jerky breaths.

Now that I was inside the library, away from the crowd of men, I was appalled at what I had done.

"I can't," I said.

Then I heard the roar outside, getting louder. It scared me so bad I ran over and flipped the bolt. Immediately, the door began to shake. The knob rattled.

"Unlock that door!" somebody shouted.

I looked over at the window. Someone was peering in. The teacher was cowering against the wall, still clutching her books with white knuckles. I didn't want to look at her.

I ran over to the desk and picked up the telephone.

"Who you calling?" the teacher whispered.

"The police."

"No. Don't. No. No."

She was scared for sure.

But I had already stopped dialing and was staring at the window. It was Jimmy's face, paler than usual, and he was frowning and motioning with his hand for me to come to the window. My first thought was, he's coming to help me. So, I put down the phone and walked, in a daze, toward the window.

I raised the sill just high enough to hear Jimmy. His face was pressed close to the windowpane. Behind him, I could see the men standing out there on the green lawn, waiting. They were yelling something I couldn't make out.

"Unlock the door, Mama," Jimmy said.

His voice was deep and calm. Like his dad.

"No," the teacher screamed. "Don't."

"I can't do it," I told Jimmy. "I'm scared of those men out there."

"I know, Mama," he said, "but I'm here. I'll protect you. You just gotta unlock that door."

I looked over at the teacher who was still clutching the books.

"They'll kill me if you open that door," she said. "You know they will."

I looked back out the window. This time I saw Tony Watson from Jimmy's baseball team and Curtis Morris, the catcher. They were at church every Sunday. They weren't going to kill anybody.

Jimmy was pleading.

"If you don't unlock that door, they'll break the window. I'm the only thing keeping 'em back."

"What's going to happen if I unlock it?" I asked.

"They won't hurt you."

I looked over at the teacher.

"What'll they do to her?" I asked.

"What do you care?"

She was standing up straight now, looking hard at me, like I was her only hope.

"You got to believe me," she said.

Her voice was squeaky, like it was when she had demanded the books and wouldn't leave. For just a moment, we stood there, that black woman and I, locked in that room together, both of us terrified of the yelling and banging outside.

Then she said, "They'll kill me" and looked right in my face.

And I said, "I know."

"I can't do it," I told Jimmy, turning back to the window.

Over his head, I could see the men moving toward us. They were chanting something that sounded like "Whites only," and several of them were waving those sticks. Then somebody yelled, "Out of the way. Mama's boy."

Jimmy turned back toward the crowd.

"Hell no," he yelled back. "I'm with *you*. I'm just trying to talk some sense into her."

Then they were grabbing Jimmy, pulling him away, knocking him down. Men I had never seen before. Big men. I started screaming. I don't remember unbolting the lock. I just remember the men, so many of them, streaming in the door, knocking down chairs, brushing books off the tables. All I could think about was Jimmy. I forced my way through those men, out the door, to my boy. I found him struggling to get off the ground, his face bleeding, his tee-shirt torn.

"You crazy Mama," he said. "You almost got me killed protecting that bitch."

"Hush," I said.

I put my arm around him and led him away from the crowd, back toward home. I could hear the whine of the police siren. Thank God, I thought. They can't hurt her now.

It wasn't until the next afternoon that I heard the teacher was in jail, charged with disturbing the peace and trespassing.

"What about those men?" I asked Jimmy. "What did they get charged with?"

"Why would they get charged?"

"Well, they beat you up."

I looked him over. His face was scratched up, but otherwise he looked normal.

"I was in the way. Look, Mama, it's lucky they didn't charge *you* with anything."

"Me? Why?"

"You let that bitch into the Mansion. But you're okay. I fixed it up," Jimmy said. "They won't touch you."

"How'd you do that?"

"I told the police she forced the door open, and you couldn't stop her, then she bolted the lock."

"That's not what happened."

"That's what you'll say at the trial."

"I can't lie, Jimmy."

"Who says you got to lie? I was at the window, watching. I gave my statement. You're not gonna contradict me."

I didn't answer. But I felt sick all over.

The teacher's coming up for trial. They're expecting me to testify against her. Jimmy, the lawyers, the church, everybody. I keep seeing her, standing up so straight in the corner of the library in that blue-flowered dress, looking hard at me with her dark eyes and hanging onto *Great Expectations* like her life depended on it. I can hear those men yelling outside, and I feel the terror as that teacher and I stood locked together in that room.

I can't let her go to jail.

But then I think, she started it. She's the one that got me into this mess. And if I tell the truth about that awful day, that I opened the door to her and locked it, my boy will be in trouble. And all he did was tell a white fib to protect his mama. That's all he did.

But she's a teacher. All she wanted was books.

Strangers in the Garden

Bluestem, June 2014.

"There'll be rats," she said, facing him over English muffins at the red Formica-topped kitchen table. She noticed, not for the first time, the decided slope of her husband's once broad shoulders, the skin sagging at the corner of his right eye. From the open kitchen window, she breathed in apple blossoms, freshly turned earth.

"It's scientific," he said. "Read the book."

She stared at the liver spots on his hand as he shoved the book across the table. A slight figure, just over five feet, she had more gray now than red in the twist of hair fastened on top of her small, compact head.

"I don't have to read a book to know about rats. You remember Craighead Grocery. It took us years to get rid of those rats. They'll be back if you take to burying garbage in the yard."

"It's scientific," he repeated, as though he hadn't heard her.

"Maybe so. But in this yard, it's unsanitary."

"Read the book," he said and got up from the table.

"Stubborn old *man*," she muttered.

She peered over half-glasses at his faded blue slacks, stained with the black dirt of the garden, the moth holes in the sleeve of his navy wool sweater.

His thick white hair hung ragged on his neck.

"Look at you," she said. "You're a mess."

He turned and fixed her with the light blue eyes she had fallen in love with forty years before.

"Goddamn it, Lucy! Be nice to me."

That made her look, really look, through the battered clothes, through the years, to the intense lean face, the thin prominent nose, the sudden, unexpected smile.

"It's not easy," she said, smiling up at him.

"Read the book," he said.

Forty years ago, it had been easy. Forty years ago, she couldn't take her hands off him. She was teaching seventh grade and had run the gamut of the so-called eligible bachelors in Spotswood, Virginia. They were a dull lot, and she was hungry for a fresh face.

"I hear there's this new man in town, buying that printing business over on Loyal Street," her friend Elsie told her.

"What'd you hear about him?"

"Name's Frank Stamps, and he's back from the war. I've seen him. He's tall, about six feet, and his hair's naturally curly and coal black."

"How come he'd want that print business? They say it's about to go under."

"You can ask him yourself. I hear he's coming to the Victory Ball."

"You think so?" The city was putting on a dance in the City Armory that weekend to celebrate the end of the war. Everybody was coming.

"What else do you know about him?" she asked.

"He smokes cigars."

"Yeah?"

"He likes whiskey."

Lucy smiled.

"And he cusses."

"I want to meet this man!" she said.

Elsie laughed.

Well, you couldn't miss him at the ball. He stood a head taller than almost everybody, and he looked like victory itself in his Army uniform. His black hair was shiny. She could tell he'd tried to slick it down, but sprigs of it kept springing up. His face was red, not like he was blushing, but a healthy red, like he'd been in the sun a lot. And his large nose was thin along the ridge and straight.

Right away, he asked Lucy for a dance. She didn't remember much of what they talked about that night. She just remembered that he danced like he was in charge, and he smelled of cigars, and she couldn't take her eyes off of him. He was that powerful.

The very next night, he showed up at her house in navy gabardine trousers, worn shiny at the knees, and a white dress shirt that was frayed at the collar. He later told her he'd worn that Army uniform for the last time and good riddance.

"I've just had raw onions for my dinner," he said, holding out a peeled onion. "Better take a bite, or you won't be able to stand me."

Lucy took one look at that curly hair and those light blue eyes, and she bit down on that onion like it was ambrosia.

It was true. He liked his whiskey, and he cussed, and he smoked cigars, and he was more fun than anybody she'd ever met. She loved the way he spun her around when they danced, loved the easy way he laughed, his head thrown back. Loved the way he touched her with his square-shaped hands and blunt fingertips. He didn't have much money, but he had the smell of the future on him. She married him six months later and never looked back.

———

She read his book and admonished herself for being so cranky. Composting seemed harmless enough. But then a month or so later, as she was standing at the kitchen window. She saw him rummaging through the garbage, picking up egg shells and rotten tomatoes and dumping them into a blue plastic bucket. He carried the bucket over to the composting pit he'd dug, and then, like in a fairy tale, a large gray rat streaked out of the pit and ran for the fence.

She stormed out to the back.

"I told you there'd be rats," she yelled.

But he just stared into the tangle of red tomatoes and eggshells on the ground.

"What are you hollering about now?"

"Are you blind? A huge rat just ran practically over your foot."

And he started laughing. Laughing!

"Well, I'll be," he said. "And I didn't even see it."

"It's not funny," she said.

They stood facing each other over the open pit. She crossed her bare arms in the cool September air.

"You have to cover up that hole," she said.

"Why?"

"Why?" She couldn't believe him. "Because it's unsanitary. Because there are rats. Because it's crazy."

"Stop yelling," he said.

"I'm yelling because I'm scared," she said.

He frowned.

"Of a rat?"

"No. Well, yes. Of course, I'm scared of rats."

He laughed again.

"They won't hurt you."

"It's not just that. You scare me."

"Me?"

"Not you exactly."

She didn't know how to say it. She didn't even know what she meant. It was something about that laugh. Not his usual belly laugh with his head thrown back. It was like he was embarrassed or confused. And he hadn't even noticed the rat.

"Forget it," she said. "It was the rat."

"I'll get some poison," he said.

And then he stood there, waiting, watching her.

"No!" she cried out, close to tears. "No rats, no poisons."

And she rushed back to the warmth of the kitchen, leaving him standing there, the blue bucket dangling from his hand like a child's Easter basket.

It wasn't his to poison. The garden was hers too. Before they married, Frank had never even touched a spade, but Lucy had learned to grow vegetables from her father. So, in those early, giddy days, she taught her new husband to make a vegetable garden. They dug up the entire back yard of their recently purchased house and planted carrots, tomatoes, squash, cucumbers, parsnips, onions, even corn. Their Forest

Knolls neighbors peered over their hedges from their identical squares of green grass and tulip borders, staring at the two of them, the tall, dark-haired man and his young, red-headed wife, groveling in the dirt, laughing, kissing. But before long, the neighbors were grinning down at them, shouting advice, and taking home buckets of vegetables.

Lucy remembered one summer evening early in their marriage, Frank bursting into the kitchen, his fingernails black with dirt, holding up in the sun-washed air a perfect sphere of an onion. Their first.

"Open up, Red," he said, thrusting it at her.

"Let me sauté it first."

She was laughing, kissing his neck, his chin, his mouth.

"Nope. It's the very first onion from the Garden of Eden. We don't even have fire yet. We eat it raw."

She started to peel it, when he shouted, 11Wait!" and reached under the kitchen sink for their bottle of Jack Daniels.

"Sit down, Red. We're celebrating."

And he poured two full glasses of bourbon, put thin slices of the onion on toast, and they celebrated right into their second-hand brass double bed.

Frank took to gardening with the same zeal he applied to everything: printing, dancing, chatting up customers. He had bought the printing business with a little inheritance from his granddaddy down in South Carolina. The business was heavily in debt, but Frank figured that the country was coming out of the Depression, and with luck and hard work, he could turn that shop into a thriving operation. Which he did. Stamps. Printing. First, he figured out all by himself how to use a Linotype machine to set type. Before long, he knew everybody in town and had more business than he knew what to do with. He was thirty-five at the time, seven years Lucy's senior, and a ball of fire. Running the press, talking to customers, racing about town drumming up business, always laughing and joking and smoking those cigars. His energy never flagged. He served on the school board, ran the Community Fund Drive, and was president of Kiwanis. The only organization he didn't run at one time or another was First Baptist.

God's got enough soldiers in his army without *me,*" he'd say when the preacher tried to recruit him for the Board of Deacons. "Besides, I'd have to cut back on the whiskey and the 'goddamns.'"

The three children they brought into the world rebelled against all the weeding, watering, and picking they were forced to do. The garden was a chore, not a passion. And so, it was left to their parents to tend with all the love they felt for each other. But after the children left home, the garden began to overwhelm them. There were just too many zucchinis and eggplants, cabbages and carrots, beans and peas, raspberries and strawberries. Lucy cooked and canned and froze, shared with the neighbors, and gave to the soup kitchen at First Baptist, but the vegetables kept multiplying. She insisted on planting a smaller garden, and Frank agreed. But by then, he was retired and had more time, and the garden grew even larger, the yield more abundant. Lucy had nightmares of rotten vegetables spilling out all over the yard. Frank seemed unaware of the burden he was placing on his wife, even though she was getting older and was constantly reminding him.

And then the people started appearing.

First, a woman, somewhere in her late fifties, showed up wearing faded pink cotton slacks and a lime green, tie-dyed shirt, with a cloth bag dangling off her skinny arm.

"Who's that?" Lucy asked Frank.

They were standing at the kitchen window watching the woman pick green beans off one of the bushes.

He smiled and nodded in her direction.

"Her name might be Page or something like that."

"You know her?"

He thought for a minute.

"I could have met her at the soup kitchen."

"What do you mean, you 'could have met her at the soup kitchen?'"

"I suppose I did."

"What's she doing here?"

He shrugged.

"I guess she's hungry."

"What's wrong with the soup kitchen?"

"Nothing, I guess."

"Then why's she here?"

"I must have invited her."

"Well, did you or didn't you?"

"I'm not sure."

"Come on, Frank," she said. "You know we can't have strangers rummaging around in our back yard."

"She's not a stranger. I told you, I'm pretty sure I met her at the kitchen."

He went back to reading the paper.

"It's my garden too, Frank."

Her voice was high-pitched, shrill.

"Why are you fussing at me?" he asked.

It was a good question. He was only being generous. So, why was she begrudging this poor woman a few vegetables? She liked her privacy. That was part of it. But it was more than that. She felt irritated at Frank when she should have felt proud of him for being kind, and she didn't know why.

The next day, a couple of teenagers showed up. She said nothing while they picked their fill of berries, but afterward, she called the Reverend Lee at First Baptist.

"If it's alright with you," she said, "I'd rather send vegetables and fruit to the soup kitchen than have folks show up in our garden."

"Of course, Lucy, and thank you. You can call anytime, and I'll have somebody pick up whatever you're donating."

"Frank says he invited folks from the kitchen to our garden. Did you know that?"

"I *have* heard him inviting folks to your garden. He's so generous, but I did wonder."

The Reverend Lee hesitated.

"You know, he's been hanging around the soup kitchen a lot lately."

She tried to hide her surprise.

"Cooking?"

"Not exactly. He's been mostly chatting with folks. Eating with them sometimes."

Lucy felt something inside her chest tighten. She told herself that there was nothing wrong with going to the soup kitchen, being friendly with all those hungry people. She could imagine Frank cooking or hauling a truckload of corn up to the church. He'd done that frequently. But it wasn't like him to sit around just talking to a bunch of homeless people.

The preacher echoed her thoughts.

"I'm probably off base here, but Frank doesn't seem himself."

She wanted to say, you're right. He's luring rats and strangers into our garden and doesn't remember it. But she wasn't ready to admit she was scared.

So, she said, "I'd appreciate it if you'd talk to him. Maybe you can find out what he's thinking."

Later that night, she brought up the subject with Frank, but he got defensive.

"Can't I help out at the soup kitchen without you nosing in?"

"I'm sorry," she said. "You're right."

For several weeks, no more visitors appeared. Then one evening just before dusk, a young man with a mean looking dog, part German Shepard, part mutt, showed up in the garden, a paper bag tucked under his arm, and started picking raspberries. He had a scarred-up complexion and a skinny blond ponytail, and his tee-shirt didn't quite cover his bulging white belly. Lucy saw him from the kitchen window and came running out of the house.

"Who's that?" she hissed at Frank, who was stooped down in the cabbage plants pulling weeds.

That started the dog to growling.

Frank looked up and frowned.

"Hey there!" he called out.

The man watched Frank for a minute then unzipped his baggy khaki trousers and started to urinate on the berries.

"Oh, my God," Lucy muttered and turned away. The dog bared its teeth and growled even louder.

But Frank just laughed.

"What're you doing?" he asked, as he struggled to his feet.

"You said I could pick all the fruit I want," the man said, zipping up his trousers. He sounded defensive.

"Well, I'll be damned. When'd I say that?"

"Yesterday."

Lucy stared at Frank. Suddenly the dog lunged at Frank, barking and snapping at his pants, and knocked him into the cabbage plants. The man grabbed the dog by its collar and smacked it hard on the nose.

"Shut your face, you bitch!" he yelled, and he headed out to the street without another word, yanking the whimpering animal by its collar and picking up his bag of berries with his free hand.

Lucy took Frank by the arm and supported him as he struggled to get up. After several attempts, he pulled himself to his feet while she dusted him off.

"Are you okay?" she asked.

He managed a laugh.

"That was some dog," he said.

"That man was lying, wasn't he?" Lucy asked, her voice shaking. "Surely, you didn't invite that man in here?"

Frank was staring at his trousers, which the dog had ripped.

"I might have seen him in town. He had a sign."

She exploded.

"You invited that man into our yard?"

"Like I said, I might have. I don't remember. You keep telling me we have too many vegetables. I was trying to help. He had a sign that said he was hungry."

"What he is, is dangerous. Frank, look at me."

He turned to face her. His shoulders were sloping down. His light blue eyes searched Lucy's face for approval.

"I've been trying to do what's right," he said.

His usually deep voice ended on a high note, like he was asking a question.

She stared up at him.

"And you think bringing stray men with dangerous dogs into our garden is doing what's right?"

He didn't answer. Instead, he said, "Don't be angry."

"I'm more scared than angry," she said. "I don't know what to do."

They stood there for a long time, looking at each other, not saying anything. Finally, she took his hand and walked him back into the house.

They sat in the kitchen, where they had sat for over forty years, at the Formic-topped table, facing each other.

"Lucy," he said, "What's happened to us?"

She searched his old man face, sagging around the eyes, still dominated by the straight, thin nose.

"I told you before. I'm scared."

"Scared of what?"

Suddenly, she had the words.

"I'm losing you," she said and started to cry. "It makes me sad. It makes me angry. I don't recognize you anymore."

He took her face in his hands with the blunt-edged fingers she had loved, still loved.

"I don't either," he said.

What You Made of Me

Quiddity, Fall/Winter 2013

Parachuting globs of jellyfish surrounded her, purple tentacles swaying. She shuddered. How like Johnny's law firm to throw their Christmas party in an aquarium. It was beautiful, she supposed. But the place was too dark. The corridors too narrow. It gave her the creeps.

"Hi, Kathryn."

Startled, she whirled away from the glass wall and bumped headlong into a young man.

"Oh, I'm sorry," she said, laughing self-consciously. He was African American, and something about his forehead and the way he narrowed his eyes when he looked at her struck her as familiar.

"What brings you here?" he asked.

"I was about to ask you the same thing. My husband works here."

"In the aquarium?"

She smiled.

"In the law firm."

"Oh. I didn't think you were a lawyer," he said.

"Are you?"

She still couldn't place him. A new associate, perhaps? His white, V-necked sweater and navy blazer suggested it.

The dark eyes searched her face.

"Give me time," he said. "I've only been out six months."

She was too shocked to hide her surprise.

"Oh, my God," she said, grabbing his hand and shaking it forcefully. "Congratulations!"

"Rama," he said. "English 101."

"Of course," she said. "I know you. I just didn't ..."

"Yeah, well here I am."

"That's wonderful. What are you doing...with yourself?"

"I'm in business," he said.

"Good. Business."

Her mind was scrambling to make sense of it.

"Me and my uncle scout around for old cars, fix 'em. I learned to do that in prison. You know, rehab? Then we sell 'em."

He surprised her with so much talk. It was not what she remembered.

"Well, that's just great," she said. "And college?"

He hesitated.

"Yeah. I'm planning on it."

But before she could probe further, a young woman in a turquoise dress swept him off into the crowd.

Later, as Kathryn was about to leave the party, Rama suddenly surfaced from out of the dark corridor of fish tanks.

"Oh, good," she said, offering him her hand. "I was afraid I wouldn't get a chance to say goodbye."

She smiled up at him.

Without warning, he disengaged his hand and wrapped his arms around her.

She fought the impulse to pull away, to escape the strong hands gripping her back, the warmth of his breath. He was taller than she remembered, more massive. She told herself, "Hold on. He's just another man at a parry, saying goodbye, being friendly." She forced herself to relax, to respond as she would to any casual hug. She didn't want to hurt his feelings. But her arms remained limp at her sides.

Her husband saved her.

"Hello," he said, holding out her raincoat, ready to leave. "I don't believe we've met."

Rama dropped his hands. For a second, his lips froze into a thin line and his eyes narrowed. Then he was smiling and reaching out to shake Johnny's.

"Johnny, this is Rama," Kathryn said. "A former student."

Johnny smiled and took his hand.

"From ...?"

She interrupted.

"One of my very best students."

"Do you work here?" Johnny asked.

Kathryn suddenly remembered she had never asked why he was at the party.

Rama laughed.

"I wish I did. It's a cool place. But I'm with Lavonne."

And there she was beside him, the girl in the turquoise dress.

"Lucky you," Johnny said. "She's terrific."

Three years ago, Rama had turned up in her English composition class. By that time, she'd been teaching in the prison college program for a couple of years and knew more or less what to expect. A dark basement room with thickly painted white walls and bars on the dust-streaked, frosted windows. Thirty or so men, all ages, all races, dressed in blue jeans, blue work shirts, blue wool caps, seated at long tables arranged haphazardly on the cracked concrete floor. Not looking at each other, carefully spacing themselves so as to leave the seats between them empty as long as possible. Breathing room was a valuable commodity.

She had heard that many of them had "taken a life." Most had known violence. But she never asked how they had ended up in that dreary place and few of them told her. She only knew that decades earlier, they had failed in school, had poisoned their own lives, and all but lost hope but then had risked starting again, risked writing essays about their failures and poems about their dreams, had tackled algebra and geometry and the dictionary.

"But aren't you afraid?" friends would ask.

"Not really," she always answered. "The guards are vigilant. Besides, the men are just people, like anybody else, but maybe more intelligent than most."

They were certainly as intelligent as the young students she taught in her regular job, at Bon Tempe Community College, and more perceptive about the complexity of life. That realization still excited her.

Rama stood out from the beginning. He was younger than most, in his early twenties, with a scrubbed look about him. His blue shirt was tucked neatly into his jeans, not hanging in large folds as was customary. He never wore a cap, and his arms were clear of the tattoos that squirmed up and down the limbs of many inmates. In class, he kept to himself, even after the other men had loosened up and begun to chat with each other. He never initiated conversation, never volunteered in class discussions. She learned how bright he was from his first essay on the dark and light imagery in the James Baldwin story "Sonny's Blues." His analysis was thoughtful, his sentences crisp, his grammar perfect, his vocabulary extensive. And he knew how to spell. She scrawled a note at the bottom of the last page.

"This is just brilliant. Why don't you talk more in class?"

But he continued to sit stiffly silent in the classroom.

Then, about halfway through me semester, he just disappeared. She waited three weeks, no Rama. Finally, she sent him a note.

"Please come back to class," she wrote. "Your essays are an inspiration. You mustn't let yourself fail."

A week or so later, he reappeared. He didn't offer an explanation or acknowledge her note. He didn't ask for additional help. He just showed up and handed in all of his missing assignments, which were as thoughtful and skillfully written as the earlier ones. She felt triumphant. She had given him a future. It was why she continued to volunteer without pay in the prison program even after she had obtained her PhD, even after she had landed a tenure-track position at the community college. She always left the prison feeling exuberant, excited by the lives she had touched.

But that's not the only reason Kathryn remembered Rama. It was the poem.

At the end of the semester, she always gave the men a small collection of poems to read. At first, they resisted. They claimed to hate poetry. But once they started reading Langston Hughes, Pablo Neruda, even Blake and Frost, their resistance melted. And when she asked them to write their own verse, they bent to it with unexpected vigor, mixing metaphors in jolting rhythm and rhyme. On the last day of class, they read their poems aloud to high fives and cheers. It was the climax of the semester, and she loved it.

All but Rama. He refused to read his poem, and Kathryn didn't question it. But at the end of the period, he suddenly stood up. The men were talking and laughing, relieved to have cleared this first hurdle of their college careers. So, Rama just stood there, his head bowed over the paper he held in his hand, waiting. Suddenly, everyone was watching him. The room was stone silent. And he began to read:

> My life is not a metaphor or simile.
> It's what you made of me
> Behind closed doors
> The cuts and bruises that I bore
> The public smiles and secret sins
> The scalding iron, the idle whim.
> You know. You left your mark.
> You think you left me in the dark
> You think your secret's safe
> You think I can't escape.
>
> My life is not a metaphor or simile
> It is the poem you made of me
> Harsh lines and jangled melody
> Shout out your secret and set me free.

For a minute there was complete silence. Then one by one, the men stood up and began to clap, louder and louder, without a word. Rama slowly raised his eyes from his poem and looked around the room. Kathryn thought he looked stunned. Then, while the men were still clapping, he handed the poem to Kathryn and left the room. She had not seen him since.

On the way home from the party, Johnny pumped her about Rama. What had he done? He looked so clean cut.

She didn't know.

"You're clearly important to him."

"What do you mean?"

"The way he was hugging you."

"Oh, that wasn't personal," she said, hoping it was true. "There's a total taboo against inmates touching the teachers. We can shake hands. That's it. He was probably making some kind of statement with that hug."

"Like what?"

"He's like everyone else. Old friends hug each other. He can do that now."

It sounded right to her, but she remembered the way her body had stiffened when he had appeared out of nowhere, his hands on her back, holding her close. Too close. She hated herself for the feeling, but there it was.

"Who's Lavonne?" she asked.

"She's my new secretary. Quiet, unobtrusive, does her job. She's nothing like the dress," Johnny said. "I was glad to see her stepping out of herself tonight."

Kathryn tried to bring up a memory of the woman inside that shiny fabric. Dark skinned, she thought, hair that fell to her shoulders in stiff lines. A little heavy. She couldn't remember the face.

"He's smart," she said and elaborated with obvious pleasure on her success in bringing Rama back to school.

"I'm proud of him."

"No wonder he likes you," Johnny said.

"Yeah," she said.

One day toward the end of March, Johnny came home from work later than usual.

"Secretary problems," he said. "Lavonne came in this morning with a cut over her eye."

"You ask her about it?"

"Yeah. It looked nasty. She fed me the classic line about bumping into a car door."

"You didn't believe her."

"It's happened before. One time, a swollen cheek. Another time, a gash on her ear."

Kathryn guessed where this was headed.

"She'd been to the doctor and gotten stitches," he said. "It's delicate. I asked her if there was a problem at home, and she said no."

"She's not a child."

"Right. But she's my secretary, and I think someone's beating on her."

"I know what you're thinking."

She could hear the defensive note in her voice.

"Yeah. That convict. What's his name? Krishna?"

"He's not a convict, and his name's Rama. Come on."

She could feel herself getting angry.

"You get out of prison, find a decent job and a girlfriend, and the first thing that goes wrong, you're the one they accuse."

"My wife, the bleeding-heart liberal," Johnny teased.

"I guess. But I happen to believe what I say."

And yet, how did the poem go? "Behind closed doors the cuts and bruises that I bore." She didn't want to admit it, but she felt uneasy.

"Get off your high horse," Johnny said. "I'm not accusing your friend, but if he's abusing her, it's got to stop."

"So, why not ask her directly?"

"I did. I didn't name him, but I asked if someone at home might be hitting her."

"And she said no."

"Right."

"That's it then."

"For now. I just hope to hell it doesn't happen again."

But, of course, it did happen again. Three months later, Lavonne took a couple of weeks of sick leave, and when she returned, her mouth was swollen, and she was missing a tooth.

Once again Lavonne had an explanation. Her teenage brother, Jamel, who lived with her, had run the car into a tree. She hadn't been wearing a seatbelt. Johnny remembered Jamel from one of the firm picnics as a large, fleshy boy with outsized jeans belted low on his hips and dark eyes that shifted from person to person, looking more frightened than bored.

"When did this happen?" Johnny asked Lavonne.

"Last month some time. I forget the date."

"What happened to the car?"

"It was totaled."

"That's terrible. Did you report it to the police?"

"No."

"Did you go to the hospital?"

"No."

"You've been gone two weeks, Lavonne. Have you been at home?"

"Yeah."

"Did you see a doctor?"

"I saw a dentist. He's going to fix my tooth."

The extended leave got the partnership's attention. They were unfazed by cuts and bruises but paying subs for an employee's undocumented sick leave affected the bottom line. They didn't want to fire Lavonne. They just wanted her to come to work. And so, the focus turned to possible physical abuse. Johnny volunteered to talk informally to a policeman he knew, a neighbor, to see what he knew. Domestic violence calls were a matter of record.

"You can't just do that!" Kathryn was furious. "Ask the police to check into someone's private life like that."

"I just had a little neighborhood chat with Tim. It wasn't official. He didn't have to do it. My motive's pure. The firm's worried about her."

"I bet. What did you tell him?"

"I just gave him the name and phone number and asked if there'd been any calls."

"You didn't mention Rama?"

He avoided her stare.

"Not by name."

"You didn't! You told that law-and-order Nazi that Lavonne had an ex-con living with her?"

"Not in so many words. Look, they found nothing. No calls. Don't worry. It's okay."

A month later, when Lavonne once again missed a week of work without an explanation, Johnny had to let her go. She didn't contest it but just packed up her make-up kit and box of tissues, which she kept in the desk drawer, and left the office.

"I feel rotten," Johnny told Kathryn. "She's a first-class secretary, but, bottom line, she has to come to work."

"You didn't ask her about Rama, did you?" Kathryn asked.

"No. She did tell me that Jamel was in trouble with the law. That could be why she missed work."

Several months later, Kathryn was at the prison helping a student with a rough draft of an essay, when he suddenly asked, "Is it true you snitched on Rama?"

She froze.

"Of course not."

"It's what I heard."

"Heard where? He's not back in here, is he?"

"No, ma'am."

She realized she was holding her breath, steeling herself against news of Rama's return to prison.

"What did you hear about him?"

"Just that you ratted on him."

"It's not true."

Her voice was so loud, so emphatic, that several students looked up.

"I saw him once, on the outside, that's all."

"Yeah. That's what I heard."

"Did you hear it from Rama?"

The student, Kevin, smiled.

"No, ma'am."

It troubled her that she didn't believe him.

And then one day in early November, Rama showed up at her house. Kathryn was bent over the computer in the small front room she used for an office, writing up lesson plans for her class at the community college, and there he was, at the front window, his hands cupped around his eyes, peering in. She involuntarily jumped back in her chair. Rama pointed to himself and then to the door. What was be doing here? She sent Johnny a quick text message.

"Call me. Rama's here."

Dropping her phone and keys in the pocket of her cardigan, she stepped out onto the front porch, into the weak winter sunlight, and shut the door behind her.

"Hope I didn't scare you," he said. "I rang the bell, but you didn't seem to hear it."

"It's broken," she said. "How'd you know where I live?"

She tried to keep her voice light.

"The law firm directory."

"You're still with Lavonne?"

"Sometimes."

Kathryn wrapped her arms around her waist. It was cold on the porch, and she regretted not having picked up her coat

"What can I do for you?"

She smiled when she asked him, but her voice sounded cold.

Rama laughed.

"I thought we might have some small talk before getting down to business. Maybe even a cup of coffee."

He looked meaningfully toward the door, but Kathryn pretended she didn't understand.

"Hey, I'm sorry. I don't mean to sound unfriendly, but this isn't a good time for a visit. I'm really busy."

"I didn't come for a visit," he said. "I came for a recommendation."

She smiled, this time more warmly. This was something she could do.

"Recommendation for what?"

"A job. I had to quit the car business."

Had to quit? What was he doing here?

"I can say you were a good student," she said. "I don't really know anything about your job qualifications."

"That's okay. Look, can't we go in? It's cold out here."

He was right. It was freezing on the porch. But all she could think about was how tall he was, taller than she remembered. He had looked up her address, had walked out to the suburbs in search of her. He was here on her doorstep.

"I'm sorry, but I'm really busy. Why don't you give me the information, and I'll mail in a recommendation."

It sounded so lame.

Beethoven's Fifth rang out from her pocket. She flipped open her phone and saw Johnny's private number on the screen. Thank God.

"You okay?"

"Hi. Guess who's here? Rama. He's leaving in a minute. I'll get back to you."

Rama laughed.

"It's that husband of yours, isn't it? You emailed him."

"No," she lied.

She felt shamed but also relieved that Johnny bad gotten her message.

"If I'm leaving in a minute," Rama's voice was mocking, "I better get on with it."

"Sure." She put her phone back in her pocket, but she didn't cut the connection.

"Okay. The recommendation was an excuse. I came here to set the record straight. About Lavonne. That brother of hers, Jamel, beat her up. He does coke, gets mean when he's out of money. I had nothing to do with it. I wanted you to know that. I tried to protect her, but I had my own interests to consider. You know, I'm still on parole. I couldn't get caught fighting that stupid kid."

Whether or not it was the truth, it didn't matter. She wanted him to leave.

"I didn't think it was you," she said.

He narrowed his eyes.

"Of course, you did."

"Come on, Rama. Who do you think I am?"

He suddenly reached for her wrist and closed his fingers around it. She yanked her arm away, but he held fast. His face was close to hers. She could smell the cigarettes on his breath.

"I think you told that cop I was an ex-con."

"I did not," she said, pulling back from him. She could hear Johnny's voice, squeaking from the depths of her pocket. She reached into her pocket with her other hand.

Rama stood watching her, holding her arm, waiting.

"He lives around here, that cop. I checked it out."

She closed her fingers around the cold lump of metal and slowly lifted it out of her pocket.

"Rama, let me go. Now!"

It was her best schoolteacher voice, loud enough for Johnny to hear.

He loosened his fingers.

"It's just that bastard almost busted me," Rama said. "I thought..."

She pulled her arm away from him and stepped back toward the door. It was over.

"I know," she said, "but I never said a word to him. You have to believe me."

It was true, but she felt like she was lying.

"Okay," he said.

He stood there on her front porch, his hair trimmed short, his face clean-shaven, his khaki trousers pressed. He dressed up for me, she suddenly thought, amazed, ashamed. This young man, this college boy, was trying to impress me.

She said the first thing that came to mind.

"Look, Rama. I've told you. I'm very proud of you. You're one of my successes."

The minute she said it, she regretted it.

He laughed.

"'My life is not a metaphor or simile.' It is the poem *you* made of me? Is that it?"

"I'm sorry," she said. "I'm really sorry. I don't think I've done anything wrong, but I'm really sorry."

"Sorry for what?"

"That you thought I talked to that policeman."

He laughed.

"No. That's not it. You're sorry I'm not still inside, aren't you? Sorry I'm not still your star pupil."

"That's not true!" she snapped.

He stood there, not moving, watching her.

"Can I come in?" he finally said.

She wanted to say, Yes. Come in.

"I'm afraid not," she said. "I'm sorry."

"You said that before."

He turned and walked down her steps. She waited until he had turned the corner of her street before returning to the house. She never saw him again.

At the end of the semester, she stopped teaching at the prison.

Waiting for Rose

Forge, Issue 7.1, June 2013

Your life can change in a split second. I know. It happened when I was seven.

Daddy was at the stove fixing my breakfast. He was wearing his blue striped pajama bottoms and no top, and he was barefoot. His chest, which doesn't have any hair, was so pale, he looked almost sick. And his face needed shaving.

"Here you go, Toots," he said. "French toast with lots of butter and jelly."

My name is Teresa, but everybody calls me Toots. Everybody except Grandma Charlotte.

That's when I heard Mama coming down the stairs. I could tell she was wearing her pink satin bedroom slippers with the pompoms and the wedge heels because she was making a loud clomp with each step.

The minute she came in the kitchen, I knew something was wrong. Her old navy terry-cloth bathrobe was hanging open over her nightgown, which had a big yellow stain down the front. And her hair stuck out in different directions.

Before that day, Mama dressed for breakfast. At least that's how I remember it. There was a bright blue cotton blouse, that smelled like lemon soap and the starch she always used, and she wore her hair, which was red and wavy, brushed back from her face and held in place with little curved combs. She would come to me first thing and take my face in her soft, soft fingers, and kiss me on the top of my head. She was so pretty, and she smelled so good.

"How's my tootsie-roll?" she'd ask.

"Sweet as pie," I'd answer.

But that morning was all wrong.

She didn't even look at me. Instead, she said to Daddy, "How come you're not dressed?"

Which was strange, since *she* wasn't dressed.

"Don't rush me," Daddy said. "I got to get some coffee. My head's killing me."

"Well, no wonder," she said in a voice I didn't recognize. "You know, they're gonna fire you one of these days if you keep being late all the time."

I thought, they can't fire him, can they?

I watched Daddy pour himself a cup of coffee. He sat down next to me at the red Formica breakfast table and snapped his newspaper open. He didn't look at Mama.

"Get off my back," he said.

She stomped over to the Frigidaire, pulled out a package of bacon, and threw a couple of pieces into the skillet which Daddy had used to fry my French toast.

"What's going to happen to these girls, huh? When your mother's finally had enough and fires your ass."

I had never heard her talk like that before. I wanted to tie the belt of her robe, and turn her around, and say, "Mama, go back upstairs. Come down again, all dressed and pretty."

"Stop screeching!" Daddy said without looking up from his paper.

He wrapped his bare feet around the aluminum legs of the chair.

"I'll screech as much as I like," she said.

"Go ahead, then."

His voice was the kind of calm that tells you a person's really mad but holding it back.

I started to get up from the table. I could tell something terrible was about to happen and I didn't want to be there.

"I wish your precious mother could see you now," Mama said.

"I wish she could see *you*," Daddy said.

He made his voice go up high like Grandma's.

"'I warned you, didn't I? I told you she was no good before you married her.'"

Then it happened. She grabbed that hot iron skillet with the bacon still sizzling in it.

"Mama," I screamed. But she didn't stop. She walked over to where Daddy was sitting. He just sat there and watched her. And then she hit him. Right on the head with that hot frying pan.

"Rose!" I screamed. "Rose! Rose! Rose!"

It was all confusion after that. Daddy was hollering and wiping hot grease off his bare chest. Mama was crying and saying she was sorry. The ambulance showed up, loaded Daddy in, and took off, with the sirens screaming. My sister Rose went too. She told me later that Mama was too upset to give a straight story, so she had to go. She told the doctor that Daddy had hurt himself cooking. She was fifteen years old.

Nobody even thought about getting me to school that day.

As I said, everything changed in a flash. But Rose told me it had changed before that. I just hadn't noticed. Or maybe I didn't want to. I was too happy being the baby of the family.

Take the time I sang "Onward Christian Soldiers" for Sunday service in front of everybody. I was six, and I wore a white organdy dress with a sash tied in the back and puffed sleeves. Mama brushed my hair over a broomstick that morning into dark ringlets.

When the time came for my solo, Grandma took me by the hand and led me up from our family's pew onto the stage next to Reverend Parker. The sanctuary was almost full, and I could see red and blue patterns on the wood floor from the sun shining through the stained-glass windows. I looked out at all the people, mostly grownups but some children, and wanted to run off that stage. But then Grandma started playing the organ, real soft, and I began to sing as loud as I could. I put my hands together, the way she had showed me, like I was praying, and looked up at the picture of Jesus on the Cross which is hanging at the back of the church.

When the service was over, everyone came up to me and hugged me and told me how pretty my singing was and how I might become a gospel singer someday. And when I got home, Mama made me an ice cream soda and made a fuss over me. That's what my life was like then. If sometimes Mama's laugh got a little too loud or Daddy looked like he was sick in the mornings, I paid no attention. I was their Toots.

Daddy didn't lose his job, although he's still late to work a lot of the time. My Grandma owns the Spotswood Hotel where Daddy's the manager, and she wouldn't dare fire her only son. Grandma is a very large person, not fat exactly, but when she comes into a room, everybody stops talking and listens to what she says.

And she hates my mama.

"You made your bed," she'd say to Daddy. "And the only way you're going to be able to sleep in it is to make that woman behave."

"How am I going to do that, Mama?" he'd ask.

"You know what I'm talking about," she'd say.

He'd wink at me.

"I think she wants me to bring your Mama to a WCTU meeting, Toots."

Grandma's the president of the WCTU in our town, which is the Women's Christian Temperance Union.

Rose is eight years older than me. After the bad day in the kitchen, she tried to explain it to me.

"Mama was sick," she said. "She didn't know what she was saying to Daddy because she was feeling so bad."

"She hit him," I said.

I couldn't stop seeing it, my own Mama in that dirty bathrobe clomping across the linoleum floor, with that hot frying pan in her hand.

"She didn't mean to. She didn't know what she was doing."

That made no sense.

"She sounded more mad than sick."

"I guess she *was* mad. But the sickness made her mad."

"Why was she mad?"

"She wasn't mad at you, if that's what you think."

"Why was she mad?"

"Grownups sometimes get mad."

"Is Daddy going to be okay?"

I was worried about him. He seemed so helpless beside Mama and Grandma Charlotte.

"Sure. You saw him when he got home from the hospital. They put a bandage on his head and some medicine on his burns. He's fine."

"Will she hit him again?"

I wanted her to say, no, never. But instead, she hugged me.

"I hope not," she said. "But I'll take care of you, Toots, whatever happens. I promise."

It was the best I could get. And she was true to her word. Whenever Mama started drinking orange juice and smelling funny, I'd find Rose, and she'd take me to Ballou Park or buy me an ice cream cone at the Dairy Korner or take me to her room for a story.

Another way my life changed was that Grandma Charlotte started coming to our house in the afternoons. A lot of the time Mama was upstairs in bed with the door closed, and Grandma didn't bother her. She always brought ginger cookies, and she'd ask me to play something on the piano, hymns mostly, and she'd quiz Rose about school. She never stayed long.

One afternoon, she showed up when Mama was downstairs fixing me an ice cream soda and pouring herself a glass of orange juice. She was wearing her old blue bathrobe, which I was getting used to, although I missed the pretty blouses. I missed them so much.

"Well, what a surprise!" Grandma said when she walked into the kitchen.

"I'm just fixing myself a little juice," Mama said. "I think I'm coming down with a cold."

I could tell she didn't like Grandma being there, but she was trying to be polite.

"Orange juice and what?" Grandma asked.

Mama glared at her and laughed.

"None of your business," she said.

"It *is* my business the way you're acting. It's very much my business."

Mama looked up at the ceiling and said in a low, steady voice, "Please leave my house."

I wanted to get out of there, but Mama put her hands on my shoulders and kept me in my seat.

"I will not leave until I've had my say," Grandma said. "You have no idea what's happening to these girls. I won't even mention the way you treat your husband. He should be able to take care of himself, although I sometimes wonder. But these girls need a mother."

I could feel Mama leaning heavy on my shoulders.

Grandma said, "Sit down and listen to me."

"I guess I don't have much choice," Mama said. "Do your worst."

"Do you know where Rose is right now?"

"With friends. She's sixteen, Charlotte."

"Do you know with what friends?"

"Of course, I know her friends," Mama said, although it made me wonder. Rose rarely brought friends home, and when she did, Mama was usually in bed.

"Teresa, honey," Grandma said, "now that you've finished your ice cream, maybe you should go. Your mother and I have some things to discuss."

I looked at Mama. I didn't want to abandon her to Grandma, but I was dying to get out of that kitchen. She didn't say anything. So, I left. But I heard Grandma say the name "Cory" as I was leaving. Cory was one of Rose's friends, and I didn't like him. I didn't like the way he put his hands on Rose, and I didn't like his laugh, which sounded rude. When I asked her, Rose said he wasn't her boyfriend, which made me feel better.

I was looking for Rose when Grandma pushed past me. Mama was standing at the door of the kitchen yelling, "Get out of here and don't you come back."

"Rose!" I called.

And there she was, standing right by the front door, her eyes on Grandma, her shoulders stiff like a soldier. I could always count on her to be brave.

"You heard Mama," she said to Grandma. "Leave us alone."

"Oh, sweetheart, if only I could."

"You only make it worse," Rose said.

I stood there looking back and forth between them, wanting them to stop, wanting all of it to stop.

"I'm going to speak to your father," Grandma said.

"You do all the time."

After she left, Rose stooped down next to me and hugged me so hard we fell on the floor, which started us laughing.

"The old goat," Rose said. And that made me laugh really hard.

And then one day, when I needed her and called and called, she didn't answer. Mama had picked me up from school. She was supposed to take me to my piano lesson, but she drove home instead. I figured she was having one of her spells, because she was driving slow, and she didn't say anything. By that time, I knew it wouldn't do any good to ask questions.

The first thing I saw when we got home was Rose's red sweater hanging on the banister. Mama went right to the kitchen and poured herself a big glass of orange juice. She sat down at the table and laid her head down on her arms. I called Rose, but she didn't answer. So, I went over and touched Mama's back.

"What's wrong?" I asked.

She looked up at me like she was surprised to find me there.

"Why don't you go play?" she said.

I didn't feel like playing, so I went upstairs to look for Rose.

The door to her room was shut. I didn't hear anything, but I figured she had to be in there.

"Rose?" I whispered through the door. "It's Mama. Something's the matter."

She didn't answer. So, I opened the door. At first, I couldn't see anything. The blinds were drawn, and there weren't any lights. Then I saw Rose on the bed. And someone was lying on the bed beside her, face down.

"Go on back downstairs," she said. "I'll be there in a minute."

But I just stood there. I couldn't move. Because she didn't have her blouse on. She had one arm crossed over herself, and she was pulling at the sheet with her other hand, but I could see her nipples.

"Jesus, Rose, you said nobody was home."

It was Cory.

Rose pulled the sheet up around her.

"What are you doing?" I asked.

"I'll tell you later. Just a minute."

I watched her get herself dressed and we went down to the kitchen. Mama was on the floor, lying in a puddle of juice and broken glass.

"What's the matter with her?" I asked, squatting on the floor beside her.

But Rose didn't answer. Instead, she said, "Come on, Toots, let's get her upstairs."

She was pulling on Mama's arm when we looked up to find Cory staring down at us.

"Oh, my god," he said. "She's dead drunk."

"No," I told him. "She's sick."

"Alcohol poisoning," he said.

"You're wrong," I said. "I hate you."

"Just give us a hand," Rose said. She sounded so tired.

When they had gotten Mama into her bed, I stayed behind, gazing at her face, patting her cheek, and saying over and over, "What's wrong, Mama?" until Rose took me by the hand and led me from the room.

Then she was gone. Daddy drove her to a hospital where he said she would get well. I wrote letters to her at the hospital, and she sent me postcards with pictures of dolphins and giraffes. She said she loved me and missed me and would come home soon. I pasted the postcards in my scrapbook. And most nights, I slept with Rose to keep from crying.

And then one day, when I was sitting with Rose on her bed, she started to tear up a letter she was reading.

"What are you doing?" I asked.

"It's from Mama."

She looked really angry.

"Let me see."

I tried to grab the paper.

"She's not getting well."

I started hitting her with my fists.

"That's not true," I screamed.

Rose put her arms around me.

"Poor little kid," she said.

She looked like she'd been crying.

I wiggled away from her and picked up the pieces of Mama's letter that were scattered all over the bed.

"Read it," I said, holding out the scraps of paper.

"You poor little kid," she said again.

I laid out the scraps of paper on the bed. Too many pieces were missing to read it, but I pretended.

"It says she's getting well and is coming home soon."

And I left the room.

Mama did come home. And the first week or two were pretty good. She was dressed and smelling nice every afternoon when I got home from school, and she made dinner for us.

"Whoopee! No more Grandma," Rose said.

Mama laughed her old laugh.

"Ding-dong, the witch is dead."

But one afternoon, soon after she came back, I burst open the door to her bedroom, where Rose said she'd gone to take a rest. The blinds were drawn, and the room smelled like cough syrup.

I tiptoed over to the bed and whispered, "Mama?"

She propped herself up on her elbow and tried to straighten the sheet which was tangled up in her legs.

"Hi Toots," she said. "How's my baby?"

I took hold of the sheet and pulled it off of her.

"Please get up," I said.

But she flopped down on her back.

"In a minute, honey."

"Please," I begged.

She didn't answer. I stood there watching her face for a long time, but she didn't say anything else. I left the room when she started snoring.

After that, she was usually in bed when I left for school, and her door was closed when I got home. She still came downstairs from time to time, but she was usually in her nightgown, and the gray showed in her hair. Daddy told me it was taking a long time for her to get well. And then he took her to what he called a "rest home."

Of course, she came back again. And again. But she always went back to the rest home.

Each time, I cried less.

That's when Grandma Charlotte took over.

"How come she's here all the time?" Rose asked Daddy.

"Toots needs her."

"I'll look after her like I've been doing for the past year."

"You're a kid."

"Suit yourself," Rose said, "but it's me or her."

And she meant it, because with Grandma hanging around all the time, Rose stopped coming home after school. She slept at our house, of course. Otherwise, Grandma would have called the police. But she never turned up until after dinner.

"Where have you been?" Grandma would ask.

"With friends."

"You'll end up just like your mother," Grandma would say.

"Good."

Occasionally, I'd see her in town with Cory, their arms around each other's waists, talking and laughing. I'd run up to her and beg her to come home.

"It's awful without you," I'd tell her.

"Not now, Toots," she'd say. "I'll be there tonight."

And she'd give me a big hug and off she'd go with Cory. I hated him.

After a while, we only saw her on weekends. Grandma called the police, but before they showed up, somebody's mother would telephone and ask if Rose could sleep over.

"She's okay," Daddy told Grandma. "Lay off her. She's a teenager. Right now, she'd rather be with her friends."

"Do you even care what happens to your child?"

"I won't dignify that with an answer. Rose's had a shock, and the last thing she needs is to have the cops trailing after her. Give her time. She's a responsible kid."

"She's seventeen, Herman."

"Just leave the police out of it," Daddy said and disappeared into the kitchen.

"Don't you pour yourself another drop of that whiskey," Grandma said.

And Daddy just laughed.

Finally, Rose's high school counselor reported her missing from school. Grandma telephoned all of her friends, but no one knew where she was.

"She's with Cory," I said.

But Cory didn't know where she was.

"Search me!" he said.

"She's a runaway," the policeman said. "She'll turn up when she needs money. They always do."

But she didn't. Every afternoon, Grandma would telephone the police to see if anyone had seen her. I always stood beside her while she phoned, listening as hard as I could. Then I would go to her room and close the door. And I'd write letters to Rose. I would tell her what was happening in school and what songs I was learning on the piano. I'd tell her I loved her. I'd hear Grandma outside the door. "Teresa, honey, can I come in?"

"Leave me alone," I'd say.

"Let's go to the Dairy Korner."

"Leave me alone."

I kept all the letters in a box in Rose's room for when she turned up. She'd promised to take care of me.

Grandma got Daddy to work on me, but I could tell his heart wasn't in it. He was drinking a lot of whiskey by then. He had to hide the bottles, because Grandma poured the whiskey down the sink whenever she found them.

I'm ten now. Mama comes home now and then, but she doesn't stay for long. I try not to think about the time before she got sick. Grandma's pretty nice to me. She's probably afraid I'll leave. But I'm only ten. So I go to school, I go to First Baptist, I play the piano.

And I wait for Rose. I have my suitcase packed. Because some day she'll come for me. I know she will. And she won't be with Cory. She'll come for *me*.

The Bread Knife

Summerset Review, Summer 2012

The first time I saw her, she was dripping blood. On the floor, on her jeans, on her bare feet.

"Oh no," she said, as she opened the door to their apartment, "I thought you were the ambulance."

She stressed the last syllable of ambulance. A southerner. We stared at her left hand, enveloped in a bulging dishtowel, streaked crimson.

Her husband, Riley, had invited Gerald and me to their place for dinner. Gerald had taken him under his wing at the law firm. Thrown choice assignments his way, treated him to lunch, that sort of thing. Gerald thought he was a comer. So, when Riley got married, he invited us over. I wasn't looking forward to it. I've had my fill of law firm dinner parties in my many years of marriage. The lawyers dominate the conversation with talk about work, and the food invariably looks better than it tastes. But Gerald said I'd like Riley, said he was friendlier, more open than the usual run of new associates. So, we went.

Riley suddenly appeared. He was in jeans too, and a white tee-shirt with a faded, colored picture of the Grand Canyon on the front. He's about six feet tall with a thick neck, a slightly bulging forehead, and a stand of straight brown hair.

"Oh, God," he said, when he saw us standing there, a bouquet of tulips in my hand, a bottle of zinfandel in Gerald's. "Come in. I'm sorry."

"This looks bad," Gerald said. "Tell us what to do."

"Just make yourselves at home, I've got to run her to the emergency room, I'll be right back. No problem. It's a new knife. I think it's okay."

"We'll come back another time," I gasped.

"Oh, no, no," Riley said. "Dinner's ready. We'll be right back. Come on in. There's lots of books and magazines here. We'll be right back."

We edged into the room, clutching our offerings, apologizing. The place was barely furnished, a few folding chairs, a black leather sofa, new from Ikea, a card table, U-Haul boxes everywhere. The young wife stood at the open door, peering expectantly into the hallway, cradling her wounded hand in the crook of her arm.

"Here they are," Riley announced, holding up a set of keys. "I'm not waiting a minute more for the fucking ambulance. I'll take you."

"We'll go with you," Gerald said.

"No."

Riley was already out the door.

"But don't leave," he called back to us. "Dinner's nearly ready."

And they were gone.

"Well, it's not boring anyway," Gerald said.

We spent the next hour debating whether to stay or go. Gerald wanted out, but I insisted that it would be rude to leave them in the lurch, unkind even. And so, I rummaged around the cluttered kitchen until I found a large water pitcher for the tulips and a couple of juice glasses for the wine. Gerald opened the zin, and we waited.

Riley returned alone. He looked beat.

"She's okay," he said and collapsed on the sofa beside me. "Thank God. She'll hop a cab home."

That's when we noticed, for the first time, the bandage on Riley's left forefinger. A large bandage.

"What happened to *you?*" I asked.

"A little nick. Nothing serious."

"Are you two trying to kill each other?" Gerald asked.

He was making a joke of it. It didn't seem funny to me. But Riley smiled, his face still pale.

"It's the bread knife. A wedding present. It did us in, one at a time."

"How is she?" I asked.

"She just needed stitches. She's okay. Let's eat."

We ate the dinner without her. It wasn't very good, a crab salad with too much celery and mayonnaise and not enough crab. A sourdough baguette, unsliced of course, which we tore into pieces and dipped in melted butter with garlic powder. The zin was delicious. Riley pretended to listen as Gerald and I made feeble small talk, but he kept ducking his head to check his cell phone, and his laugh was a beat late whenever Gerald attempted a joke.

"We should leave," we kept repeating. "You need to be at the hospital."

But he wouldn't let us.

"Gemma would be so disappointed," he said. "It's our first dinner party."

Just as we were finishing the pecan pie—her specialty we were told—she suddenly appeared at the front door, a huge mitt of a bandage wrapped round her left hand, her arm in a sling.

"Darling," Riley jumped up from the table, knocking over his chair, and rushed to her side, his hands stretched out awkwardly as if he were unsure of what part to touch.

"Hi," she said, looking over his shoulder, smiling at Gerald and me. "I'm Gemma. Would you like a piece of chocolate?"

I couldn't resist her. She was pretty, of course, like a child, with a blaze of strawberry blond hair, tender pale skin, and widely spaced blue eyes. But that wasn't it. As she stood there that night, smiling helplessly and clutching her wounded hand, I could see she needed to be taken care of. And with our only son out of the nest, I was ripe for the task.

We began with cooking. She had obviously not learned the basics, or anything really, from her mother, who remained a mystery, along with the rest of the family. When I inquired, she brushed off my questions.

"Where do your parents live?"

"Florida."

"What does your father do?"

"Something with insurance."

"Does your mother work?"

"Sometimes."

"Do you have brothers and sisters?"

"One each."

"Where do they live?"

"All over."

"Do you go back there to visit?"

"No."

I figured it was a painful subject and eventually gave up.

Gemma's only culinary accomplishment, the pecan pie, consisted of a store-bought crust and the ingredients listed on the Karo syrup bottle. She loved sweets. And I love to cook.

So, we began in my kitchen with Julia Child's pie crust recipe, the five-page one. Gemma studied the drawings, measured the flour, chilled the water, rubbed butter and flour between her fingers and thumb, the thumb with the angry red scar that circled the base and made tracks over her knuckle, rolled out the dough, and she baked a perfect pie crust.

After that, I invited her every Saturday morning to come cook with me. She would show up at our front door, her pale face slightly flushed, her eyes questioning. Would I really give her a lesson? I couldn't wait. You see, like many women of my generation, I've never had a real job. But I'm a star in the kitchen.

So, together we would chop and carve, bake bread, reduce sauces, sauté vegetables, and whip soufflés light as air. She was a quick learner.

After a couple of months, I told her, "You have a career, here."

She was that good.

"A career," she said. "You think so? I never figured myself with a career."

"Why don't you take classes?"

"Yeah?"

"There's this place called the Culinary Academy in San Francisco. Julian did that for a while."

"Your son?"
"My son."
"Did he like it?"
"For a while."

Like everything else he tried. He had chopped veggies at a high-end downtown restaurant for several months. His dad had wrangled that gig for him. Before that, he bagged groceries at Whole Foods. That was after he quit making jewelry—earrings from abalone shells, silver pendants with moonstones on leather straps. I had several. And before that, college. First, university, then state college, then community college.

At the time, Julian was in Tahoe, Bear Valley. I always felt a jolt of excitement when I heard his voice.

"How's it going, Mom?"

"We're fine, sweetheart. How's my boy?"

"Great. Just great."

"Did you find a job?"

"Yep. A couple, as a matter of fact. I'm teaching snowboarding at the lodge and waiting tables."

"Oh."

"It's just for the season."

"I see."

"Look. It pays the bills."

"Is that all you want?"

I could hear the disappointment in my voice, but I couldn't stop.

"You know, honey, you're going to wake up one day and wonder what happened to your life."

There would be a silence, then, "Yeah. You said that before. Well, right now I need to be at work."

And he would be gone.

I always spent the afternoon digging in the iron-dark earth of my back garden after those conversations. Blaming myself. Trying to figure out where I had gone wrong.

"Leave him be," Gerald would say. "The kid lacks backbone. Nothing you can do about it."

Gemma had backbone.

"I did it!"

She called out before I could even open the door that glorious Saturday morning. The blinding sun lit up her tangle of red-gold hair. The Japanese maple in my front yard glowed in autumn flame behind her, framing her.

"The Culinary Academy."

She twirled about the deck, head thrown back, arms waving.

"I made it. I'm in."

"You're taking classes?"

I grabbed her round the waist. She felt tense, wiry, like she might explode at any minute. My gem, my Gemma.

"Full-time."

"This calls for champagne!"

"At ten in the morning?" asked Gerald.

"You bet."

And so, Saturday night dinners replaced Saturday morning lessons. Always at our house. Daube de Boeuf. Roast Goose with Prune and Foie Gras Stuffing. Orange Mousse. Whatever she was learning in school.

"What do you think, Riley?" I asked during one of the many such dinners.

"I love it," he said, smiling, his eyes devouring her as she served quenelles or spooned out bouillabaisse or dashed in and out of the kitchen in her white coat and chef's toque.

I did too. I couldn't help it. She lit up the room with her blazing hair, her quicksilver movements, her nervous giggle as she lifted the lid from the terrine and leaned forward to breathe in the sauce. I was in love.

Riley involved himself in Gemma's cooking with the same intensity he brought to his legal practice. He did most of the shopping, arriving at the fish market before daylight each Saturday, sniffing the freshly caught salmon, supervising the cleaning, squeezing the tomatoes and avocados at the farmers' market, scouring Chinatown for fresh crab. I know because I was often with him, carrying the bags, arguing with the vendors. Riley also served as Gemma's sous chef, chopping, tasting, hauling, adoring.

I told everyone I knew about Gemma, I was that proud. And soon partners in the law firm began hiring her for the elaborate dinner parties they gave for clients. Riley backed her up, working behind the scenes, anticipating her every move, basking in her glory.

If sometimes she seemed impatient with him, criticized the cut of meat he brought from the market, pressed him to hurry his chopping, even occasionally spit out some broth he had prepared, we forgave her. She was an artist.

It's hard to explain my own excitement at Gemma's success. To watch her evolve from the bewildered child I had met that first night into a creative genius was breathtaking. I felt like I was part of it, that I had made it happen. I had a mission now, to make sure she had everything she needed to be the best chef, maybe in all of San Francisco. I was that ambitious.

The next time the four of us had dinner together—roasted artichoke, Veal Prince Orloff, Green beans a la Provençale, Reine de Saba for dessert, I came out with an idea I'd been mulling over.

"I think it's time you began working in a restaurant."

"I like what I'm doing."

"You're too good for it, honey. What I'm talking about is one of those haute cuisine restaurants. The menu changes with what's in season. The chefs are all first-rate. You'd learn a lot."

"I like doing the private dinners. It's more my style. I'm my own boss."

"It's going to get boring. Not to mention the people."

"What about them?"

"Lawyers, businessmen. How do you stand them?"

"They are my customers," she said. "I like them. And it's my way of doing things."

I should have let it go.

Instead, I said, "But you're missing a great opportunity."

She stared at me, hard, the line between her eyes deepening. I was surprised. I hadn't seen that line before.

"How do you like the veal?" she said.

Once Gemma was fully launched as a private chef, we no longer saw her on Saturday nights. But occasionally on her nights off, Tuesdays, she would concoct elaborate gastronomical experiments for Gerald and me to taste and judge. We always feasted at our house, where she had the luxury of my six-burner Wolf range.

But one Tuesday night, she invited us to her house.

"It's an anniversary," she said.

"Whose?"

"Our first dinner together. It's been two years."

"Just two years," I marveled. "And look at you."

"No blood this time, I hope," Gerald said.

"Only in the duck. You haven't seen the place in ages," Gemma said. "You'll be surprised."

She was right. The two of them had completely transformed the apartment. The living room walls were plastered end-to-end with tacked up photographs, some in black and white, some in color, of dinner parties Gemma had catered, plates garnished with Technicolor food, laughing guests toasting the chef, Gemma in white coat and chef's toque, grinning at the camera. There were no photos of Gerald and me.

"You're getting to be quite a star," I said, pretending a generosity I didn't feel. Who were all these people?

Riley had knocked out a wall between the tiny kitchen and the dining room, creating the illusion, if not the expanse, of a farmhouse kitchen. Charming, but cramped. We had to duck our heads to keep from crashing into the heavy skillets which dangled from hooks in the ceiling. Stacks of cookbooks spilled over the counters. Two gleaming white refrigerators, one on each side, guarded the door to the bathroom, a recent addition off the kitchen. Riley's home construction had left uneven edges of sheet rock and unpainted surfaces, lending a slightly off-center, rakish air to the place.

Perched on stools at a round table in the middle of the room, Gerald and Riley sipped champagne and chatted about work. I tried to make myself useful, chopping onions, quartering tomatoes, beating eggs. But Gemma was too fast for me. I kept bumping into her as she moved briskly from mandolin to boiling pot to mixer to frying pan.

"You're a guest," she finally said. "Why don't you sit down and enjoy yourself?"

Her voice had an edge.

The food was, as always, magical. As I took my first bite of duck breast with raspberries, I said, "I don't know how you do all this in your kitchen."

She shrugged.

"Think what you could do in a real gourmet kitchen."

She put down her fork. Her face was flushed.

"What's not real about it?"

I could tell she was annoyed, but I had an answer.

"The stove for a start."

We all glanced over at the small stove, glazed black with hardened, accumulated grease. All four burners were blazing.

She was staring at me.

"Do you think the sauce would taste better with a *real* stove?"

I had never before heard sarcasm from her, and it should have stopped me. But it seemed so obvious, what I was saying.

"Don't be silly. Don't you want a commercial stove? Like my Wolf range?"

"Not now."

I looked at Riley who had stopped eating and was watching me.

"You mean it's too expensive?"

"That too."

"It's a business expense, Gemma. Get a loan. At the rate you're going, you'll pay it back in no time."

She didn't respond.

"Look," I said, "You've got a wonderful thing going. Gerald and I know all kinds of people who could help you with a loan. You could even get a bigger place, design your own kitchen."

My mind was racing.

I reached over and squeezed her hand. It lay there, soft, warm, unresponsive.

"This *is* my own kitchen. I designed it. I like it."

"Look, honey," I said, "you're big time now. You've got to think big. If you can make this kind of food on that antique, think what you can do on proper equipment."

What did I expect? That she would throw her arms around me, and laugh and prance about, as excited as I was? It didn't happen. Without looking at me, she slid her hand out of my grasp and sat there, very still, not eating, staring at her plate.

Gerald finally broke the silence.

"This duck is to die for."

"Fuck the duck," Gemma said.

I almost giggled. But then she was standing up and holding her plate high in the air. Without another word she hurled it to the floor with a loud crash and left the room.

No one spoke. I couldn't take my eyes off the thick white china fragments, the slices of rosy-colored duck breast and bright red raspberries. I jumped up from the table and started dabbing at the berries on the floor with my napkin.

"Don't," Riley said.

He towered over me, his forehead furrowed, his eyes dark, frightened.

"I'm sorry," I said.

"Don't be. She's overworked, that's all."

Then he turned his massive back to me and headed down the hall to his wife.

"What did I do?" I kept asking Gerald all the way home.

"Let it go," Gerald said. "She's a chef. It comes with the territory. They're a temperamental lot."

She came over the next day and apologized. Told me she'd had a stressful week and hoped I wouldn't take it personally.

"I'm really embarrassed," she said.

"Don't worry," I said and put my arms around her. I was relieved. Somehow, I thought it was my fault, that I should be apologizing. But I didn't know what I had done wrong.

She handed me a dish of the floating island we had left untouched the night before.

"A peace offering?"

I hugged her.

"Of course."

Neither of us mentioned the stove.

But I couldn't get that beat-up black oven of hers out of my mind. You have to understand how disgusting it was to even think of cooking on that thing. Besides, I knew just where she could squeeze a Wolf range into that jumble of a kitchen. So, two weeks later, without telling Gerald, I arranged to have one delivered to Gemma's house. It was a crazy thing to do. But at the time, I told myself I was being generous. I kept seeing Gemma holding that plate of pink duck high above her head, then dashing it to the floor. I could tell she was on the verge of destroying her career, and I couldn't let her do that. I told myself, with the proper equipment, she'd be herself again. And I was in a position to help. I knew she couldn't afford it; Riley was still paying off student loans. So, I ordered it, had it sent anonymously. She'd know, of course. But I fooled myself into thinking she'd be pleased.

A week passed with no word from Gemma. She didn't answer my emails or return my phone calls. I asked Gerald if he'd heard anything about her from Riley. He hadn't.

And then, early one morning, when I opened the front door to fetch the *Times*, there she stood, like some pre-Raphaelite virgin caught in my garden, her wan face diminished by untamed gold hair. Instinctively, I wrapped my arms around her thin shoulders, thinner than I remembered.

"Come in, come in," I said. "I'm so glad."

I could feel her resistance, but she followed me into the front hall.

I waited for a response which didn't come. She just hovered there on the deep blue of the Persian carpet, looking as if she might at any moment go under.

I took her in my arms. You see, I still believed I had done the right thing, that she would thank me, that I would continue to guide her, to love her. Because I did, I loved her so much.

"Don't," she hissed, pushing hard against me, accidentally hitting my shoulder with a sharp wrist bone. She was staring at me, her eyes wild.

"My dear," I said, backing away, rubbing my shoulder.

"I couldn't believe you were so stupid." She spat out the word.

"Send it back," I whimpered.

"I'll think about it." She laughed then, mocking me. "You don't get it, do you? This isn't about your fucking stove or your plans for me. It's not about *you*."

"I know."

"You don't know anything. Just stop. Stop trying to live my life."

It was too much to take in.

"You're exhausted," I said. "You need a break."

I ached for her to nod, to rush to me, to ask for help. But she just stood there, her pinched face looking for the first time frightened.

"I'm sorry," she said. "That's what you want me to say, isn't it?"

"I don't know," I said.

But she didn't hear me. She had pushed open the door and stepped out into the blinding summer sunlight. I was too stunned to follow.

That night Riley met us at his front door. He was still dressed for work, his dark blue suit sharply, incongruously pressed, his tie, a fashionable red and purple, drooping at an angle from his collar. His arms hung leaden at his sides as if his hands were weights holding them down.

"She's gone."

His voice had no expression.

"But I just saw her," I said. "This morning."

His large face looked crumpled, like he was about to cry. Without a word, he led us to the kitchen.

The first thing I saw was broken glass, on the table, on the counters, all over the floor.

"What on earth?"

"It's not the first time."

"I'm sorry."

I was ashamed at how inadequate I sounded.

It was then I saw the stove. I hadn't noticed it in the chaos of glass. But there it was, the Wolf range, immense, dominating the tiny kitchen. But something about it was wrong. It should have been shiny. I edged carefully around the shards of glass to get a better look. There were deep cuts carved in the surface of the enamel.

"Jesus," said Gerald, staring at the floor.

He pointed to a knife lying there.

Riley was leaning against the sink, his white face blank.

"Where is she?" I asked. "I have to see her. Maybe I can...?"

"Stop it!" He hissed.

His voice was hoarse.

Afterward, they wouldn't even let me visit her in the hospital. They were right, of course. I mean, I hadn't made her the way she was. But whatever she had, I'd made it worse.

These days when Julian telephones, and I'm thinking how he's wasting his life and how much I want to tell him to go back to college, to do *something*, I don't. I just think about that stove. Seeing it, all black and scratched and scarred, was the scariest thing that ever happened to me. And I hold my peace.

Drawing Lily

Forge, March 2012
Also published in *Spotswood Virginia,*
Stephen F. Austin State University Press, 2021

They were out on the porch at the sun-bleached table, their heads close, almost brushing, the boy Julian chattering away, the grandfather Carl nodding, his narrow hazel eyes and full, chapped lips expressionless. Both had pencils and paper. Both were drawing. Out of the corner of his eye, the old man saw his daughter, Ellen, pull a crumpled tissue from her pocket, then disappear into the dark pine-scented beach house.

Was she crying? He couldn't tell. And anyway, it made no sense. She'd known for months. Lou Gehrig's disease. There was a fancier name, but he could never remember it. And it somehow made him feel better that somebody famous, the baseball player, had died of it. Made the mumbling and the drooling he tried to conceal somehow less shameful.

He studied his grandson. Julian had his mother's high cheekbones and sharp chin. Her same colorless eyebrows and lashes, her lank blond hair. The boy was asking questions, staring at his grandpa's drawing, talking, talking as if his talking could fill the space left by the old man's silence.

"Is that Lily?" Julian asked, smiling at the cow his grandfather had drawn.

A really good cow, not a milk-carton cartoon cow, but a lumbering field animal with lowered head and wet black nostrils and a bulging udder.

Carl's wiry, tapered fingers added the tail, filled in the black spots. He bit his lip and squinted at the paper. The lines in the translucent skin of his cheeks deepened as he concentrated.

"Tell me," Julian begged.

Carl shook his head and pointed at the boy's bare narrow chest.

"You want me to tell it?"

Carl nodded. He had told it so often, first to Ellen when she was Julian's age, over and over, and then to his grandson.

"She was a good milker, Lily," Julian said, imitating the slow, flat cadence of Carl's southern speech.

The old man smiled, revealing a dimple that quickly disappeared into the deep lines of his cheek. He pulled a handkerchief from his pocket and patted his mouth.

"Your papa got her at the county auction, and he was right proud of her. You had to fetch her from the pasture every night before dinner."

The boy paused.

"How old were you?"

Carl pocketed the damp handkerchief and held up both hands, fingers extended.

"Ten? Like me."

Julian paused for a minute as if to let that piece of information sink in.

"You were worried you'd be late that night, weren't you? Your mama didn't like you to be late for dinner. You were standing up close to Lily about to take her lead rope when something spooked her. Something loud. And all of a sudden, she just took off down the hill. You felt a powerful tug on your leg, then a stab of pain that knocked the breath out of you."

Carl smiled at the boy's recollection, not just of the story, but of the exact words Carl always used in telling it. Words like *fetch*, *spooked*, *powerful tug*. Words from the hill country near Spotswood, from the farm.

"Then you fell flat on your face with your left leg twisted under you."

Julian stared down at his own skinny legs poking out of his bathing suit.

"You had managed to tangle your leg up in that lead rope without knowing it, and Lily had yanked you over when she charged down the hill."

He imagined he could still feel it. Luckily the rope had slipped off early on, and he hadn't been dragged far. He had rolled over on his back, hollering out, trying to get up. But every time he tried to put weight on his left foot, the pain shot up his leg so bad he had to give it up. He lay there on that hill, pitying himself, for what seemed like hours, sure that Papa or Willard would come looking for him.

"You were all by yourself and nobody came."

Carl felt the boy's hand, warm on his back, protective.

Nobody came. After a long time, he got up on his hands and his good knee. He could still feel it, the sharp knife of pain as he dragged his hurt leg behind him up the hill toward the house. About halfway up, he found a stick strong enough to bear his weight. He fell a time or two, calling for his mama. But finally, he opened the kitchen door and crawled inside. She was washing dishes. She took one look at him and screamed. All the family ran in from somewhere and just stood there staring at him. Then Papa picked him up and carried him to the front room and laid him on the couch.

"Your mama was scared you had broke your leg," Julian continued. "But they didn't take you to the doctor, did they?"

Doctors cost money they didn't have, so they put it off. And next morning, he was feeling better, except every time he tried to stand up the pain was so sharp he had to hold his breath to keep from crying out. So, they let him stay on the couch for a week or so.

"But it didn't get better."

It felt a little better. Papa said it was a sprain, and it would take time to mend. Told him to take it easy. But there was work to do. So, when he could stand it, he got up and hobbled around as best he could. But it kept hurting and after another couple of weeks, he knew something was wrong. Not just a sprain. He'd had his share of sprained ankles. They hurt in a particular place when you moved a particular way. Papa would ask him where it hurt, and he'd point to the place. This pain wasn't like that. It was all over his leg, and it hurt all the time. There was no way he could move to get away from it. When it got that bad, he couldn't even get out of bed. Mama kept asking wasn't his leg getting better, but he told her it was about the same.

He couldn't remember much of what happened next, except that in the middle of the night, his mama got out the truck and drove him to Spotswood, to the hospital.

"The doctor said you had a bad break. And he had to break your leg again before he could set it. He said the bones had started to knit back together crooked, and you'd have been a cripple if they'd left it like that. How'd they do it? Break your leg?"

Carl walked across the porch and picked up a pine twig that had fallen into the sand. He snapped it into two pieces.

"Wow!" Julian breathed. "They knocked you out with ether, didn't they? Then they put you in a cast from your hip to your toes for six months. And you were on crutches for longer than that. After that, you limped for years and years."

Carl was drawing again. This time a boy with his mouth turned down, walking on crutches.

"That's why you never played baseball."

The boy thought for a moment.

"Did Grandpa say he was sorry?"

The old man laughed and shook his head. Not a chance. His papa had said he was a damn fool to let that cow tangle his rope 'round his leg. They didn't have the money for doctors, and the bad leg set them back considerably.

"But you got well, didn't you?"

The boy was no longer imitating his grandpa's southern cadence. His voice was urgent now, insistent.

"Your leg's perfect now, isn't it?"

Carl ran his hand through Julian's silky blond hair and kissed the top of his head, breathing in a mix of salt and sweat. He nodded.

"You got well," Julian repeated.

They picked up their pencils and began drawing again.

He could still draw anyway. Lou Gehrig hadn't robbed him of that. That's how he thought of his disease, as a personal tormentor.

He'd first noticed it a year ago, in the spring. That he was slurring his words. His daughter kept after him to speak more clearly, and he tried. But his tongue didn't work the way it always had, and his throat felt tight. He tried to ignore it. He'd never been much of a talker anyway. But his daughter Ellen made him go to the University Hospital in Charlottesville for some tests. The doctors there told him.

So, he was going to die. They didn't say that. They talked instead about medicines he could take to slow the process. They told him that the rest of his body, the parts that weren't his throat and tongue, were still sound, but he might need physical therapy. He could still draw pictures and write words even though his voice would soon be silenced. They didn't mention what he'd already figured out, that he would eventually lose the ability to swallow, that before it was over, he wouldn't be able to breathe.

In some ways, it was a relief not to talk. He didn't have to discuss his symptoms with Ellen, who watched him, birdlike, fear deepening the lines between her eyes. He could get on with the parts of his life he had always loved.

This summer, for instance, he had rented this cottage at the beach for a month, the way he had always done. Year after year, when his wife Jane was still alive, and later, with Ellen and her family. Only for the first time, Max wasn't here. The discarded son-in-law he continued to love even though Ellen no longer did, the missing father Julian telephoned every night but never talked about.

Carl could still take short walks on the silky white sand on legs that were functional, if not strong. He could roll up his pants legs and wade in the sunbaked ocean.

And he could draw, the way he always had, with confident strokes of the pen, with reckless joy. He was a draftsman by trade, had spent his years working in an architect's office. He sat now on the front porch of the cottage at the picnic table, with Julian, drawing. The noonday heat swirled off the sand in front of him, distorting the string of cottages that followed the curve of the beach.

Carl was absorbed in his drawing when Julian jumped down from the porch onto the hot sand and headed off in the direction of the surf. Every few minutes, the old man shaded his eyes with his hand and looked out over the stretch of inert bodies clogging the shorefront. He could make out Julian standing about fifty yards away at the edge of the water, facing the panorama of surfboards, floats, girls in bikinis, splashing children. He knew Ellen didn't let Julian go it alone, but he trusted the boy to stay safely on the beach. At the same time, he knew how much Julian loved the water, loved running into the crashing waves and being knocked under, loved feeling the heavy water rolling over him, the sand scraping his skin. Together they had been knocked over countless times, but they always bounced back to the surface, laughing, spitting out brine. Carl knew the ocean current was unpredictable. Knew that on rare occasions an undertow could carry you out without warning. But to him the ocean was familiar, warm, playful.

And then Julian was gone. Carl pulled himself to his feet and peered out into the shimmering sunlight, searching the spread of red and yellow beach towels where Julian had just been standing. He wasn't there.

Carl looked around for Ellen, but the cabin was empty. He thought he remembered something about her going shopping, but he wasn't sure. At any rate, she wasn't here.

Panting heavily, he scrambled down the weathered porch steps onto the hot sand, weaving clumsily through the baked bodies strewn out on towels, through the children splashing water onto sandcastles. At the water's edge, he peered out beyond the swimmers, scanning the waves for this most precious of boys. No Julian.

I won't panic, he told himself. He's somewhere on the beach.

A man, deeply tanned with wind-blown white hair, approached. "You okay?

Carl mopped the saliva running down the ridges beside his lips with his crumpled handkerchief.

"My boy," he mumbled.

The man peered at his face.

"How old?" he asked.

Carl held up both hands, fingers extended.

"Ten?"

Carl nodded.

"Look, I'm sure he's okay. The current's been moving sideways up the beach. No undertow. Your boy's probably having too much fun to notice."

The man paused.

"He's not alone, is he?"

Carl didn't answer but headed up the beach in the direction the man pointed, splashing the shallow water, pounding deep footsteps in the wet sand. His breath was ragged, and his throat burned. Every minute or so, he had to stop. He scanned the surf, his hand shading his eyes from the blinding sun. There were so many people out there in the waves. Too many. Had he missed him in all those bodies? Beyond the waves, the water was black and vacant. Not a soul. He tried not to think about that.

He told himself that Julian was too sensible to swim by himself, too cautious. He tried to pick up his pace, glancing wildly around, but he stumbled and fell to his knees. A woman, too large for the bikini she was wearing, pulled him clumsily to his feet.

"Julian!" he tried to call out, but the word came out jumbled, broken.

"Are you alright?" she asked, her round face close to his, frowning.

He shook his head and tried to run, but he was unsure about the direction he should take, so he stood there in the hot sun, looking everywhere, seeing nothing. So that he almost missed him when Julian came wandering up the beach, his thin sunburned shoulders shaking from the cold water, strands of his wet hair streaking into his eyes.

"I'm okay, Grandpa. I'm okay."

The boy grabbed him by the shirt and plunged his wet face into the old man's soft chest. Carl could feel his slight body trembling, could feel the tears.

"I know," he tried to say but couldn't. And so, he wrapped his arms about the boy and held fast for a long time.

That night Carl sat with Ellen on the stiff mattress next to Julian who was absently picking up the colored pens and paper that floated over the surface of the lightweight summer blanket. The room was just large enough for the bunk bed and a small chest, and, like the rest of the cottage, smelled of pine.

"Why did you do it?" Ellen asked.

"What? Do what?"

"Go out there by yourself? You know better."

Her voice carried an edge of anger.

"I know," he said.

"Then why?"

She took his face in both of her hands and looked him in the eye.

"I don't know. I meant to stay on the beach. But then I was in the water. And a big wave came, and I couldn't touch bottom."

He started to cry.

"I'm sorry."

Ellen put her arms around him and held him against her.

"What happened?"

"I was drowning," he said, his voice breaking.

"How did you get back?"

"I don't know. I was on the bottom. It was dark, and the water was in my nose."

Ellen rocked him in her arms. The anger was gone.

"You're safe now," she said.

Carl put his arms around his daughter and cradled both of them against him. His eyes stung from all the things he knew and couldn't say.

Julian pulled away from his mother.

"This is going to sound weird," he said, "but I have an idea about heaven."

"Heaven?"

Carl was surprised. He couldn't remember the subject of heaven ever coming up before.

"I don't know. It's just an idea I got."

"Okay."

"Well, not exactly heaven. But a place you go, you know, after you die."

"Yeah?"

"Here's my idea. You go there sideways. Not up like heaven or down like hell. But somewhere different, and you go there sideways."

He was fiddling with the colored pens, avoiding his mother's questioning gaze.

"Okay."

"Do you know what I mean?"

He faced his grandpa.

Carl shook his head. He stroked Julian's cheek. It was so soft, so smooth. His beautiful Julio.

"It's a world like this one, and you meet a lot of people in that place, your family and people you knew a long time ago."

His eyes were fixed on Carl's, silently pleading.

"It's a lovely idea," Ellen said.

"I don't want it to be lovely. I want it to be true. I want Daddy to be there all the time, and you and Grandpa."

Carl pulled the boy to him, felt the soft flesh of his shoulder, felt his resistance.

"It's a lousy idea," Julian said, breaking away from his grandfather and sinking down into the covers.

Ellen bent down to kiss him.

"No," she said, "It's a beautiful idea. I wish I could tell you it was true. I wish it were true. And maybe it is."

"Forget it," he said and turned away from her.

The next day, they were back on the porch, each absorbed in his own drawing. And Carl had once again, without meaning to, drawn Lily. But drawing wasn't enough. He wanted his voice back. He had things to say. Things his grandson needed to hear. And sitting there, mute, impotent, he had drawn the cow. As if to remind himself, not of his broken leg and the months of wearing a cast, or the years of limping, or of sketching the baseball plArey he watched from the sidelines. But of something else, a memory he had pushed away, of lying in bed under a feather quilt in an empty house. Aching not just in his leg but in his whole body. Shaking with cold in the warm spring afternoon. Calling out to his mother. But there was nothing, only silence, and he knew it was too late. They wouldn't get back in time.

He had no memory of their finding him, shivering, burning with fever, no memory of the ride to the hospital in the pickup. They had told him that part. What he remembered now, what his body remembered, was the tightness in his throat, the sharp sting behind his eyes, the crush of darkness, the terror. No light anywhere, even from the window where the shades had been drawn.

He called out, "Mama, Mama!"

Silence. He held his breath, listening. Nothing. And he knew, right then he knew, he would die.

His hands were shaking, and the space behind his eyes stung. To keep from crying, he looked over at Julian, absorbed in his drawing. This, he thought, this boy. He was what it was about, what he would miss. This very boy.

Carl ducked his head and reached for his handkerchief. Then he began to draw. A series of pictures, cartoon-like, of waves. Blue waves, black waves. They covered the entire page. Then there was a head, just a small head, barely visible above the breakers. He added a new frame to his cartoon. The head belonged to a boy. His arms were waving. Over his head was a moon, and a cow, just like Lily, was jumping over the moon.

Julian put down his own pencil and began to watch his grandpa. In the next frame, Lily jumped down to the ocean and started swimming toward the boy. A balloon came out of the boy's mouth, "Help! Help! I'm drowning!" The cow was getting closer.

"Grandpa," Julian laughed. "Cows can't swim."

The cow stopped swimming in front of the boy and wrapped the chain from her neck around the boy. She then began swimming back to shore towing the boy behind her. When he was safely on shore, the boy got up on Lily's back and rode off down the beach.

Julian laughed.

"That's awesome, Grandpa. Do another one."

Carl placed a fresh piece of paper in front of Julian and pointed to him. And Julian began to draw.

Alphabetical Index of Stories

Made in the USA
Middletown, DE
13 May 2023

30511610R00258